RED WIZARD OF ATLANTIS

Ravek Hunter

I0665633

First Edition, March 2018

Copyright © 2018 Ravek Hunter Literary LLC

ISBN:

978-1-948782-07-4 (paperback)

978-1-948782-05-0 (ebook)

www.WorldsOfAtlantis.com

For Mrs. Wife,
who gave me two incredible boys
that I hope will be proud to read their father's work one day.

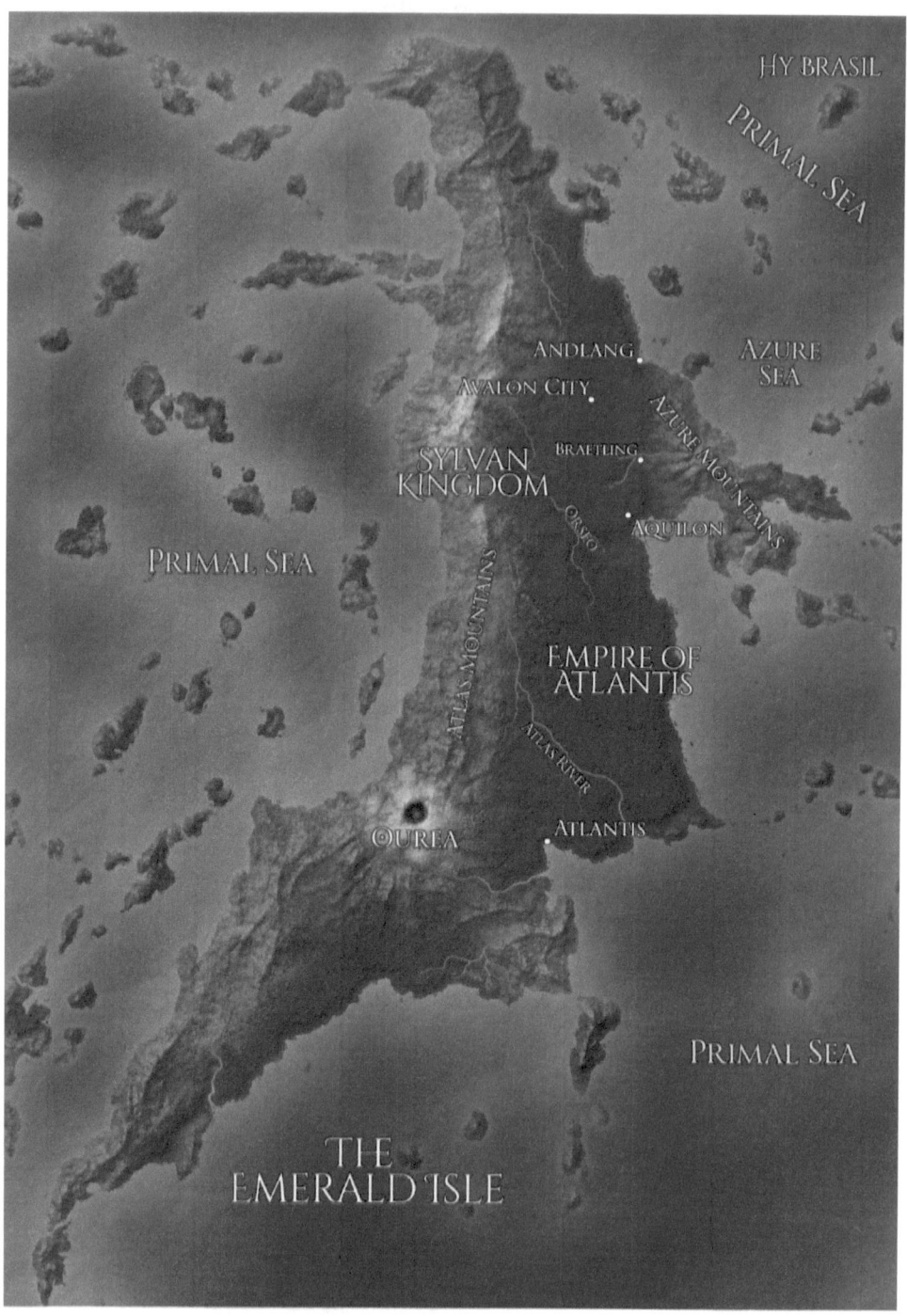

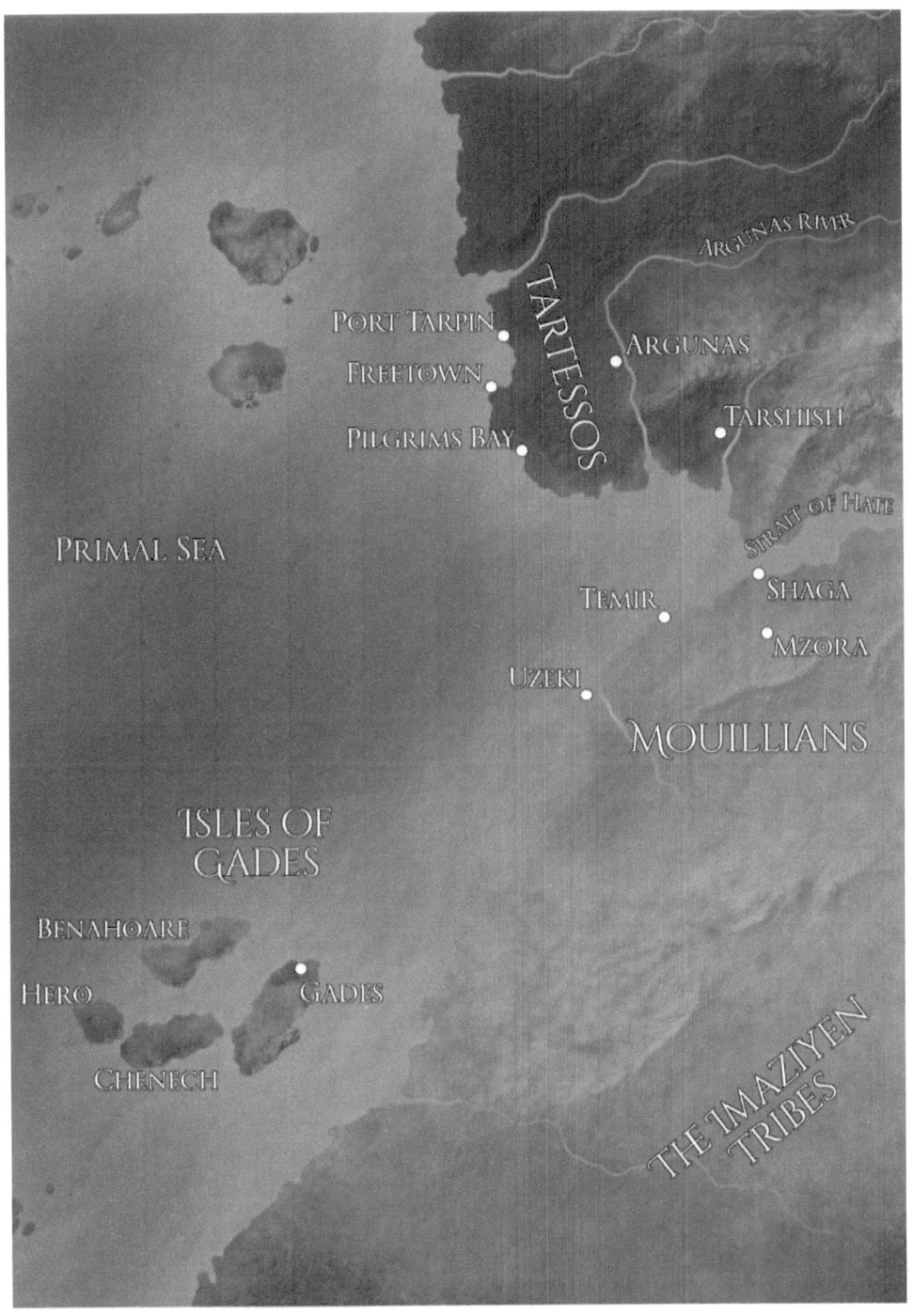

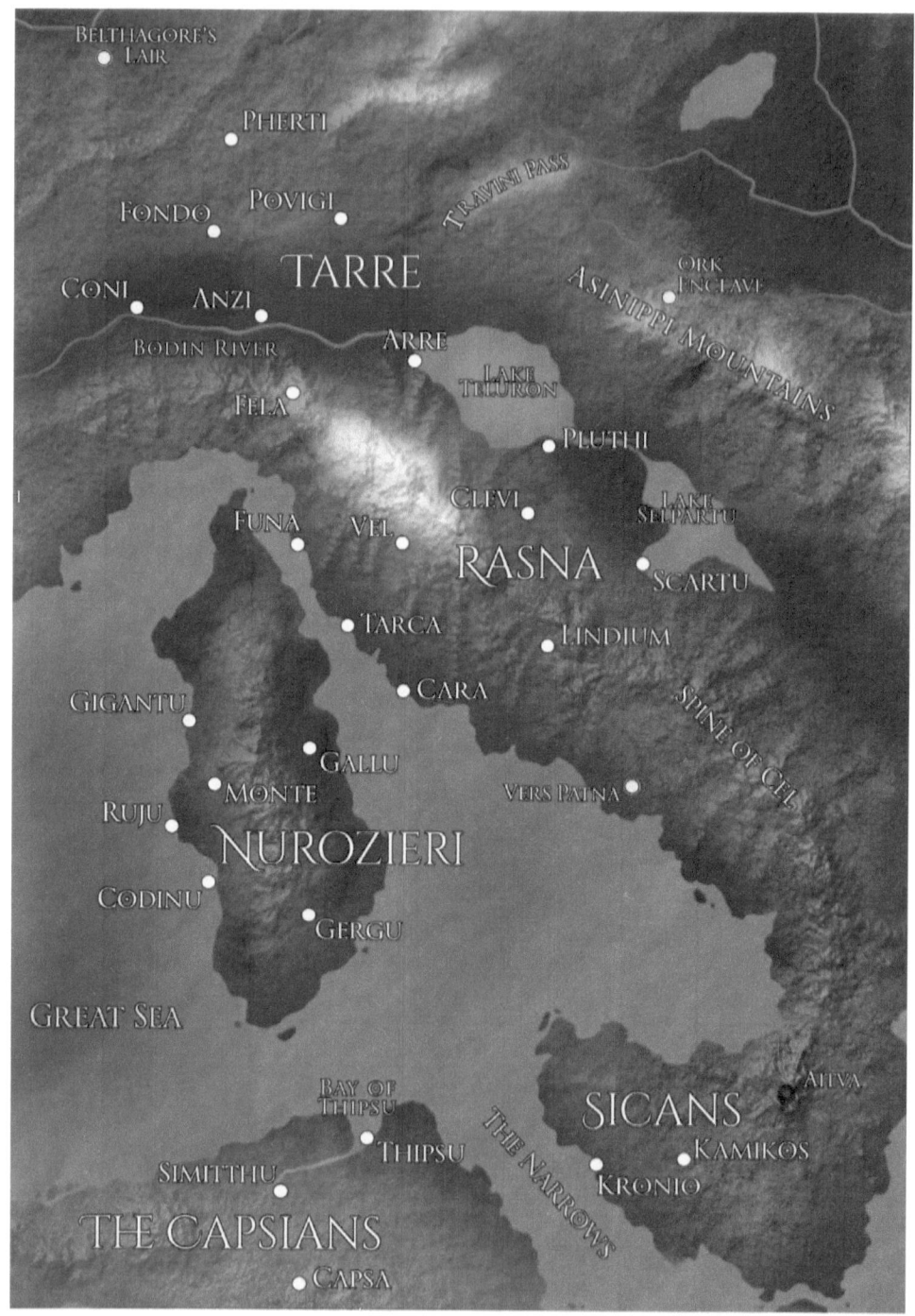

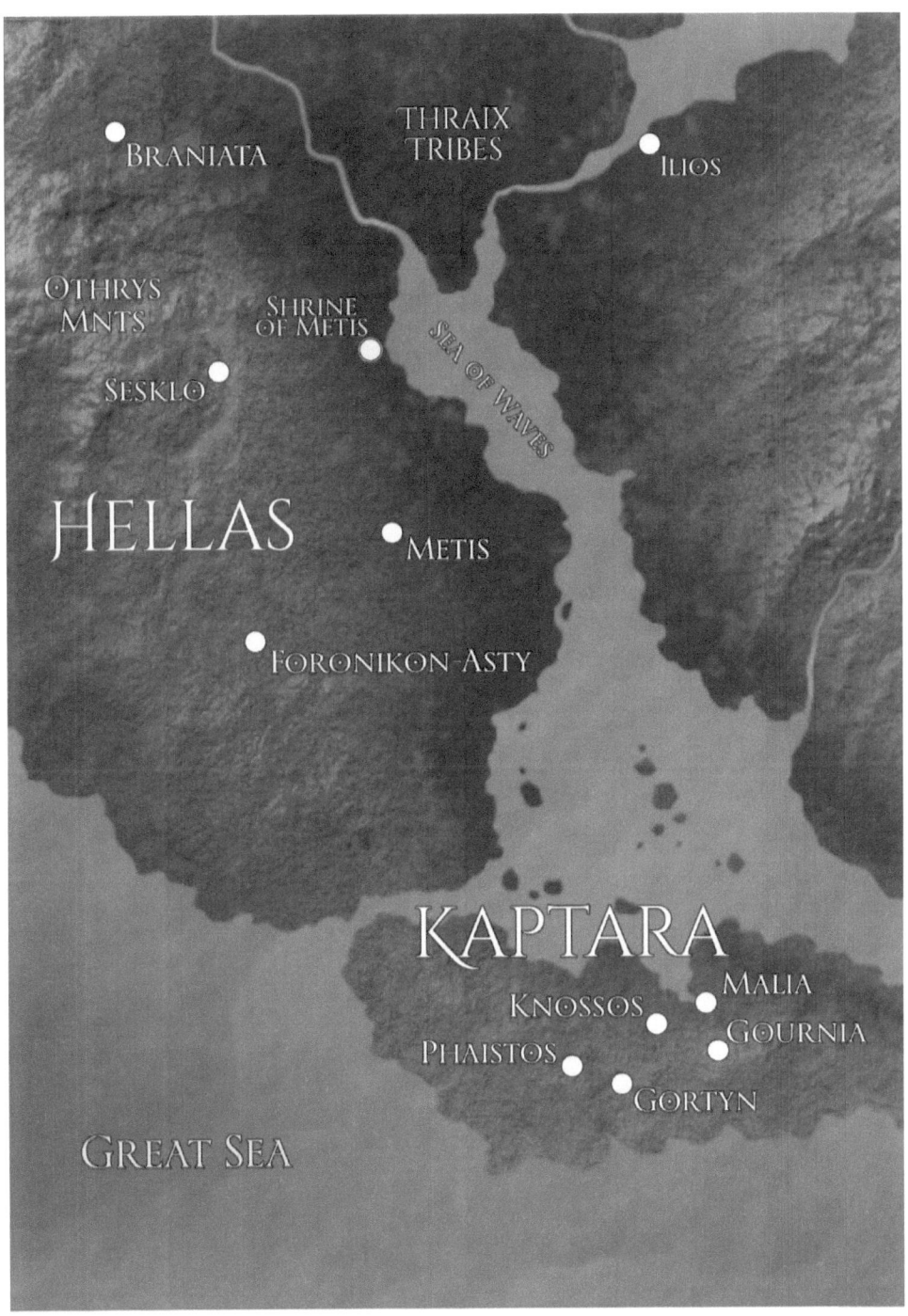

Fantasy Novels by Ravek Hunter

Red Wizard of Atlantis

The Fallen

Saving Eridu

The Imaziyen Druid

Shadows of Lyonesse

Beasts of Courth

Ys (Coming in 2022)

If you enjoy reading books by this author, please remember to leave a review at your favorite bookseller!

To learn more about the backstory, mythology, and character development in these stories or to view world maps visit us at:

https://www.WorldsOfAtlantis.com!

Table of Contents

Children of Atlas

It was from the stars they came, out of the vast darkness of the Primeval Cosmos, plunging from the sky in a great wingless beast consumed by smoke and fire. It fell with a thunderous crash upon the earth plowing a long black rift across the open plain before it came to rest in a final shudder of sparks and lightning. The smoking shell of the massive creature lay shattered, yet from its broken maw came hundreds of odd-looking figures that crawled through the acrid haze and stumbled disoriented onto the lush green grass of a new world.

The Sylvan watched the arrival of the newcomers from the quiet repose of the forest. They scrutinized these strange bi-pedal aliens with blue-tinted skin and elongated heads and large almond-shaped eyes that had come uninvited to their tranquil isle, until now isolate and protected from intrusion by the vast expanse of the Primal Sea. They observed how the slender forms worked as a collective to remove the shiny scales of their battered host piece by piece to make shelters, how they buried their dead, how they mourned their passing.

When that was done, they brought red glowing crystals that shown bright even in daylight from the metallic frame of the silver beast's remains. The crystals they handled with great care and reverence, depositing them in caverns deep in the earth near an inlet on the coast. It was there too, that they began to build with stones.

These were a people with no hope of return or rescue, determined to survive and resolute in their struggle to make a place for themselves. A permanent place that would bring irrevocable change the Isle. To the land, to nature, to a way of life that had existed since time began.

Still the Sylvan watched.

The prophesies spoke of events such as these that would herald the beginning of the Fourth Age, the Age of the Golden Aspen, the Age when the winds from the north would bring an icy chill even in the summertime. And end the elves isolation from the rest of the world forever.

In time the Sylvan learned that the unusual blue-tinted people called themselves the followers of Atlas, the one who had risen among them and offered up hope for a new future. They would name the spine of the island in his honor and build a shining city on the sea that would become known as Atlantis.

And they thrived.

**Recorded in the Fourth Age of the Golden Aspen
by Watcher CrellianRafkarSil of Avalon**

Prologue

Sylvan Year (SY) 4088

"Hold the damned shield, Laghfrin!"

"You worry about that demon, Dhroghan! I will see to the shield!" Laghfrin had to scream to be heard above the noise of battle. She glanced at her fellow Tuatha De maintaining the enormous bubble that formed the invisible prison waiting to capture the last Demon Lord. Only seven Tuatha De remained of the original sixteen that held the magical sphere in place. The others had fallen to the perils of the demons and their minions or to pure exhaustion. And with each loss, those who persisted had to work that much harder to keep the prison from failing.

Laghfrin could feel the ebb and flow of magical power from each one of her companions across the link they shared. She knew how much strength they had and which ones would fail first. With so many losses, she couldn't afford to lose even one more. It was a race against time; either the last Demon Lord would be trapped or one of Laghfrin's comrades would fail and the shield would collapse releasing all the demons they had trapped thus far. It would bring a catastrophic end to their endeavor to rid the world of these evil beasts that might never be repeated. There wasn't much time left. Everything depended on these Tuatha De of the Blood, pure born with no corrupt interbreeding with humans or any other species. They gave their lives dearly for this world, knowing that there were no others to replace them.

Not since the Breaking had a Tuatha De of the Blood been born.

"Zamfer!" Dhroghan yelled to a man Laghfrin knew to be the Atlantean emperor. "Watch your flank! The demon has summoned more fiends against you!"

The Atlantean emperor, fiercely beautiful despite the long dark hair over his elongated skull matted with blood and sweat that ran down his blue-tinted angular face, hefted his glass-like Aurinium blade coated in the black blood of demons and spun on his heels in the direction Dhroghan pointed. With him turned a hundred warriors, powerful men and women themselves outfitted with magnificent Aurinium armor and long curved blades, to charge against a cluster of terrible beasts all horns, teeth and claws, rushing mindlessly forward without regard for their own lives.

Laghfrin felt helpless. All she could do was focus on the magical prison while the others battled the last Demon Lord. If they failed, she would die standing there, wasted and useless. She had no choice. Over the past several days they had lured thirteen Chaos Demons and six Demon Lords into the prison she and the others held, but not without a terrible price. Thousands of bodies littered the battlefield over at least a league. Most of them were humans, but there were more than a few non-human allies scattered among them . . . including nine of her own.

"Brak!" Dhroghan cried desperately. "To the north!"

A company of several dozen dwarfs streamed around her, led by the Mountain King, Brak Iron-teeth, lord of the Dvergr. They were solely tasked with defending the Tuatha De keeping the spherical shield from failing. So far, they had performed valiantly against the terrors conjured by the Demon Lords. Laghfrin reluctantly acknowledged that without the protection of the short, ugly creatures, the Tuatha De would have been over-run long before they ever had the chance to capture even the first of the dreadful monsters.

Laghfrin was exhausted. For nine days the combined armies of the humans, dwarfs, elves, Tuatha De and Atlanteans had fought the demons. First, the Chaos Demons were rounded up. They were uncomplicated and simple-minded compared to what was to come. Dhroghan brought them in groups of three or four until all thirteen were safely inside the prison. Then he lured in the Greater Demons one by one.

Each of the Demon Lords brought new horrors that had to be overcome. They were physically enormous with the ability to invoke powerful magic and conjure nightmarish terrors from the Infernal Planes to aid them in battle. Worst of all, they had psionic abilities— mental powers that allowed them to dominate and destroy another creature's mind with their own. Atlantean wizards of the Yellow Hall had similar aptitude and they kept the Demon Lords psionic command at bay. It was a titanic struggle, invisible to everyone around them, that left more than a dozen of the yellow-clad Atlanteans with broken minds driven to madness from which there could be no recovery.

A jarring shock rocked Laghfrin's body. Her weary legs no longer had the strength to support her body and she found herself on her knees. For too long the demons had been free to terrorize the world and do as they please. They sowed chaos, destruction and death in every corner of the world. It was a constant battle between good and evil with far too much grey in between and they were finally on the cusp of ending it all. If she could just hold on a little longer . . .

"Dhroghan, take care with your fire! My Tree Guardians are coming in!" It was the lord of the Sylvan Kingdom, High-King RalnapianCalithIlon, that shouted in the distance.

The Demon Lord was close, Laghfrin could feel him. Glancing quickly to the east, she watched what looked like a forest moving into position in front of the fearsome beast towering over the trees by a factor of three. Its body was red, like the crimson of human blood, with a muscular, humanoid body that bore no clothing at all. And just like the others, it was the head of the creature that sparked the fear in one's soul. Laghfrin looked away quickly, but not quick enough to avoid the dreadful visage bearing down upon them. The great mandibles that clacked mercilessly over a wide maw filled with row up row of teeth longer than the longest broadsword, eyes bloodred and split in the center like those of a snake and long pointed horns protruding from the top of its head completed the perfect nightmare. All the Demon Lords were distinct from one another in their appearance in terrible, unnatural distortions of the physical world and Laghfrin knew she would have horrendous dreams that could be attributed to each and every one. If nothing else, Laghfrin had the satisfaction of knowing that the process of trapping the Demons in the bubble stripped them of their corporeal state, leaving only their consciousness or spiritual essence alive. That was the best the Tuatha De could do short of sending them back to the Infernal Planes and that was now impossible with the rift permanently closed.

Laghfrin checked the link to her companions and adjusted the balance and flow of the magic they shared to give relief to the weakest. It would just be a little longer. She knew that Dhroghan and the others were preparing to bring it in. Already, the Demon Lord had sent waves of conjured fiends that nearly overwhelmed them. She feared that many more would sacrifice their lives before this last horror was contained in her prison.

She regretted that they did not have enough time to learn more about the Demon Lords. She was aware that they all had a True Name, but not even the wisest among them knew of a way to ascertain what they might be. Such knowledge would have made their task far less hazardous. According to the ancient texts, a Demon Lord could be quickly banished back to the Infernal Planes if his True Name were known. As it was, the best she and her confederacy could do was trap them so they couldn't cause any more havoc upon the world.

A group of two-hundred human warriors moved to confront the Demon Lord, supported by several dozen Atlantean wizards and elven archers. Dhroghan was right in the center of them, conjuring lightning strikes and doing his best to keep the demon focused on him and moving forward. It wasn't an easy ruse. If he overplayed his deception, the Demon Lord would suspect he was being led and their plan would fail. That's where all the other combatants came in . . . to execute a deadly charade.

The Demon Lord waded through the Tree Guardians, setting many of them ablaze and still they fought on. Dhroghan's overall strategy was a retreating action that would draw the Demon Lord into the invisible sphere of the prison that held its brethren. Fortunately, the ego of the demons worked against them and they couldn't see past the illusion of their quarry in retreat—even when it was a methodical withdrawal.

"Forward to the line!" Brak Iron-teeth's commanding bellow carried over the field of combatants sending his company of stalwart dwarfs charging toward the front.

Laghfrin felt a sick mixture of relief and panic with the Demon Lord so close. In seconds, everything could go disastrously wrong. And this was the last one. After nine days of constant battle with no sleep or reprieve, she had precious little left to give and she desperately wanted it to be over.

The image of a wretched fracture torn across a vast expanse of earth like a gaping wound flashed in her mind.

Barely a month ago, Laghfrin stood at the edge of the rift that had somehow formed between the Infernal Planes and their world—she and fifty more of the Tuatha De Blood. No one could say why the breach had so suddenly appeared; only that it was there and it had to be closed. The thirteen Chaos Demons and seven powerful Demon Lords that escaped through it were causing mayhem across the globe and if they didn't close the rift quickly, there would be no force on earth that could stop the hundreds more that would soon follow.

The rift was a remarkable thing, spanning over three hundred leagues northwest to southeast and fifty leagues roughly east to west. The Tuatha De took positions around the massive expanse and linked their power between the leagues that separated them. The vast energy they applied pulled molten rock from the earth's core to fill the fissure which they vitrified and cooled creating, in effect, a massive glass sea sealing the portal into their world forever. Even still, a strong aura of evil pervaded the section they had covered and Laghfrin knew that any civilization, even twenty thousand years to come, would suffer the blight of its corruption if they settled close to it.

"Parm, apachama! Zir Teloc!" The Demon Lord's obscene bellow echoed over the commotion of battle followed by screams of agony and death that rose to a high pitch wrenching Laghfrin's attention back to the present.

Nearly all of the humans sent to defend against the Demon Lord's minions were dead or dying. *Such a pitiful, primitive species,* she lamented silently and *yet we give our lives for them.*

The Atlantean and elven warriors skillfully fell back with Dhroghan and the dwarfs. They were so close Laghfrin's heightened senses could almost smell their fear and uncertainty. Even these ancient and noble warriors barely held their panic in check.

Another contingent of several hundred humans came forward. Many immediately ran away in fear, as might be expected from a primitive species, but one group had a charismatic leader at the front urging them forward. His name was King Anlawd Dormont and despite knowing the grisly fate they must face before them, his brave warriors followed without the slightest hesitation.

The Demon Lord broke the earth underneath the humans sandaled feet sending dozens into fiery crevices and still they rushed against it fighting with nothing more than spears and clubs. And heroic spirit. Six times before, Laghfrin watched this same display of courage. Each time she was impressed with the fortitude of the humans and their selfless determination. The intelligent ones knew what was at stake instinctively, like animals and they feared the consequence of loss. If ever a people deserved admiration, it was this strange race and if Laghfrin lived to see the end of this endeavor, she would weep for these people and devote her life to their evolution.

"Micma a ialpon a unph!"

She felt heat on her face as fire erupted everywhere, but Laghfrin and her Tuatha De were harmed by none of it. Dhroghan was protecting the bearers of the shield from the Demon Lord, who was by now, nearly on top of them. Just one more step and it would be over. The Atlanteans, elves, dwarfs and humans fell back along the perimeter of the shield that only they could see while Dhroghan stood immediately in front of it, taunting the Demon Lord forward.

It came. It came willfully and with fury. Dhroghan smiled.

Laghfrin watched in disbelief as Dhroghan abruptly disappeared into the confines of the shield. He had not done that with the others. It horrified her to see him vanish into the swirling mass of energy. The Demon Lord followed.

They had him.

A roar of cheers rose from thousands when it happened. *But what of Dhroghan?* They had no way of knowing what was happening inside the magical prison.

"It is time."

Laghfrin was shocked by the sudden appearance of a woman standing next to her. "Who are you?"

"I am Metis. And it is my task to watch over and protect the confinement of the demons." She waved her hand and a beautifully engraved pithos the size of a human man appeared nearby. "Shape your magic to confine them in here."

"What about Dhroghan?" Laghfrin heard herself scream. They couldn't leave him to the fate of the demons!

"He has made his choice . . . and his sacrifice," Metis calmly replied, beckoning again toward the pithos.

Laghfrin was overcome with emotion. "No! We cannot leave him!" Only she knew that they were lovers. *How could she abandon him to such a fate?* The pain of his loss would be intolerable.

Metis was unrelenting. "Do it now! Your companions are on the verge of collapse and the loss of even one will cause the barrier to fail and undo everything thousands have died to accomplish!"

Recognition dawned on her. Laghfrin knew this woman, this is Tuaha De of the Blood. And she also knew that Metis was right—they had to finish this. She looked down the length of the line of Tuatha De holding the magical constraint. Like her, to a man and woman they were on their knees holding on to the last vestiges of their power by a thread that she alone maintained tenuous control over.

Laghfrin had no choice.

Tears of anguish fell down her fair cheeks and in a voice thick with despondence, Laghfrin issued the command that would release the shield into the pithos, *"Saanir oi sor ol zonrensg a loagaeth piadph coraxo bahal de allar a babalon pir pambt oi zizop bagle tol cocasb."*

The audible shrieks from the demons forced into confinement were almost maddening, especially since she knew that one among them could have been Dhroghan. When it was done, Laghfrin collapsed to her knees from exhaustion and despair, weeping bitter tears.

Metis quietly completed her part, applying the final seal, trapping the demons in the pithos forever. "Over time you will learn more about these demons, maybe even their True Names. Fortunately, with prolonged confinement and the rift closed, they will weaken and lose much of their power. Pray that this world will never suffer their kind again." And then Metis and the pithos holding the demons were gone.

Laghfrin stared at the spot where Metis—she knew that woman by another name once—stood for a long time and then she was startled by a hand gently touching her shoulder. Turning to see who it was, her heart nearly leaped from her body.

It was Dhroghan.

"Where did you come from?" Laghfrin jumped up and hugged him tightly. "I thought I trapped you with the demons when we collapsed the shields into the pithos!"

Dhroghan kissed her passionately before he answered. "Aww, dearie. I teleported myself away just before the Demon Lord was on me. I guess I went farther than I expected. It took me a while to get back." He winked at her flippantly. "I am touched by the display, though. Unless you are mourning another of your lovers?"

"So sure of yourself," Laghfrin chided and kissed him once again before turning serious. "Phalaeh was the one who brought the pithos. She calls herself Metis now. I thought she died in the Breaking."

Dhroghan shrugged. "She escaped the Breaking and spends most of her time in Hellas now. They worship her as a goddess there. You know how vain she is. Besides, these humans need guidance."

19

Laghfrin knew well his vanity also. "And what do they call you there?"

The question apparently caught him off guard and his cheeks flushed a little. She expected him to lie, but to her surprise he was forthcoming. "Aether, god of light."

"Perhaps I will accompany you to Hellas sometime and become a goddess as well," she teased, barely suppressing a sarcastic laugh. "But first, we must honor the men and women who died here."

"Yes," Dhroghan agreed sadly. "I will create a monument in this place so that no one will forget what happened here." He turned and spoke to the human King, "Have your people collect the dead and bury them a pace apart, in rows of ten. When you are done, I will mark their graves."

King Dormont nodded thoughtfully before he barked orders to his commanders, "Organize your men into teams and start a line of trenches here where I stand!"

Two days later Laghfrin was standing on a low hill beside Dhroghan, looking down at the shallow graves of thousands in rows that stretched at least a league to the east. Laghfrin didn't need to say anything. She knew Dhroghan was just as upset about the loss of life as she was. No Tuatha De wanted to revisit the stain of the Breaking, which had cost them so many lives less than two thousand years before.

"Link your power to me," Dhroghan said quietly.

Laghfrin nodded to the Tuatha De and Atlantean wizards standing behind them. To her surprise, several dozen human druids stepped up to join them. They all opened themselves to Dhroghan and allowed him to pull their power into himself.

Even as exhausted as everyone was so soon after the battle—she could feel each individual's weariness through the link—they still tendered an enormous amount of energy as a whole. With what he was planning, she expected that Dhroghan would need every ounce of it.

Hands tightly clasped into fists, Dhroghan held his arms crossed over his chest, concentrating on the task at hand. Except for his low chant, there was not a sound, not even from the hundreds waiting for what he would do. Laghfrin felt the anxiety of uncertainty unsure if what he attempted was possible.

Dhroghan's hands glowed with a golden yellow luminescence and his chanting became more insistent. He drew massive amounts of power from those linked to him, perhaps more than what they could give. Then the earth beneath their feet began to tremble, subtly at first, rising to a level of violence that had them all struggling to stay on their feet.

Dhroghan lifted his glowing hands slowly into the air while stone edges forced their way above the surface of the dark soil at the head of each of the earthen graves. The stones grew out of the ground like weeds, thousands of them, as if Dhroghan were physically pulling them up from the dirt. In a very real way, he was. And as the stones rose, the earth and the bodies slid beneath them, filling in the space and solidifying into perfect tombs. When it was done, a massive stone monolith twice the height of a human man stood to mark the grave of each man and woman who had died there.

On shaking legs, Dhroghan turned to those assembled around him. Those brave people of every race that stood with him against the terrible evil that they were never sure they could defeat until the end. Laghfrin was never prouder to be anywhere in her life.

"As long as there is life on this earth, this place will be marked by these stones in remembrance of our brothers and sisters who died here. Even many thousands of years from now, when their meaning is a mystery and their names are forgotten, the stones will stand for them." Dhroghan paused to raise one golden-glowing fist into the air. It shown like a beacon of beautiful light in the hazy dusk before the final minutes of nightfall. "From now until the end of days, this place will be known as Carnac!"

Chapter 1

Visions

SY5489

Four men and a woman sat in comfortable chairs evenly spaced around the circumference of a dimly lit circular room. Two paces behind each chair, almost as if set into the wall like a picture frame, was a florescent oval portal tall enough and wide enough for any one of them to walk through. The surface of each gateway concealed its destination with a swirling white fog that never dissipated or left the confines of its border. Three more chairs were conspicuously empty, but none paid any attention to those except for one.

Wodanaz, where are you?

Myrllin glanced around the shadowy chamber dimly lit by magical light-globes floating at varied elevations in the open air vacant of a ceiling, at least not in any ordinary sense—instead, the clear unimpeded starry night shown down from high above through an invisible bubble of energy protecting those inside from the elements without. Below his feet, solid black obsidian with lightning-like trails of red glowing Orichalcum formed the entirety of the circular floor from edge to edge, easily twenty paces in diameter.

Busy. Leave me alone, brother.

Briefly, Myrllin squeezed his eyes shut in frustration. Known as the Chamber of Portals, at least to those who had intimate familiarity with it, was the meeting place for a few powerful individuals who influenced life and events throughout the rest of the world. They called themselves the Assembly of Nine. In this room all persons were equal and decisions had to be unanimous among those present to put them into motion. Located in the highest tower of the Imperial Wizards Enclave in the City of Atlantis, no more than a dozen people alive were aware that it even existed.

I know you heard the Calling. This is important, you should be here.

The group met regularly every ten years on the eve of the seventh full moon and in rare events of crisis with regional or global reach. The last such predicament resolved in this room was the Oak War, a conflict between two factions of druids devoted to the goddess Eriu, over six centuries prior. It was determined in this room that one of the factions represented the faithful reflection of the Goddesses harmony with nature and thus it was decided they should prevail in the conflict.

Catch me up on the details later . . .

After the silent words played through his mind Myrllin nearly slammed his fist on the arm of his chair. This night was no regular meeting. Something momentous had occurred or would occur and a *Calling* was sent out to bring the Assembly of Nine together. Well, most of them anyway.

A tall, lean Atlantean stood from his shadowed chair, silhouetted against the glowing portal behind him and addressed the small group, "We have gathered in accordance with the Calling. Who wishes to bring an issue before the Assembly?"

It was Liltanian, Emperor of Atlantis that opened the discussions. He was the sitting Supreme of the Assembly of Nine responsible for conducting the meetings and following the established agenda.

Frustrated with his brother's indolence, Myrllin stood from his chair and walked to the center of the chamber, where the illumination from the light-globes were greatest. In a robust, confident voice that rumbled with age and wisdom, he made a reply, "It is I, the Mad Bard."

There were chuckles throughout the room. Those who had either lived long enough or heard the stories knew of his sense of humor, often forgetting the serious truths behind his witticisms.

"Then I surrender the stage to you, fair bard," The Emperor nodded with a smile and resumed his seat.

A female voice rang out sweetly in the dark room, "It is good to see you well, son of Dhroghan. Will your brother be joining us?"

She was the Dagda-Dana Laghfrin, the Tuatha De Wizard Queen of Falias in the North.

Myrllin pulled at the layers of his flowing gray robes with agitation. *Wodanaz should be here.* He raged at his brother on the inside while he returned her beautiful smile, "It warms my heart to see you as well, Dagda-Dana Laghfrin," he bowed with a flourish, "and all of you, of course. Sadly, I have not had the time to locate Wodanaz since my return; however, I will be sure to make it my priority once I am done here."

"You have slept since the end of the Oak War. Have dark visions once again disturbed your slumber?" Laghfrin raised one thin eyebrow high upon her forehead..

"I have had visions," Myrllin confirmed. "One of which concerns all of you here."

Silence hung in the air as they waited for him to continue. Instead, he stood thoughtful and contemplative, considering the best way to proceed with the dire information he must impart. He must not appear too eager to get to the point without the proper set-up underscoring the certainty of his prediction. They had to believe him, take him seriously and plot their course accordingly.

"By Buri, get on with it, thaumaturge!" a deep voice roared from a stout, broad-shouldered, short man whose feet did not touch the ground from the height of the chair where he sat. He was the Mountain King, Sulyen the Breaker, Lord of the Dvergr Dwarfs in Tirnan Yog. His bulbous and bearded features were contorted in a fierce display of impatience.

"Quiet, Sulyen. Let him choose his words. You know how important his visions can be." In contrast to the dwarf, this man's voice was a serene calm of almost poetic timbre. He was the High-King TatharonCalithIlon of the Sylvan Kingdom.

Hardly noticing the exchange, Myrllin stood in the center of the room a moment longer before he slowly began to speak. "What I reveal shall come to pass. There is no doubt of it, nor is there any way to change or avoid the outcome."

He waved his arms in the air and muttered a few arcane words, conjuring before the assemblage a sizeable luminescent globe representing the world they inhabited. *Better to show them,* he thought. The complexity of details was striking: vivid oceans sparkled against the rich terrain of landmasses below clouds that appeared like stretched cotton circulating beyond the horizons of the slowly rotating globe.

"I have seen death from the sky," Myrllin intoned darkly. "It will come in a fiery ball larger than the Great City itself."

Everyone knew that the 'Great City' he referred to was Atlantis. Not even the civilizations of the Western Kingdoms or the multitudes in the far east could rival her influence. The City of Atlantis was the hub of power for the Atlanteans, the source of their supremacy from whence they subtly reached out and touched organized societies in even the most remote corners of the world.

Myrllin clenched his fingers into a fist and spoke a charm evoking the image of a pitted rock to appear next to the globe. He waved his hand and the rock entered the atmosphere of the earth where it burst into flames as it fell leading a long fiery trail behind it.

"It will impact the Ourea with unimaginable force, causing the earth to erupt, splitting the island from end-to-end to the lowest depths of the Primal Sea, forcing open a rift deeper than any other to swallow what remains whole. The Emerald Isle will perish and fall below the waves, never to rise again. All who stay will perish." Tears came unbidden to his eyes as he created images upon the globe reflecting the horrific violence of his words. "Walls of water leagues high will rush upon the lands of the Olmec in the west and the Ugarit in the east, and over the ice in the north to the ice in the south. Intense heat from the boiling sea will rise into the air above the earth melting huge swaths of ice and raise the levels of the oceans across the world to flood millions of leagues of land. Many civilizations will be lost, along with countless lives and the Enlightened Times will come to an end."

Myrllin wiped the moisture from his face. Everything he described was illustrated on the rotating globe. When he finished, the world looked much different than it had moments before. There was silence in the room, a collective pause of disbelief, every eye stared wide at the changed planet, the newly drawn coastlines, the unfamiliar regions once covered by glaciers and the absence of a continent.

Several long moments passed before the Atlantean Emperor Liltanian broke the silence with a heavy voice, "You say this vision is a certainty and that nothing can be done to change the outcome?"

"That is the truth of it," Myrllin nodded.

"Then Atlantis is doomed." The Emperor's tone was somber.

"As are many multitudes on this planet," added the lilting voice of High-King Tatharon.

Then a new voice spoke, the Arch-Druid Caomh of Eriu, "Perhaps it is important to know when this will occur, wizard."

"Ah, yes that is important," Myrllin was surprised he had not mentioned it in his presentation. He was sure that he meant to. "A little over two millennia from today."

"Two millennia? That's generations from now," exclaimed the druid.

"Not for all of us, Caomh. It is the time of my grandchildren," countered Tatharon.

Sulyen, clearly agitated, spoke up gruffly, "Aye, not so long for my people as well. So what's the point of telling us all this? If it is, as you say, unavoidable, what can we do about it?"

Myrllin banished his glowing globe, returning the room to its former dim illumination. "To prepare for the survival of humanity. They are the future of this world and there are dark times ahead long after the Sylvan Elves, Dvergr Dwarfs, Atlanteans, Tuatha De and even wizards like myself have long become myth and legend."

"And why should we care if they survive?" demanded Sulyen.

Almost annoyed, Myrllin turned to the bitter dwarf. "For the preservation of life, for one. And for another, they are all you have to carry the memory that your people ever existed."

Not wanting to get into a debate over the merits of saving humanity, Myrllin spun on his heel and strode back to the center of the room. "I am not here to convince any of you of anything. What will be will be. Each of you must decide how your people will spend the remainder of the time you have. Perhaps some of your people will somehow survive and thrive, but that was not in my vision."

"We have much to consider," Laghfrin's beautiful brown eyes shined with intensity. Myrllin new there was vast power behind those dark orbs, but not even she or her kind could stop what was coming. "Will you stay with us awhile and offer your wisdom to our deliberations?"

Myrllin laughed at the suggestion as he made his way toward the portal behind the chair he once sat. "I am a terrible advisor and there is much that I must do in this age. I can only offer this: keep a watchful eye on the stars for you will see the harbinger of your fate long before it arrives."

Liltanian rose from his chair and hastened to speak. The Atlantean Emperor apparently wanted more from the sage before he departed. Myrllin couldn't blame them; they would likely not see him again anytime soon. "You mentioned that you had other visions while you slept?"

Myrllin stopped and turned to face his peers once more. He had forgotten the other vision in his haste to warn them of the impending apocalypse. "Yes, there were others," he admitted. "One, in particular, may be far-reaching. Something ancient and evil has been awakened while I slumbered. My vision suggested that great misfortune will be visited upon the world unless it is stopped. All I know is that it is a subtle thing that will creep among those unaware seeking to devour civilization from the inside. I don't understand what that means yet, but I do know that each of you must be vigilant against abuses of

27

power and other egregious activities within your realms. There will be chaos in many parts of the world that will require heroes equal to legend to overcome. The other visions do not concern any of you."

With a shrug, Myrllin cast his gaze over them impatiently, tapping one foot as he leaned on the long staff he carried. If they expected more from him, they would be disappointed. Rarely were his visions very specific. It was one frustration he shared with the rest of them.

Tatharon stood up from his chair and stretched his slender limbs apart, "So what now for you, Myrllin? Will you sleep again for another millennium or stay with us for a while?"

"I have an important line of succession to prepare for, in addition to many other tasks. I will be around if you need me." Picking up his wide-brimmed floppy hat from his chair, Myrllin started again toward the portal. Just before he entered, he paused one last time, "Consider carefully the future of this world and the millions of lives that weigh upon your shoulders. This is not the time to think only of yourselves."

Not waiting for a reply, he stepped into the swirling clouds and misty vapors hell-bent on tracking down the infuriating scoundrel he called brother.

Chapter 2

Awakening

SY5379 (One-hundred years earlier)

"I am here, my love. Have you forgotten me?" She was the very nature of perfection and harmony, even with her beautiful lips puckered in a sad pout that broke his heart and filled him with sorrow. "Of course, you have forgotten me. You think of me only in your dreams, even though you know I wait for you. If you loved me, you would be here with me."

Was that a tear that slowly crawled down the perfect pink flesh of her cheek? Her silky blonde hair flailed across her face and neck, driven by invisible gusts of wind, removing the lone tear. Would there be more?

"Shall I wait for an eternity, my love? Or die here alone and wanting?" She tensed her body causing it to appear stiff and rigid, crossed her hands over her chest and assumed a very serene expression of one no longer living. Her white peplos, so sheer, billowed around her with the wind, revealing hints of her splendid curves in a mockery of her death shroud.

"Here lies the poor, wretched Anesidora; she died with a broken heart, with un-kissed lips and the frozen stare of sadness in her eyes. Weep for her now, oh gods, that she never felt the tender touch of her lover!"

Sadness, utter sadness and loss. Akakios felt it deep within his soul, if he had one. How could he leave this divine being to such a sad ending? How could he tell her that she was only a fantasy in a dream?

Akakios awoke sobbing into his blankets. It seemed so real. He felt her emotion and longing raw and unfiltered by shame. Was she real? If he did not find out soon, he would go insane from never sleeping. Weeks had passed. How could he face her night after night and endure her pleas, her pain, her suffering? Dreams of Anesidora had been his singular obsession for too long. He had to find out if she was a vision sent by the gods or a demon of his mind's own making.

———

The summer morning was cool and breezy, a very comfortable time of the day that Akakios enjoyed more than any other. He was leaving his home earlier than usual to perform the rite of sanctification over a new forge built for an impatient blacksmith who would be anxious to begin his work. Akakios strong point had never been walking and certainly not running. It was the unfortunate side effect of an imperfection from birth that had produced a shriveled and useless stump in place of his right foot. Despite the disability, he was able to walk with the assistance of his staff, half dragging his deformed foot along with him. He snorted top himself. Why should he be in a hurry anyway? He was the Ta Hera of Kronos after all. The blacksmith would just have to wait. With slow determination, he descended the front steps to the street below where two acolytes from the temple waited for him outside.

"Eukomai se, Ta Hiera," *I pray for you, Holy One*. They greeted him humbly, in near perfect unison.

"Eukomai se," Akakios replied without slowing his awkward gait.

"We have brought a gift for Kronos today, Ta Hiera," the younger of the two acolytes piped with excitement.

Akakios regarded the boys, who were only around ten years old and still many years away from becoming priests themselves. They were of an age that the ancient stories and mythos inspired their imagination to flights of fancy. Stories that Akakios was only too happy to pass along to the next generation of young followers.

"Show me the gift you bring, child, so I may judge the blessings you shall earn with it." Akakios couldn't hold back the slight smile he felt on his face. He was pleased they were eager students.

Each of the boys produced a small sculpture made from wood. One represented the patriarch god Kronos and the other portrayed the wise goddess Metis. Akakios knew their forms well and was stunned by what they presented to him. *The gods must be speaking to me through these children.*

He recovered quickly. "That is fine work I see from both of you. We will sacrifice the figures to Kronos at the dedication this morning. Now let's be away. Master Kyros will be in a foul mood if he wastes his entire morning waiting for us."

The boys smiled enthusiastically, put their figurines away and took up positions two paces behind him, as was considered appropriate in public.

Akakios did not think of himself as a feeble man for his age. In fact, despite his incapacitated right foot, he was fit and generally energetic. He liked to walk the city meeting people and enjoyed the thin mountain air. For some reason, he felt especially invigorated today, as if he were subconsciously anticipating something special that would occur without having any idea what it might be. Whatever it was, or even if it was anything at all, he would enjoy the feeling while it lasted, especially since at his age nearly every day was a little more difficult than the one before.

He turned onto a wide street that ran through the center of the city. He considered the sharp incline and how far he had yet to go and wished he would have instructed the acolytes to bring his carriage. It wasn't that his deficient foot caused him any pain or distress, it was just that he misjudged the distance to his destination. He always hated showing up to a dedication flush and soaked with sweat if he could help it.

The people he passed made reverent signs to him and often touched his clothing for blessings. He was used to it and waded through them as if they weren't even there. Most interestingly, his god Kronos also suffered the affliction of a shriveled right foot and given Akakios's elevated position in the temple, many believed him marked by Kronos lending much credence to his close relationship with the deity. Of course, he knew it was nothing more than an odd coincidence, but how could he dissuade the faith of the believers?

Besides, it had favored him with advantage more than a few times politically within the temple as much as with the faithful.

Akakios acknowledged many people on the street this morning. Working people dressed in light chitons, the length of which was typically short this time of year, with a tunic fastened at the shoulders and belted at the waist. Most of their attire was a combination of dull colors with sandals or boots typical of tradesmen, farmers, shepherds and a hundred other occupations in the labor class. There were a few merchants out as well, distinct in their appearance by colorful chitons of fine fabric and a few pieces of jewelry. And of course, there were the servants. Lots of servants running this way and that, stopping long enough to offer their respect as everyone did, no matter their social status, when Akakios passed by.

The old priest's mind wandered while he waved and smiled. He'd lived in the mountain city of Sesklo all his life and he knew practically every one of the thousands who called this beautiful city home. The majority of them worshiped Kronos as he did, but there were many gods and goddesses of Hellas to chose from without exclusivity. Every city-state in the Confederation of Hellas revered a particular deity as their patron and protector above all others. In the case of Sesklo, it was Kronos, patron of blacksmiths, artisans, fire and harvests. These were the domains of his god.

Slowly winding his way higher and higher on the main thoroughfare, Akakios was reminded why he loved Sesklo so much. It was a city of many elevations with grand vistas, beautifully sculpted marble carvings and white stone buildings held up by high, fluted columns set adjacent to stone-paved streets lined with life-like statuary. An industrial city of sorts, Sesklo was reputed to have the finest metalworkers, sculptors, craftsmen and artisans in all of Hellas. Their master-works were exported well beyond the city, well beyond Hellas, even as far as the courtyards of the Emerald Isle a thousand leagues to the west.

On nearly every surface of every building he passed there were beautifully chiseled artworks dedicated to a god or hero with scenes from mythology - each one telling a familiar story. Not a single sign creaked on rusty hinges over a doorway announcing the trade within like other cities, rather, their stone walls and doors were adorned with the artistic representation of their craft and the god that it was dedicated to. Akakios had to admit that it was a little confusing for foreigner visitors unfamiliar with their ways, but it was a small sacrifice for the lack of clutter and over all splendor that was unique to their mountain dwelling.

His mind continued to wander as his feet guided him to his destination. Some said it looked as if he walked in a trance. It was often like this of late because of his sleep deprivation and although the whispers of the faithful were not meant for him to hear, he knew that when the people observed him in his current state, they speculated that he must be in communion with the gods. For once, the rumors might be true. There was only one thing that Akakios was troubled by and it consumed nearly every waking thought. Because of it, he hadn't slept fitfully for the better part of a year.

It started with a recurring dream night after night. But unlike normal dreams, the images were vivid and memorable. They involved a distorted vision of Kronos and the distant figure of Metis, the goddess of wisdom. The dreams hinted at a union between the two, not as a sexual act, but as a creation to beget something or someone. Later, the dreams evolved to include the result of their union and eventually the identity of their creation was revealed to him - Anesidora.

In his dreams Kronos told him that her name meant "all-gifted," and Akakios was shown images of Kronos, Metis and other gods he could not see clearly bestow gifts upon her. Not gifts of a material nature like gold and silver, instead, favors of character, persuasion, the power of speech and a way of speaking, needlework, weaving . . . and above all else, beauty. It was her mother, Metis, who lastly gifted her with fine clothing and jewelry. In these dreams, it was as if Anesidora was being presented to him and that's when Akakios first started to feel the tug of a deep sense of love growing for her. Sometimes the dreams included the appearance of Metis with a saddled, winged horse from legends called a Pegasos ready for flight. For what reason, he did not know. None of it really made any sense at all.

The dreams continued to evolve over the months and soon Akakios found himself engaged in mundane discussions with Anesidora. She made him feel like a young man again, huddled together like lovers, laughing over follies in poetry or weeping with the tragedies of literary prose. Before long, Akakios could not deny that he had fallen deeply in love with this fantastical figure and felt compelled to find her. And each morning after he awoke, he would once again realize that it was only a dream and thought himself a silly old man. Why would he have such fanciful dreams? They were more fitting to young men looking for adventure or the pursuit of whimsical adoration. Yet the feelings for her grew stronger in him each day and lingered long into the day. Akakios feared that soon he would be unable to resist the power they held over him and he would be compelled to go on some fool's journey in search of a fantasy that didn't exist. How the gods toyed with their disciples, but why him?

The dream he had the previous night was the most distressing yet. As usual, Anesidora appeared to him in all her beauty. The peplos she wore, a long garment pinned at her shoulders and cinched by a gold chain around her waist, was nearly sheer, revealing the perfection of her body. She stood in front of a temple at high elevation with winds that blew her silky blonde hair and silvery garments one direction and then another. Yet most disturbing was that she was reaching out to him, not to an image of himself in his dream, but to him directly, saying, "Come to me."

The dream repeated over and over during the night and by morning Akakios decided that he must speak with the Hierophant, Head Priest of Kronos, about these dreams. Perhaps the two of them could interpret their meaning together and bring him peace.

"Ta Hiera, we are here," the sweet voice of one of the acolytes broke through the cacophony of noise in the busy street.

Akakios, deep in thought as he walked, was startled to see that he was only a few strides away from Master Kyros's forge. He smiled warmly to himself, for he knew this family well, one of which he was always glad to see. Entering by way of the storefront, Akakios's gaze skimmed over the metal tools, parts and weapons displayed on a number of crowded shelves and racks. Even at this early hour, there were several patrons making various selections with the help of shop stewards. He was glad to see that Kyros's business was prosperous enough that he could afford the building of a second forge, bringing on two more apprentices.

Barely two steps inside, he was greeted warmly by Kyros's wife, Theokleia. With long blonde curls and a shapely figure hardly concealed by a sea-green peplos, she was considered one of the natural beauties of the city.

She bowed to Akakios and kissed his hand. "Eukomai se, Ta Hiera."

Her smile seemed to light up the room and lift up his heart. Akakios took her by the shoulders and hugged her warmly. "Eukomai se, dear one," he returned. He'd known Theokleia since the day she was born. In fact, he was the priest who presided over her naming ceremony.

"Kyros is enthusiastically awaiting your arrival!" she told him with a mischievous grin.

Akakios smiled, still holding her hands. "You mean he is impatiently pacing and cursing the late arrival of the club-footed Ta Hiera!"

Theokleia laughed an amiable, lilting laughter that had change little over the years. "You're so bad," she whispered and kissed him on the cheek. "I have missed you!"

Theokleia had grown to be a beautiful and vivacious woman, but to Akakios she would always be the happy little girl with blonde curls who listened so intently to the ancient stories he used to tell the children on the steps of the temple every week. That was a long time ago. Too long.

With childlike enthusiasm, Theokleia ran ahead of him. "Kyros! The Ta Hiera is here! Be on your best behavior now, or he might just crack your new hearth!" She giggled.

Akakios and his acolytes followed her through the back of the storefront and out into a large courtyard beyond. On one side of the spacious area was a forge in full operation attended by two young apprentices. On the other side was the new forge, freshly constructed and cold to the touch. The entire area was covered by a thick leather canopy that kept the sun and rain off the forges and their workers. Sitting adjacent the new forge was a small portable pen holding a single pig. Everything looked to be in order. Reluctantly, his gaze shifted to rest upon Master Kyros, who was standing in front of the cold forge next to his wife with his arms folded, clearly annoyed and anxious to get the ceremony over with.

Akakios was always impressed by the figure of Kyros. He was a large man, typical of a blacksmith, with short brown curls that fell shoulder length from a full head of hair and intense brown eyes. He wore a basic chiton and a protective leather apron to keep the hot metal sparks from burning holes in his clothing. Akakios could see by the ash on the man's arms that he had been hard at work for hours already. Although impatient to get done with the dedication, he showed Akakios proper respect with a quick bow and the proper greeting.

"I know I'm a bit early, Kyros, but I have a very busy day, so why don't we get started," Akakios announced in mock self-regard.

Kyros blinked and then moved away from the cold forge, doing his best to hide his embarrassment, efforts that were completely blown by Theokleia's giggle.

The Ta Hiera directed the two acolytes to take positions on each side of the forge. However, before getting started, he quickly whispered to the boys, "You have your gifts handy?" Of course, they did and they smiled proudly when Akakios placed the figures within the forge.

While Akakios prepared for the Ritual of Fire, everyone in the courtyard began to gather to watch. Kyros and Theokleia had invited several friends and patrons and by the time Akakios was ready to start, the open space in front of the forge was crowded with onlookers.

The Ta Hiera signaled one of the acolytes, who retrieved the pig and tied it squealing onto the newly cut block anvil. Everything prepared, the acolytes positioned themselves a step behind Akakios and initiated a rhythmic chant that rose and fell in a low, measured cadence. The chatty spectators in the courtyard immediately went silent, eager to watch the ritual unfolding before them. It was a rare thing for a new forge to be dedicated by the Fire-Bringer and most never had the opportunity to witness it in their lifetime.

Akakios commenced by calling out blessings from Kronos for all the elements of the forge—hammer, tongs, paddles, the whetstone, sharpening and sanding implements, molds made from ingots and clay, the block anvil, slack basin, bellows, crucible and most importantly the stone hearth. He called out the blessings in time with the acolytes chanting that increased in volume and cadence, rising higher and higher, faster and faster. All around, the onlookers stood transfixed wide-eyed and hands over gaping mouths. Even Kyros watched with a mixed expression of fear and awe.

"Bring forth thy hand unto me! I am your vessel, the instrument of your power!" Akakios shouted the appeal to the clear sky above.

An audible crackling filled the air and Akakios could feel the power of his god running through him, standing hair on end, like an electric charge waiting to be released. The intonation was nearly a constant high-pitched scream drowning out the squealing of the terrified pig. Akakios called forth his final blessings on the hearth, raised his arms into the air and with a roar like an avalanche falling down a mountainside, his hands erupted in flames.

Startled cries burst from the crowd and they took a collective step backward away from the heat of the flames. Some froze in place transfixed with fear while others fled the courtyard altogether. If any were expecting a bromide ceremony with tiresome oratory, sedate smiles and platitudes, they should of thought first why the Ta Hiera was sometimes called the Fire-Bringer.

Akakios cried once more to Kronos thrusting his hands into the charcoal-filled hearth. The chanting abruptly ceased and there was a collective inhalation from the crowd. It was said that only a hearth in service to a worthy metal worker would ignite, although if the truth were to be told, Akakios never had one *not* light. Immediately the hearth blazed to life as the flames withered from his blackened hands and the Ta Hiera stepped to the side so all could see that the forge had passed the Ritual of Flames.

A hush cloaked those that assembled to witness the miracle that day. More like a stunned silence. Akakios was not surprised, the reaction was always the same. He waited patiently for the moment to come and when it did, it was a euphoric rhapsody of voices raised in adoring devotion to the god of fire, the god of blacksmiths. This was his favorite part. Not only because he basked in the adulation poured upon him, but also because of the glorification of his role in the temple. It gave him purpose in his old age, reminded him that he was useful and unique, that he was valued by the faithful for more than just his rhetoric on holy days.

When the crowd eventually settled, Akakios stepped to the block anvil to perform his final obligation. It was called the Rite of Purification with the purpose of bringing the blessings of Kronos upon it so that it might never break and as far as he knew, none ever had. He took a wide-bladed knife offered by one of his acolytes and without ceremony plunged it into the heart of the pig tied to the anvil. With one sharp squealing shriek and a few seconds of reflexive twitches and kicks from the swine, its life essence flowed over the block saturating the hard stone in a final sacrifice of blood to Kronos.

The ritual complete, the crowd in the courtyard cheered appreciatively, kissing the cheeks of Kyros and Theokleia in congratulations on their new forge. The blacksmith appeared genuinely grateful and Theokleia reflected the joy of her husband. Akakios watched the young couple with pride. They worked hard to build a prosperous life and pay homage to their god and it left him wondering how soon they might have children to join him for stories on the steps of the Naos. Servants appeared and removed the pig to the kitchen. They would slowly cook its meat all day in a pit and serve tender pork pulled from its bones with legumes, olives and cheese at the feast of celebration later that evening, while its inedible parts would be returned to burn in the hearth in honor of its sacrifice. Those festivities went far too late in the night for his aged constitution and he imagined that by then he would be dozing on a padded lounge, as he did every night, dreaming. That last haunting thought compelled with it a sense of urgency.

The Ritual of Flames had taken Akakios's mind off of dreams for a while and brought him out among people to socialize. He was more than a little pleased with the distraction. Even so, Akakios said his goodbyes and with his acolytes in tow, departed for the Naos of Kronos. He was eager to see the Hierophant and work out what to do about these dreams.

Chapter 3

The Naos of Kronos

Beautiful cities of white marble columns, grand fountains and life-like statuary are shrouded in clouds at high elevations as if to conceal the perfection of their artistic expression. Indeed, it is like strolling through a metropolis of the gods! Their legends come alive in this land where creatures from mythology are spoken of as commonplace and their culture is reflected in painted carvings on the side of every structure big and small.

True or not, the folklore seems real enough when one walks among them. I would have enjoyed seeing much more of the beauty of Hellas if it didn't require the talents of a mountain goat to get to so much of it!

Wodanaz the Wanderer

Akakios admired the Naos of Kronos as he approached the colossal temple. He was impressed by its structure, even after so many years. Tall columns supported the massive marble facing with larger-than-man-sized carvings of Kronos demonstrating the activities that represented his province. Each was a masterpiece of sculpture in white marble highlighted with accents of red-gold in each scene. There were the hearth and hammer with Kronos as the metalworker, the hammer and chisel with Kronos as the sculptor, the scythe and sickle with Kronos as the harvester and flames held in his hands as Kronos the bringer of fire. Akakios paused a moment before entering to behold the miracle of stonework that could only have been accomplished with divine conveyance to guide the artist's hand to shape the stone with such eloquence and virtue.

The entire foundation of the Naos was elevated on a high stone base and carved with steps that Akakios and his acolytes climbed up to the grand entrance of the temple. Set atop the landing in front of the entry was a large brazier that continually burned with a red flame day and night all year long, even with high winds, snow and driving rains. Akakios knew it was no natural flame, ever-burning and unquenchable; it was powered by the undeniable will of Kronos through the priests who attended to it and served as the hallmark of the temple perched high above the city. Ensconced on each column around the circumference of the landing several smaller ever-burning torches illuminated the temple at night, reflecting off the red-gold accents making the temple appear as if it were engulfed in flames from a distance. Akakios often mused that if the temple ever did catch fire, no one would notice.

Beyond the brazier, Akakios led the acolytes through the open doors of the Naos, which were lined in more red-gold and polished to a degree of diligence that they reflected smoothly in the light of day. Farther inside, the passage widened into a long hall and he passed rows of columns decorated covered floor to ceiling with carvings by master sculptors depicting Kronos posing or performing various activities he was known for.

Akakios brought his retinue to a stop at the end of the hall where sat a simple altar with a small bowl that held the sacred red flame. Astride the altar two guards stood in full bronze armor, holding a rounded bronze shield and a deadly-looking sword forged with a protrusion in the shape of a sickle near the tip of the blade, that they called a Harpe. They were highly trained warriors who would not hesitate to swiftly strike down anyone foolish enough to defile the flame or the altar.

None had ever been so foolish.

Speaking a quick prayer to Kronos, Akakios admired the wall behind the altar carved to look like flames then pressed and smoothed with red-gold to give the illusion of life and movement cast by the real flame in the bowl set before it. This was the most holy space in the Naos. The blaze here required no attending from priests or anyone else. Akakios knew there was no trick to this fire. It just was and always would be, as it had been from the beginning.

The Naos was oriented in such a way that on the summer solstice, the sun would shine through the open doors of the wide hall and onto the gold flames, setting off a display that lent the appearance of fire flickering and dancing across the entire wall. Akakios was intimately familiar with this hall, for it was here that the Fire-Bringer conducted the Ritual of Fire on the summer solstice. Akakios couldn't begin to recall the number of he had done so. The last time had been only a few weeks previous. Kronos indicated through omens and images in the fire that there would be a continuation of blessed prosperity and bountiful harvests to the good fortune of Sesklo and its people.

Akakios cast all thoughts aside regarding rituals and omens, he wished to find the Hierophant to discuss his dreams. He left his acolytes behind in the main hall and made his way into the private sections of the temple where only the priests of Kronos could tread. The hallways and backrooms of the Naos that outsiders would never see were no less spectacular than the public areas of the temple. Most of the lower-level priests had regular jobs in addition to their duties to Kronos and given the god that they had chosen to follow, almost all of them were talented sculptors, craftsmen, blacksmiths or artisans in the city. Akakios admired their work and dedication to their god. Many of them enjoyed prosperous businesses and traveled to far-off lands trading their goods while serving Kronos at the temple in conjunction with their personal affairs.

The Naos provided large rooms and courtyards for the priests to pursue their chosen craft, Akakios passed by many on the way to the Hierophant's office and spied new works that would soon be released for display in the temple or sold to a wealthy noble in some far-off destination. As massive as the temple was, it could hardly hold anymore new art. Every wall was covered with marvelous works by generations of priests who had left their artistic mark and the storerooms were bursting with hundreds of masterwork-level sculptures and carvings. The Naos made a spectacular business of the crafts and often sent groups of priests appointed to conduct trade for the temple's benefit into foreign lands to sell-off the excess. It was the main revenue of the Naos, although few knew it. Most believed the temple operated on the relatively meager sums donated by the populace.

Akakios found the Hierophant, Miltiades, exactly where he expected the man to be this time of day - in his private office. There was a sleepy-eyed acolyte outside the door who immediately perked up and rushed inside to announce the Ta Hiera. A moment later the boy held the door open for Akakios to enter.

Inside, the Hierophant was sitting at his desk reviewing various documents probably related to trade. A grey-haired man only a few years older than Akakios, the Hierophant had the strength and build of one much younger. Before he rose to the top leadership position in service to Kronos, he was an accomplished blacksmith with a thriving business. To this day he still took a hammer to anvil every opportunity he could, but Akakios was sure his blacksmithing days were far behind him. Today he wore his usual chiton and kolpos, all white except for a thin line of red trim that added a just a hint of color that appeared to stretch across his chest and shoulders. Akakios envied the Hierophant's physique, considering that he was almost the exact physical opposite. His deformed foot would not afford him much in the way of exercise or sports to develop an athletic frame. Instead, long walks and a proper diet kept him in reasonable health.

The room was illuminated by candles and the afternoon light that filtered through a single window, under which sat two acolytes dozing in chairs while awaiting any task the Hierophant might decide to send them on. Along the walls and scattered around the room were many tables and shelves cluttered with scrolls and tomes that gave the large room a slightly musty smell that many of the acolytes joked was actually the old Hierophant himself. Akakios also found the humor in that one and secretly wondered if it might be true.

"Eukomai se, Hierophant," Akakios greeted the Hierophant before taking a seat in front of the ornately carved wooden desk. Even that showed numerous scenes of Kronos enmeshed in his trade among his devotees.

"Eukomai se, Ta Hiera," he replied distractedly while moving papers here and there on his desk.

"Is this not a good time, Hierophant?" Akakios asked politely.

"Yes, yes—I mean, of course not, Ta Hiera. Are you well today?" he asked, putting aside the papers and looking up at Akakios for the first time since he entered.

Akakios replied with a small smile, "I am well, Hierophant, but I have a private matter to discuss with you."

Tapping on his desk to get the acolytes' attention, the Hierophant pointed to the door and the two boys hastened to leave his chambers.

Once the door had closed behind them, the Hierophant leaned back in his chair casually and smiled. "Kyros didn't give you fits for not dedicating his forge two minutes after dawn did he, Akakios?"

Akakios laughed. "No, Miltiades. Kyros is a fine man. He just expects the world to revolve around his timetable."

"To be so blessed with youth and arrogance again." Miltiades almost sounded nostalgic. "I may not know much, but I am sure the only timetable we can count on is that of the gods and they are very avaricious with the details."

Akakios would usually quip back and forth with his friend about the gods and their absurd demands, but not today. He was eager, almost desperate, to discuss why he had come to see the Hierophant and it wasn't to exchange drollery about gods and men. He allowed his voice to take on a more serious tone, "There is something important I need to discuss with you. I believe I have been having . . . visions."

"Visions?"

Akakios leaned forward and rested his arms on the Hierophant's desk. "Of a sort. Perhaps we can work out their meaning, if you suppose there is one."

Miltiades lifted an eyebrow with interest. "Please go on."

"It's the vision of a beautiful woman, somehow beget by a collaboration between Kronos and Metis. She has been bestowed with gifts by many other gods as well and now she asks me to seek her out,"

Akakios was certain his tale sounded far less ludicrous when he rehearsed it in his head earlier, "and I wonder: is this a fantasy of an old man or a directive from our god's creation?"

To his credit, Miltiades did not immediately burst out laughing and even appeared to be listening very carefully. He remained silent for a long moment after Akakios stopped speaking before he replied, "Did the woman reveal her name to you?"

"She did," Akakios confirmed. "She said her name was Anesidora."

Miltiades stared at him, unblinking, almost stunned. "Come with me," he abruptly rose from his chair, put on his gold headband with flaming sickle and scythe, the sign of Kronos and a symbol of his office and opened the door.

The acolytes waiting outside immediately jumped to assist him with whatever he needed, but the Hierophant quickly waved them away. "Stay here until I return."

Taking an oil lamp from a small table outside his office, the Hierophant led Akakios through several dark hallways and down a stairway leading below ground level. This part of the Naos had not been used for many years other than storage for dust and cobwebs and not a soul was seen along the way. In all his years spent working and praying in the Naos, Akakios did not think he had ever been down here before.

At the bottom of the narrow stairway was a door thick with heavy wood that looked as if it had not been opened in decades and the undisturbed dust on the floor before it appeared to confirm Akakios's presumption. The Hierophant pulled a key hanging on a long silver chain from around his neck and after a few tentative turns, unlocked the door.

Inside, the light from the oil lamp illuminated a plethora of scrolls, texts and tomes organized neatly on bookcases along the wall and in baskets lined up against the shelves. "This is the secret library of sacred texts." The Hierophant waved away the cloud of dust the opening door stirred up in the room.

"I always wondered what was down here," replied Akakios.

"As my successor, I should have brought you here years ago, but for some reason I always put it off until the next year or the year after. We all think we will live forever, until we don't." The Hierophant blew dust from a tome and then returned it to the shelf. "I've spent thousands of hours in this room over the years trying to understand the gods and I still find it beyond my grasp. I don't recommend that you follow my poor example," his wan smile in the dim light made him look older than he was. "There is something here you must see. I believe it will help you make a decision about the meaning of your visions."

For over an hour the Hierophant searched through a number of texts looking for something he might have recalled reading once. Then abruptly he stopped as if impaled to the floor. "Here it is. I don't know why I remembered this. When I read it previously, it was meaningless, barely a fragment of the original text and I didn't give it another thought until today. Now I am confident that it is the single most important piece of knowledge gained from all the writings in this room."

The Hierophant turned the pages until he found the one he was looking for and handed the tattered book to Akakios to read for himself. There was a partial passage on a fragment of page that remained and could have easily been overlooked had Miltiades not known it was there.

Akakios read it out loud, "And there was a communion not of divine flesh between Kronos and Metis that begot their progeny. They named her Anesidora and she—" That was it, no other reference. He kept reading the short passage silently over and over trying to make sense of the meaning and what else there could have been.

The Hierophant, realizing Akakios must have finished reading the passage a dozen times, quietly spoke, "It was written by Eusebios over a thousand years ago. The gods were giving you a glimpse of the past, perhaps to validate the legitimacy of their issue. It makes me pause to wonder why, after so many years, I would recall what I have always thought was an obscure and insignificant passage in a forgotten text. It's humbling to think that even a Hierophant might be nothing more than a pawn in the great game of the gods."

Akakios thought for a moment, "Then it must be a vision rather than a fantasy. I am encouraged to find Anesidora as she has implored me to. Now the question: How do I find her?"

Miltiades considered the question. "In your visions of Anesidora, what were her surroundings? The lighting, sounds and any environmental factors that stood out.

"She seemed to be high in the mountains where it was cold, with her hair and clothing buffeted by winds constantly changing directions." He remembered it clearly.

"Hmmm, that could be anywhere in the Othrys Mountains." The Hierophant sat on a lone stool while Akakios paced the small room, leaving footprints in the thick layer of dust on the floor.

"My impression was that she dwells in a temple, perhaps her own or one of Kronos or Metis?" Akakios offered while trying to remember more details.

"There are no temples to Kronos at a very high elevation that I am aware of." Miltiades thumped his fingers on a hardbound book he held. "Although it is said his palace is built among the highest altitudes of the Othrys. And there is also a legend of a shrine to Metis atop the eastern peaks near the Sea of Waves. That would seem the more likely place to find this Anesidora."

"Then that's where I shall begin." Akakios was excited about pursuing his vision now that he believed it might be more than just a dream.

"I caution you in this, my friend," Miltiades eyebrows creased with worry. "The Othrys Mountains are a dangerous and mystical place where the gods' creatures ply their fancy. Would you consider an escort of priests and explorers for your safety? It would devastate our community if the Fire-Bringer never returned from his calling."

"I must do this alone. If I am to find and rescue Anesidora from her turmoil, it would not look well upon me to have brought an army to do so. Don't worry," Akakios played a series of flames across his fingers, "Your old Fire-Bringer still has a bit of heat in his belly from the old days."

Miltiades clasped him on the shoulder. "Well then, as you wish. But when you return, I am passing on this key. I have learned everything the gods choose for me to know. In the meantime, let's return to my office and decide who will oversee your duties while you are away."

———

Akakios dismissed his acolytes and walked the way home alone. It was nearly evening and the temperature had dropped to a crisp chill. The sun setting behind the mountains to the west bathed the city in the last illumination of the day casting a vibrant, reddish-orange light reflecting off the white marble, stone buildings, statuary and columns. At this time of the day, Sesklo was at its most beautiful.

Akakios passed a row of temples on his way home. There were many small temples in the city dedicated to Gaia, Nyx, Ourea, Aether, Hemera, Metis and others. They were the gods of Hellas's pantheon, known as the Protogenoi. They formed the elements of the universe that included the domains of earth, air, water, sky, darkness, light, the Underworld, night, fire, procreation and time. All were revered throughout Hellas, yet only Sesklo claimed Kronos as their patron deity, while the other cities chose patrons of their own.

Or rather, the gods chose them.

Out of all the gods, Akakios elected to stop only at the Naos of Metis and say a prayer. If he was going to find one of her earliest shrines from antiquity, it might go easier for him if the goddess favored his cause. There he stayed only briefly, showing respect to the lone priest on duty and making an offering of sanctified water blessed by the Hierophant himself.

Akakios arrived at his home a short while later and slowly climbed the steps to the front door, which was promptly opened by one of his servants. He was exhausted by the event of the day and excited about the journey he would undertake the next. Eating only a little dried fish and a honey cake to satisfy his sweet tooth, he washed and immediately retired to his bed. Sleep came quickly as he slipped quietly into the nether of his subconscious. He looked forward to telling his young love that he would finally be on his way to find her.

Chapter 4

Paein

Akakios awoke early and prepared supply packs for his pilgrimage into the Othrys Mountains wilderness. Knowing only vaguely where he was going to search for the Shrine of Metis, he was resigned to the idea that it could very well take half a lifetime time to find, if it existed at all. That's where his faith would sustain him. During the dark hours when doubt crept in, he questioned his resolve and wished to quit and go home, he would depend upon his faith to see him through. He was no stranger to impossible quests and how they wore on one's determination; it had just been a few years since had joined one.

The boys that served as his acolytes arrived cheerful and innocently oblivious just like they did every morning. They knew he was going on a journey, but not the reasons. Akakios envied their blithe unsophistication and purity of soul and silently lamented how soon it would all change for them. Youth was such a pitiless and wonderful thing.

"Strap the bags on tight, boys," He called cheerfully. "And don't worry about Tella, she won't bite or kick."

The night before, Akakios spent several hours with the Hierophant discussing the best way to approach the hunt for the shrine. Wandering the Othrys near the coast would be time-consuming and likely futile. Fortunately, there was a mountain road through the passes and valleys all the way to the cliffs overlooking the Sea of Waves and it had several villages along the way so he wouldn't be entirely in the wilderness the whole time. And Akakios knew well not deviate from that path until he had reason to do so. Of course, the burly Hierophant tittered at him like some hand-wringing old lady reminding him of the dangers in the mountains and imploring him to take a small retinue of attendants for protection. Akakios had already expressed his reasons for going alone and politely refused all the while silently hoping he was not acting as reckless as Hierophant made it seem.

With one last glance back to the comfort of his home, he departed with a wave and a smile to his two young acolytes. Their youthful exuberance had them running behind him until he crossed the outermost boundaries of Sesklo, leaving them staring after him as he continued on alone down the desolate East-Way Road and into the unknown. How they would wonder at the adventures that lay ahead, Akakios chuckled to himself.

He took a deep breath of the cold mountain air. The summertime was the best time to travel the mountain routes of Hellas considering the weather was dry and the conditions favorable with little snow except at the highest elevations. Even so, the East-Way Road was far less traveled, benefiting from little upkeep throughout the year and few travelers that journeyed to and from the outlying villages mainly for trade.

Within a few hours, Akakios spied carts ahead and joined a small convoy of merchants bearing loads of wheat and grains and other mundane items for the outlying villages. He enjoyed the company of the traders, but after a day of slow travel he realized that with their wagons and trailing livestock, it would take him twice as long to reach the coast than on his own. Reluctantly, Akakios left them the next morning, although he would miss the convenience and security of camping together at night and socializing around the campfire. Not that the East-Way mountain road was a terribly dangerous road to travel, since there was little profit for bandits and the wild animals generally stayed away from anywhere people tread. Still, one was always more vulnerable alone than when traveling in a group. He hoped to reach the next village, where he could stay overnight if he didn't come across a friendly campsite, before nightfall. Given his position and reputation in Sesklo, which was the closest city to any of the villages, he was sure there would be no shortage of invitations for the Ta Hiera of Kronos to stay at someone's home or inn and offer a blessing in his passing.

As many years as Akakios had lived in Sesklo, he had traveled this road only a handful of times in the past and most of those times no more than a day out of the city. To his chagrin, he had forgotten to bring along the map that he and the Hierophant had plotted the locations of villages between Sesklo and the sea. He could imagine the parchment sitting on his writing desk where he had left it. Ah, his mind might not be quite as sharp as it once was, but surely he could rely on other travelers and locals for directions along the way. Besides, it wasn't as if there were any other roads branching in another direction or intersecting the one he was on, not a single one – the East-Way ended at the last village closest to the sea, so he was not likely to lose his way.

Near to nightfall, the late afternoon sun, having lost all of its warmth, cast a broken array of horizontal beams through the thick boughs of trees lighting up wandering specs of dust like gold and stretched his long shadow forward onto rough trail. Akakios followed around a bend where the terrain transitioned into a forest dense with heavy coniferous undergrowth and pale-barked aspen with bright green leaves that rose steeply above him on each side, following the form of the sloping pass. His legs and hips were sore, he was not used to riding for long hours and for a while thought to lead his horse through the pass and allow his cramped legs some exercise. Akakios wasn't far along when he felt the small hairs on the back of his neck rise with the eerie sensation that he was being watched. Without slowing his awkward pace, he invoked a quick spell to expand his awareness and soon identified what, or rather who, it was that observed his passing. It was trick he learned from a druid of Sunna during his more adventurous years, decades ago and it had come in handy quite often.

"I know you are there." Akakios, alone on the East-Way Road, felt the unseen eyes of his adversary watching him from the thick growth pines and firs. He was sure there was more than one.

"Look at me," he dragged his club foot along beside him, using his long hardwood staff to support his weight. "I must appear weak to you, easy prey."

There was a low growl from somewhere to his right. Akakios allowed himself a brief smile. What a clever ruse. He was sure it wasn't him they wanted as much as the ample meat of his horse, but

Akakios was not about to give up his prized animal to the wild frenzy planned by this lot.

"Consider your options, Great Mother. This forest is filled with prey for your taking." Akakios continued his slow trek. "I know you cannot speak so that I could understand, but I feel your uncertainty."

Another growl, this time from a different direction, confirmed his suspicions. He knew their plan now, thanks to the second one giving away his position. If that one survived this encounter, he would pay for his undisciplined behavior later. None disrespected the Great Mother without cost.

Akakios stopped in a small clearing where the trees grew a few paces back from the road and planted his staff in front of him with both hands. "Now is the time for a decision, Great Mother. Do as you may, or leave me in peace."

Gray blurs of sodden fur shot out from the dark forest on each side of the trail. They came for him baring long white teeth, sharp and biting, in muzzles that snapped with the power to rend flesh from bone and wide eyes intent with the need to kill. They were the legendary Dire Wolves of the Kryos Forest and their Great Mother was known as Aukokhi.

His horse screamed and reared before attempting to run back down the way they had come. Akakios held firm to the reins and paid it no mind. Time slowed. Still leaves on smooth bleached branches almost glowing in the fading light stood in stark contrast to the black clouds of dry soil tossed violently into the air by the massive claws of the approaching Dire Wolves. Unnatural strength filled him, euphoric power surged through his veins and the rapture of Kronos poured out in a rush of glorious intensity.

And there was fire.

Without thought or plan, tall flames sprang up around Akakios and his mount, so intensely hot that they instantly consumed the space where they appeared and like the snap of a tree struck by lightning, they rent the air with a deafening crack. The Dire Wolves tried to stop their charge, they tried desperately to alter their course, but it was too late, they were too close. With barely a yelp, they disappeared into the flames leaving no hint they ever existed, no patch of fur or scorched bone to eulogize their absolute incineration. Releasing his mount to run freely, Akakios deliberately walked through the ring of fire and allowed the flames to die down around him, not a hair singed on his body.

"You are brave, Aukokhi," He spoke to the air, not knowing exactly from where in the forest she still watched. There were others with her, many others. "You are the bravest of beasts and you are a wise pack leader, but I will not be your prey today." Akakios raised his voice, angry that he had been forced to take sacred lives so unnecessarily. "I know you understand my words, Aukokhi! Go away with your children and find other prey to satisfy your hunger, or I will destroy you and all that are with you, for I am the Fire-Bringer!" Akakios staff burst into unnatural flame in his hand and he held it aloft in dramatic fashion for emphasis.

There was no sound, not even a rustle of leaves, yet he knew they were gone, like an elusive breeze. Alone again, Akakios lowered his staff and relinquished the flame. With a shrug of his shoulders and a dismissive grunt, he whistled for his mount. Moments later Tella came back up the pathway at a fast trot and stood nervously before him. Akakios was quietly thankful she had not run off too far after the flames died. He gave his old horse a pat on its nose, calmly mounted and continued on his way.

It would be fully dark in an hour and Akakios was getting concerned that he had not seen anyone on the road nor any signs of a village for quite a while. He began to regret leaving the slow-moving convoy and wondered if he had made a bad decision in his haste and resigned himself to camping off the road when darkness fell. If it came to that, Akakios hoped Aukokhi and her pack would not return for another try at him during the night when he was more vulnerable. He would take precautions in any case. Keeping an eye out for a good place to stop, he soon heard a welcoming tune being played on shepherd's pipes not far ahead down the road. His heart leaped with the prospect of company at camp or at least someone who could tell him what was a little farther down the road.

The sun retired from the sky allowing the cold gloom of the forest to press in all around when he found the source of the music. In the distance, he could see the camp lit up by a small fire just off the road in a clearing with the backdrop of thick brush and trees. Dancing around that fire were two silhouettes, each with pipes, playing a rousing tune back and forth and then together in a harmonious chorus that was very catchy. When he rode closer, he could see that the revelers were two short figures wearing odd breaches, short tunics and some sort of adornment on their heads. Akakios smiled to himself. Perhaps they were traveling hypokrites who would entertain him with ribald comedies and forlorn tragedies. The two men stopped playing and stood together when they noticed his approach. To his relief, they began to wave in a friendly manner and he waved back.

At least they seemed affable and from the spirited tunes they played and danced to, they must be a lively duo that would share easy conversation. Akakios had been alone on the road all day with no one to talk to except for Tella and the animal wasn't much of a conversationalist. He mused at what fun it would be if animals could speak, then immediately rejected the idea. They would surely curse all Hellenes for their tradition of sacrificing them to the gods!

When he arrived at the edge of their camp, Akakios dismounted and walked his horse into the light of their campfire. What he saw next made him freeze in his tracks. The odd clothing he thought they were wearing earlier was now clearly something else entirely. The two creatures had the torso, arms and face of a typical man, but the coarse tight curls of the hair covering their hindquarters, long cleft hooves bereft of boots and smooth horns curved above their heads were that of a goat. With a start, he recognized them as the mythical Paein.

"Have no fear, good traveler! My name was Agreus and this is my brother Nomios. You are welcome to join our camp, join our company and join our songs!" If the small creature weren't so strange to his eyes, Akakios would have been comforted by the Paein's cheery demeanor.

Nomios joined in with a trill on his pipes, "And look, good sir." He motioned to rabbits on spits over the fire. "My brother is an excellent hunter with a fortunate bounty to share with another!"

Akakios could not believe what he was seeing. Two cheery Paein wearing fine tunics in a camp with roasting rabbits. For a moment he thought maybe he had fallen asleep on his mount having another unusual dream, except that he wasn't and it was really happening. The two brothers stared back at him with broad smiles on their faces, politely waiting for him to accept their offer of hospitality.

With no little effort, Akakios finally found words in his throat to speak, "Thank you, brothers Paein. My name is Akakios, Ta Hiera to Kronos in Sesklo. Your offer of accommodation at your camp is appreciated and welcome on this dark night."

Nomios played another trill on his pipes and exclaimed with excitement, "A Holy One, Agreus! How fortunate we are! And to Kronos of Fire and Field! We are honored by you!"

"Please sit by the fire with us and enjoy the bounty of my hunt! We will play many tunes and tell wonderous stories! A time we will have!" laughed Agreus.

"A time we will have!" Nomios repeated excitedly.

Akakios tied his horse to a nearby tree and joined them at the fire. He was still stunned at meeting these mythological creatures. The stories that spoke of them described the Paein as the children of the deities Eros and Rhea. They lived in the mountains and forests and were said to help shepherds find lost charges wandered from their flock. Yes, to those living in the mountains of Othrys, these stories were familiar, if not taken very seriously. Yet here they were, vividly undeniable and impossible to explain.

Grateful for the warm meat, Akakios consumed the rabbits while Agreus and Nomios played their pipes and danced around the flames, acting out comedies in vulgar form and verse about promiscuous gods and dryads eager to please. Apparently a favorite storyline often performed by the brothers as demonstrated by their skillful delivery of the vivid imagery. The night went long with laughter and honey mead that flowed freely and frequently, before Akakios's vision blurred from too much drink and he fell fast asleep.

With the passage of darkness to dawn, Akakios half expected to awake from a curious dream, but the Paein were still there. Eager to please as ever, they beseeched Akakios to allow them to travel with him and play their pipes for his entertainment. He was glad for their company. Thus far their conversation has been about music, poetry, art, love and the gods; however, Akakios had thus far held back the reason for his pilgrimage.

Back on the road, the Paein again amused him with their pipes and prose and somehow kept pace with Tella even as they danced around the wary mare. The day and the leagues slipped by in their company and oddly Akakios did not recall a single traveler or village passed during the day. It was just as well, as he was enjoying himself immensely in the company of his new companions.

As darkness once again fell over the heavy boughs of the deciduous forest that crowded close to the road, the Paein found the perfect spot to camp and set up a campfire to warm Akakios's travel-weary bones. Agreus disappeared for a while and returned with more rabbits, quickly gut and cleaned them and spit them over the flames while Nomios played the pipes and danced around in fits and twirls. From somewhere, Agreus brought a large amphora of the most exceptional Oinos wine. It was a silky burgundy produced in the city of Metis that rivaled the famous and expensive Mekali Red the Heirophant sometimes imported from the Emerald Isle. The Paein took a long draft, then passed it over to Akakios.

"Do you know about the nymphs, Ta Hiera?" Agreus leaned back on his furry elbows and hiccupped.

Akakios nodded. "I have read about them but certainly never met one."

The Paein jumped up, clapped his hands and spun in a circle. "Yes! They are certainly difficult to find and it's even more difficult to convince them to lay with you!"

"I see." Akakios hadn't expected the conversation to take such a risqué turn, yet the wine that warmed his belly elevated his spirits and he found it quite humorous. "Is it your objective to philander with the maidens or to convince them to be your mate?"

Agreus sputtered and squawked, "Mate! Never!" and happily proceeded to go into exaggerated detail about the philandering he would like to do with a nymph, causing Akakios to blush more than once and drink frequently of the Oinos to cover his embarrassment.

"I have heard that the nymphs in the Sylvan Kingdom and Eriu are particularly amorous." The Paein danced from hoof to hoof while he spoke and Akakios briefly wondered if the creature could keep still for even a moment. "Whom do you think would be most offended by my exploits with the nymphs? The elves or the druids?"

The thought of the Paein asking either for permission made Akakios laugh. "Maybe you should stick with the nymphs in Hellas, wherever they might be."

The rabbits were steaming over the low flames, dripping their winter fat into the sizzling embers to cloud the air with a delectably roasted scent. Akakios could not remember eating anything the entire day and his stomach churned in fits of loud growls from the delicious fragrance. Taking pieces of the tender cooked meat, he barely let them cool before he eagerly consumed the first few bites, all the while marveling at how satisfying they were.

With the Paein finally quiet and eating their rabbits, Akakios thought it would be a good time to casually pry for answers to some of the questions he was seeking. "Have you heard of a Shrine of Metis in the high peaks of the Othrys near the sea?"

Agreus and Nomios replied at almost the same time, "Of course we do! We know the Othrys, every league of it! Are you going there, Holy One?"

A thrill of excitement ran through Akakios, still, he tried not to let it show in his controlled response, "I was thinking to visit and pay respects to Metis while I was in the area. It's more of a pilgrimage, I suppose."

The two Paein looked at each other and then tumbled around on the ground laughing hysterically, "You are a funny Ta Hiera!"

Of all the replies Akakios might have expected, this one was not one of them. What was so funny about a priest paying homage to a goddess? He wanted to ask, but the Paein were rolling about in complete hysterics.

Agreus finally stopped and took a breath, "We will give you directions once we get closer to the sea!"

Exasperated, Akakios didn't question the brothers Paein further. It was enough that they claimed to know the location of the shrine with a promise to tell him how to get there. He fervently hoped they did not also expect to accompany him there. If Anesidora was waiting for him, he imagined how ridiculous he might appear showing up to rescue her with these two giddy creatures.

That night, while Nomios played his pipes, Agreus whispered to Akakios that he had the gift of prophecy. It was a rare lucid moment devoid of levity that hung heavy in the fog of wine that congested his mind and dulled his senses. The Paein divulged a dark foretelling of forbidden love, sins and deceptions that didn't at all make any sense or illuminate for whom the fortune might apply. Even so, the music was as intoxicating as the Oinos and the prophecies intriguing if only Akakios could have remembered much of them the next morning.

Just as they did the day before, the Paein traveled with him all the next day, never passing a single soul or village on their way. Akakios knew there was something unnatural going on, it was almost like a dream, except that he was awake and everything that happened was vivid and real. New suspicions about the true nature of his companions obsessed his mind, but since he estimated that they were not far from the coast, he planned to be leaving them soon anyway and he didn't want to upset them. He still needed their help to find the shrine and the odd little creatures had done nothing so far to warrant his interrogation.

The evening began the same as the last with a campfire, music, Oinos and rabbits. This time, however, Agreus was not in his playful mood and continued to whisper dark prophesies and dance around the fire casting long shadows against the stands of trees that loomed like goliaths in the chill night. For the first time since he left Sesklo, Akakios felt small and vulnerable. The mood of the spirited Paein had turned ominous and before he bolstered his courage with too much Oinos, he decided to ask again about the shrine.

"Seek a clearing within a wooded grove of oaks in the highlands on the western slope of the coastal-facing escarpment of the Othrys," Agreus spoke cryptically. His lips kept twisting to form a smile, as if there were something irresistibly funny that he did not wish to divulge.

"How will I know I have found the right grove?" Akakios tried to remain focused. He had to get the details right. There must be hundreds of groves in the Othrys.

The Paein waved his arms in a grand flourish, as if unveiling the apparent truth. "A sign from Metis will be waiting for you, oh Holy One!"

Akakios tried to ask more questions, but Agreus jumped up and joined Nomios in playing his pipes and dancing around the fire. The gloom lifted and the brothers returned to laughing and telling their lewd tales. Akakios, unable to keep his eyes parted, fell asleep dreaming of dark prophesies that only hinted at something dreadful just beyond his mind's eye. Something that would change everything if he could just part the haze for the briefest glimpse.

When he woke the next morning, the Paein were gone as if they were never there and Akakios felt terribly alone. They had consumed so much of his attention that time flew by like a flight of fantasy during their journey together. Aside from the darker moments, he had actually enjoyed their entertaining company and looked forward to telling the Hierophant all about them on his return to the Naos. On the other hand, if his journey continued with such meetings, the Hierophant would probably think his Ta Hiera had gone half mad. Just the thought of it made him laugh out loud, reminding him again of his isolate journey.

Akakios rode at a steady league-churning pace the first half of the day when, just a few leagues from the coast, he came across a rough game trail leading into the sloping forest on the side of the road disappearing into the elevations of the Othrys. It was the first of its kind he had encountered and decided it was probably the best route to follow into the tangled wilderness to the place described by the Paein He knew from experience that game trails were more reliable than not and this one looked particularly well-travelled. Too dense to ride, he dismounted and led Tella up the narrow pathway

Hours passed before the terrain underwent a dramatic change. Akakios's calves and thighs were burning from the constant climb made all the more difficult by his malformed foot. Not far ahead, the forest made way for jagged, rocky terrain quilted with clusters of thickly wooded copses standing at extreme angles on the steep westward-facing mountainside. It was some relief that Akakios could at least ride his mount where the ground was stable as often as walk it where it was not. By the time night fell and he made a camp, Akakios thought he might be in the general area where he expected to find the clearing within the wooded grove if the Paein had been truthful and he managed to remember everything they said.

That night, he had another dream. Whereas his previous dreams of Anesidora had been about love and longing, tonight his dreams were dark and frightening. Anesidora appeared to him in distress. Noticeably frightened, she begged Akakios to come to her urgently. She whispered of specter in the dark stalking her relentlessly, threatening to do her harm. With a start, Akakios awoke in his own sweat and was unable to settle his mind enough to sleep again, so he lay with eyes wide in the dying firelight until it smoldered and the sun peeked above the horizon. For the first time, he felt a lucid fear that he would not be able to find his love in time to save her.

Chapter 5

Beasts of Legend

Akakios was impatient to leave camp. As soon as there was enough light to travel over the rocky ground and through the copses of dark, tangled timberland, he would be on his way. He knew that he must get to a higher elevation on the western slope where there were fewer trees and his vision would be unobstructed over the vast stretches of the forest below. Akakios was looking for oak, but so far all he had seen was poplar and cypress. He started a slow climb up the escarpment, leading Tella behind him, to where he thought he spied a ridge jutting out from a web of branches far above. In the shadow of the trees, it was cold, tempting Akakios to set a pace faster than he should to keep his limbs from becoming stiff as much as to cover ground a little quicker. In his haste, he stumbled over exposed roots and loose rocks, relying on his staff to keep him upright until he finally came across a rocky clearing with a fantastic view in every direction.

"Thank Kronos," Akakios muttered to himself. He was no longer a young man and the climb had nearly exhausted him.

He sat to rest on the outcropping overlooking the expanse of the sloping forest below and basked in the warmth of the sun on his face even while the chill wind cooled his cheeks. Not having slept well the night before, Akakios dozed, allowing his grip to relax on Tella's reins. He was vaguely aware that his horse wandered freely, but he was unconcerned that she would go far, so he remained within the comforting swaddle of half wakefulness without stirring. Akakios had reached the tree line where the ground was strewn with loose rocks and the few clumps of grass and weeds scattered across the slope squeezed through jagged cracks for his horse to pick at, sometimes kicking the ground to move the stones and gain access to the tender roots. It was the only sound except for the occasional rustle of wind through the trees. Akakios was sure there could be no more comfortable place in the whole of Hellas.

Sometime later, he knew not how long, a terrifying scream ripped Akakios out of his light slumber to fully awake. Disoriented at first, he wondered if he could have imagined the sound. Then the cry came again, a bestial sound not human, full of terror and pain. He jumped to his feet and looked around wildly. Everything was as it was before he dozed off, except that his horse was not within sight. Where was Tella? She must have wandered away further than expected looking for the choicest sprouts among the greenish ophiolite that formed the primary characteristic of the terrain around him. He called to his mount with the distinctive whistle it was trained to respond.

Nothing.

Another desperate scream broke the serenity of the still mountains not far over the ridge above him. A chill streak of fear raced across his spine. These were not the cries of an animal with a hoof stuck in a furrow, rather, a creature in mortal danger, maybe beyond his help. Akakios scrambled up the rock-strewn slope using his staff to keep from slipping and sliding on smaller stones while dragging his deformed foot behind in his rush. He clawed his way over the ridge on all fours and gazed down into the shallow ravine below that held a clear-blue pool fed by a fresh spring surrounded by an expanse of tall grass and tender foliage.

Akakios's mind took in the beautiful landscape, although it might as well have been the hot geysers of hell, for his focus was riveted on the terrible scene unfolding before him. Tella struggled to run with only the use of her front legs, the flesh from her hindquarters ripped away, trailing a wide swath of blood through the vibrant green grass, while her eyes rolled wildly over a crimson snout bleating a desperate squeal fraught with panic as she tried to escape her attackers. Akakios knew immediately that it was a hopeless flight.

Three terrible creatures that Akakios immediately recognized from legend flapped erratically in circles around the disabled horse. Each of them easily half the size of Tella, with the wings and talons of a monstrous eagle and the head, torso and breasts of a woman. He read once that they were called the Harpyia. And to see first hand what shocking destruction they wrought on flesh and bone was terrifying.

The beasts screeched at the dying horse as much as one another, lunging at the poor animal, tearing off chunks of living flesh with their razor-like claws. The quivering meat they shoved into unhinged maws eager to consume it raw. Incredibly, they fought against each other in a kind of aerial frenzy for their turn at the horse that only added to the frantic chaos playing out below. Petrified at first, Akakios's anger quickly rose like an erupting volcano. To see his horse slaughtered in front of his eyes by these hateful creatures was more than he could bear.

Rage pounded through his temples and his vision restricted casting everything around him into darkness except for the Harpyia. Those three Akakios kept solidly within his narrow circle of sight as he stood up boldly, perhaps stupidly, on the ridge and slowly made his way down into the ravine. By the time he got to the bottom Tella was no longer screaming. Exhaustion, shock and loss of blood left her with barely the strength to toss her head back and forth in pain. Crimson foam sprayed from her mouth as she bled out, while the Harpyia continued to devour her alive.

Akakios stood at the edge of the ravine and leaned heavily on his staff to catch his breath. He knew there was nothing he could do for his pitiful horse, but he wasn't about to allow the monstrous beasts to finish their meal in peace. His mind raced with tactics of old on how he would destroy them, until one of the Harpyia happened to glance in his direction.

"Sisters!" she screeched. "We have new prey!"

The Harpyia that spoke turned to fly toward him while the other two continued to fight over the remains of his horse. Akakios, at first stunned that the creature spoke with that he could understand, paused a second before fury over the loss of his horse and the fast approaching Harpyia compelled him to action. Raising one hand on outstretched arm, palm forward, he lashed out with a fierce bolt of flames that struck the Harpyia square between her feathered breasts and exploded violently over her body. Consumed in a ball of flaming flesh and feathers, her dying shriek was satisfying to Akakios's ears as was the sight of her flapping around aimlessly on the ground kicking up the gravel-like dirt until her body lay smoldering and lifeless. The pungent stink nearly made Akakios gag.

The spectacular end to their sister did not go unnoticed by the remaining two Harpyia. Screaming furiously, they abandoned their feeding frenzy and hurtled toward him with deadly purpose blazing in their angry eyes. Akakios sent a wave of flames rolling in their direction. With surprising speed and agility for their size, the Harpyia easily maneuvered around the fatal fire and gathered momentum. Akakios knew he could only get one before he was face to face with the other and settled on the Harpyia on the right to be the next recipient of his bolt of fire. The flames struck true, consuming the creature in a conflagration, but her forward momentum nearly toppled him over in his quick scramble to get out of the way and before he could right himself again, the surviving Harpyia slammed into him.

Screeching wildly, she knocked Akakios off his feet and onto his back plunging her long claws deep into the muscle and sinew of his chest. The Harpyia was surprisingly light, but it wasn't her pressing weight nor the buffeting of her powerful wings that caused his distress. It was the intense pain from her claws firmly entrenched in the fleshy parts between his ribs that filled his awareness. The Harpyia screamed and raged, flexing her claws, causing the wounds in his chest to bleed that much more. Akakios felt like he might pass out and knew that if he did then his pilgrimage to save Anesidora would be at an end.

He had one chance to survive and worked to concentrate through the pain and violence to cast the only spell he could think of. Meanwhile, the Harpyia, having dug as far into his chest as it could, set about furiously lifting his body and slamming him to the ground again and again, inflicting torturous agony on the old priest's frail body. Akakios struggled to stay conscious. Black spots crowded his vision and he knew that he was almost lost. With titanic effort he reached up and grabbed the Harpyia's stick-like legs just above her enormous claws and willed his hands to come alive with white-hot flames. The Harpyia's screams transformed from fury to howling pain. In an attempt to flee, she lifted Akakios off the ground several feet. Still, he held firm, ignoring the pain that wracked his chest, knowing she didn't have the strength to carry him far. Seconds later he was falling. Just before he hit the ground, he heard the intense cries of the Harpyia diminishing into the distance, then darkness took him completely.

———

It was dark when Akakios next opened his eyes. He was surprised at the multitude of stars that littered the heavens above too numerous to count. He had not expected the Underworld to have stars. Then he became aware of the numbing cold and how stiff body had become and he realized that he must not be dead after all. How long had he lay there? His hands held tightly to a pair of rods above his chest. When he looked down to ascertain what they could be, he was horrified to see that he held the legs and claws of the Harpyia with its talons still embedded deep within his chest, but that was where the Harpyia ended as the rest of the body was no longer attached.

Slowly Akakios sat up and gingerly removed the claws from his chest one stubborn talon at a time. It was a torturous process that nearly drove him mad from the agony of it. Fortunately, he had unintentionally cauterized his wounds and stopped the bleeding when he severed the Harpyia's legs with his flaming hands. That was probably the only reason he was still alive, he thought bitterly. When he was finally free of the devilish claws, Akakios breathlessly stumbled to his feet to survey the darkness around him.

In the light of the waning moon on the horizon, the indistinguishable bodies of the two Harpyia that died by his flaming bolts were still where he remembered they fell. Beyond them, rising from the shadows, lay the remains of his horse, its body rigid and contorted in final repose. The black stains all around it had long since dried ruining the grass where it pooled. There was no sign of the third Harpyia. Akakios was certain it would not live long without its only means of defense and feeding. He almost felt sorry for it.

Almost.

Akakios picked up his staff and carefully hobbled over to his poor Tella removing the tattered packs that hung tenuously from what remained of their frayed straps. The sturdy leather bags were shredded nearly as bad as the animal that carried them and much of what they held proved to be damaged and useless. He salvaged what he could in one small bag that had suffered only mild damage and then whispered a short prayer over the body of his faithful mount.

Akakios sat heavily on the ground and wept dry tears. The ache of his injuries was almost unbearable and he needed to rest. Gloomy despondence wrapped him like a shroud sucking all the strength from his bones and the hope from his heart. The Hierophant was right. He should have brought a retinue of guards and servants to keep him safe. A few decades earlier, he could have sustained an injury such as this and more, healed himself and been on his way not much worse for the wear. These days the healing took longer and the healing magic granted by his god would leave him exhausted. For the first time since he departed Sesklo, Akakios wondered if he wasn't just some old fool trying to relive his youth.

Refusing to stay among the carnage longer than he had to, Akakios cast the few healing spells he remembered upon himself and worked his way back to the overlook where he had sat napping earlier. The little healing that he could provide for himself would be enough to dull the pain and allow him to sleep. He consumed the last of the artos, a loaf of wheat bread, he found stashed in a pocket of his robes and curled up behind a large boulder for protection from the wind. The only cover he had was a strip from a bloodstained blanket he managed to recover, but it would have to do.

So many years had passed since his last expedition into the unknown. He thought about those days, the companions found and lost, the thrill of mystery, triumph over adversity and countless close calls with death. This felt nothing like that. He just felt miserable and cold. Perhaps he would wax nostalgic about this adventure one day as well. Memories had a funny way of leaving out the hardships. Akakios eyes grew heavy with fatigue and he didn't fight the urge to sleep.

Anesidora found him in his dreams once more.

She was frightened and pleading for Akakios to hurry to her. She was at a temple high in the mountains, windy as before, but her surroundings were darker and more foreboding. There was a sense of danger and fear and when he woke with the daylight, the palpable emotions conjured in the dream were still with him.

Akakios knew right away he was going to continue his journey. There was no going back. The rest and healing had been enough to give him the energy to continue his search for the grove of oaks and despite everything he was more determined to find them than ever. Anesidora had a way about her that rekindled his spirit and bolstered his resolve. He walked along the ridge, carefully avoiding the ravine where he encountered the Harpyia the previous day and carefully made his way farther up the slope to a higher elevation. The day was bright with the warmth of the sun, but the higher Akakios climbed, the colder it became and the gusts flowing down from higher altitude brought a biting chill. Pine was the dominant tree as far as he could see causing doubt in his mind that he would find a grove of oaks so high up the mountain. He considered descending to the line of deciduous trees below where there was a higher likelihood of oak and protection from the wind, but his vision would be limited to his immediate surroundings and he might pass within a few spans of an oak grove without ever realizing it. Instead, Akakios decided to stay at the same approximate elevation for a while longer and hike in a roughly northeastern direction parallel to the ridgeline. As long as the sun was up, he could see over the tops of the trees and far into the distance down the forested slopes and if nothing else, he still had a pair of sharp eyes to spy out any of the elusive oak stands. The thing that worried him the most was how exposed he was on the predominately barren mountainside. There were a few clusters of trees here and there as well as a number of massive boulders scattered about, but if he encountered any more of the Harpyia he might be hard pressed to take cover before he was spotted. He supposed there was little he could do about that and simply resolved to keep his eyes peeled for any movement that might give him enough warning to escape.

By late afternoon Akakios was on another ridgeline surveying the treetops when he discovered a stand of tall oaks a little below and to the east of his position. Thrill and relief flooded through him. *Finally, a tangible sign,* Akakios thought. The oaks had to be the ones he was looking for. They were the only oaks he had seen since he entered the mountain forest!

"Kronos, don't torture me with the sight of these trees," Akakios prayed wearily. "Grant that this grove is the one I have been searching for."

After resting a little while, Akakios started down the hazardous slope in the direction of the oak trees. From what he could see from above, the grove was not very large and even with his deformed foot he doubted it would take much time to walk from one end to the other. It took only an hour to clamber down to the edge of the grove where, to his pleasure, there was minimal underbrush and level ground that yielded to soft earth which was far more comfortable to walk upon than the jagged ophiolite that dominated the ridge.

Cautiously, Akakios slid between the trees as quietly as possible and soon found a narrow clearing about a stone's throw wide and maybe twice as long. The clearing was illuminated by the sun on its final descent to the horizon, that cast shadows on the carpet of short green grass dotted by random mushroom rings. It looked for all the world like the perfect place to take an afternoon nap. And he might have if a flash of movement on the far southern end of the clearing didn't cause him to practically jump out of his skin. There, still and quiet, stood a beautiful white steed grazing gracefully in the narrow pasture. Akakios rubbed the exhaust form his eyes to see it more clearly and gasped in disbelief. It was a magnificent white steed all right . . . with *wings*.

Akakios's knees nearly buckled, he couldn't believe what he was seeing. It was a Pegasos, another creature of fantasy and storybooks. Often the animal was represented in sculpture and relief in Sesklo, but to see one in the flesh was astonishing. If he thought the Hierophant would think him mad before, he was confident of it now.

With a start, he realized that the Pegasos had a riding harness and immediately became alarmed that there might be an unfriendly rider close by. Akaios froze where he stood, but saw no one else around. Just to be safe he waited and watched the incredible creature for a while longer before he crept forward a few more steps. He feared that at any moment its rider could strut from the dense camouflage of the forest and find him standing there. Who new what manner of being could ride a Pegasos? Certainly, a god . . . or a devil. Akakios stayed in the shadow trees for cover, moving as quietly as he could, trying not to spook the creature or unnecessarily announce his position. Despite his best efforts, somehow the Pegasos was aware that he was there, casually watching him with an idle eye as if he were no more of a concern than a chipmunk. Akakios was not sure how close he should get to the animal, but he was starting to feel ridiculous trying to sneak up on it while it watched him so passively.

He paused to consider his plan. What was his plan? Walk up to the Pagasos, hope that whatever rode it didn't show up and then what? Was this the sign from Metis that the Paein had referenced? It must be. He had seen the goddess with a Pegasos in his dreams. Maybe it was an ally. Maybe it would take him to Anesidora. Gathering his courage, Akakios approached closer. The Pegasos seemed completely indifferent to his presence or proximity. Most unsettling was the intelligent look in its eyes, far more than any horse he had ever known, it seemed to weigh and measure him with each hesitant step of his advance.

Only a stride away, Akakios stopped and waited. It wasn't fear that held him back, he was nervous to be sure and wary about what might happen next, but out of respect for this elegant creature. The Pegasos lifted its head from the grass and looked down its long muzzle scrutinizing him fully. It was a strange thing to be so utterly inspected by an animal he might otherwise consider a beast of burden, a thing for him to control and claim mastery over. Not so with this one. This was a creature of the gods.

The Pegasos pulled its feathery wings in close to its flanks and performed a sort of bow with its front legs bent and its weight on its knees. Akakios did what he might consider a mortifying thing at any other time in his life and bowed in return. The Pegasos replied with a grunt and tossed its head toward its back.

Confused at first, Akakios's cheeks soon reddened with embarrassment as it dawned on him what the Pegasos was expecting. "Shall I climb atop you then, fair beast?"

The Pegasos repeated the gesture toward its back.

Akakios slowly inched forward and gingerly touched the fine arch of its neck. The hair was coarse like any other horse, but its long white mane was soft, well-oiled and properly groomed. "Did Metis send you here for me?"

The Pegasos brayed with impatience.

By Kronos, he thought, *it really does expect me to mount.* Gathering every ounce of courage he could muster, Akakios cinched his belt tighter around his heavy himation and anxiously climbed atop the winged beast.

Not hesitating a moment, the Pegasos turned and sprinted down the center of the clearing with shocking acceleration. Akakios, caught completely off-guard and still in the process of adjusting his staff over his shoulder, fumbled the supporting strap on the riding harness and flipped off the fantastic steed's back.

Akakios tumbled and rolled and then came to rest in the soft grass with the wind knocked out of him, gasping like a hooked fish. Halfway down the meadow, the Pegasos stopped short of flight and briskly trotted back to where he lay. It stood nickering above him, which, to his embarrassment, Akakios could only interpret as a laugh.

"That wasn't funny," he stated flatly after recovering enough to stand.

The Pegasos simply tossed its head and knelt again for him to mount. After a passing hesitation, Akakios drew a deep breath and slowly climbed on telling the beast, "Wait a moment while I get settled, if you don't mind."

The Pegasos stomped once with one mighty hoof, but otherwise stood patiently while Akakios secured himself to the riding harness.

When he was all set, he nudged the regal beast gently in its flanks like he would a regular riding horse, indicating that he was ready to go. Just as before, the Pegasos was quick to respond, bolting into a full gallop before it opened its majestic wings and lifted off the earth. Akakios was sure that if the straps on the harness had been oranges, he would have squeezed out every drop of juice. The sensation of being pressed and lifted at the same time while the ground demised below him was terrifying. Akakios felt completely out of control, his stomach churned with nausea and his body was petrified with fear. He had experienced many wondrous adventures in his lifetime, but this was the first time he had ever flown through the air and he was already sure he wasn't going to like it.

The oak grove surrounding the small meadow rushed away below them as the Pegasos ascended at a steep pitch to gain altitude. Within seconds the trees below looked like toys from a child's playset and the terrain appeared to him like an incredibly detailed map. To Akakios's great relief, the angle of ascent soon leveled off to a gradual lift. Far above and ahead of them, he could see the highest peaks of the snow-capped Othrys with the last rays of the sinking sun fanned over them like the wings of an enormous butterfly. Akakios had a feeling that was where they were headed. It was nearly nightfall and at the heights they were climbing he was glad for his heavy wool himation. The air was becoming colder and the wind sharper as it cut through the gaps in his clothing.

Akakios settled himself and endeavored to calm his nerves. He was still terrified that he might fall, but the nausea had disappeared and in its place he began to experience a heady exhilaration. Despite the fear of falling and the cold and the thin air, soaring through the sky filled him with a dangerous excitement that made him feel young again. He knew now the secret only birds knew, why they sang their joyful songs and flitted about with boundless energy full of life! Only they could experience the euphoric freedom unbound by the shackles of gravity, dancing among the stars, diving through puffy billows, traversing the realm of the gods.

The Pegasos banked sharply. Every ounce of enthusiasm in Akakios was suddenly replaced by panic, adrenaline flooding into his veins. He held tightly to the straps, pressing his body close to the Pegasos and only began to relax after he realized they were ascending in a wide spiral stealing lift off the wind currents that pushed them ever higher. Akakios dared to glance over the Pegasos withers. At their dizzying height objects on the ground were indistinguishable one from another and the failing light obscured any detail he might have been able to discern beyond the shadows. Moments later the ground disappeared altogether when they entered the rolling brume between the dark clouds stretching to the ends of the earth in every direction.

Akakios did his best to quell his rising panic. They were too high and he could no longer see the ground or anything around him. The sudden disorientation was terrifying. He had never been a fan of high places to begin with and this was taking it to the ultimate extreme. To fall from this height, which was his real fear, would leave him nothing more than an unrecognizable spatter on the earth, betraying not a hint to anyone of what had become of him.

Then suddenly the Pegasos broke through the clouds and into the magnificent firmament of the cosmos. All his stress and anxiety were quickly forgotten, replaced by a rapturous wonder at what he witnessed in the vast dome above. The air was clean and clear, with no obstruction or haze to diminish the beauty of the multitudes of the heavens spread out to the edges of eternity. There were so many stars, some floating among clouds of their own, infinite in number, more luminous that he had ever seen them and impossible for his mind to fully comprehend. And there were other things. A trail of clouds like the dust from the wheels of a chariot cut a wide swath through the dark sky and a tiny fireball that shot over the horizon. His eyes welled with cold tears, so blessed above all mortals for the chance to behold the miracle of the gods dominion. Below the churning hooves of the Pegasos the clouds were so thick that Akakios wondered if he could walk upon them, the reality of their elevation an illusion of his imagination, nothing more than a dream. He was in the province of the gods and it was humbling.

For the first time in his life, Akakios suddenly felt like he could understand the gods' perspective on the world below them. If it were a cloudless sky in daylight, everything on the ground would appear so small and insignificant. A city must look like a colony of ants with people crawling all over themselves, each one filled with self-importance as if anything they did actually mattered. Never again would Akakios think of his life in Sesklo in the same way as before. He was sure of it. All he had to do was look up to the sky and remember this moment and everything in his life would all import. Except the gods.

His gaze fell back to the peaks of the Othrys cutting through the clouds in the distance. Akakios could just see a light coming from a structure built at the pinnacle of the highest mountaintop nearest to them. It had to be the shrine of Metis. Only the gods could have constructed a shrine in such a place. Akakios felt a surge of excitement and anticipation. Anesidora was there waiting for him to save her and he was more determined than ever not to let her down. How could he? He was a young hero again, the Bringer of Fire, riding in on a Pegasos with the blessings of powerful gods!

Akakios laughed in the bluster of the bitterly cold wind that assaulted his face and tore at his himation.

Still some distance away from the shrine, Akakios felt the Pegasos abruptly tense under his thighs followed by an aggressive snort blowing hot steam from flared nostrils. He followed the steed's gaze over the clouds to a spot above the temple and just below the mountain peak that held it. Something dark moved steadily across the silhouette of the mountain too fast to be crawling. It had to be a flying creature, perhaps another Pegasos. He wondered if they might be territorial the way his own reacted to its presence.

"Easy now," Akakios pat the Pegasos thick neck, not sure if that would do any good at all.

The creature disappeared behind the peak above the temple and moments later re-appeared around the other side. A sudden burst of fire erupted from the thing down toward the temple and Akakios's heart nearly leapt from his chest. The flames briefly illuminated the awful truth of this creature and it was no Pegasos. Underneath him, the Pegasos snorted and kicked excitedly. It postured confidently in their ascent and to Akakios's terror, he realized the Pegasos intended to confront the beast orbiting the shrine above them.

"No, no, no," Akakios pleaded with the Pegasos. He tried to make it turn by applying pressure with his thighs and pulling at the reigns. The Pegasos ignored him as if he wasn't even there.

As the Bringer of Fire, Akakios had always been confident in his abilities. He knew that his god, Kronos, prepared him well in this regard. However, battling mythical creatures straight out of legend at this insane altitude mounted on the back of a winged creature he did not control did not appeal to him in the least.

And the beast was huge—easily twice the size of the Pegasos.

More fire sprang forth from creature, pouring over what appeared to be an open landing in front of the shrine surrounded by tall white-marble pillars in the shape of a half moon. He was still too far to see it clearly or if anyone was on the landing, but he was sure of one thing - it had to be the thing that Anesidora feared would take her. Akakios must have arrived just in time.

The creature had not reacted to their approach and Akakios suspected it had not seen them yet. If he only knew what the Pegasos was planning. What could a Pegasos do to a thing that size, breathing fire and whatnot anyway? Maybe the Pegasos was expecting *him* to do something. Akakios had to come up with a strategy of how to overcome the monster that didn't result in sending him plummeting to the earth. He watched it carefully, looking for any weakness he could exploit as they drew closer.

Only a few hundred spans from the shrine, the creature finally noticed that it wasn't the only thing in the skies and broke off its assault on the temple, slowly angling its heavy bulk toward them. Akakios still could not see the beast clearly in the dark, but he assumed it had to be some kind of dragon and desperately hoped they were out of range of its fiery breath. Inexplicably, the Pegasos continued to fly higher than the shrine, presumably in an attempt to gain a height advantage on the approaching monster. To his surprise, the slower creature did not pursue and instead returned to circle above the shrine. It must have thought it had scared them off.

Akakios sighed in frustration. He wanted to be off the Pegasos with his feet planted firmly on the stone pavers in front of the shrine where he could utilize his talent to greater effect and at the same time protect Anesidora. The Pegasos clearly had something else in mind. Whatever happened, the steed better know what it was doing since aerial combat was entirely out of his knowledge or experience.

Up they went, higher and higher until the wind was no more than a light breeze and Akakios thought himself so close to the stars that he might easily reach out and scoop up a handful of them. It was a labor to breathe at this altitude and he feared he might lose consciousness if they stayed too long. He cast his gaze around admiring how the horizon was visible in every direction, disrupted only by the mountain peaks to the west . . . and something else.

Lights.

Scrutinizing them closer, Akakios realized that they were not just lights, but beautiful light cascading from enormous windows and what he earlier thought of as mountain peaks were actually massive walls and towers built upon the highest reaches of the Othrys Mountains. Akakios stared in wonder at the colossal structure with the revelation that it must be the palace of Kronos. Nearly overcome by elation and lack of oxygen, Akakios was euphoric at the thought of coming so close to his god. For a moment he forgot everything else, even Anesidora and tried to compel the Pegasos to take him there, but his mount had ceased it's ascent and slowly turned into a steady circle forcing his eyes back to the shrine below. Not so quick to forget what he had seen, Akakios resolved to rescue Anesidora and plead with the Pegasos if he must, to take them to Kronos's palace where he would formally present himself to his deity.

Turning his attention back to the shrine, the details of the beast below resolved with alarming clarity against the backdrop of torches flickering calmly around the landing. Akakios caught his breath at the sight of it. The beast had the body and head of a lion conjoined by a *second* head, that of a goat, protruding from its back, wings of a bat and the writhing scaley body of a snake in place of its tail. It was a Chimera. Another in a string of creatures from legend that none had claimed to see in over a thousand years! The Pegasos pitched its wings and rocked back and forth briefly. Akakios interpreted the move as a warning and promptly secured himself in the harness so that he would have full use of his hands without the necessity of holding onto the reins and then he pulled the staff from the straps on his back. The Pegasos carefully folded mighty wings tight over its flanks and pulled its legs up close to its body as it angled into a downward dive. Akakios felt no fear. He was bolstered by the sight of his god's domain and whether it was divine inspiration or something he had gleaned from the past, Akakios instantly realized what he must do.

Chapter 6

Anesidora's Pithos

Akakios stoically regarded the Chimera, watching it slowly turn its awkward frame to face the diving Pegasos. They dove at terrific speed through the icy atmosphere and despite the unpredictable high winds buffeting the Pegasos from one direction or another, his winged mount expertly kept them on target. Akakios hardly noticed the cold. His focus was locked on the terrific beast below, calculating in his mind every possibility, every chance that might see them through this deadly encounter alive.

Only seconds remained.

He clasped tightly a small lead coin brought forth from his robes moments earlier and framed in his mind precisely what he expected to happen with it. The coin instantly grew into a large lead spearhead which he softened with concentrated heat conjured through his hands and forcefully affixed to the end of his staff. It was no mean task to accomplish this simple chore on the back of a plunging Pegasos even with both hands free. More difficult still, was the complex set of spells he cast next to transform the staff into the sleek lines of a perfectly balanced spear. Through it all his concentration never wavered, his intellect was quick and sharp, his mind functioned with clarity of purpose he had not experienced in years.

"*Phero Pyr,*" Akakios raised the spear above his head and spoke the evocation willing it to burst into flames.

The Chimera gathered speed and rose fast to meet them, roaring with fury, tongue flicking from its wicked snake-head tail, lethal claws extended forward. Akakios maintained his poise and prayed. If he had guessed wrong . . .

Fire erupted in a blazing stream from the toothy maw of the Chimera's lion head.

"Predictable," Akakios muttered gratefully.

The two great beasts were dangerously close, the threat of impact imminent and yet Akakios kept his gaze steady and his breathing calm—he wrapped himself in an impenetrable cocoon of concentration. It was only in this state that he could react with the precision needed to make his plan work. The Pegasos must have understood as well, for it did not waver in its flight, even in the face of fiery death. Akakios hurled his flaming, lead-tipped spear directly into the oncoming stream of fire. It left his hand at an incredible speed, with far more velocity than he could have possibly managed with his feeble physique and passed through the fiery breath softening the lead to a near liquid state. Akakios held his breath and prayed that Kronos would guide his throw to its mark.

Kronos answered his prayers that day.

The spear flew straight and true, splitting the fiery breath into several splintered streams that shot around the Pegasos missing it entirely and lodged deep inside the throat of the Chimera's lion head. The creature coughed and sputtered and tried to swat at the fiery conveyance, but the spear had already consumed itself, leaving only the molten lead that was rapidly cooling within the enraged monster's throat and lungs.

Akakios felt triumphant for only a second before he realized that the Pegasos was too close to avoid the floundering beast. The two creatures crashed into one another with a terrible jolt that shook him to his core and rattled his teeth.

The Chimera, unable to draw breath, frantically latched onto the Pegasos with its powerful front claws and urgently attempted to expel the solidified lead from its lungs with a series of violent coughs and hacks. The goat head sprouting from the back of its lion body snapped and bit at the Pegasos's wings whenever they came close spitting out long feathers with each success while the snake-headed tail struck with venomous accuracy along the poor beast's haunches.

It was everything Akakios could do to avoid the thrashing of both embattled creatures and he feared one or the other would kill him incidentally before he could release the straps that held him fast. The

Pegasos tried to pull away screaming savagely from the vicious bites and penetrating wounds caused by the Chimera's long claws holding it fast, ripping deep into the Pegasos barrel chest, as it furiously responded with sharp-hooved kicks and fierce bites of its own

Yet even the powerful wings of the Pegasos was unable to bear the additional weight of the heavier creature and they began to fall, end over end, tumbling in a chaos of blood and feathers trailing behind. The Chimera's lion head thrashed wildly back and forth, unable to inhale the sweet air its lungs so desperately desired and still, it held tightly to the Pegasos. Akakios managed to loosen the harness enough to free himself, but to what end? To jump and save himself from getting battered between the two beasts only to fall to his death? His only hope was to hold on to the Pegasos and try and do something to separate them.

They were falling faster and faster and with every rotation of their embattled frames Akakios could see the shrine's landing rising up to meet them. He prepared himself to jump unsure if they might miss the landing altogether in their twisting descent. Panic rose within him waiting for the right moment. It was taking too long for them to spin around enough for him to see the landing. He thought to hazard a reckless jump before the fall was interrupted by the jarring impact of the two beasts' heavy bulks crashing down near the edge of the landing. A half-turn more and Akakios would have been crushed beneath them. As it was, even cushioned from the fall by the Pegasos, Akakios was dazed and disoriented. Still, the struggle between the beasts never ceased. The wildly flapping wings of the inseparable creatures twisted the pair so violently that they rolled closer to the edge of the landing. Akakios, with his wits scrambled, but free of the constraining straps took the chance and jumped clear of the Pegasos praying his blind leap, propelled by the tumbling brutes, sent him in the right direction.

Akakios landed hard on the unforgiving stone pavers drawing harsh scrapes down his face and arms and nearly shattering his kneecaps. He hardly cared—he was alive. Glancing back toward the edge of the landing he watched the gravely injured Pegasos vigorously pumping its legs, struggling to gain traction on the polished stone in a futile attempt to stand up as the much weightier Chimera pulled it over the side. The shrill scream of the poor animal diminished as they fell farther through the clouds until it was drowned out completely by the rushing winds below.

Akakios sat up and cleared the blood from his eyes with shaking hands. He was acutely aware of how quiet and serene the shrine was in contrast with the life and death struggle he endured just moments before. It was odd that the strong gusts outside the landing were somehow kept at bay allowing the torches to hold their flames with the barest flutter. It was like he had just awoken from a violent nightmare into another dream, it felt so surreal. He stood up on trembling legs, adrenalin fading away leaving him exhausted and shivering violently in the frigid cold that not even his heavy grey himation, now stained with the Pegasos blood, could keep out. His gaze panned around the landing searching for a place to get warm and found a welcome sight.

Braziers set within a cavernous opening framed by massive oak doors set into a white marble propylon burned bright with scant a flicker, beckoning to him with the promise of warmth. Akakios recognized the landing as the backdrop from which Anesidora called to him in his dreams. Yet she was not here. He supposed that she must be waiting for him somewhere within the shrine, scared and alone, fearing that the Chimera would soon come for her. He dragged his malformed foot wearily over to stand in the comforting heat of the braziers, gathering his strength, marshalling his courage, preparing to meet the woman in his dreams. She was more than that, he knew. The time they spent together was real. He could recall every moment vividly; her touch was like silk, the timbre of her voice soft and feminine, the fragrance of narcissus on her neck, the scent of berries on her breath . . .

Akakios stared down the wide passage. It ran straight into the side of the mountain lined as far as he could see with dozens, maybe hundreds, of braziers to each side. It did not turn or twist and there were no doors or hallways that intersected as far as he could see, only a brilliant light in the distance that must lead into another room. That was where he would find Anesidora. He was certain of it.

"What am I waiting for?" he chuckled nervously to the empty hallway.

The journey to get to this point had been long and arduous to say the least with fantastic beasts, bizarre travel companions and dreadful loss. To take the next few steps meant that was all at an end. He would embrace Anesidora, kiss her sweet lips and . . . what? There must be a way down from the shrine that didn't involve riding a Pegasos. At least he hoped so. If he could survive the tests he overcame to get here, he would survive the way back and this time he wouldn't be alone on his journey home. Excitement broke the lonely stalemate pushing him forward; one step and then two. He moved slowly at first, pulling his deformed foot forward clumsily without his staff to give him support and with a little effort, he found a regular cadence that was faster than a crawl if not less cumbersome. Akakios fantasized about his meeting with Anesidora over and over during the long walk down the tedious hallway. He imagined her running to embrace him extolling his heroics or weeping with relief prostrate at his feet or gleefully raining kisses over his face and neck unabashed. That last one was his favorite.

He must have been deeply engrossed in his own fancies, for he was abruptly aware that he had come to the end of the hallway. He gazed into a wide circular room capped by a domed ceiling filled with wonderous things. Statues of Metis in stately poses circled the perimeter and to his utter astonishment, life-size sculptures of the Pegasos and the Chimera, each standing defiant and regal on his right and stone effigies of the two Paein and the three Harpyia on his left. Akakios had to pause and wonder what game of the gods he found himself embroiled in. Thinking back on his experiences over the past few days with the Paein, the Harpyia and now the Pegasos and Chimera, the presence of the statuary made it all feel contrived.

Akakios looked up at the massive domed ceiling, half expecting to see the gods staring back down at him, laughing at his folly. Instead, the dome was covered with beautifully carved and painted reliefs reflecting stories about the gods he had known from childhood, stories that were comfortable and familiar. He still couldn't shake the feeling that he was being watched, but with the exception of the lifelike vacant eyes of the statues, he saw nothing alive.

And no sign of Anesidora.

He walked toward the center of the room and came to seven steps that led up to the highest platform of a raised dais. There stood a large pithos almost the height of a man and too wide at its midsection to put one's arms around. Upon its blue-and-ivory painted surface were figures and symbols showing scenes of people acting in sinful displays. To look at them made him blush. Not that he was a prude or had any moral objection to what the scenes were acting out, he just hadn't experienced much intimacy in his lifetime, at least not since he retired from his days as an explorer.

Akakios ascended the steps to stand next to the large pithos. He noted that the lid was sealed with wax and stamped with a medallion carved with the face of a Demon that he didn't recognize. He certainly wasn't an authority on Demons, he mused to himself, but many of the more important ones' likenesses were depicted in the old legends and this was not one of them. Perhaps it was just a symbol to frighten away anyone who was curious about what was inside.

Startling him from his thoughts, a delicate feminine voice from nowhere whispered, "Free me, my love."

His heart almost leaped from his body at sound of the familiar voice, his blood pounded with exhilaration he had not felt since he was a youth and his head swiveled around like a snowy owl trying to look in every direction at once. She was here! He knew from his dreams that this voice was his beloved Anesidora. But, where was she?

"I am here for you, love!" Akakios shouted to the room. "Call to me again and I will find you!"

The voice of Anesidora came again, weaker this time, fearful and distressed, "Here, my love." *She sounded so close.* "I am imprisoned in the pithos," she cried piteously. "Please release me! Hurry, there is little air remaining and I cannot breathe!"

Without thought or hesitation Akakios broke the Demon head medallion and evoked fire from his fingertips, weaving it like thread around the wax seal over the lid skillfully melting it away without causing the air inside the pithos to heat up. There was something strange about the seal, an urgent warning nagged at him from the recesses of his mind. No one could reduce the powerful magic that sealed the pithos, not the most potent wizard or priest from any kingdom, not even an Atlantean. Only a Fire-Bringer of Kronos had the power. The nagging became a scream, the scream became a shriek, but it didn't matter; it was nothing more than an annoyance, he had to save Anesidora! In seconds the wax fully melted away and the lid sat waiting his final touch.

This was it. Everything was silent, even the cries inside Akakios's head had ceased. It was as if the entire world held its breath, waiting for what was to happen next.

Akakios knew what would happen.

He was about to release his love and they would be together forever. It was like wonderful a dream. He knew he was old and she was young, but what did it matter? They were kindred souls. She loved him and he loved her. He was finally on the cusp of his life changing forever. He didn't care if he was the Ta Hiera anymore or even a priest of Kronos. He would be a lowly shepherd for all he cared as long as they were together. Nothing mattered anymore, except removing the lid . . .

Firmly gripping the heavy ceramic cover between his knobby fingers, Akakios pulled forth the lid and opened the pithos.

The rush of air that erupted outward from the pithos knocked Akakios from the dais ripping the lid from his hands to shatter on the floor. A shrill screech of thunderous voices followed so loud that the pithos vibrated furiously causing tiny fissures to spider down its length. The dais split in two with a loud *crack* and the pithos burst sending a thousand shards in every direction. Akakios covered his face to protect his eyes from the flying debris and scooted away from the steps, pushing fearfully with his functional foot.

Several large black voids and many smaller ones emerged from the shattered remains of the pithos and streaked around the room up to domed ceiling. They screamed with the shrill laughter and sorrow of multitudes that threatened Akakios's sanity. He covered his ears to keep out the sound, but the cries were in his head tearing away sound thinking and judgment, his sense of reason and all thing rational. He tried to force them out of his mind, make them stop, they held such power and at the same time he knew they were exceptionally weak. Then they were gone.

Akakios opened his eyes and watched the voids, blacker than the darkest space between the stars, dart down the long hallway and disappear. There was something purely evil about them that was so palpable Akakios was left trembling on the floor. Their tormented screams echoed with laughter into the night beyond and it filled him with dread.

The room fell silent.

Akakios fearfully glanced around at his surroundings. He was alone again, his head swimming with unanswerable questions, but mostly he wanted to know what happened to Anesidora. What had the evil things done with her? Did they take her away for some dark purpose? It wasn't her fault. They used her to bring him here; the only one alive with the power to free them. They used their love to trick him into setting them free. They used his singular desire to be with her to overcome his prudence, control his emotions and unleash something vicious and evil into the world. He could feel it in his bones and he was ashamed. It was in this moment of abject humility that he pressed his forehead to the floor praying to Metis for forgiveness and swearing to Kronos that he would dedicate his life to finding the evil beings he had released and destroy or recapture them. If only the gods would help him find Anesidora. The gods would guide him to her again. He was sure of it! Slowly he rose from the tiled floor and with strident resolve, limped back down the lengthy hallway.

Akakios was sure an eternity passed by the time he reached the opening to the landing. Stagnant chill air greeted him when he stepped outside. Everything appeared just as it was before. He decided that the first thing he would do was return to the Hierophant, tell him how he had been tricked into doing something irreversible that could change the course of history, *would* change the course of history, if he didn't find a way to stop it and implore his help. Miltiades was a good man and his friend. Akakios was confident that together, they could rally the abbas dedicated to Kronos along with an army of hoplites and the faithful to their cause and set off on a great Hellenic Quest that rivalled the ancient legends of old.

He hobbled around the landing, anxiously seeking a way down. There must be a way. So engrossed in his search, he noticed the heavy fog rolling down from the Othrys only after it nearly covered the landing. There was something unnatural about how it broiled over the pavers and slowly enveloped him that gave Akakios pause. Then his eye caught a shadowy form move smoothly out of the shrine passing in front of the hazy light of the braziers and stopped on the far side of the landing. A slight luminescence surrounded the figure in a blue glow without revealing a hint of who it might be. It looked nothing like the black voids he had released, nor did it radiate the paralyzing fear he experienced when they were near. No, this one moved with the gentle, stately grace of a noble woman and even at a distance he felt comforted by it's presence.

Akakios dropped to his knees touching his forehead to the cold tile, "Hieros, Metis. Your humble servant beseeches your forgiveness."

The goddess responded with a lilting giggle. Confused, Akakios dared to glance up at the divine being. The fog swirled around her form, faded enough to reveal the almost ethereal curves of a woman within the flowing confines of a gossamer gown worn more for decoration than modesty. His eyes rose to her smooth shoulders where golden locks played across creamy alabaster skin and up the long curve of her neck to her pouty sanguine lips, perfectly straight lines of her nose and large round blue eyes edged with long thick lashes. Akakios recognized the figure as Anesidora, solid before him, more real and beautiful than even the vivid memories of his dreams.

She lived!

Akakios's mind raced. She must have escaped the wicked voids. She must have fled the pithos and hid within the shrine, unable to find him until now. He was electrified by the sight of her, his hopelessness turned to euphoria, unable and unwilling to pull his eyes away from her for the briefest second for fear she might disappear.

Anesidora extended her arms toward him and spoke in a voice overflowing with love and joy, "Come to me, my beloved, so we may finally embrace and be together for all eternity."

Akakios enthralled by the sudden revelation of her presence and overwhelmed with a tangle of emotions found no voice to reply. It was all he could do to rise clumsily to his feet and slowly make his way toward Anesidora, dragging his useless foot behind him. He no longer had his staff. It was somewhere far below, ashes in the maw of the fallen Chimera. He moved in jerks and fits from the other side of the landing toward her, ignoring the fog, his eyes fixed upon her and her alone.

"A gift for you, my love." She clapped her hands and held her arms out to receive his embrace.

A sensation ran through his club foot like a feather across his skin and his movement became steady and assured. Akakios stopped and looked down at his feet, nearly bursting into tears when he saw it; his useless foot was mended and formed fully like the other.

"Come, my love. Quickly now." Anesidora beckoned reassuringly.

Akakios, so focused on his need to join her, pushed aside the unusual events that brought him here. Yet somewhere, in the deep recesses of his mind, his subconscious ticked off the subtle clues. There were the odd inscriptions on the pithos, the medallion embossed with the likeness of a demon, the urgent pleas of Anesidora herself to free her from the pithos, the evil that emerged from it, the unusual nature of Anesidora's current appearance, the odd words she used to bring him to her and the precarious nature of his current location. Any one of those details should have provoked alarm bells compelling his wary nature to bring them to the surface for clarity and careful consideration. None of that mattered now, not with the lovely being standing in front of him, so willing, so available, to be his. Nothing would distract him from this perfect moment.

Only a pace away, his feet felt as if they were walking on air when he reached to embrace her. A part of Akakios's mind registered that his arms closed through her a split second before the sensation of falling. He was confused and unable to comprehend that in seconds he would be dead. As he fell, laughter reached his ears. It was pure and innocent, distinctive of his love, Anesidora. And it filled his heart with joy.

———

Kyros was startled awake in the middle of the night by a loud noise. He was sure it was the sharp crack of lightning, but there was no sound of rain or thunder. Maybe it was his imagination or the ringing in his ears, but the sound seemed to echo off the mountains surrounding the city.

Theokleia was lying next to him, she was also awake and she sounded fearful, "My husband, are you awake?"

"I am, wife."

"Did you hear that sound, or was I dreaming?"

"I heard it as well, unless we were in the same dream."

She scooted closer and lay her hand on his chest "Maybe someone broke down our door? I am frightened, Kyros."

"Do not worry, love. I will check the house." Kyros rolled off the bed picked up the heavy forge hammer on the floor against the wall.

He walked through the small house, his senses heightened, ready to lash out at any sudden movement against him. Everything was quiet. From what he could see in the darkness, nothing was disturbed. He continued through the connected storefront and there too, all was well. Kyros lit a lantern and strode into the large back courtyard where his forges stood. The nearest was the older forge and everything was in order as he would expect, except for a tong that was on the ground. It must have fallen off a hook. He left it where it lay. It would be an excellent excuse to lecture his apprentices on the care and organization of the forge tools in the morning. Somewhat agitated, he inspected his newest forge and everything appeared in order there as well.

And then his stomach dropped to his feet.

In the flickering dim light of the lantern, he beheld the impossible. His new block anvil, so recently sanctified by the Fire-Bringer, was cracked through and through.

———

In the Enlightened Times, she was known as Anesidora, daughter of Metis and beloved by all the gods. She was perfection of beauty, grace and poise and her elegance outshone all above and below, yet none were jealous of so many flawless attributes. It was because her every perfection was a gift from one god or another and they all claimed a part in her form and making. What none of them knew was the depth of her cruelty, as none of them thought to bestow compassion in her creation. And this pitiless vice she turned upon those weakest to defend themselves—humanity. By many names has she been known throughout the ages, once as Anesidora of Hellas and most recently as Pandora, yet her story is the same and her fateful actions that altered the destiny of civilizations two thousand years before the Cataclysm of the Younger Dryas resonate still to this day.

Wodanaz the Wanderer

Chapter 7

Graduation

SY5490

The Imperial Order of Wizards, as the purveyors of magic are known in Atlantis, fancy themselves quite the organized and disciplined collection of intellectuals. Over the years I played for them, sang for them and demonstrated my own sorcerous skills for their entertainment. Although they seemed decidedly unimpressed with my conjuring, it felt more like a jealous acknowledgment of superior competence in a craft that for them was entirely dependent upon a bunch of rocks. I must admit, to their credit, that they were always quite polite about it!

Wodanaz the Wanderer

———

Qellel of House Mekali sat at his small writing desk working on a solution to a difficult problem assigned by his master. From his first day in the Tower he had been challenged by a complex question each morning in class and expected to come up with the solution before midnight. At first, weeks went by when he solved only one or two in the time allowed. Now, twenty long years later and in the final month of his training, he solved them consistently. Still, they were never easy and these days the problems that appeared deceptively simple were always the ones that ended up with the most highly convoluted solutions. The one he worked on today was a mathematical calculation of the heat index of a charge in relation to the amount of magical power invested into it. His master was a stickler for not wasting more energy than was required to accomplish any particular task. He always told Qellel that energy conserved was energy available for use another time. Qellel knew the solution involved something to do with the heat from the conjured charge rising exponentially and he was on the verge of an answer when his concentration was interrupted by an abrupt knock on the door. He ignored it knowing it had to be an initiate or apprentice looking for advice or tutoring. A master would not have bothered to knock.

To his surprise, the door creaked open hesitantly. "Qellel?" It was a first-year initiate boldly peeking in. "Master Ampher requires your solution now."

"Shush, I need just a moment, longer. I'm almost there."

"But Qellel," the young initiate pleaded. "Master Ampher has summoned you and any delay will reflect upon me."

"The master is old and does not count the time the way we do. One more minute won't matter a wit to him, Daerys. Sit in that chair and be still."

The initiate did as he was told and sat in the chair clutching his white linen robes nervously. Qel knew the boy was between a rock and a hard place. Either delaying the command of a master or defying the order of a graduate apprentice could get him a week washing dishes in the kitchen. Qel didn't care about that at the moment. He had been subject to those quandaries enough times in his first years in the Tower. Daerys would have to just deal with it. All that mattered at this second was unravelling the solution to the problem.

"Got it!" Qel lifted the page and showed it to Daerys. "Now we can go."

With a huge sigh of relief, the initiate jumped up and quickly smoothed his white robes before he led the way out the door. Qel was curious about the problem he had received today and wondered if it had anything to do with the vast power grid that covered the whole of the earth. He knew that one of the primary responsibilities of the Atlantean Imperial Order of Wizards was to maintain and protect the pyramids and towers that housed the Orichalcum Source Crystals that provided the magical energy to the network. Because of this, Atlanteans and non-Atlanteans alike were able to access and use magic from anywhere if they had the talent and training to do so.

The tallest of all the towers in the Wizards Enclave, where he walked now to see his master, was one of those connected to the Source Crystals far below the ground beneath their feet. It radiated power for leagues in every direction before connecting with another structure of similar construct. From what he had learned in his studies, Qel knew the edifices were constructed under the supervision of Atlantean Wizards with labor native to the societies where they were built. In nearly every case, the structures mimicked the architecture and tradition of the local peoples and often doubled as a temple to their prevailing deity. Once built, the Atlanteans would transport Orichalcum Source Crystals from the caverns below the Wizards Tower to the buildings via one of the Imperial air ships magically powered to sail on the sea or through the air. When the Orichalcum Crystals were secured deep inside the bowels of the pyramid or tower where they would reside forever, a quartz-crystal cap carved in the shape of a pyramid was placed at its apex to amplify the magical power for leagues in every direction. From then on, a small group of Atlantean wizards or priests would staff the site in perpetuity. The wizards who performed this duty were known as Wizards of the Source and Qel dreamed that one day he would be one of them.

Qel knew that his master and the masters of every Hall for that matter, was always on the lookout for students who had the intellect and talent to become Wizards of the Source. It was well-known that they were a rare find and for more reason than just their intelligence. Wizards of the Source were said to possess a natural physical resonance that matched the frequency of the Orichalcum Crystals. Qel really didn't understand it very well. What he did know was that the Wizards of the Source were highly revered and enjoyed the novelty of residing among foreign peoples in distant lands until they were discharged by the emperor.

He longed for the day when he would be tested against the Source Crystals. The idea of traveling the world and living among exotic cultures was intriguing. Either way, Qel wanted to be an explorer. At every opportunity he and his best friend Havacian spent long nights reading stories from illustrated tomes under the dim illumination of floating light-globes in the Enclave's extensive library or mused over tales sung by visiting minstrels. He would miss that after they graduated.

Almost without realizing it, they arrived at Master Ampher's office. Daerys opened the door and Qel walked inside alone, the door closing quietly behind him. His aged master was sitting at a very large desk strewn with dozens of scrolls in various states of undoing. He did not look up when Qel entered. Instead, he continued writing and waved him to a nearby chair with his free hand. It was getting late in the day and Qel could see the light fading from a large window directly behind his master's chair. Almost as if reading his mind, the old man raised his fist and opened his hand releasing small balls of fire that swiftly streamed toward a dozen candles and sconces around the room, igniting them to bring additional illumination to the dim chamber. Still, his master did not look up and Qel absently wondered why the old man preferred flame to the more commonly used light-globes scattered throughout the Enclave. Well, maybe being the Master of Elemental Flame had something to do with it.

While he sat, Qel thought back to the time he had spent at the Tower. He had been an apprentice for twenty years. Training, training and more training. That had been the crux of his life and the rewards were fleeting. Sometimes he was allowed to spend a day with his family or walk a few hours in the city, but it was always back to the training. Then there was the research. Hours in the sacred library among the tens of thousands of tomes, books, scrolls and clay tablets copied from originals around the world, searching for the smallest of details to solve the problems given to him by his master. And so it went, day after day, week after week, month after month, for years.

He considered himself lucky in a way. Master Ampher was firm but not harsh and as long as Qel followed his instruction and made the expected progress his life was not too difficult. Looking at his master now, a man in the twilight of his life at nearly one hundred and eighty, he was glad for the opportunity to learn from one of the most brilliant wizards of his day. Rumors supposed that he had once been a great adventurer who explored the wonders of the lands west of the Emerald Isle. Qel heard there was a series of books written of his exploits but so far had not found them. He wished to ask his master about them one day when the time and subject was appropriate.

Master Ampher finally lay down his quill and fixed his gaze intently on Qel. "You're late."

"My apologies, Master, I needed just a minute longer to solve today's problem." How did he always know?

"Give it to me." The master held out his hand and Qel promptly placed the page on his palm.

Glancing over it, Master Ampher scratched his elongated bald head and absently stroked his long gray beard. His blue-tinted skin was heavily wrinkled and pale against his white robes, which hung loosely over his gaunt frame.

"So, you solved it. Impressive." He leaned back in his chair and the page burst into flames in his hand leaving not the slightest hint of ash behind. "You are the first apprentice of mine to solve that problem in many decades and nearly within the time I allowed."

"Thank you, Master. I defer to your proficient training that has allowed me to grow in my talents and education."

His master laughed weakly, a rare and unusual sound to Qel's ears. "I have been merely your guide. It is the talent and drive within you that has powered your progress." He stood then, slow and a little unsteady, reaching for his walking staff propped against the side of his desk. "Qellel of House Mekali, it is my pleasure to congratulate you on your upcoming graduation and Journey of Discovery thereafter."

His master extended a hand forward, his long knobby fingers clutching a small black box. Qel quickly stood and accepted the box with shaking hands and carefully opened it. Inside was the object he had most coveted since the first day he was brought to the Enclave— an Aurinium chain necklace from which hung a red Orichalcum Crystal twice the size of his thumb.

"As of tomorrow, you will officially become a Wizard of the Red Hall, or a Fire Wizard. However you wish to be known. Perhaps someday you, too, may be acknowledged by the Grand Wizard as a master." He smiled warmly and put a hand gently on Qel's shoulder. "Long after my time has ended, I'm sure, but I believe you have it in you."

Qel was overwhelmed. Everything in his life was about to change. No more schedules or problems to solve, no more supervision by his master or anyone else. He would be free to do as he liked. Go where he liked. Now he was faced with his dream of exploring the world and from this moment forward he would have the time and reason to do so. In just a few short days, he would be off on his Journey of Discovery, five years for him to go out into the world and experience life, utilizing the skills he had learned to survive and hopefully flourish in the ultimate practical test. After that, he would return to the Enclave to test for Source resonance and either begin training to be a Wizard of the Source or continue on the long road of perhaps, one day, earning the title of Master.

———

The Orichalcum Crystal reflected fractals of light across the walls from the illumination of the light globe floating in the air nearby. It was beautiful and the thrill of power that the small crystal generated was nothing short of euphoric. More than anything, he was in awe of what the crystal on the Aurinium chain represented—that he was no longer an apprentice.

Aurinium, what a strange material it was. This was the first time he had the opportunity to handle and inspect it. From the look and feel, it might have been glass. Except that glass was brittle and would certainly break if any force was pressed upon it. His father had explained the metal once. He called it metal, but Qel wasn't sure if it really was. He said the Atlantean Forge Wizards combined ground-up shells, quartz crystal and other rare elements into an intensely hot forge causing a magical reaction that turned the material liquid. Then it was poured into molds to produce armor, weapons, jewelry and certain tools. Only Atlantean warriors were permitted to use the armor and weapons made from Aurinium and under no circumstances could it be sold, given away, or traded, especially to foreigners. There were very strict laws regarding the use and possession of Aurinium products and Qel felt fortunate to possess a small piece of it. Aurinium was highly prized by Atlanteans and foreigners alike and it was so rare because only the Atlantean Forge Wizards were capable of creating it.

The necklace made him think of his parents. Qel looked forward to finally presenting himself to his family as a graduate and a member of the Imperial Order of Wizards. He was sure they would all be proud. He had not often seen them during his apprenticeship and hoped to spend a few days at his family's home in the country before he departed on his journey of Discovery.

Qel glanced at the water clock on the table. It was getting late into the evening and he still had not heard from Havacian. Earlier he had left a note in his friend's room telling him to come quickly when he returned. Havacian's master must have kept him working late on a project. Sometimes the Wizards of the Blue Hall carried out activities that could only take place after dark. The last time Havacian was so late, his class was doing research with florescent algae. Qel couldn't remember precisely, but he thought it had something to do with deep-water squid. It all sounded uninteresting to him, but Havacian could speak enthusiastically about it for hours if Qel would listen. He supposed that was why Havacian was a Water Wizard and he was not.

The element of fire was Qel's specialty and he was as passionate about it as Havacian was about water. It was strange, in a way, that the two of them had become such good friends with professional interests that couldn't be more adverse. But since the first day they met, they had gotten on well and enjoyed each other's company. Qel hoped his friend would be graduating with him the next day. Although an apprentice never knew for sure until the day before graduation when, or if, they would receive the Aurinium necklace. The two of them always dreamed of traveling the world together, exploring strange cultures and places and discovering new things at every turn. If for some reason Havacian's master did not think he was ready to graduate, then Qel would be forced to spend the first year of Discovery on his own and anticipate that Havacian would join him the following year. It would be a disappointing start for sure.

Qel took a book from the shelf and began to read. It didn't take long before sleep overtook him and he was dreaming of the places he would go, the strange creatures he might encounter and the even more unusual people would meet. It was a good dream until it was suddenly interrupted.

"Qel! Wake up!" a voice whispered hoarsely above him. "Qel! It's Havacian, wake up!"

"Havacian?" Qel stirred sleepily. Was he still dreaming? No. "Havacian!" Qel sat up quickly. "Are you OK? How late is it?"

Havacian was laughing. "It is almost morning! Master Curatei had me charting squid all night, only Pontus knows for what reason and you wouldn't believe what happened at the close of my duties."

In dramatic fashion, Havacian pulled his hand from inside his robes, dropping the heavy end of an Orichalcum Crystal on the length of an Aurinium chain to leave it swaying in the dim light. Qel just stared at it a moment before he pulled out his own, tucked under the collar of his robe. They were almost identical. Spontaneously, they both burst out laughing. Qel had no more worries. They would be graduating together and travel the world on their Journey of Discovery just as they had always planned.

———

Grand Wizard Tochthon stood in the center of the impressively spacious, cylindrical room that formed the base of one of many towers in the Wizards Enclave. His long black robes trimmed with gold trailed behind him while he paced across the rich purple-red porphyry floor polished to such sheen that it appeared as if it were dusted with the stars. Physically, he looked like any other Atlantean; nearly seven feet tall, an elongated skull with long gray hair to his shoulders, sharp features, distinctive oversized eyes, blue-tinted skin and lean physic. Qel always regarded the Grand Wizard as a venerable reflection of the office he represented, but more than that, to be this close was to feel the power of his presence.

Qel listened attentively while the Grand Wizard spoke to the apprentices assembled for graduation—there were only seven this year—extolling the virtues of their elevation to a Wizard of the Imperial Order. The masters whose apprentices were graduating looked on proudly from high-backed chairs set a few strides behind him. Master Ampher was there, as was Master Curatei and two others.

Qel stood next to Havacian and the other five graduates, all of whom he knew well, nearly twitching with excitement, pride and a host of other emotions. He stood there listening to words of encouragement from one of the most powerful beings on the planet. Perhaps more than anything, he was inspired by the raw power of the men and women assembled in the room. It was a rare thing for any Atlantean other than the masters to interact with the Grand Wizard. For that matter, he was rarely seen around the Enclave. Qel heard rumors that the long periods of absence were due to his travels between dimensions and gateways that could take him to other worlds. He always laughed at the idea of it. But what if it were true . . .

The Grand Wizard was coming to the end of his speech. He gestured to the row of masters sitting behind him. "You have joined a very exclusive group of some of the most exceptional Atlanteans of our time. All of whom carry the burden of a long and accomplished history. Dedicating their lives to educate and prepare the next generation of wizards to whom they will eventually pass the torch of responsibility. It is through our order's efforts that you can feel the power of the Source Crystals no matter where you may travel in the course of your time dedicated to Discovery." He stopped pacing and looked them over with an intense gaze that sent a shiver through Qel when the Grand Wizard's eyes flickered over him. "Never forget that the Crystals are our primary concern at all times and if there is ever a need to protect or defend them, wherever you may travel, it is your duty to do so no matter the cost." It was a stark reminder of their purpose that left a chill in the pit of Qel's stomach. A heavy silence oppressed the room in the seconds that followed emphasizing the serious nature of the moment. If he remembered anything about his graduation in the years to come, it would be those few words and the weight of responsibility they carried.

Then the old wizard smiled in a fatherly way that made Qel feel warm inside. "I wish you all safe and productive travels and I look forward to seeing each one of you again in five years. I will leave you now with Master Curatei for final instructions before he releases you upon this unsuspecting world." A few chuckles echoed from the masters before the Grand Wizard concluded his speech. "Welcome to the Imperial Order of Wizards."

There were no wild cheers or celebrations. That would have been undignified. However, Qel felt it inside and by the broad smiles reflected by the others around him, they were feeling it too. Grand Wizard Tochthon quietly glided from the room through a side door while Master Curatei took his place in front of the line of graduates. The old master had overseen Havacian's apprenticeship in the Blue Hall and also served as the Keeper of Records for the order. He was reputed to be the most learned man in all of Atlantis, with an unrivaled depth of knowledge of not only the places and cultures of the present day but most recorded history as well.

Like all the masters, Curatei was very old and what little hair remained on his elongated head was gray and perpetually out of place. He walked with a noticeable limp that caused him to rely on a cane and his once straight posture was bent by a permanent hunch from untold hours leaning over writings of every form and medium. Despite his physical appearance, Master Curatei's disposition was generally good-natured and approachable, with a penchant for finding humor in almost everything. His apprentices, including Havacian, always spoke highly of him and enjoyed his often-lengthy lectures and extensive studies of aquatic elements. Even with the little exposure Qel had to Master Curatei, he often found himself laughing at the old man's anecdotes and ramblings.

"Good afternoon, my young and newly appointed wizards," he greeted them all. "I will try to keep this short and to the point." There were smiles and muffled snickers from the graduates and masters alike. Master Curatei was never short and to the point about anything.

Master Curatei smiled with them. "The world as you once knew it outside this Enclave will not be the same as when you first arrived here many years ago. Not because the world has changed so much, you've all been out enough to know that, but because *you* have changed so much. When you walk out those doors today, you carry knowledge and power with you as well as the responsibility that goes with it!" The master waved his hands dramatically when he spoke, emphasizing his words with exaggerated gestures. "We can't have you running around blasting down trees and recklessly putting others at risk, Atlantean or otherwise. There are grave consequences for those that abuse their endowment!"

He raised his cane and pointed it at them causing the medallion of his office to sway on the thick Aurinium chain around his neck as he adjusted his balance. "Take everything in moderation, whether it be drink, lovers and most especially hubris! Your character reflects fully upon the order and you *will* be judged for it!"

For nearly an hour, Master Curatei listed what seemed like every possible situation they might get into while on their Journey of Discovery before he finally came to the end. "Just a few final items of importance." He cinched his luminescent blue belt, which had loosened under the torrent of his gesticulations. "You will have a weekly stipend available for you to withdraw wherever you find a Source structure or one of the Order's many towers in the more advanced kingdoms you may visit. Also, when you mingle with the peoples of other cultures, you may dress as you like. You are not required to identify yourself as a Wizard of the Order unless you choose to."

Master Curatei's voice turned uncharacteristically grim, "Finally, as powerful as you all are, it is a dangerous world out there and sadly we lose one or two of you every year. Remember that the purpose of your Journey of Discovery is to gain practical knowledge and understanding of your abilities. Those of you who survive will return to us mature and wizened in ways you could not possibly understand right now." He waved his hands in a final flourish of dismissal. "Be careful and may Pontus guide and protect you on your travels."

Qel quietly filed out of the room with the others, pausing to glance over at Master Ampher as he left, receiving a confident nod and a wink. It all felt so surreal to him. This had been his home for two decades and soon he would be leaving. Outside the tower, Qel and Havacian bade farewell to the other graduates before they walked together toward their rooms.

"So, we are in agreement?" Havacian asked.

Qel nodded. It wasn't really much of a plan, but it was a plan. "To Avalon"—he smiled broadly— "and then we'll go where the wind takes us."

"Good." Havacian clasped Qel hand. "I'm off to see my family and I expect to find you here when I return in two days. Are you sure you don't want to come with me since your own family is at their summer estate in the country?"

"I have a few things I need to finish here before we leave and I don't want to delay our departure any longer than necessary," Qel sighed. "I'll make sure I collect all the supplies we will need for the journey north. We can resupply at my family's home since it is not far from the border with the Sylvan Forest. Wish your family well for me."

"Will do!" Havacian slapped his back and then hurried off toward his dormitory. Qel smiled, watching his friend's departure. There was a skip in his step and enthusiasm to match. Somehow, he knew that they were going to have grand adventures together and just like Havacian, he couldn't wait to get started.

Qel fingered the Orichalcum Crystal that hung on his neck underneath his robes. His one disappointment was that his own family was so far away and he was eager to tell them of his accomplishments. It had been several months since he had seen them. Their estate in the north was where he grew up during the cool summer months before he was taken to the Wizards Enclave. His family was highly respected and relatively affluent merchant landowners who cultivated a well-regarded stock of wine from obsessively tended vineyards. He considered going to stay at his family home on the inner ring of the city—certainly there would be a few servants to keep the house clean and maintained while the family was away—but he would be lonely there by himself. At least here in the Enclave he knew nearly everyone and there would be no end of activities to keep him busy until Havacian returned. Then they would begin the journey that he hoped would be the adventure of their lives.

Chapter 8

Uneasy Farewell

"Master Curatei told me that we will immediately be elevated to Class Four when we return from our Journey of Discovery," Havacian was saying excitedly as they rode through the Wizard's Enclave.

Qel laughed without much humor at that. "Well, that assumes we safely return from our journey and gain the knowledge and experience expected of us."

"We've been cooped up within these walls for so many years that at times I wondered if the masters would ever let us out." Havacian twisted the length of his newly acquired Aurinium chain, which hung around his neck, biting on it occasionally. Qel knew it was a sign of how nervous his friend really was about leaving the comfy confines of the Enclave and the only home they really knew.

"It seems the masters are very generous to those who manage to graduate." Qel shook the pouch of mixed gold, silver and copper strips that he had withdrawn as his first stipend. "If you recall, there were more than fifty of us in our first year and only seven at the end."

Outside of the supplies of food, blankets and packs, their only significant purchases were the two horses they rode. Qel was sure they wouldn't have enough money to buy them, but apparently, the Imperial Order of Wizards had a pre-negotiated price with certain livestock traders in the city for graduates going on Discovery. To his surprise, the horses were quality Lambei with light-colored manes and tail hair. The powerful steeds were known for their strength and constitution, although they were not the fastest horses and tired quickly if not paced properly. The livestock vendor, an Atlantean with corrals outside the city, explained that the Lambei originally came from the western continent and now he bred them on his farm here on the Emerald Isle.

That was one thing the Atlanteans were very good at—bringing the best of everything they found back to the Emerald Isle to replicate for their own people's convenience and enjoyment. The Imperial Order of Wizards was the only class that encouraged its members to get out and see the world. Most other Atlanteans, except for the merchants, preferred the comfort of their island home and rarely traveled beyond it. Avalon was the notable exception, where many vacationed. His father used to quip that there were very nearly as many Atlanteans in Avalon as there were elves.

"Did you calculate the time it would take to travel to the border?" Havacian asked.

Qel had. "If the weather is good and the road is not congested, we should arrive at my family's home in about twelve days. It's another two days more from there to Aquilon."

"We have a long journey ahead of us, but I am looking forward to every moment!" Havacian practically beamed with enthusiasm.

Qel nodded his agreement while gazing out over the vast, circular array of the city beyond the gates of the Enclave. It would take them half the day just to get to the northern road on the mainland from here. The Wizards Enclave was constructed on the central island at the same elevation as the palace and just below the Temple of Pontus. Glancing up he could see the massive temple complex between two of the high towers of the Enclave. The central island was basically the pinnacle of a massive dormant volcano, according to the Dvergr Dwarfs and the temple was built upon the highest peak. Over the years, Qel had attended many religious ceremonies in its expansive courtyard said to hold as many as five thousand citizens. It was a beautiful temple profuse with towering columns easily ten times his height, fountains that spouted rivers of water and sculptures intermingled among buildings covered with carved images of Pontus and the Oceanides. The entire complex was constructed of beautiful bright white marble and red Orichalcum. Yet, as impressive as the temple might be, the overwhelming feature that could be seen for leagues in every direction, was the truly colossal sculpture of Pontus rising from the central courtyard to thrust his golden trident toward the deep blue depths of the Primal Sea. Somehow, the Earth Wizards had managed to tint the marble sculpture blue and his glistening trident was reputed to be made of pure gold. It was an extraordinary sight by any measure.

He considered the six imposing towers of the Wizards Enclave. There was a tower for each hall that overlooked the clusters of one- and two-story buildings between them. All were constructed of white marble to match the palace and temple, although they looked diminutive compared to the effigy of Pontus that rose above them. Even the emperor's palace on the opposite side of the center island was outshone by Pontus. *And perhaps that was the point,* Qel mused. Below the elevation of the Wizards Enclave and the imperial palace were the estates of the wealthiest Atlanteans and then finally, near the base, were four ports, each located at the cardinal points of the compass. Between them, one could find exclusive shops, taverns and imperial storehouses. Wide swaths of manicured parks, amphitheaters, an arena and a racetrack filled the remaining spaces on the island that was just shy of three leagues in diameter. Some of Qel's favorite books in the Enclave described cities from around the world. A few included magnificent illustrations, but not a one matched the scale and beauty of his city—the City of Atlantis.

Riding out through the gates of the Enclave, they passed several imperial soldiers, resplendent with their translucent blue Aurinium armor and spears, guarding the front entrance. They were entirely symbolic, as there was almost no crime in the city and on the rare occasion something happened it was usually committed by a human or a drunken dwarf on the outer ring. The road they followed took them down to the foundation of the island where the ports were located. They could exit the city by way of bridges that traversed the three land rings, each separated by water, or by direct ferry to the outermost ring. After some quick discussion, Qel suggested they take the boat, even if they had to wait a little while for its arrival.

As luck would have it, by the time they reached the busy north-facing port, the ferry was taking on its last passengers. The pair paid for passage and climbed on board with only minutes to spare before the wide-bodied ferry departed across the nearly crystal-clear blue waters of the wide canal. Qel watched the port slip away behind them and admired the white marble estates that dotted the once violent peak of the volcano. There was so much on the island to hold his visual interest, but his gaze kept wandering back to the towers rising from the Wizards Enclave. He felt a pang in his stomach watching his home for the past twenty years slowly diminish in the distance.

"Master Curatei told me once that the old volcano extends another league under the surface of the water on the south side of the island," Havacian remarked. A quiver in his voice betrayed his nervous excitement in contrast to Qel's desire to wax nostalgic over their old life. "Apparently it is one in a chain of ancient volcanos, including the Ourea, which caused the Emerald Isle to come into existence in the first place many millions of years ago."

One of the things Qel liked most about Havacian was that his craving for knowledge was not just restricted to the school of his hall. He had a lot in common with Master Curatei in that way. *Who knows?* Qel thought. *Maybe Havacian will find himself Keeper of the Records one day.*

They traversed the quarter league of water quickly. The ferry was propelled by a magical means Qel was not familiar with, but he guessed it was like the disks and horseless carriages that the wealthier Atlanteans used for transport. He and Havacian moved to the front of the ferry and watched as they passed through a wide break in the first land ring that surrounded the main island. It was on this ring that most of the affluent Atlanteans lived alongside a few foreign merchants, the embassies, libraries and local temples. Here the buildings were constructed of polished white granite and marble and the streets were laid with roughly textured gray granite that tempered the starker white buildings and conveyed a soft, elegant appearance. If nothing else, his people had a penchant for consistency. His parents' home was located on this ring, although it was out of sight of where they passed into the next channel of water.

Qel pointed in the distance to a watery figure, three times the height of a man, gliding across the water. "Tell me about the Oceanides, Havacian. I have always been fascinated by their odd nature."

Havacian smiled. "Well, you know the legend of the Oceanides and how they are asserted to be the children of Pontus. That may be true, as they are an enigma even to the Water Wizards. Of course, some in the Blue Hall are capable of summoning water elementals, but they are a very different creature," he shrugged. "The Oceanides apparently exist for one reason and that's to protect the waterways of Atlantis. We have not been able to control them in any way nor compel them to go beyond the outer ring. The only record of them doing anything beyond their endless patrols was during the Vikja raids a few centuries ago. They devastated every Vikja ship that managed to fight its way into the waterways. Since then, the Vikja have given the city a wide berth. As you know, the Vikja are a very superstitious people and the sight of an Oceanide is terrifying to them. That's why they won't even come here for trade under the flag of the Dvergr, preferring to use the port of Andlang instead."

Qel had read a little about the Vikja. The Eriu poet Vyvyan described them as a fierce, almost barbaric, seafaring culture that lived on a frozen island in the northern most reaches of the Primal Sea just below the glaciers. They had a proclivity for seizing merchant vessels and raiding the coastal villages of the Western Kingdoms when they weren't plying trade for the Dvergr Dwarfs. Vyvyan often glamorized the atrocities of the Vikja in his songs and poems pointing out that they were simply a passionate people misunderstood by the rest of the civilized world. Qel wasn't sure if the poet really meant it or if he didn't quite understand Eriu humor.

Soon the ferry was passing through the break between two wide segments of the second ring. Flanking the cut on either side stood a pair of magnificently colossal stone creatures, half-fish and half-man, holding implements of trade and craft. They were known as the Telchines. Nine of their sculpted likenesses dominated the architecture of the second ring and according to the priests, they represented yet another group of unusual children from Pontus. The mythology suggested that the Telchines were exceptionally skilled in metallurgy and that they lived on an island far to the west near the Confederation of Hella where they worked their forges in service to their divine patriarch. It was from them that the secret of Aurenium was said to derive. As far as Qel knew, no Atlantean had discovered this island, but he was hardly privy to anything the emperor chose not to announce publicly.

The further out from the center they travelled, the more crowded the channels became with other ferries and ships of trade. Each segment of all three land rings that surrounded the central island of Atlantis embraced a port near one of their breaks and two bridges that connected it to the parallel section of the adjacent ring. None of the segments of the same ring had connections via a bridge over the breaks between them so as not to impede the movement of ships into the interior. The second, or center, ring was similarly constructed as the inner ring. Here, however, the population was more balanced between Atlanteans, affluent humans and a few dwarfs. Qel noted that the ports on this ring were much busier than those of the inner ring and island. Of course, the population increased in proportion to the escalating diameter of the rings as they went farther out. He could see fewer disks and more horses carrying humans and Atlanteans, some with carts pulled by Hydruntin here and there along the stone-paved streets. While the second ring was almost entirely residential, with upscale markets, temples and taverns to serve those that lived there, it was also the location of many of the schools and trade institutions with the best reputations. Qel never spent much time on this ring, but two of his older sisters had attended one of the schools here when they were young. The eldest became an administrator of land grants for the imperial government and the younger one studied economy and trade, eventually returning to help his father manage the family business.

The ferry continued on, pausing several times for other water traffic on its way to a port on the final land ring that surrounded the city. Qel was patient, knowing that the water channel between the second and third rings was always busy, as were their ports. The segment of the outer ring where they would dock was on the north side of the city and the only segment to be built upon the mainland. The other three sections were like the rest of the rings: fully surrounded by water and connected to the inner rings by bridges arcing high enough above the water to allow a ship of nearly any size to pass under. Unlike the center and inner rings, the segments of the outer ring were connected by two sets of colossal gates that could be closed to protect the city from weather and intrusion. Always they were guarded by imperial soldiers on land or in ships as well as an Oceanide or two that always lingered nearby.

Qel watched the details of the third ring resolve on their approach. It was dominated by taverns, inns, trade houses, pens for livestock and public buildings. There were several clusters of residences inhabited mostly by humans who could afford to live inside the walls as well as a few Atlanteans. Qel was always astonished at the mass of people who went about their business on the third ring. Before entering the service of the Imperial Order of Wizards, he grew up in his family homes in the country or on the inner ring where there were never more than a handful of people within view at any given time. The press of people on the outer ring seemed chaotic and confounding to him. It would have been much worse if not for the smaller canals that spidered along the main thoroughfares and back alleys. These narrow waterways served as the main trade line for goods and livestock transported around the city from the main ports. Moving trade goods in this fashion kept the streets and alleys of the city clear of merchant traffic and uncluttered for pedestrians to enjoy. Even so, he was glad they would be passing through it quickly once they docked on their way to the north road.

There was one feature of the outer ring that had always fascinated Qel and that was the high curtain wall surrounding the city. It was made of Bluestone enchanted by the Earth Wizards that caused the wall to glow with a silver-blue luminescence at night and appear as beautifully polished silver during the day. What the purpose of the enchantment was he did not know and for once, neither did Havacian. Qel supposed the emperor would do everything possible to keep their home safe and the secret of the outer wall was probably just one of many exceptional protections very few knew anything about.

"It looks like we are near to port," Qel observed from the railing when the ferry angled toward the outer ring on final approach to the dock.

Havacian pulled on his sleeve. "Let's go claim the horses so we don't have to wait long to get off."

Qel thought that was a good idea too, so they walked to the center of the ferry where the animals were penned. Once the boat docked, they were able to disembark right away and join the flow of people that moved in the general direction of the north gate. Glancing around at the unusual faces and costumes they passed, Qel recognized many different cultures from near and far. There were people from Ys in their colorful corsets and smartly tailored jackets, knights from Lyonesse wearing the white-with-gold-fringe cloak of their station, Mouillian traders, a number of Gadesians and even a few broad-shouldered dwarfs from Tirnan Yog rumbling by. Of course, the Atlanteans towered above them all and except for the few dwarfs and even fewer elves, the majority in the crowd were human.

Turning from the port road onto the broad boulevard that ran straight and true in the direction of the north gate, Qel noted that here, too, white marble and granite dominated the architecture. All of it was enhanced by hanging gardens, grand fountains and impossibly life-like sculptures of exotic creatures real and imagined. They passed through the outer ring, where trade and mercantile served its purpose, yet even among the apparent clamber of traffic and people, Atlantis displayed its undeniable beauty at an unrivaled scale everywhere.

Qel suddenly realized how much he would miss not just the Wizards Enclave, but the City of Atlantis itself. It wasn't like he was going to the family's country estate with the knowledge that he would be returning in a few months. No, this time he might not return for years. Qel looked over at Havacian, intending to comment on that thought and quickly decided otherwise, not wanting to dampen the joy and enthusiasm clearly visible on his friend's face.

The busy boulevard became less crowded once they passed through the gargantuan city gates guarded by a score of mounted and unmounted imperial soldiers diligently observing everyone who passed through. Qel knew the way well and led Havacian onto the sloping incline of North Road beyond. They would follow as it curved its way through the interior of the Emerald Isle, rolling through leagues of agricultural estates until it terminated at the city of Aquilon about one hundred and eighty leagues to the north. Along the way, Qel planned for them to stay at any number of inns, way stations, or estates willing to board travelers that he was familiar with.

At the top of a ridge about a league outside the city, Havacian abruptly pulled his mount off to the side of the road and gazed back at the glistening City of Atlantis in the distance. Qel stopped with him, observing the western-leaning sun reflected brightly off the silver curtain wall that surrounded the counterposed rings of white stone and deep blue channels of the sea converging on the center island of more white stone and the imposing semblance of Pontus himself. Seagoing vessels moved purposely throughout, bringing people and prosperity to every part of it while imperial flyers mounted on trained Rocs circled high above, keeping a protective watch.

"It's beautiful, isn't it?" Havacian said with a hint of sadness in his voice.

Qel presumed that his friend had just now begun to realize what he had understood earlier and the emotion was weighing heavily on Havacian. He felt sorry for his friend, having already experienced the nostalgic pang himself, although it was probably worse for Havacian since his family was down there in Atlantis, while Qel was on his way to see his own.

"You know we can come back here at any time we wish." Qel tried to sound supportive.

Havacian nodded slowly. "That's true, but will we?"

Qel had no answer for that. Pontus only knew where their travel and adventures would take them. For a while, they watched and silently reminisced about the life they were leaving behind until Qel patted his friend on the back, startling him back to the present.

"We're proper explorers now," Qel announced gallantly. "Let's go find our destiny!"

Havacian smiled at that and the two turned their mounts north, racing up the wide road as fast as their sturdy Lambei would carry them, laughing with the rush of youthful exuberance and throwing their cares to the wind.

Chapter 9

Child of Gold

SY5485 – Five years earlier

Lysithea was standing alone in the dark in the heart of her beloved apple grove. She stared up at the stars that shone bright in the blackness of the cloudless sky. The evening was mild, allowing her the opportunity to wear one of her favorite outfits—a very long, light blue evening gown with many layers of solid and sheer silks that trailed behind her wistfully when she walked. Despite Lysithea's outward appearance of serenity, her delicate hands were clenched together tightly in front of her gown, betraying her anxiety.

This was going to be a special night. That was her hope anyway as she nervously muttered a quiet prayer to the goddess Gersemi that it would be so. The apple grove where she waited was considered a sacred place by here people, it was also her home and on any other night she would have been entirely at ease here. She was the queen, after all and it was the time, late in the evening, when she would meditate on the essential challenges facing her realm. At least that was what her closest staff and advisers thought she was doing. It was only a small lie and it relieved her of explanations that she was not ready for yet, *especially* right now. Besides, why shouldn't she be entitled to a little privacy in her life when she wanted it?

Queen Lysithea barely had to reach with her mind to feel every branch and leaf stimulated by the light breeze so clean and fresh during the springtime eve. Even the soft soil beneath her feet that nurtured her grove felt comforting and warm. Long ago, the elves from Sylvan Kingdom gifted this grove to her ancestors and the first Nymph Queen of Gades built a fabulous palace around it from which to rule. According to legend, the goddess Gersemi— a nymph herself— blessed this grove, altering the fruit it bore to produce a very particular golden-hued apple with unique properties that would benefit the nymphs and those that pleased them. The apple became known as Gersemi's treasure and it was the nymphs' most prized possession. Just as it had been for her mother and grandmother and every Nymph

Queen that came before her, the grove was part of who she was, a physical extension of her well-being. And so it would be with her daughter one day. *Her* daughter. She smiled at the thought.

She passed one of the giant white owls that perched motionless nearby, a silent guardian dedicated to the protection of the grove. There were many of them among the trees, each nearly her height and three times as wide. Their glowing, seldom blinking eyes were the only warning that they were real and not decorations for her amusement.

A sudden rush of wind rustled the leaves through the orchard from somewhere beyond Lysithea's sight. The owl rotated its head swiftly in that direction, flapped its wings as if it were going to take flight and then settled again unperturbed. Lysithea immediately sensed the presence of something else in her grove and her anxiety heightened further with expectation. She didn't need to see the source of the disturbance to know who it was that so boldly trespassed in her private orchard. She waited patiently, even with the troupe of butterflies fluttering endlessly in her stomach, knowing it approached. Then, more silent than a shadow, a beautiful man of pure perfection, garbed in flowing robes of silken gold, emerged from the darkness to stand close in front of her. Without a word, the queen rushed to embrace him, to trade soft and subtle kisses with hot breath upon each other's lips. The all-seeing owl, perhaps discomfited by the lurid display by its master, looked away.

After a while, they separated just a little and the man in gold spoke in the perfect tone and timbre of one who could sing melodious ballads or the honey-coated prose penned by Vyvyan, "How are you this beautiful evening, my queen?" The words barely parted his lips before he was planting small kisses down the length of her long neck.

Lysithea shook with a lilting, playful laugh. "I am very well now that you are here, my love."

She led him to a stone bench, where they sat close and spoke at length about many things, from the mundane to affairs of state. She loved this man her people knew as Senjit, a Golden Dragon currently in human form. He had been Queen Lysithea's secret friend, advisor and lover for more than a century. They often met just as they did this night to keep each other's company and enjoy their love together. This night was different, however; she had something important to tell him that would change both of their lives forever.

Senjit seemed to sense her anxiety. "What troubles you, beloved? You appear unsettled tonight. Much more so than usual when my touch causes your flesh to quiver," he smiled at the joke.

Lysithea didn't know the best way to say what was occupying her mind, so she just came out with it. "Senjit, I am with child."

"Pregnant?" He appeared shocked and elated at the same time. "I never considered that would be possible. But it is wonderful news!" Senjit pulled her close and kissed her deeply.

Lysithea was relieved that he was happy but terrified by the unknown. "What do you think it could mean? Will the baby be a nymph or dragon? Or some monstrous hybrid of both?"

"We will simply have to wait and see," he assured her enthusiastically. "Each of us has a special innate power within and I am sure that our purity of love will create a beautiful being beget from the two of us. Whatever it is, it will be our child and we will love it,"

"I know what 'it' is, dear. Would you like to know? Or shall I just wait and surprise you?" she asked him playfully.

"Do you now? I suppose I should know so not to waste time on my knitting," he teased back.

She smiled broadly. "A girl. We will have a daughter."

"That is wonderful! Not really a surprise considering you are a nymph." He laughed. "In any case, I hope she is just like her mother. Unless she's a dragon. Then she can look like me. There is no more beautiful Dragon in the world than me, you know!" he laughed as if he were joking. Lysithea knew better than that. Senjit, at least in dragon form, considered himself one of the most beautiful creatures on earth. And perhaps with just a tiny bit of jealousy, she had to agree.

She kissed his cheek. "And that's just one reason I love you."

Feeling alive and excited, the lovers fell into each other's embrace and celebrated their joy together. Senjit's acceptance of their child gave her comfort, a box checked off her long list of boxes needing checking, albeit one of the most important ones. She hoped that her people would be just as accepting of a child of a dragon.

———

Dawn broke, sending its first rays of the new day through the open window of Lysithea's bedchamber. She was awake already, unable to sleep much after Senjit departed. She couldn't stop thinking about all the things they talked about. They speculated endlessly about what their daughter would be like, her personality, her physical characteristics, what powers she would carry within her. That last part scared Lysithea a little for some reason.

So much talk about the future sent her mind wandering back to the past. Lysithea considered what she really knew about her lover. Someday their daughter would ask questions about her unusual parents and Lysithea was determined to have the right answers. She tried hard to remember the stories Senjit had told her over the years and piece them together as best she could.

She recalled that he was raised by the centaurs on the island of Chenech, one of four islands that comprised the Isles of Gades, until he was old enough to fly. The legend of his arrival was simple and well-known by the people of Gades. Senjit assumed it was true, but she didn't think he really cared if it was or not. Apparently, his mother was an ordinary dragon that arrived at Chenech Isle already pregnant and on the verge of labor. It was said that she was a very intelligent and kind dragon who quickly befriended the gentle centaurs on the Isle she settled.

Sadly, she lived only a few weeks after giving birth to Senjit for reasons unknown and the centaurs raised him as their own in deference to his mother, whom they held in high regard. Senjit never knew her by more than her name and the few stories the centaurs passed down. She was called Findyl, which was inscribed on a small monument at the site of her burial. Often, Senjit would visit the secluded glen within the forest and trace the name on the granite stone with his finger as if it brought him some sense of comfort. Lysithea had accompanied him there on several occasions, but she worried that the infrequent visits brought him nothing more than sadness and regret. Lysithea never pressed Senjit to know more about his past. Maybe there wasn't much more to tell other than that he was raised well by the centaurs, considered them his family and forever indebted by their kindness. That was over four hundred years ago and in terms of dragon years he was still young.

Although the Isles of Gades, her realm, had always been Senjit's home, Lysithea knew that he would regularly leave his lair on the nearby island of Hero to travel the world. In the century she had known him as more than just a casual acquaintance, Senjit often spoke of the unusual people he met and the strange cultures he experienced in obscure, far-off regions of the world. Oddly, he was known in those foreign lands more as a dragon than a humanoid. Some of those peoples even worshiped him as a god, although he didn't seem to take that very seriously. Once Senjit made a vague reference to a child and a family he was close to in a kingdom somewhere to the east, she couldn't recall the name, but he never said more about it. Lysithea suspected that he had sired human children on more than one occasion and was perhaps even married previously, but he was reluctant to speak of it. What did it matter anyway? They were in love and having a child together. Besides, relationships with humans were always so temporary considering their short lifespans.

One of the most important matters Lysithea and Senjit discussed was how to explain her pregnancy to her people. It was common knowledge that the queen consorted with Senjit and that he was a Golden Dragon. However, it was unlikely anyone expected anything to come of it. The human and elven populace in Gades, as well as the centaurs scattered around the isles, could care less, but the nymphs that made up the ruling class were a much more exclusive group and preferred to keep outsiders at a distance. Of course, it was not uncommon for a nymph to take a human male, conceive a child, and then either never tell him about the pregnancy or, in the rare case of love, allow the male to live in her household without any actual titles or authority. The nymphs on the Isles of Gades were culturally matriarchal, although they did not require the same of their subjects.

Fortunately, nearly every child born to a nymph was a girl and on the odd chance a boy was born, the offspring never acquired the female nymph's natural abilities. Instead, he was likely to have potential in the magical arts. These rare males usually grew up in the household of their mothers and then were sent to the Wizards Enclave in Atlantis or the Demesne of Magic in Avalon to apprentice to a wizard once they came of age. Unfortunately, the male offspring almost always lost their sanity before the age of thirty and either ran away into The Wilds or got themselves killed before they became a danger to society. Lysithea was glad they did not have *that* complication to deal with. As it was, she worried her sister nymphs would not accept her daughter as the next in line to rule given the nature of her father. A child from a union with a Golden Dragon might be a source of considerable controversy.

That evening they met in the grove again and as expected the conversation turned to their future together.

"We should announce the pregnancy openly," Lysithea suggested to Senjit after a short debate. "You are well liked and it would be better not to hide it. If it causes any concern among my sisters, I will just have to deal with it."

It was no secret that her sisters all liked Senjit and openly suggested that he become her consort. His charm was one of his most endearing qualities. However, their opinions might change once they found out she could have a child by him.

Senjit looked amused for a moment, then asked, "Shall we join in the bond as man and wife?"

Lysithea laughed. "So, you want to be king?"

Senjit took on a tone of mock indignation and snobbery, "I am known as Huanglong by the Huaxia, Culebre by the Astriense, Ladon in Hellas, the World Serpent by the Vikja, Usum by the Kur-gal, the Earth Monster by the Olmec and many more titles by peoples all over the world. The last thing I need is another appellation! Except for husband. I wouldn't mind the title of husband."

In a high, royal resonance, she teased back, "So be it! I grant you the title of husband." They laughed together and she hugged him rigorously. She couldn't have been more thrilled with the outcome. If only her sisters would share her enthusiasm . . .

Lysithea knew Senjit couldn't care less about earthbound power. He was a Golden Dragon and he considered the sky his realm. Besides, he told her many times how much politics of the earth-bound bored him. They bored her too, most of the time. She decided it was time to take a gamble.

Within a few days, the announcement was made that the queen was taking a companion. A huge ceremony was planned with a public celebration to take place afterward. To Lysithea's relief, the nymphs and general citizenry of the Isles of Gades responded to the news happily. Her closest confidants advised her that while it was true that Senjit was a wildly exotic magical beast, her sisters agreed that the match was far more befitting her station than a mere human or elf. Her more substantial fear about whether or not her child would be accepted was also allayed. It seemed that her sisters expressed more curiosity than concern and looked forward to witnessing the results of the union. In other words, they were reserving their judgment until they found out what they were truly dealing with.

Two weeks later, Lysithea was bathed and dressed in a beautiful flowing gown of white and gold for the wedding ceremony to be held on the rolling grasslands outside the City of Gades. It was open to any citizen who wished to attend and they came in droves to see their reclusive queen bound in union to a dragon. Nobles from the nearby kingdoms, centaurs, elves, druids, nymphs and commoners alike mingled side by side in joyous celebration of their nuptials. Senjit was not an uncommon curiosity to the populace, as he was often seen flying high above the isles going someplace or other, although he was rarely viewed up close. His arrival for the ceremony was a spectacular show for those fortunate enough to arrive early and watch him fly from the sky in dragon form landing transformed in the figure of a human.

With little pageantry, the Arch-Priestess conducted the simple ceremony, blessed their unity in the name of the goddess Gersemi and announced that they were husband and wife. Then there was a massive celebration with an abundance of food, dancing and gifts commemorating the day.

Lysithea had never been happier in her life.

A few days later, she hosted a private ceremony at the palace, within the sacred apple groves, for her sister nymphs to accept her new consort. Senjit, as expected, was accepted unanimously. Inasmuch as he was an impressive Golden Dragon, the nymphs loved their queen and showed unequivocal trust in her judgment. Lysithea knew how vain nymphs tended to be, she was vain herself and she expected that her sisters secretly liked the idea that her consort was a powerful dragon who would contribute to the influence and security of their small island nation.

During the small reception afterward, Lysithea and Senjit announced her pregnancy publicly and that the baby would be a girl. The news was received in all parts of the Isles with enthusiasm and with a quiet undercurrent of speculation as to what form the child would emerge as. From that time on, Senjit became a familiar and welcome resident of the palace and close companion during the term of her pregnancy.

All seventeen-months of it.

Nymphs did not often get pregnant and when they did, it was almost always by choice. When Lysithea went into labor, the Arch-Priestess of Gersemi was again summoned, along with the queen's birthing attendants – young nymphs trained for just such an occurrence. A few hours later, the child was born and a gasp rippled through those gathered to witness the birth and attend to the queen.

"Extraordinary." Senjit was standing next to Lysithea when the child came.

She immediately looked up at him with fear clutching at her heart. "What's wrong?" she begged, not having seen the baby yet with so many huddled over the newborn, cleaning and evaluating its health.

A sharp cry abruptly broke the quiet of the room. Relief flooded through Lysithea and she forgot all about Senjit's odd reaction moments earlier. The Arch-Priestess gently handed the newborn to her mother. When she looked upon the face of her baby for the first time, she didn't need to see more to know that she would be beautiful. And different. She had skin the color of liquid gold.

Before Lysithea could say anything, the Arch-Priestess was standing over the two of them. "This child is strong and healthy," she announced to the room. "I bless her in the name of Gersemi and in accordance with the wishes of the goddess, the child will be known as Alseid."

The awkward uncertainty of the nymphs in the room turned to jubilant laughter and celebration. The Arch-Priestess had claimed the child for Gersemi. That meant her daughter was not only healthy, but just as importantly, she was a nymph. Later the baby would be washed in the spring that fed the sacred grove and a slice of the golden apple would be placed on her tongue to establish a bond with the orchard that would last throughout her entire life. For now, the Arch-Priestess and the rest of her sisters left the room so Lysithea could rest and enjoy a little privacy with her new family.

"She is so beautiful," observed Senjit. "We will have to keep a close eye on her to avoid surprises by any unexpected abilities that she doesn't know how to control. When she is a little older, I will probe her mind and discover what I can. Alseid. What is the meaning of her name?"

Lysithea couldn't take her eyes off the now sleeping infant. "It means 'of the grove,' and you are right, we will have to watch her carefully.

"'Of the grove,'" Senjit chuckled. "She *was* conceived in that venerable orchard!"

Lysithea rolled her eyes. "I'm sure Gersemi had a different reason for choosing that for her name. Although, who could know the mind of a goddess?" She laughed.

Lysithea and Senjit studied their child closely over the next few months, wondering what strange abilities might manifest themselves in the child they brought into this world. So far, she had not displayed any unusual talents; in fact, with the exception of her golden skin, she was a completely typical nymph. Even Senjit's gentle mind probing only confirmed her Sylvan nature and magical potential. Perhaps they had nothing to worry about after all.

Chapter 10

Going Home
SY5490

"What is that thing?"

There was fear in Havacian's voice. Qel felt it too, laying in the damp grass on top of a hill, overlooking the broad swath of the savannah that stretched out for leagues before them. Their attention was riveted on the grotesque scene playing out below.

"I don't have any idea," Qel whispered. "Look at the size of it." He honestly wasn't sure what he wanted to do more, watch with morbid curiosity or run away like the hartebeests.

Less than an hour had passed since the pair strayed from the North Road half a league from where they lay now to take a break from their journey and nibble on a snack of mahiz. It was a nice summer afternoon with a warm breeze from the east that softly teased the dark shoulder-length hair over Qel's elongated skull that left him touched by a lethargic sentiment on the soft cushion of grass where he sat propped up on one elbow. In the distance, an endless herd of hartebeests grazed their way across the landscape so numerous that they flowed like an ocean of fur and flesh for leagues on the expansive plains of the Emerald Isle. Qel loved to watch them as a child and he loved to watch them now. He was fascinated by their methodical purpose of consuming the long grass, yet remain in a cohesive group, leaving a broad swath of lighter-colored short grass in their wake that they would revisit in the next season after it had grown tall again. He knew the hartebeests destruction upon the savanna was only temporary as the roots of the weeds they consumed remained intact and renewable.

Qel was drowsily half-listening to Havacian chatter about something to do with the way water condensed to form clouds, or some such, when he noticed a disturbance at the edge of the hartebeest herd not a stone's throw from the hill where they sat. At first, it was just a confusing burst of sudden movement, with hartebeests running a short distance in every direction. The brief frenzy drew the attention of the entire herd and like the ripple of a wave across a lake, thousands of the hartebeests stopped cold in their tracks, swinging their heads up to listen. For a brief moment, the silence was profound. And then a sharp, primal scream rent the still air before it was cut short almost instantly. The reaction by the herd was electric. They bound away virtually as one, springing high into the air at sporadic intervals and thundered west at fantastic speed.

What was left behind was shocking. The area where Qel noticed the initial disturbance was covered in blood that contrasted sharply with the bright green grass. Of more immediate concern was the large creature bent over the mutilated body of a full-grown hartebeest. Qel urgently gestured to Havacian to be quiet and move back down behind the hill so as not to be noticed. Fortunately, the horses were a short distance away and out of sight as well. Without speaking, Qel crawled on his belly to the summit for a better look at the terrifying beast. Havacian was right beside him.

The creature was bipedal, with greenish-brown leathery skin and patches of dark red fur all over. Parts of its body were clothed in mismatched scraps of fabric that didn't quite fit and were loosely cinched at the waist by a wide belt from which hung a large leather sack. Qel had the impression that it might be an intelligent thing and he wondered idly if it could speak. Although, conversating with the awesome beast was not high on his list of priorities at the moment. There was a massive spiked club on the ground beside it that was stained with crimson and appeared well worn with use, but it used its massive claws to tear through the hide of the hartebeest easily as if it was sheer gossamer silk.

"Do you think there are more of them?" Havacian sounded on the edge of panic, his eyes wide with fear darting this way and that.

Qel glanced around as well, but he saw no other movement. "I don't think so, but we should probably leave in case there are."

Just as they started to back down the hill the thing's head shot up and it sniffed the air. Qel pressed a hand on Havacian's back and they both dug their chins deep into the soft soil and watched. The creature gazed around the immediate area and continued to sniff at the air as if it were looking for something. Not the hartebeests. They were long gone toward the horizon and out of sight. Nothing else moved except their horses quietly grazing down the hill behind them. Qel prayed to Pontus that they wouldn't make any noise.

At times looking in their direction, Qel got a good look at it's strange features. It was an ugly creature, to be sure. Blood covered its face entirely and a formless strip of red flesh dangled sickeningly from its toothy maw while it chewed distractedly upon it.. Bushy red eyebrows matched the hair on its narrow chin defining a heavily muscled jaw under large pointy ears that resembled those typical of an elf. But it was the thing's eyes that struck the most fear into Qel. They were red, so red that they seemed to glow from the inside.

The monster sniffed around a bit more, then dropped the bloody remains it held in its claws and loped a short distance in one direction and then another seemingly in time with the shifting breeze. When it ran, it crouched and its long thickly muscled arms grabbed the earth and pulled itself forward as much as its legs propelled its heavy bulk. Qel was surprised by how efficient the movement was and guessed that it could run extremely fast for at least a short distance if it wanted to. It had captured a hartebeest, after all.

One of the horses stomped a hoof and snickered. Qel froze, ice replacing the blood that ran through his veins. The awful thing turned and looked up the hill precisely where they lay hidden. Qel's heart pounded like drums in his ears. The creature stood very still and quiet staring up in their direction for a long time, often sniffing at the air. Qel was never so terrified in his life. He had to clench his teeth together to keep them from chattering so the thing below them might not hear. It squinted in the bright sunlight as if straining to see clearly, but Qel guessed that however deficient with sight the beast likely compensated with sharp ears and sense of smell. The breeze shifted again, this time down the hill from their position and the creature sniffed again . . . emitting a low, guttural growl.

Qel realized it could smell them, or the horses, but before he had time to react, the thing was bounding up the hill toward them at a fantastic sprint. Qel grabbed Havacian and pushed off the incline sending them tumbling down the back of the hill. When he was able to look back the beast was crouching in the spot they had just vacated, sniffing alternately at them and their horses as if to determine their identity by scent. The horses saw the massive creature as well, reacting with nervous stomps. Neither of them was hobbled or tied to a branch. Their muscles twitched on the verge of panic.

Qel barely had time to stand up when the creature sprang down the hill and smashed into Havacian's horse, knocking it prone. The poor lambei never had a chance, it's screams falling on the pitiless ears of the monster tearing out its bowels. Qel's horse, seeing the danger, immediately took flight, to where Qel didn't notice, his eyes were glued to the carnage taking place before him. It was all impossibly unreal and savage. Only minutes earlier the afternoon was so perfect . . .

Havacian slowly stood up and the two backed away from the violent scene, shocked and staring. Qel's mind was spinning. *That could have been one of us*, he thought. *It will be one of us if we don't do something.* Thinking fast, he summoned his strength and focused as best he could. A thin jet of flame shot from the palm of his hand and struck the creature on the thigh. It responded with a sound Qel vaguely interpreted as surprise and turned its fierce gaze on them. All he had succeeded in doing was getting the monster's attention. Now it would come for them. Yet it paused, regarding them as if evaluating the threat they posed. *Had it faced their kind before?* Then the moment passed and it barreled toward them. Qel had only seconds to act. He quickly conjured a ball of flame and sent streaking forward. As he did so, he felt as much as heard lightning crackling from the fingertips of Havacian. The elemental magics landed squarely causing the charging creature to throw its arms up in front of its face. The monster barely lost its stride and kept coming, seemingly more annoyed than harmed by their assault.

Nearly upon them, Qel hopelessly fumbled for another cast. He knew the spell he needed and the calculation for the power required to destroy his attacker, but fear crowded out his concentration and wrecked his confidence. His mind screamed while his body quivered. This was how he was going to die, barely a week out of the Enclave, an example of failure to future graduates. A disgrace to his family.

Something dropped from the sky in front of him and he fell backward expecting an impact, but none ever came. To his utter astonishment, Qel looked up at the backs of two Imperial Warriors. They took the full force of the creature's charge on their Aurinium shields just steps away, pushed off the beast and lashed out with their glass-like longswords, scoring hits on its arm and ribcage that caused green blood to spout from deep wounds. The monster roared and struck back, grabbing the edge of one warrior's shield and pulling forward while the other warrior danced around its heavy bulk, landing horrific slashing blows with every step.

Qel struggled to stand without taking his eyes off the battle raging only steps away. He had to help these brave men. A line of fire shrieked over his head and between the two warriors, hitting the creature in the chest. Qel instinctively ducked and jumped away. The flames exploded over the beast's entire body, the blast knocking the warriors off to the side and slamming Qel back on the ground next to Havacian. A second shriek of flames followed and another as more fire engulfed the thing now screaming and flailing wildly in every direction. The stink of putrid burning flesh was nauseating and the sight of it was . . . nearly too much for Qel to take. *Why wouldn't the thing die?* The warriors, apparently unaffected, stood back a few steps and watched until the fire did its work and the creature was reduced to nothing more than a unrecognizable charred mass on the ground. They cautiously strode over and poked the corpse with their blades to ensure no life remained, but it never so much as twitched.

"Why are you here?" a powerful voice boomed from behind, nearly causing Qel to jump out of his boots.

He spun around quickly where he was sitting on the ground to see who had spoken and was amazed at what he saw. A man in black robes hovered shoulder height above the ground on a luminescent disc. The expression on his face was stern and serious. Qel did not have to study the symbol on the gold medallion hanging from a thick Aurinium chain to know that he was in the presence of a Battle Wizard.

Havacian spoke first. "We were resting on the hill there when that thing came upon us. It killed my horse and was intent on killing us when you arrived, Exalted One."

"And where are you going?" The intense gaze from the Battle Wizard demanded that they tell him whatever he wanted to know.

"We are on our way to the estate of my family, House Mekali, two days north of here, Exalted One," Qel spoke up, his voice cracking from nervousness.

The Battle Wizard studied them for a moment, then pointed to the charred remains of the beast. "Do you know what that creature was?"

"No, Exalted One," they almost replied in unison.

"It's called a Mountain Troll. Normally they keep to the Atlas Mountains and away from the edges of civilization, but every few centuries their population grows to the point that their territories overlap and a few of the smaller ones are forced closer to the roads and villages to find food." He sighed. "We have been looking for this one for several days."

The grim warriors, one a man and the other a woman, walked up beside Qel without the smallest acknowledgment of his presence. The female addressed the Battle Wizard, "Exalted One, the troll is irrevocably dead."

"Good," he replied. "Let's complete our patrol before it gets dark."

The warriors jumped on discs floating nearby and rose up next to the Battle Wizard. Still glaring down at them, the wizard turned his disc to leave when he abruptly stopped. "If you do not learn to properly defend yourselves, you will both end up being the meal of another Troll or Ogre or something else before you are a month into your Discovery. I am called Traegarlin and I will see you again in three days at the estate of House Mekali."

There were no farewells or words of thanks. The Battle Wizard simply departed, followed by his escort of Imperial Warriors.

Qel looked at Havacian. "We have nearly managed to get ourselves killed already."

"I didn't expect to be fighting for our lives just days out of the city," Havacian laughed anxiously. "Fine adventurers we have turned out to be."

"And a Mountain Troll at that! Did he say it was a *small* one? Imagine the size of a big one! The last time I read anything about trolls was in a children's storybook before I was brought to the Enclave! I never imagined I would ever see one for real."

"We have been sheltered in the Enclave for too many years," Havacian conceded. "I hope that Battle Wizard keeps his promise and comes to teach us a few things."

They gathered up Havacian's pack from his dead horse and went in search of Qel's Lambei. Half an hour later they found it shivering in a stand of trees, its eyes still wild with fright. Qel couldn't blame his poor mount. He, too, was nervous and jumping at every shadow or sudden noise from behind every knoll or stand of trees they passed.

It was late afternoon by the time they were back on the North Road. Only a few hours of light remained before nightfall and with both of them riding his horse, they would be lucky to make it to the next inn before dark. To pass the time, Havacian spoke excitedly about the Battle Wizards, much of which Qel already knew mixed with and a few interesting things he did not.

"Everyone knows that Battle Wizards are trained specifically in the art of combat and war, charged by the emperor with the task of safeguarding the city and patrolling Atlantean territory on the Emerald Isle. They are also ever-present in the palace and provide protection for the emperor wherever he goes." Havacian always took on an instructional tone when he was fully into his commentary on a subject. Qel didn't mind. He enjoyed learning the little-known details that his studious friend always seemed to know so much about. "What is not well-known is that they do not come from a specific Hall. They could come from any of them. And there is no tower dedicated to their class. Rather, their training and administration take place in a segregated, nondescript section of the Enclave that only they are permitted to enter. The honorific of *Exalted One* is similar to that of the most accomplished scholars and teachers, who are traditionally referred to as *Revered Ones*, signifying their elite status. The Masters of the Imperial Order of Wizards are among the latter."

"You know, until today I had never considered the possibility of joining the Battle Wizards," Qel said.

Havacian snorted. "If they would take you."

"You don't think they would take me?" Qel was a little offended.

"Master Curatei says they only take the most talented wizards with the ability to perform under the most extreme pressure. Based on our recent performance, I doubt either of us would stand a chance."

Qel couldn't deny that. Not that he had any real interest in becoming Battle Wizard anyway. At least he would have a better idea about them after a little training from Traegarlin, even if he only learned enough to stay out of some horrid creature's stew pot.

———

Qel was happy to get an early start the next morning. If they didn't take any detours, it would be early afternoon when they arrived at his family's estate, even sharing the one horse. He hadn't seen his family in nearly a year due to his demanding schedule in the months before his graduation and he barely had time to send letters. They knew he was on his way—he sent a pigeon before he left—and he was looking forward to spending a few days at home.

"Does your family trade in goods other than wine?" Havacian asked when they were on the road.

"Wine is the primary trade. Although we also produce dates, olive oil and dyes for textiles in the city, but not enough of it to export. Mekali wine is what our grove is known for and it is well regarded in the Western Kingdoms. Even as far away as Tarre and the Mouillians!" Qel was proud of his family's business.

Havacian began speaking about something regarding the Mouillians, but Qel was hardly listening. His mind wandered back to his childhood, when his whole family used to come to the estate during the summer months. He was the youngest of three sisters and a brother and was considered the intellectual one of his siblings given his talent for mathematics from a very early age. By the time he reached puberty, he had mastered trade accounting and was working with the accounting staff in the family business keeping the books accurate, although he considered it very dull, tedious work.

There was one interest Qel enjoyed above all others and he relished the rare occasions to pursue it during the time before he was taken to the Enclave. He was always fascinated with astronomy and spent almost every night as a youth staring at the cosmos with a telescopic device amplified with lenses and magic. It was a gift from his parents on his seventh birthday. Qel studied the intricate movements of planets and stars across the night sky and kept extensively detailed logs that were likely still collecting dust on shelves in his old room.

That was also the time in his life when he started to notice a capacity to visualize and focus with incredible intensity. He was capable of performing completely different tasks independently, like writing and reading at the same time, to his parents' astonishment. It was perhaps only a year after that when his desires involving natural elements began to manifest themselves physically. It might have been something as simple as wishing for a fresh wind and having one suddenly manifest, or he would think to start a fire and a flame would appear at his fingertips. Once he even wished to dig a hole and one appeared where and how he wanted it. He could never conjure anything very grand, like a pet hartebeest, or wings that would allow him to fly. It was probably a good thing, he laughed to himself, considering his age and the fantastical things he would wish for.

"Do you remember when they took you for Assessment?" he asked Havacian.

"How could anyone forget a gang of strangers showing up at your door and whisking you off to the Enclave, where the Yellow Wizards poked and prodded at your mind for several days? I was ten and scared to death."

"All those concentration and focus exercises controlling small feats of magic that went on endlessly." Qel barely suppressed a shudder. "Although I have to admit that I did enjoy the ride on the flying disc. That had to be the most exhilarating time of my life up until then."

Even though Qel had known he would be assessed by the wizards at some point, he didn't know exactly when it would happen. No one ever did. All Atlantean children were assessed at around the age of ten for skills and abilities that might lead them into the temple or the Imperial Order of Wizards. If a child had passing abilities that would soon disappear, they would be sent home. If the wizards detected an attunement with the Atlantean Sea God Pontus, the child would be sent to the priests. If a child had an affinity for the physical arts associated with the elements, then they would go to the Wizards Enclave. His sister, fifteen years his elder, was sent to the Temple and eventually became a respected high priestess of Pontus. Qel was in the third group. The wizards didn't even let him go home to say goodbye to his parents. They were summoned to the Enclave where they shared a few tears and words of encouragement before he was left in the wizards' care. It was especially hard on his mother. From then on, he would see them three or four times a year if he maintained his studies at an acceptable level.

He always did.

Qel was eventually found to have abilities in line with the Red Hall and that's where he was sent. It was an exciting change from the mundane life he led at home and he embraced it. At the hall, he learned to do new tricks and to control his abilities the first year. It was a fun time with few responsibilities and he was a young boy exploring a new world. It became much more difficult the second year and each year thereafter.

Twenty years later he was going home, no longer a child, the last of his siblings to find a calling. With one sister as a high priestess, a second working as an imperial administrator, a third that handled the distribution for Mekali wine and his only brother as an architect and builder, his family would now have a Red Wizard to count among them. He hoped his parents would be proud.

A few hours later, Qel and Havacian were in sight of his family's estate perched atop a high rocky ledge amid row upon row of vineyards that covered the south and southwest slopes of the hills all around them. A few Atlanteans tended the vines on their floating disks, checking for air flow and water drainage, inspecting roots and monitoring the health of the crop. Qel knew the work well. These were not servants. They were experts in their field and respected professionals. If servants were ever required, they hired humans to fill those roles. No Atlantean could ever be counted among the servants of any house.

Qel turned the lambei to follow the tree-lined road through the open gates in the wall that surrounded and protected the estate. In the distance the familiar shape of the main house came into view. It was fronted by high marble columns and a pair of heavy wooden doors flanked by tall curtained windows. A complex of smaller outbuildings stood together behind it where the work of the winery took place. Two Atlantean warriors clad in Aurinium armor stood casually at the bottom of the steps leading up to the house. The guards hailed them when they came to a stop and a older human man stood ready to take their horse.

"Your business today, sirs?" one of the guards inquired.

Qel dismounted and handed the reins of his horse to the stableman. "I am Qellel of this house. Please advise my parents that I am home."

The guard smiled. "We have been expecting you, but you do not look like the young boy who left here years ago. Please follow me inside for refreshments while your mother is informed of your arrival. Your father is out of the house at the moment. Welcome home."

They all walked through the thick double doors of the main entrance to the house and into a comfortable sitting room where a human servant brought a bowl of water and wash towels for them to clean up. Another servant soon arrived with a flagon of wine, glasses and a plate piled with olive bread drizzled with olive oil.

Washing his face and arms quickly, Qel was excited and nervous at the same time. Once his mother acknowledged him as her son and Havacian as a guest, the guards would allow them to freely go about the property. He sat with Havacian in comfortable chairs and sampled the olive bread.

"I missed this," he said between bites. "Nothing reminds me more of my home than the freshly baked olive bread and Mekali wine."

"It is delicious," Havacian agreed.

"Thank you," a female voice came from the doorway. "It is my own recipe."

"Mother!" Qel jumped up and embraced her.

She hugged him tightly. "It has been too long, child. Are you well?"

"I am perfectly well. How are you and Father?"

She smiled. "We miss our children."

Qel turned to Havacian, who stood awkwardly with a piece of olive bread stuck to his cheek. "Mother, this is my good friend Havaciante of House Talika."

His mother walked over to Havacian and removed the bit of bread to his obvious embarrassment and then hugged him warmly. "I am pleased to finally meet you. Qel has always mentioned you in the few letters we received from him over the years."

Havacian placed his hands over his heart in a formal greeting. "It is my pleasure and gratitude for your hospitality, Honored Mother."

She sat in one of the plush chairs and motioned for them to sit as well.

"House Talika is a banking family, is it not?" Qel was sure his mother already knew the answer to any question she might ask about his friend's family. She had always been very protective of him, even from afar. Anyone Qel ever mentioned as a friend or associate she would know more about them by the end of the day than he would in his lifetime.

"It is, Honored Mother. For many generations now. One of my brothers and a sister will continue the tradition."

"Your family is very well-known and regarded in Atlantis. Please convey my respects to your parents when you next write to them."

"I will, Honored Mother," Havacian promised.

She turned then to Qel. "Your father and sister are out looking after a new harvest of grapes for next winter's ice wine. They should be in soon. Your old room has been prepared and a guest room for Havacian is nearby. Will you be staying the summer?"

Qel looked at his boots. "No, Mother, just a week or so. The Enclave has released us to pursue our Journey of Discovery. We plan to travel the world if we can."

"A week?" Her tone was anything but approving. "After twenty years away from home, you will stay only a week? Qellel, I am disappointed. I had hoped we could spend more time together."

Qel could feel the guilt mounting. His mother was very good at getting her way when she expertly applied guilt on her children's consciences. "I'm sorry, Mother, but we have a duty and only a limited time to learn what we need to before returning to the Enclave." He gave her a besieged look, his counterbalance to her guilt. "But I will be sure to see you much more often now that we are no longer tied to the masters."

To his relief, she relented. "Very well, my child, but I expect letters more frequently from now on."

"I promise." He smiled.

She stood and Qel and Havacian stood with her. "Go get cleaned up and rested before the evening meal and we will talk more then."

Pleasantries exchanged; his mother breezed out the room. All in all. Qel thought it went rather well. Maybe she had come to grips with the fact that he was no longer a child. He could hope anyway.

Qel led Havacian to the guest room before going on to his own. Memories flooded back with every step and Qel truly began to wish that he could spend the summer here, but he also knew that it was not enough for him to go back to his family and continue in the role he held previously. Nor did he desire that life anymore. He and Havacian had a plan that would begin in Avalon and then move on to someplace new. It was an exciting time in his life that he would not squander.

He resolved stay long enough to satisfy his mother and learn what they could from the Battle Wizard Traegarlin, if he indeed arrived. Then they would be on their way. His mother would continue to goad and guilt him into staying longer no matter how long they were there and a subtle battle of wills would play out. As the youngest child, she had always babied him and tried to keep him close. If it weren't for the Enclave, he was sure he would have been smothered. That's how it stood, he thought. Fend off his mother for a week or two while learning something useful from a Battle Wizard that might save his life. He wasn't sure which part of that thought might be the larger challenge.

Chapter 11

Lessons

The Battle Wizard, Traegarlin, arrived at the Mekali Estate just as promised and proceeded to engage Qel and Havacian in a rigorous training schedule. Qel decided in advance not to mention to his family the incident with the Mountain Troll that prompted the circumstance of their meeting. He didn't want to worry them, especially his mother. Qel explained the Battle Wizard's appearance as a planned part of their training and his father was more than happy to welcome an Exalted One as a guest in his house.

"I observed your pathetic attempts to affect the Troll with your feeble magic before I saved your skins." Qel felt himself cringe under the Battle Wizard's intense gaze before it shifted to Havacian. "And you! You might as well have been meat on a stick served up for that creature as much as you did to help."

"Well, I—" Havacian began to protest.

"Be quiet and listen!" the Battle Wizard snapped. "What I teach you over the next several days will save your lives. Neither of you fools has any idea what the real world is about outside the cushy halls of the Enclave where you were pampered with ideology and little practical advice. Look at the way you handled yourselves only a few leagues out of Atlantis!"

They were gathered in the early morning a league west of the main house on a flat grassy plain that abutted the shore of the broad, lazy meandering of the Orseo River that coursed over the savannah from the northwest. It was a cool, breezy day with the scent of field flowers in the air that reminded Qel of his childhood. He recalled memories of swimming with his brother and sisters in the Orseo, camping under the stars at night and telling stories huddled around a bonfire. Now, here he was, learning how to properly defend himself with his magical talent under the spontaneous tutelage of a Battle Wizard who saved he and his best friend from a monstrous Troll.

Despite the cantankerous nature of their teacher, Qel felt good this morning and looked forward to the lessons.

Until now.

Traegarlin paused to study them both a moment and Qel caught his breath. *Did I miss something with the distraction of my brief daydreaming?* From the absence of sound coming from Havacian, he guessed that his friend was doing the same.

To Qel's relief, the Battle Wizard continued on. "I will have each of you tell me why you failed with the Mountain Troll and then we will begin the appropriate exercises. We have very little time and you two need a mountain of work, so we will get right into it. Qellel, I'll start with you."

Qel was starting to feel like a first-year apprentice again, regardless, he was determined to learn what he could from this man. "I have difficulty drawing significant power quickly. It always comes, but it takes time to build to a sufficient level." It was always a deficiency for Qel with anything that involved conjuring magic. Master Ampher was never overly concerned about it and suggested that it would eventually come with time and practice. Unfortunately, when it came down to just seconds, defending his life or another's, Qel now realized that he didn't have the luxury of time.

"And you, Havaciante?" the Battle Master prompted.

"I just freeze up," Havacian responded meekly. "I don't know why."

Qel averted his eyes staring down at his boots to avoid compounding the embarrassment his friend must have been experiencing with the blunt admission. The two of them were devoted students and researchers exploring the magical arts in the Enclave, that was true, but Qel had never felt pampered. To the contrary, he was constantly challenged and worked sometimes days at a time without sleep to please his master. Not once in the past twenty years had there been a single minute devoted to using magical force in self-defense. He wondered, had any graduate ever received such training? Perhaps that was a deficiency in the Enclave that needed to be addressed. Maybe that's why the mortality rate for wizards on their Journey of Discovery was so high.

Traegarlin nodded in silent contemplation as if reading Qel's thoughts. "Neither of your conditions is unique and fortunately the solution is the same. I expect you both to put every effort into the skills that I teach you. I will not waste my time. If I believe you are not prepared to adequately defend yourselves on your own, I will send you back to the Enclave for further training." He looked them each pointedly in the eyes. "Yes, I can do that. The Imperial Order of Wizards would far prefer to interrupt your Journey of Discovery and train you to live in the world than leave you on your own to die in it. The masters have softened too much over the years and focus far more on the academics than practical survivability beyond the walls of Atlantis. Now let's begin."

The training commenced with exercises that emphasized focus and concentration while enduring stress and distraction. Qel committed himself to everything Traegarlin asked of him. Both he and Havacian were used to the rigorous discipline required in the Enclave and this would be no different. Qel put every effort into mastering the shortcuts and techniques supplied by the Battle Wizard and by the end of two weeks of intensive practice, they had made significant improvement. Initially, Traegarlin said he would spend no more than a week training them, but by the end, he was so impressed with their progress that he decided to extend the training by another two weeks. Qel was proud that they had impressed the Battle Wizard and grateful for his time. It also pleased his mother that they would be staying a few days longer.

On the last day, they stood together on a hill overlooking the grasslands, quietly taking in the beauty of the setting sun behind the far-distant Atlas Mountain Range. Without turning to look at them, the Battle Wizard spoke softly, as if to honor the last light of the day and spoke into the wind. "Your advantage will be in the water," the Battle Wizard addressed Havacian. "You have the skills and the tools to sink ships and control the waters around you. If you returned to the Enclave to be a Battle Wizard, your place would be on a naval ship patrolling the waters around the Emerald Isle or protecting imperial merchant ships that ply the Primal Sea."

"And what about on land? Will I be at a disadvantage then, Exalted One?" Havacian asked.

"You will be fine in most situations. You are quick with the lightning and energy bolts—stick to those. Your disadvantage is that you have fewer options on land than you would in an aquatic environment because of the focus of your training."

"Now, Qellel." The Battle Wizard still stared out over the plains. "You have made tremendous progress since I arrived. Your advantage is the huge breadth of tools that you have available to you, whether it's controlling the environment, utilizing the elements around you, or causing damage to your opponent with fire. Especially fire." The Battle Wizard did turn then and put his hand on Qel's shoulder. "You must continue the exercises that I have taught you every day and soon you will be fast-casting equal to Havacian or anyone. It's within you to do it. I have no doubt about that."

"Thank you for taking the time to train us, Exalted One." Qel bowed respectfully to the Battle Wizard. "I promise to be diligent and practice what I have learned." He glanced over at Havacian. "I am now more prepared to face those who intend to cause harm to the people that I care about or me."

The Battle Wizard smiled. His upturned lips had an unusual effect on the lines of his hard face. "I believe you will. When you return from your Discovery, find me in the Enclave if either of you has interest in joining our elite group. If you are worthy, I can help."

That evening, the Battle Wizard departed. From out of nowhere, his two Atlantean warrior escorts showed up on their floating disks and without a hint of social grace, they all flew off into the darkness together. Qel was eager to get underway as well, except that he and Havacian had agreed to spend one more week at his home to satisfy his mother and rest after the arduous training of the past three weeks. Under the guidance of the Battle Wizard, Qel was nearly proficient at fast-casting powerful spells in about half the time of when he started.

He still needed to cut that time down another half if he was going to be as capable as Havacian. The Battle Wizard had also recommended that he learn to utilize the energy of the Source Crystal he wore around his neck. Qel agreed, but it would require a shift in the way he summoned the power and might, for a while, cost him a little more casting time before it helped. Despite this temporary hindrance, with everything he had learned, Qel felt confident that he would achieve a respectable skill level with a little more time and a lot more practice.

———

Qel rode at a moderate trot over the stone-paved road that led north through the hills and valleys of the open countryside. He was happy to be back in his comfortably fitting travel attire as opposed to the formal robes the Battle Wizard insisted they wear during their training. The leather trousers, white silk tunic with turned-up collar and smartly cut long coat trimmed with leather made him feel like a proper explorer. Flung over his lap he carried his heavy cloak in case it became cold in the early mornings and evenings when the sun was at its lowest. Havacian was outfitted much the same and rode beside him on a Lambei that Qel's father was generous to provide after hearing that Havacian's horse had been injured and put down after breaking its leg in a foxhole. Qel didn't like lying to his father, yet he liked less the idea of them worrying about him all the time.

They had departed the Mekali Estate two days previous, packed with fresh supplies and warm farewells. He promised to send messages via pigeon as often as possible detailing his travels and he meant every word, especially after the tight hug from his mother that lasted far longer than it should for his age. When she embraced him, he felt like a little boy again and was sad that as a man he had to think differently about such things. Fortunately, his father was more pragmatic, having traveled to many lands beyond the Emerald Isle and offered up some pragmatic advice when they stood alone together.

"Be careful of whom you trust, son," his father said. "Our own people and the elves will not deceive you; the dwarfs are very literal and will usually mean and do exactly as they say, but the humans are different creatures altogether. You will find some that will fear you, take advantage of you, revile and revere you. There is no consistency whatsoever when it comes to their behavior."

"The humans in Atlantis seem kind enough," Qel had challenged.

His father laughed at that. "That's because they have to be. Otherwise, they would not be allowed to stay. I know it seems harsh but, as a rule, distrust them all, yet try not to prejudge them."

It sounded counterintuitive to Qel, but after some thought, he understood the wisdom in his father's words. He always did eventually. His father had taught him much about respect and honor, while his mother had opened his heart to love, kindness and compassion. He was grateful to them both.

Havacian piped up, excitement in his voice, "By the looks of it, we should be in sight of Aquilon soon."

Qel stirred from his reflections and scanned the road ahead. It was busier now that they approached the city, with many locals moving along the broad highway in cart, on horse and on foot. Some of the wealthier Atlanteans glided by in floating carriages or disks, although there were far fewer of those here than in the City of Atlantis. The foreigners they passed were mostly merchants and tourists from the Western Kingdoms. People from outside the Emerald Isle were welcomed and allowed to freely travel where they liked within the Territory of Atlantis as long as they obeyed the laws and conducted themselves properly. However, they were cautioned to stay within the settled areas and near the main roads because the lands away from the cities and estates were wild and dangerous. Even the Atlanteans could not protect the foolhardy adventurer who traveled the untamed lands, especially near the mountains, where indigenous dangers such as the long-toothed lion, giant boar, great wolves, bears and others were numerous. Then there were the unnatural terrors like the Mountain Trolls and Ogres that had somehow managed to find their way from Fomoire, where they were banished by the Tuatha De over three millennia ago. An involuntary shiver shot through Qel at the thought of Trolls.

The trees around them became more numerous as they rode north, to the point that they were almost always in the shade of an increasingly thick forest, the expanses of farming and agriculture left far behind. Qel had never been this far north and the unfamiliarity of it made him feel, for the first time, like he was on a true adventure. He knew that feeling would only intensify as they traveled farther and farther away from home. The anticipation was almost electrifying.

"There it is, Havacian! I can see it now through the trees ahead. We are finally here."

Qel was surprised that Aquilon was not surrounded by a wall or moat and there was no gate to bar entrance. Havacian explained that it was an Atlantean trade city open to anyone that wished to conduct business on the Emerald Isle and the primary gateway for trade between Atlantis and Avalon. There were several imperial soldiers casually standing on either side of the road where the city began, observing those that entered, but no one was stopped. Like the City of Atlantis, Aqualon's buildings and architecture were of clean white stone and marble construction with broad paved avenues between them.

Riding deeper into the city, Qel appreciated many of the differences from Atlantis. Here, there was a more fluid balance of construction and nature. They passed beautiful, well-tended gardens; a park filled with towering ancient trees and numerous ponds—stocked with fish that jumped at insects—connected to a slow-moving, narrow, winding river that flowed through the city. Precisely manicured hedges lined every street and many of the buildings somehow incorporated trees into their planning with them growing into, out of and on top of the marble structures.

Havacian pointed to one of them. "That must be the Sylvan influence. I read about how they use nature in their construction. I look forward to seeing how they do it up close."

Just then a group of elves passed them in the opposite direction. They were men and women dressed in earthy tones of greens and browns. The men's trousers and jackets were finely tailored and the women modeled loose gowns of gossamer and silk that flowed elegantly behind them as they walked. Qel was always stunned by their natural beauty. Of course, he had seen elves in Atlantis, even in the Wizards Enclave, but they were rare occurrence.

The diversity of the population was striking as he observed more of the slender Elves, broad-shouldered dwarfs, humans from lands he recognized and many more from places he did not. Among them all, it seemed the Atlanteans were in the minority within their own city. Qel and Havacian stopped at the edge of the enormous central marketplace filled with colorful stalls and storefronts. There was no way they could ride through the crowds of the market or even walk with their horses. They would have to go around it on a perimeter road that appeared designed for just such a purpose as others like them who were leading horse and cart.

Qel spotted a pair of imperial soldiers nearby keeping watch on the crowds. He dismounted and casually walked over to speak with them. "Good sirs! Could you please direct us to the Tower of the Imperial Order of Wizards?"

From his current vantage he could see many towers short and tall around the city, but there was nothing to distinguish their function one from another and only the style of their design reflected their unique features. Still, any one of them might have been the Wizards Tower and without direction, would take the better part of a day to find.

One of the soldiers pointed to the opposite side of the market. "Take the roundabout road there and when you reach the southwest corner, you will see the Tower you wish to find. It is marked by a red crystal at its peak."

He should have guessed that. It was something Master Curatei mentioned in his graduation address. Qel thanked the soldiers and he and Havacian continued on their way.

Havacian gestured to the crowded market as they led their horses around it. "I want to come back here before we leave. I can only imagine the variety of exotic goods that must be for sale here."

"I agree," said Qel. "After we stable our horses and get a room, we should return and peruse their wares!"

Just as the soldier promised, Qel could see the Wizards Tower in the near distance when they reached the southwest corner of the market. He knew it by the rotating crystal pyramid at its apex that glowed faintly red with the bright western sun sinking into the treetops behind it. Soon it would be dark and the glow from the crystal would dominate the night sky above the city if it were anything like the ones in Atlantis. The modest entrance to the Tower grounds was just a short distance away and soon they were standing in its long shadow.

The Tower complex was surrounded by a low wall that held at least a dozen two- and three-story buildings connected by paved walkways. At the gate, an Atlantean man wearing brown robes was sitting at a small desk under a sheltering overhang. He asked them to state their name and purpose when they approached.

"I am Qellel and this is Havaciante. We are on our Journey of Discovery as recent graduates from the Enclave," he offered.

"Welcome Qellel and Havaciante," the young man smiled pleasantly. "The stable is there to your left and you can seek accommodations at the building in front of the Tower. Safe travels."

At the stables, they gave their horses over to a pair of human stable boys and removed their travel packs before proceeding to the main building. Qel was surprised at the number of foreign guests on Tower grounds. There were numerous elves, a few dwarfs and several humans—all presumably wizards, scholars, or mages—talking amongst each other in the comfortably appointed common room and enjoying refreshments.

The house administrator appeared to be of the Green Hall, a Nature Wizard, from the luminescent green belt that cinched his robes at the waist and the gold medallion of his station hanging from a chain around his neck. He sat at a large table with a stack of parchment perfectly aligned on one side next to a ledger and an inkwell set off-center within easy reach.

"How may I be of service, gentlemen?" his deep tone was polite, yet formal.

"We are traveling from the Enclave and would like rooms for two or three nights," Qel answered. "If you don't have separate rooms, then we can share one."

"We have rooms for each of you," he assured them. "Tower level four, rooms seven and nine.

"Please fill in the information where indicated." The house administrator pushed forward the ledger. "The common room is open all day and night for drink service; however, the kitchens serve only during mealtimes." He continued the introduction while Qel and Havacian completed the registration. "If you require a private office or a conference room, one can be provided for you. The library is located on the second level of the Tower, as is the open laboratory. Finally, only permanent residents of the Tower are permitted access to the subterranean levels unless granted special access by the Master of the Tower."

Qel thanked the administrator, then he and Havacian went to find their rooms. They walked through the common room to a pair of massive double doors set into the curvature of the tower wall. An Atlantean wizard wearing yellow robes walked through one side of the set of doors when they arrived and kindly held it open for them to pass through with their heavy packs. Inside, the base of the Tower contained a small room and the landing for a broad stairway, which three men could easily climb abreast, spiraling up the inside the perimeter of the Tower. It was brightly illuminated by light globes set into the walls spaced only a few paces apart. Near the stairway stood a row of racks holding a number of luminescent disks similar to those Qel was familiar with as carriers. He and Havacian each pulled one from their wooden frame. The disks slid off easily floating just above waist high under their own power. Without hesitation, the men put their packs on top of the disks and pushed them forward as they climbed the stairs.

"What level are we going to, again?" Havacian asked.

"Four," replied Qel.

"I guess a little exercise will do us good after days on a horse!" Havacian chuckled.

The stairwell rose at a moderately steep angle around the wide tower that Qel guessed had a diameter of at least fifty paces. As they ascended, they passed several other wizards of different ages and halls that greeted them cordially until they arrived on the second floor where the library was located. Here a tall set of double doors stood open, revealing a massive two-level library. Qel paused to gaze into the room.

Shelves covered the walls from floor to ceiling on both levels holding thousands of scrolls, tomes and clay tablets. There were wizards everywhere in the room, sitting in lounge chairs or at tables in groups. Most were immersed in quiet conversations that resulted in a low murmur, almost like a hum, to those not immediately nearby. Light globes of various intensities floated freely around the room, providing illumination that could be moved from place to place as required by those within.

"A very respectable library," commented Qel.

"It is," agreed Havacian, "although not quite as large at the library at the Enclave."

"Yet this one seems so well attended," Qel observed. "We'll have to try to spend a little time here before we leave."

They continued to the fourth floor and found their rooms as indicated by numbers on the doors. "I'll meet you in the common room after I have settled my packs in and cleaned up a bit," Qel told Havacian before he entered his room. Havacian happily agreed. His chamber was only two doors further down the hall.

Qel walked through the unlocked door and stopped to stare in surprise even before closing the door behind him. It was huge and the furnishings were opulent. Four plush chairs, a couch and a large table that six people could comfortably sit around for dinning dominated the chamber, but there was no bed. He walked in farther and noticed two doors on his right. He opened the first. To his surprise, it was a private lavatory with both hot and cold running water! The second door led to a bedroom as large as his own at the Mekali Estate, complete with a large bed with fluffy pillows and a full-sized writing desk fully stocked with ink and parchment.

He couldn't believe how lavish the whole thing was. As an apprentice in the Enclave, he lived in a tiny room barely large enough to hold a small bed and a little writing desk. He never would have expected that wizards enjoyed luxury of this scale. It looked like a room reserved for the masters. Qel quickly put away his things, washed and put on a clean tunic. He was excited about talking with Havacian and wondered if his friend had expected such fine accommodations and neglected to tell him about it.

There was a large open window in the curved wall on one side of the room. Qel walked by, briefly glancing out and had to stop and stare again. The city was far more extensive than he had estimated. From his vantage, four stories above the ground, he could see much of the city spread out before him. It was alive with activity. People were rushing in every direction on what he was sure was important business while others strolled unhurried through lavish gardens or shopping boulevards. Looking out farther, he could see an abundance of inns, taverns, playhouses and other forms of entertainment to keep the very diverse population happy and distracted.

There was a knock at the door.

Tearing himself away from the stunning vista of Aquilon, Qel answered to find Havacian standing there in his travel clothes with a worried look on his face.

"What's wrong, Havacian?"

Havacian looked beyond him and into his room as if to confirm his thoughts. "Do you think they gave us the wrong rooms?"

Qel had not considered the disappointing possibility. "By Pontus, you might be right. Let's go speak to the house administrator."

They walked back down the winding stairs to the common room and approached the house administrator who had assigned them their rooms.

"Why would you think there was a mistake?" he asked them.

"The rooms seem more . . . spacious and well-appointed than we expected," Qel replied hesitantly

The house administrator regarded the pair with the most unusual perplexed expression on his face. Then a knowing smile began to form. "When did you graduate?"

Havacian shrugged, "A few weeks ago."

"So, you're on your Journey of Discovery." His smile broadened. "You will have to get used to the idea that you're not apprentices anymore. Wizards like their comfort, to an extreme, I might add and now you are one of them. There has been no mistake with your rooms."

Relieved there was no mistake, but embarrassed that they had to ask, Qel thanked the administrator and led Havacian into the common room. They barely sat down at a table when, seconds later, a young human girl wearing a white apron over a long blue wool dress asked them if they would like something to drink. Havacian requested a carafe of wine.

"It seems that Master Curatei left out a few important details about our Journey," Qel laughed quietly.

"I have a feeling it was by design," Havacian grinned. "He has a clever humor and loves surprises.'

Qel nodded his agreement, "We have certainly had our share of surprises,"

The server returned with the wine and neatly poured it into two glasses.

Qel raised his glass, feeling almost giddy about the luxury they were enjoying. "Here's to the start of a great adventure."

Havacian raised his glass in return and smiled. "It's good to be a wizard."

Chapter 12

Hjaltadans

There is not much I care to say about the Hjaltadans (although there is a lot that I could say about it) except one thing . . . What was I thinking? Everything always seems so much clearer in hindsight.

Wodanaz the Wanderer

———

Myrllin stood atop the tallest tower of seven that sprang from the thickly forested elevation into which his stronghold was constructed. It wasn't a fortress as much as it was a palace fortified by the natural protection of the highest mountain on the island, a mountain that formed much of the fortress's walls and foundation. Stronghold or palace, it was a design of artistic architecture beautiful to behold. From his vantage, Myrllin could see far into the Primal Sea and if he could have seen beyond the horizon, he would have recognized the coast of Eriu in the east, the island of Tirnan Yog further north and the Emerald Isle to the southwest.

This was his home—his and his brother's, if Wodanaz ever bothered to come home, but that was a rare reunion. He kept the island shrouded in mists and illusion to restrain the unwanted and curious from trespassing. Those who did have the misfortune to find their way to its shores were in for some very nasty surprises and rarely survived to tell the tale. Myrllin didn't trouble himself too much over the occasional interlopers. None had ever made it far enough into the interior to cause him any aggravation and the wild beasts that prowled the island always enjoyed the entertainment. The people of Eriu called his elusive island Hy-Brasil and he accepted that since it was as good a name as any.

Brother, I need you.

The thought appeared in his mind unexpectedly. It was Wodanaz and the message was urgent. He didn't have to wonder where his

150

brother was; each of them could point in the direction of the other at any time, no matter where they were thanks to their father and the Liafal Stone.

I'm on my way. He projected the thought back to Wodanaz.

No reply.

Wodanaz? Brother?

Nothing.

They hadn't seen each other since Myrllin roused himself from his long hibernation some weeks ago, but that was not unusual. In fact, having just recently returned to Hy-Brasil from the Assembly of Nine in Atlantis, Myrllin was planning to hunt down his brother no matter where he was and give him a good tongue lashing. Wodanaz had deliberately ignored the Calling of the Assembly which did not reflect well on either of them. His brother was so irresponsible sometimes. All the time, it seemed. Drinking and carousing with the Vikja, hanging around in taverns, sleeping in barns – it never ended! And nothing had changed during the two-hundred years Myrllin had been sleeping. He was infuriated with Wodanaz until the moment his brother sent that last message and then all of his anger drained away replaced by an urgent fear. Wodanaz never called for him like that unless the situation was dire.

Myrllin concentrated for a moment, took his bearings and determined the direction in which he must travel. He sensed Wodanaz about three hundred leagues to the northeast, somewhere in northern Eriu. He sighed deeply. Depending on his mode of travel, the distance could take considerable time to cross, especially since much of it was over the vast expanse of the Primal Sea. Still, he had little choice in the matter and so he would have to fly. But Myrllin did not have the talent to fly on his own. No, he would require the help of another. Possibly a very reluctant another. He closed his eyes and prepared the charm that would summon the beast to him.

"Tuageo wraga mewe workommendno Dergo!" he called in a voice powerful enough to echo from the lower peaks all the way to the cliffside lair where he knew that Dergo slept.

He did not need to speak the words twice, it would come as it had always come before and with its help, there would be a price. There was always a price. That's how it came to be here in the first place. They had an alliance of sorts. The creature would defend his island from intruders in exchange for a safe place to live. Later Myrllin was forced to stock the island with magically altered mammoth-sized rabbits in order to satisfy its hunger and dissuade it from rampaging across foreign lands in search of its meals. Fortunately, the giant rabbits bred incessantly, providing a renewable food source for all of the predators on the island.

Myrllin felt the wind buffet the layers of his gray robes, sending the cold air beneath its folds and causing a shiver to ripple through his body. He knew the creature was close. When he saw it, it came from below, moving fast and close over the tree-tops, up the side of the rocky incline and then straight up the tower, never losing momentum until it stopped, suspended in midair just in front of him. Myrllin was never unimpressed by the beauty of the creature and its size. A massive red claw and then another, either of which could have crushed him with little effort, came to rest on the embrasures that surrounded the landing atop the narrow tower. Myrllin was sure he felt the structure sway a little when the red-hued Dragon settled its weight upon it and wished for a moment he had the sense to summon the beast from more stable ground.

"Why have you summoned me, Myrllin?" The red worm's eyes squinted narrowly, the deep resonance of his voice sending vibrations washing over Myrllin.

Still, he faced the creature unperturbed. "I need you to take me to the northern coast of Eriu."

"What will you ask me to do when we get there?"

"Nothing, Dergo." Myrllin opened his hands in a gesture of innocence. "You only need to transport me there quickly and without rest. Then you may return."

"Very well, wizard," the Dragon's shiny scales reflected the light in flashes as he twisted his lithe neck to bring down his massive, horn-riddled head level to Myrllin's face. "It will be cold at the altitude I will need to ascend if you desire the most favorable pace. You should ready yourself accordingly."

"I am ready now," Myrllin was wearing only his layered robes, floppy hat and walking boots. They were warm enough for cold weather, but not the frigid temperatures of high altitude. He wasn't worried. "How quickly can you get me there?"

"It is a small thing to take you there, Myrllin." The Dragon shifted his weight, knocking a chunk of the parapet from the crenellations where he perched like an enormous pigeon. "Two days with only necessary stops along the way. I will decide the price later. It will be reasonable."

Myrllin liked Dergo. He was a young Dragon of the red variety with an extraordinary intellect. He arrived at Myrllin's island two centuries ago seeking protection—protection from what, Myrllin still did not know. He suspected the wise Dragon was far more than a simple creation of the Tuatha De that managed to liberate himself from Fomoire. Dergo's personality reminded Myrllin of another Dragon he knew: Senjit, a Golden Dragon sired in part by a god, whose lair was on one of the fabled Isles of Gades. But tonight, it was with this Dragon that his concerns lay, as Dergo could deliver him swiftly to his brother's aide.

"Damn your price, worm!" Myrllin snapped. "You live safe on my island with plenty to feed you. Do as I ask!"

The great red heaved his head high into the air and growled at Myrllin's aggressive reply, smoke trailing from its flaring nostrils, before the fantastic beast settled his gaze once more at eye-level. "As you wish, wizard. I sense your need is considerable, but mind your respect. I am no mere mount for your convenience."

Myrllin felt a little abashed at the Dragon's mild reprimand, deservedly so. "Forgive me, Dergo," he relented. "Wodanaz has gotten himself caught-up in something again and he needs my help. I fear it may be something very serious this time."

Dergo bent low in front of Myrllin, his deep timbre compassionate for one of his kind, "Then ascend my scales and find steady purchase so we can be off."

Myrllin pat the scales of Dergo's neck gratefully and climbed atop the massive beast. When settled, he invoked a lattice of webbing over his legs to hold him firmly against the Dragon's spine and a protective shield against the frigid cold and agitation of the headwinds they would encounter at the extreme elevation they would be flying. This was not the first time he had employed Dergo for the means of fast travel.

"I am set, Dergo. Let's be off," Myrllin announced.

And Dergo, the Red Dragon of Hy-Brasil, took to the skies with a few beats of his leathery wings soaring sharply upward into the starry night.

———

For two days and two nights, Myrllin flew atop the mighty Red Dragon, across the Primal Sea and into the north they soared. The few ships he spied below appeared small and surreal, like children's toys traveling one way or another for trade or plunder. With few prompts, he kept the Red Dragon on course and in line with the direction he knew Wodanaz would be waiting. Then on the morning of the third day, they passed over the coast of Eriu, north of the city of DunOinos. Myrllin deliberately chose a route that skirted human habitations so as not to cause a panic. They continued over the forests and vast swaths of grassy plains where the enormous mammoths grazed before the lower peaks of the Vuro-Menjo, the most northern mountain range in the Western Kingdoms, came into view through the low clouds that almost seemed to pour over its summit.

Protected by his shields, Myrllin couldn't feel the blistering cold, especially frigid at the altitude that they flew. He always worried for the well-being of his winged host, but from all appearances, Dergo was unaffected by the weather and his scales remained warm to the touch where Myrllin sat. They flew on and soon crossed the mountain range at its narrowest point beyond which the vast forests of spruce and pine came into view shrouded in the thick haze and fog typical of the sparsely settled lands of Northern Eriu.

By midafternoon Myrllin could see the coastline where the forest sloped down to Sea of Dragons. He instructed Dergo to begin his descent. There was a village on the shore, but that was not their immediate destination. Instead, the red-hued Dragon spiraled slowly down to a clearing in the forest about a league away. Whatever Wodanaz was involved with, Myrllin didn't want to risk exacerbating the situation by frightening the villagers with the sight of a Dragon. Living just across the sea from Fomoire, where Giants and Trolls and all manner of beasts that had been exiled by the Tuatha De were settled, the humans no doubt had their fair share of troubles already. It was said that the northern marches of Eriu and Lyonesse were the most dangerous tracts of land on the planet. Myrllin was inclined to agree as were many others – adventurers, explorers and fools from all parts – whose imaginations were captured by romanticized stories of monsters, treasure and exploit. They flocked here to prove their heroics . . . yet most often demonstrated only how well they died.

Myrllin dispelled the webbing around his legs and slowly, stiffly climbed down from Dergo's back. He fell the last few feet and nearly tumbled over with how weak and numb his limbs had become.

"Do you want me to wait for you here?" the Dragon rumbled.

"No." Myrllin carefully stretched to regain proper circulation. "Once I find my brother, we will stay together for a while."

"As you wish, wizard. I think I will hunt one of those mammoths we passed a few leagues back. Rabbits grow tiresome after a while and I am voracious."

"Do not stay long in the Western Kingdoms, Dergo, even this far north," Myrllin warned. "I cannot protect you here."

Myrllin wasn't sure, but he could swear he saw a look of indignation cross the Dragon's rigid features. "I can take care of myself," he growled and took off in a steep ascent, barely giving Myrllin a chance to retreat to the protection of the trees and avoid the undercurrent from his mighty wings.

Myrllin watched his friend disappear into the gloomy, cloud-laden sky above. "You'd better," he grumbled and strode toward the forest. He was a league away from the village and on foot; he reckoned it would be nightfall by the time he reached it.

After an hour of walking through the thickly wooded forest, Myrllin realized that he must be angling away from where he guessed the village was located. It was an unexpected detour, but it really didn't matter. He was following the directional sensation in his mind that would guide him to his brother whether he was in a village, a cave, or up a tree. None of which would surprise him. Although Wodanaz had a wonderful charisma, he also had a penchant for getting himself into tight spots. He enjoyed engaging with the ordinary folk and manipulating the choices they made, often becoming embroiled in their causes. Humans were a chaotic race at the core of it and Myrllin wondered how they ever managed to scratch out a civilized existence. Something more than magic was guiding their fate, he reckoned.

On almost any other occasion Myrllin might have enjoyed a walk through a wood such as the one he traveled now. It was teeming with a fantastic population of wildlife that he was rarely fortunate to observe. He passed long-haired elk munching on clover, a spotted snow leopard skulking between the trees and a pair illusive woolly rhinoceros grazing along the fringes were among the rarest sightings. None of them hindered his way, nor hardly took note of him in the waning daylight. Myrllin wondered what terrible creatures skulked these woods in the darkness at night that might show more interest in his passage. He didn't plan to meet any of them, as he expected to exit the forest well before darkness found him.

At least he hoped so.

The ground Myrllin walked over was flat and clear of brush, with the trees spaced far enough apart so that they did not delay his trespass through the wood. It was not long before the forest thinned and ended altogether at the edge of a broad, grassy plain. The wind was strong from the north here, bringing the smell of salt air that touched his tongue while the last rays of the sun bent beneath the western horizon. In the distance ahead, he could see the flicker of light, perhaps from a campfire, which seemed to blink at regular intervals as if it were being eclipsed every few seconds by someone moving in front of it.

Myrllin knew with absolute certainty that was where he would find Wodanaz.

Quickening his pace, he spoke a charm that made his eyes glow with night vision and carefully avoided the ruts and gullies that littered the soggy terrain. He still maintained his shield against the cold, even though it was technically summer, since this far north almost felt like winter. Especially at night. Had it actually been winter, the ground in this place would have been frozen and covered with at least a foot of snow. He was glad it was not winter yet.

The campfire was less than a league away. He was impressed by the maker's ability to keep it lit in the stiff breeze. It was that same bitter wind that brought a sound to his ears. Myrllin thought he heard something strange, a tune perhaps, carried across the distance from the solitary light. From the little he had caught, it sounded like a lively melody that one might expect to hear in a tavern with the aim to inspire drink and merriment.

Myrllin's anger flared. If Wodanaz had brought him here on the pretense of trouble and it turned out to be another one of his drunken binges, Myrllin swore he might turn him into a goat for a week. He calmed himself with the assurance that his brother, as much of a befuddled drunk as he might be at times, would never be that irresponsible. Then again, he might.

Myrllin marched ahead and in his anger nearly missed a pair of large luminescent orbs staring at him from out of the tall grass. They lay close to the ground about thirty paces ahead of his path on the right. The eyes shined not because they reflected the glow of the firelight—that was too far away—and not because of any illumination Myrllin carried, because he had none. The eyes were luminescent because the light came from within the creature that waited and watched. Only a creature of magic cast a glow through its eyes from within.

Had it been a beast of nature, Myrllin would have continued on and evaded it or sent it running in fear with a harmless bolt of flame, but this thing could not be avoided or frightened away, so he stopped. His abrupt action as much as trumpeted to the creature that it was spotted and it rose reluctantly from its crouch. By the blackest of black silhouette that contrasted against the darkness behind it, Myrllin could see that it was an immense creature at least five times his size that stood on two massive legs thick with knotted muscle. At that distance, his night vision could not resolve any detail, yet when it slowly approached closer, Myrllin could clearly see that he was about to encounter a nightmare. It stopped only a few paces away and regarded him with an expression of curiosity. It had not charged, which Myrllin might have expected from the stories he knew about the atrocity that stood before him, but he wasn't sure that was a good sign.

They stood staring at each other for a long moment only paces apart, neither moving nor speaking. Myrllin thought with some humor that it was like two great alpha male long-haired elk sizing each other up before the sudden violence of their enormous multipronged horns crashing against each other in their struggle for dominance. The monster could easily reach him if it chose to, but Myrllin, not knowing what to expect, was ready for that. Its knobby muscular arms were long nearly touching the ground on either side of an almost hairless torso that could only be described as barrel-chested—if barrels were ever built that large. Topping its sharp, angular head, there was a bit of spiky hair—Myrllin couldn't tell what color in the dark—with protruding brows and a long, pointed nose.

It licked its narrow lips flashing a row of long, dagger-like teeth within its wide mouth. It was the ugliest creature he had ever seen and it smelled like rot and mold. Then, to Myrllin's greatest surprise, it spoke, "What are you?" The words came out sharp and jagged in a baritone that to anyone else might have been spectacularly terrifying.

"The 'what' is not important." Myrllin showed no fear in his reply. "It is the 'who' that you address and my name is Myrllin."

"Mer-lin . . . Why do you not run in fear of me, Mer-lin? Do you not know what I am?" The creature straightened its spine from its natural bend and stood imposing over him.

"Very impressive, I must say." Myrllin really was impressed. "And yes, I know your kind. Although I have learned only tonight that the Tower of Tongues benefits creatures such as you as well. Because of that alone, I am glad of our meeting."

"You know my kind?" The beast hunched again and thrust its head forward and close to Myrllin's own. "Then you should be running in panic with the knowledge that I will tear your limbs from your body and feast on your tender innards!"

Myrllin laughed in the grotesque face only inches away, "You know that I am not without defenses or you would have already attempted what you boast."

The creature snorted and pulled away, still close enough to strike at him if it chose. "Are you going there?" It gestured to where the campfire burned brightly.

"I am," Myrllin admitted. "What do you know of it?"

The creature pounded the ground with a massive fist. "A madman has enthralled my brothers and I cannot free them, lest I am caught in his snare as well."

"I see," Myrllin shrugged. "Well, you are from Fomoire and are forbidden by the Tuatha De to leave its shores, yet here you are. It sounds like your brothers are not fated to end well."

The beast straightened again and pounded both fists this time. "We are hungry! And the animals that the humans tend are easy to kill. The humans themselves are also good to eat, if mostly less satisfying."

"Well, that 'madman' you refer to is likely my own brother, who is a traveling minstrel and he has a particular soft spot for humans." Myrllin leaned casually on his staff. "Perhaps we can arrange a bargain?"

"What sort of bargain, Mer-lin, will prevent me from eating you?"

"You assume much, Troll," Myrllin glared back. "But let's consider for a moment that perhaps I can help you."

"Speak plainly!" the Troll bellowed.

Not reacting, even in the slightest, Myrllin continued, "I will promise to spare your brothers from death and in exchange, you go back to Fomoire and never return."

The Troll nodded his acceptance. "If you lie, Mer-lin I will hunt you down and make you watch while I devour your parts."

"Fair enough!" Myrllin exclaimed. "Now stay here. I will return in a while."

———

Myrllin contemplated the scene in the "camp" that he came upon an hour earlier. Thirty-eight Trolls, he was precise about the number because he counted them many times over, were *dancing* in a wide circle around a slightly elevated hill. To complete the vision of madness, on that hill Wodanaz stood near a small fire with two shivering and exhausted humans lying at his feet. Wodanaz was aware Myrllin was there, as were the humans and the Trolls. Yet not a thing had changed since his arrival.

Myrllin watched the flows of magic to interpret the purpose of the drama that played out before him. His brother was playing a fast-paced tune on a flute made of gold that had the magical effect of causing the

Trolls to dance, a strange limping-hop sort of thing, in a circle around where Wodanaz played. From what he could gather from the humans and the intermittent, truncated fragments of thought from Wodanaz, who desperately tried not to disrupt the melody, was that they had all been there for several days. So long that the Trolls had danced a trench waist-deep into the soft earth. Wodanaz apparently had captured the Trolls with his enchanting music when they attacked the village, then brought them out to this remote location, away from the settlement. Unfortunately, the innkeeper and his wife were caught inside the ring of Trolls from the start and unable to escape. There had been one other with them at the time, a scullery maid from the kitchens, but she was torn to pieces when, in a panic, she tried to escape the ring.

The hours ticked by while Myrllin considered what he could do to save them. If Wodanaz stopped playing, even for a few seconds, the beguiling spell would be broken and the Trolls would be upon them all. Although he was confident that he and Wodanaz could kill roughly half of the Trolls in short order, the other half would surely overwhelm them. And he couldn't strike them down one at a time either. If he did so, then that too would break the spell and the creatures would be free. As best he could figure it, he only had a few choices left and none of them were good for the people stranded inside the ring.

There wasn't much time. Myrllin knew that as strong as Wodanaz was, he would fail from exhaustion sooner than some of the Trolls and it would be a risky bet that Myrllin could kill those left standing before one got to he or his brother. He considered several other options, weighing their risks in his head, before finally settling on one he thought was the best real choice for all of them to survive.

Wodanaz! Myrllin called with his mind. His brother looked up slowly from the sitting position he had assumed when he was unable to remain standing any longer. He looked bleary-eyed and on the edge of fainting. The effort of weaving the magic into the music over such a long time had taken its toll.

Myrllin just needed him to hold on a few moments longer. *I am going to cast an area spell that should encompass all of the Trolls and stop them where they stand forever! Just before I do, I will surround you and the two humans with a shield that will protect you from its effects. Take care to stay in the shield!*

Wodanaz stood up on unsteady legs while Myrllin issued instructions for the innkeeper and his wife to clear the fire and take positions, one on each side of his unstable brother. They were soon leaning upon one another for support waiting for Myrllin to commence with the miracle that would free them. The Trolls, sensing that something was happening that would not favor their survival reacted, with fits and snarls while they danced, cursing at Myrllin, spitting promises to suck the marrow from his bones.

Myrllin paid them no mind. He had to time the incantations just right. The first would protect Wodanaz and the humans, interrupting the magical tune restraining the Trolls in the process and setting them free. The second cast would have to be completed within a fraction of a second after the first to cover all of the beasts before they had a chance to escape the circle. In essence, Myrllin would have to perform the impossible task of evoking two powerful charms at the same time if his plan was going to work. He had never done anything like this before and no certainty it would work, only theory, but he had to try.

Myrllin calmed his mind, wholly concentrating his attention on the task at hand, allowing his senses to reach out and feel the energy all around him. The power was ever-present and waiting, in every tree, leaf, stone and speck of dust. And in all the spaces in-between. He gathered it into himself carefully weaving a complicated network of magical strands that would protect those within the ring of dancing Trolls. Just before he finished, Myrllin held it fast within one partition of his mind while he began the second part. Beads of sweat trailed down the sides of his face and his hands clutched tightly to his staff to keep his body steady. Again, he wove a complex snare of magic, this time over the Trolls and linked it to the casting of the first. Once he released them, there would be no going back and neither could be reversed.

He opened his eyes to survey the scene one last time. Everything was set. Myrllin could see the glowing threads of the spells he wove around them, invisible to all but him. It was so complex, so fragile, that if he made even the smallest miscalculation . . .

A misstep that would kill them all.

Myrllin would have liked a sign from Wodanaz, but his brother's head was slumped down on his chest where he stood and it was all he could do to keep playing the rapidly deteriorating melody on his golden flute.

It had to be now.

Time stood still for a fraction of a second when Myrllin raised his staff and spoke the charm releasing the power of the evocations upon the scene before him. He watched as the shield slowly took hold with a final tightening of the magical weave just as . . .

There was sudden movement from Wodanaz. Was that a stumble?

Before Myrllin could see clearly, the energy of the second spell crashed down upon the Trolls. It exploded with an intensity that instantly dried the wet soil and threw up a vast cloud of dust that rushed away from where it landed with such concussive force that it sent Myrllin tumbling to the ground, pummeled by hot fragments thrown up suddenly the earth.

He lay there until the heavy dust settled and it began to clear except for the lingering haze in the darkness all around him. Myrllin still had his night vision and quickly searched the vicinity where he had last seen his brother. Thirty-eight stone monoliths circled the mound where Wodanaz lay, the golden flute fallen by his side. Behind him rose two more monoliths, the innkeeper and his wife, who lost the protection of the shield when Wodanaz stumbled forward. Myrllin felt sadness for the pair and knew that Wodanaz would mourn them as well.

"You have not held to the bargain, Mer-lin." A thick, rumbling voice spoke from behind.

Myrllin rolled over to see the Troll he met earlier standing over him. "They are not dead, Troll." He gestured to the monoliths. "They are alive within the stone and will remain that way forever. Immortals they are!"

"You have used trickery in your dealings with me, Mer-lin and now I will keep the promise I made to you. *Zir g teloch!*"

The Troll rushed forward.

Surprised by the sudden realization that the troll was something more that what it was, Myrllin was not sure what he had left to defend himself. Hastily, he put together a fire charm. The Troll, quickly within arm's length, grabbed Myrllin's leg. He was out of time. Then there was an unexpected rush of air and a massive jaw clamped on to the upper half of the Troll, lifting him violently into the air.

Dergo.

Myrllin couldn't believe his eyes. The Dragon bit down hard, splitting the Troll in two, sending its lower half flying away while he devoured the upper parts.

Struggling to stand, Myrllin shook his head. "Foul beast," he whispered to the remains of the Troll strewn all around him, "I was trying to spare you."

The Dragon continued to pick at the parts of the Troll left behind on the ground. "Couldn't find any mammoths nearby," he said between mouthfuls.

Myrllin almost laughed, but then he heard a noise behind and quickly turned to find Wodanaz struggling to stand. With no hesitation, he ran over to see to his brother's needs. To Myrllin's relief and amazement, Wodanaz was exhausted, yet unharmed.

Together, they stood and surveyed what they had done. Then Myrllin turned to his brother. "I didn't know you could play the flute."

Before Wodanaz could reply, there was a startling roar from Dergo. Myrllin looked back in time to see the great beast heaving partially shredded flesh from its huge maw. On the ground below, where most of the Troll's remains were spewed into a slimy pile, rose a shadowy orb of vile blackness darker than the void between the stars. It hovered a span off the ground, stretching at its edges as if fighting its own physical confines.

Dergo cautiously stepped back and away from it, clearly uncertain and maybe even a little afraid. Myrllin could feel the bone-chilling fear that the orb seemed to exude from fifty paces farther away. Then with an ear-piercing shriek and an audible *pop* at the end, the thing was gone.

"Was that what I think it was?" Wodanaz asked in a hoarse whisper.

"It was," confirmed Myrllin. "The demons are loose again."

Chapter 13

Shadows

Alseid walked into Queen Lysithea's chambers to awaken her mother. Senjit was away this night, hunting for game on the Mouillian Coast to satisfy his infinite appetite, leaving her alone for a few days.

"Mommy, are you awake? Mommy?" Alseid, less than an arm's length away from her mother's ear, called out far too loudly.

The five-year-old was a beautiful little girl with long curly blonde locks and liquid-gold skin that had not changed a bit since her birth. Her skin tone was unique to anyone that saw her, but they also knew who her father was, so none thought it particularly unusual. What everyone commented on were her beautiful green eyes that looked so much like her mother's.

"Yes, dear one," Lysithea replied, rousing from a deep sleep.

"Mommy, I captured a shadow. What shall I do with him?" she asked innocently.

Lysithea thought her daughter might be confused, "Do you mean you saw your shadow? Are you afraid?"

"No, Mommy, I captured it. Come see!" Alseid was very excited, pulling at her mother's sleeve relentlessly, as if that would hasten their departure.

Lysithea got out of bed, tossed a night-robe over her shoulder's and followed her daughter back to her room to see what nonsense she was imagining this night. One thing she had discovered about her child was that she had her father's sense of playful humor, to the eternal chagrin of Senjit.

Everything in Alseid's room looked normal at first glance until Alseid pointed out a small bubble the size of an apple floating near her daughter's bed.

"Look, Mommy! Look! There it is!" Alseid exclaimed, jumping up and down with excitement.

Suddenly feeling frightened, Lysithea pulled her daughter behind her and cautiously approached the strange object.

Inside the bubble a dark mass swirled like the blackest storm clouds moving erratically as if tossed by angry winds. Even from an arm's length away, Lysithea could feel something very wrong and evil about the thing.

She partially turned to face her daughter while keeping a wary eye on the floating orb. "Calm down, Alseid, please. Tell me what happened."

"The shadow woke me up because it was trying to go inside me." She appeared curious rather than afraid at the thought, then suddenly she laughed and clapped. "So, I captured it like we do with lightning bugs in bubbles!"

Lysithea tried to press her for more details about how *exactly* she captured the shadow, but the small child was unable to explain further. After a while, Alseid eyes drooped sleepily and she became lethargic and uninterested in whatever had happened with the orb. Lysithea was just relieved that her daughter was not afraid because of her experience.

"Mommy, will you take it away so I can go to sleep? I'm tired now."

Maintaining her calm, Lysithea smiled warmly at her daughter "Go sleep in Mommy's bed tonight, dear."

Alseid exited the room at a skipping run back to her mother's chamber. The child always seemed to run and never walk wherever she went. Once she was gone, Lysithea approached the shadow-filled bubble and gingerly cupped it in her hands. She had to make sure it did not get away, yet she had no idea how long her daughter's bubble might last. She walked to her changing room and pulled out a small chest made from almost indestructible Dvergr steel. It contained her most exquisite jewelry. Aside from being well constructed, it was also shielded with enchantments against intrusion. Without a second thought, she dumped the expensive valuables on her dressing table and placed the orb inside where it would stay until Senjit returned.

———

Senjit stared at the shadow-filled bubble for a long while, probing it carefully with his psionic abilities in an attempt to gather the smallest clue as to what it was and where it came from.

With a start, he turned to Lysithea. "It's a Chaos Demon. Alseid somehow captured a Chaos Demon before it could enter and possess her mind and body."

"What is a Chaos Demon and why was it trying to possess our daughter?" Lysithea asked anxiously betraying a hint of anger.

Mindful of her temper, he spoke calmly. "It is a lesser demon with the sole purpose of causing chaos in any way it can. They are from the Underworld or the Infernal Planes, depending on what one believes. How it escaped or was released, I cannot say."

What Senjit did know was that this was a very dangerous demon that he would have to find out more about and especially why it tried to possess his daughter. Although he didn't show his emotions outwardly, Senjit was very concerned and, like his wife, nearly in a rage over it, but he didn't want to make his Lysithea more frightened than she was already. He did his best to keep the conversation calm.

"Are there others? Will more come for Alseid?" There was fire in her eyes when she spoke. The protective instinct of a mother on the edge of violence.

Senjit detected the rising panic in her voice and moved to her side holding his wife close. "Not likely. It probably found her by chance. They can sense magic and are attracted to those with great power, like a fly drawn to a light-globe. It knows that if can possess someone strong in magic or influence, then it could cause greater damage to the world around them. In any case, I will set wards of protection just to be sure and teach you how to renew them when I am not here. In any case, I will need to spend some quality time with the one she caught. Perhaps I can find out how it got here."

Lysithea, although reluctant at first, agreed to the plan and after teaching her the wards, Senjit set off to his lair in the mountains on Hero to study the Chaos Demon further. Secretly he was terrified of what he might find. No minor demon should have had the strength to pierce the dimensional barrier between the Infernal and Material planes. All he could conclude for the moment was that it must have accompanied something far more powerful. Something that could change the world.

———

Weeks passed before Senjit's tenacity bore fruit. Using his psionic talents, he first determined how to communicate with the Chaos Demon. The thing was reluctant to provide any useful information, that was not unexpected, and it took enormous perseverance and trickery before he was able to discover that it came from the vicinity of Hellas. After that, further efforts to interrogate the demon became increasingly hazardous, even for a creature of Senjit's intellect, and he decided his best course was to travel to Hellas and find out what he could there. If another rift between this world and the Infernal Planes existed, then there could be more demons, many more, to be dealt with.

"Irgil a unal chis caosg?" Senjit spoke to himself aloud. He was surprised that the words came out in the language of his father. It was especially unsettling that he could not explain how he might know his father's language since he had never met the man nor had he any idea who his father might be. It was the only clue he had that might lead him to the identity of his father one day – if he ever cared to find out.

Senjit looked closely at the bubble and wondered for the hundredth time how a five-year-old little girl with no training somehow possessed the natural ability to create one, let alone trap a Chaos Demon inside it. He would leave that to Lysithea to work out while he investigated the source of the demon. Even confined in the bubble, the Chaos Demon was still posed great danger and Senjit realized that he would have to destroy it rather than risk the possibility that it might escape. The concentration of evil, even in a minor demon, was so powerful that a lesser being than he would have been instantly driven mad had they attempted what he had done. It was a perilous thing, indeed, to allow one's mind to play so closely along the dark edges of a creature possessed of such wickedness unnatural.

Senjit took the roiling globe from his laboratory and into the vast cavern where he slept in his natural state. With barely a thought, he transformed his physical form into the great golden beast revered by so many. The slits in his dark golden eyes regarded the tiny bubble in the palm of his massive claw. *Why would the gods allow such evil to exist?* he wondered. Maybe they didn't have a choice. Right now, he did and he had no qualms about carrying through with it. With his legendary breath, Senjit spewed liquid fire as hot as the molten nephelinite deep inside the Ourea upon the dark globe holding the Chaos Demon. There was not a sound from the creature, no cry or plea, one moment it was there and in the next it was not. He knew the moment it was gone, as in a flicker of a second, the oppressive weight of malevolence and fear felt even through the barrier of the orb, simply ceased to exist. Even so, Senjit was no fool to think he had destroyed the demon, for he knew it could not die on the Material Plane and that the best he could do was send it screaming back to the Infernal Planes that it hated so much. It would have to do for the time being. He felt satisfied when it happened, even if it was just a small piece of evil removed from the world.

Spreading his mighty wings, Senjit took flight in the direction of Gades, where the Royal Palace stood high over the northern coast of the island kingdom. It was only a few hours past dawn, the air was cool and the wind from the north had surrendered it chilling bite to the warmth of the sun. He looked forward to seeing his wife. Only then did he realize how much he missed her, so preoccupied by the Chaos Demon he had been.

Far below, he watched the trade vessels from the Mouillian cities, Nurozieri, the Kingdom of Courth and parts beyond cutting through the straights between the islands of Benahoare, where most of the centaur people lived and Chenech, dominated by the smoking peak of the so-called 'White Mountain'. A reclusive race of halflings made their home within the subterranean caves and passages formed by the ancient lava flows of the volcano. They raised small goats they called Ara and a special breed of sheep with straight wool known as Hana that Senjit would filch on occasion from the rocky foothills and sparse forests that was the dominate features of Chenech.

Soon, the Royal Palace of Gades loomed out of the mists formed by the ocean waves that pounded the rocks far below. The palace was built into the cliff face and the constant spray left a perpetual layer of droplets over everything along with high humidity that the nymphs seemed to enjoy. It was said that nymphs were a magical race of fairy-like people from the sea that were related to the elves. Certainly, there was a strong presence of elves from the Sylvan Kingdom in the Isles of Gades and a highly cooperative relationship between the two kingdoms, but Senjit was not convinced of the nymphs Sylvan heritage.

He fluidly altered his shape from dragon to humanoid form as he landed on the balcony outside of Lysithea's private chamber and walked inside. She was facing away, sitting on a cushion stool at her writing desk with quill in hand when he entered. Her long dark hair spilled lazily over pale shoulders and a smooth back bare to the waist revealed by a fashionable gown of wispy silks in tones of soft blues and green sea foam. She was so beautiful and it had been so long, that he had to just stop and admire her lovely figure.

"So, you have returned," she remarked coolly without turning.

She knew he was there. Somehow, she always knew when he was close. But that thought was a distant second to the displeasure in her voice that caused Senjit's ears to twitch with trepidation. Had he done something wrong? Had something happened? Surely, she would have sent word . . .

The anxious moments stretched for what seemed like an eternity as Senjit searched his mind for an appropriate response. This cold reception was not at all what he expected. He felt his mouth working, but there were no words.

"I . . ." was all he could get out before she turned and held his gaze with her beautiful green eyes.

A mischievous smile appeared on her face and she rushed to him. Kissing his face, kissing his neck, peeling off his clothing, letting her gown fall to the floor. Touching him.

"I missed you," she whispered in his ear pulling him toward her bed.

Two hours later, Lysithea lay snuggled in his arms. It felt nice to have her there again, close to him, the warmth of her body inviting and the scent of her hair intoxicating. It was like this every time they were apart for a long period of time, usually without the theatrics upon arrival, by Lysithea had a wicked sense of humor sometimes.

He told her what he had discovered from the Chaos Demon in the weeks he had been away and of its ultimate destruction. She was concerned with the first part and relieved at the last. Senjit was relieved, in turn, when she told him that their little girl, Alseid, had not exhibited any lingering effects from the experience. No nightmares, no misbehaving beyond her usual protests against baths and vegetables, and hardly a question about it.

"I need to travel to Hellas and find out if there is a rift open to the Infernal Planes that allowed the demon to escape. The one Alseid captured may not be the worst of it."

"I wish there were a way I could accompany you," Lysithea slid her long nails gently over his chest. "Now that we have a child, our adventures together must be postponed for a while." She nuzzled her nose in between the creases of his neck and whispered, "Be careful, Great Dragon and remember there are two here that love you."

Senjit smiled. "Fear not, love, I will not be away long if it can be helped and there is no other place I would rather you be than here, with our daughter, as I know she will be safe."

He turned his head and kissed his wife, before passion once again ruled their lives for just a few more precious hours. Neither of them knowing when, or even if, they would share such moments again.

———

Senjit flew high above the Great Sea at an altitude that allowed for him to conserve energy and glide with the fast wind currents. At this height, he could see the white tips of the waves stretching on for leagues in every direction and occasionally a square-sailed Mouillian brig, a Tartessos pirate sloop, or any number of smaller trade vessels that plied the open waterways. They all looked like children's toys from his height.

He had only been gone a day and a half and already he missed his family. His beautiful Queen Lysithea looked very young by Nymph standards and her green eyes, long brown hair, fleshy lips and slender curves were naturally seductive and never far from his memory. Then there was his little Alseid, sweetly innocent and filled with mysteries that only she could know, her bouncing blonde curls, her mother's intense green eyes and her liquid-gold skin made her a unique thing of beauty to behold. Reluctantly, he put them out of his mind. They would always be in his heart, but for now, he needed to focus on the task at hand—finding the source of the Chaos Demon's entry into this world.

Senjit was unsure about what to do once he reached Hellas. The only information that he could glean from the demon was that it had escaped a pithos in which it had been imprisoned somewhere in Hellas, maybe the high mountain peaks of the Othrys Mountains. And there was another disturbing detail: the demon did not escape alone. This he had not imparted to his wife, as it would have made her terrified for the life of their child. Although he did not believe another Chaos Demon would find its way to his daughter, Senjit worried that there could be many such demons loose upon the world, sowing chaos everywhere through their humanoid or animal hosts. He had to find out the extent of the demonic intrusion and if this pithos was some sort of gateway that needed closing.

He decided that he would begin his search in Foronikon-Asty, a city devoted to Gaia, the Earth Goddess, in the southern part of Hellas. He would land out of sight and change into his human form before approaching the city to avoid causing a panic. In Hellas, his dragon form was known as Ladon. There were stories and legends about him that the people knew, but he did not travel to Hellas often and although he was not thought of as a malevolent beast, they were not used to seeing a dragon in their skies. And there was a certain ire, considering he was guilty of stealing a few goats from time to time.

As the sun rose on the third day out of Gades, Senjit spied the walls of the city in the distance and began a slow descent toward the more remote expanses of the surrounding countryside. Last time he visited Foronikon-Asty, it was the agricultural center Hellas specializing in citrus. It seemed that had not changed during the intervening years, as there were leagues of groves all around the city with many varieties of oranges, grapefruit, lemons and limes. Angling low and parallel to a line of trees, he rendered himself invisible to avoid being sighted by locals rising with the new dawn before drifting along with the fresh breeze low over the endless lines of fruit trees, enjoying the fresh scent of citrus. Not far from the city, Senjit spied a suitable copse of trees and by the time his feet hit the ground, he had transformed into his human form once again. Thoughtfully, Senjit chose the local costume of an affluent local merchant. He enjoyed his comfort and didn't see any reason why he should go about staying in hovels when he was not recognizable either way.

The early morning walk toward the city was a pleasure for Senjit. He passed many farmers and tradesmen going about their morning rituals or hurried into fields, shops and stalls. Soon, the workers would invade the groves, harvesting the fruits of their long labors and carting off the produce to market or to the docks for export to any number of foreign ports. There was only light traffic this early in the day on the westward road he followed toward Foronikon-Asty. Senjit chose the route purposefully since the east road ran down to the harbor and was quite busy in the morning. Not that he was hiding or feared being noticed; crowds were merely an inconvenience he chose to avoid.

Approaching the massive walls of Foronikon-Asty, Senjit could see that it was well defended by towers placed evenly along its length with regular patrols in between. Citizens flowed through a wide archway with double sets of gates that could be closed at a moment's notice and most of the interior buildings were constructed of white stone and timber. He followed the main avenue leading toward the more affluent section of the city, where he might find proper accommodations and better-quality food.

Along the way, he passed temples and government buildings, which incorporated white marble into their construction and adorned their exteriors with fountains, statues and wall carvings. Small shrines to various deities and gardens with even more fountains and statuary littered the city as a form of high art. Many of the walls surrounding private residences were also covered in painted carvings depicting stories about the gods, the Cosmic Egg and the creation myth.

The city was bustling and vibrant with life. From what he could see, the people of Foronikon-Asty appeared to enjoy a pleasant lifestyle with nearly no poverty in evidence. He passed what was considered to be the most famous pottery and bronze sculpting school anywhere in Hellas in addition to several pottery workshops, tanneries and clothing fabricators. There was not much that he recognized. Senjit had not graced the boulevards of Foronikon-Asty in over two hundred years and at that time it was a very different city.

Attached to one of the government buildings was a tall, slender tower built entirely of marble—if his sharp eyes were not deceiving him, one single massive column of marble. Rather than being constructed, it had been carved from the inside. But that was not the only unusual aspect of the impossible tower. At the apex of the tall structure hovered a large crystal glowing red, bright even in the daytime, and it rotated in place slowly.

Senjit could remember many details of Foronikon-Asty from his previous visit and the tower was not one of them. He wasn't really surprised to see it. He knew what it was and who built it. The Atlanteans erected similar constructs all over the planet with crystals that magnified the power of the Orichalcum Crystals stored inside the tower. The Orichalcum was the source that powered magic to all those who knew how to use it. Even Senjit drew power from them, although the vast majority of his abilities were inherent.

Further down the road, a jubilant Cryer was singing about an upcoming celebration to honor some god Senjit didn't catch the name of. The cities of Hellas were known for their festivals. Last he counted, they had at least twenty-five a year and he was sure they must have added more. He enjoyed the food, the games, the entertainers and the pretty girls. Well, not so much the pretty girls anymore. Senjit could imaging Lysithea whipping every one of them if he came back home with the smallest hint of their scent on him. Not to mention what she might do to *him*. He smiled. There would be no fear of any of that happening. She was far too precious for him to stray.

A few blocks later, Senjit passed close to the center of the city where the most important temples and government buildings were located. This was the highest point of Foronikon-Asty, atop a hill with the Temple of Gaia at its summit. There were many wealthy homes that stood near the base of the tall hill showing off impressive courtyard gardens and fountains. Each employed an army of servants in matching chitons to keep everything looking perfect. Beyond that was the merchant's district, where tradesmen from around the world plied their trade. There were many fine taverns here with men who spent money on wine to relax, and more often than not, to excess.

That was where he wanted to be.

Senjit loved to buy a few rounds and listen to the stories of well-traveled people. Perhaps something of the demons would catch his ear. Still, it was too early in the day for the merchants' tongues to loosen with drink, so he decided to take in the sights of the city until the evening when the shops closed and the taverns began to fill.

———

When the sun drew long shadows over the streets of Foronikon-Asty and the warm glow of lanterns began to illuminate the way, Senjit settled himself into what he believed would be a popular tavern. Already, merchants, tradesmen and citizens with coin crowded in and the music began to play. Foronikon-Asty was a very progressive city-state of Hellas and the varied tunes teased upon tympanon, lyre, flute and salpinx were accompanied by poems and stories of ancient deeds and legendary heroes.

Senjit purchased several rounds of drinks and enjoyed spirited conversations with several merchants from around Hellas, but none related stories of any particular interest, at least not to Senjit. It seemed that all everyone wanted to talk about were the scandals of a prominent official or despoiled lady. And there was an especially juicy tale involving a wealthy merchant's son and a priest's daughter. Senjit tried to relax and prepared himself for a journey that could span numerous nights like this across several cities, big and small, to find a hint of a clue.

Almost as if preordained, several nights and a dozen taverns later, Senjit decided it was time to leave. The next day he would travel to Metis, a larger city-state farther north with more travelers and merchants from distant locales. He certainly never expected his search to be easy, especially considering how ambiguous the circumstances surrounding demons and pithos were. He just had to be patient, keep asking questions and listen to the stories, songs, sonnets and poems, before he would find his way.

On the last night in Foronikon-Asty, Senjit sat in another tavern and cast the usual mass charm over the room to compel the patrons to looser tongues. The charm, combined with copious amounts of alcohol, usually had them talking liberally after a few rounds. It was late into the evening after the drinks had been flowing freely for several hours when Senjit was speaking with a man whose brother was a priest of Kronos in the northern city of Sesklo. He related an unusual story about something that had occurred near a village on the northern coast of the Sea of Waves.

"My brother told me a fable about a Ta Hiera of his order that had gone on a sort of spiritual pilgrimage a few years back. Now, this was not the usual Ta Hiera of any temple, but the Fire-Bringer himself!" Senjit ordered another oinochoe of wine to keep the man talking. "Somehow, no one knew the purpose of his mission, which was strange since the priesthood always promoted these pilgrimages as examples to initiates." The man shook his head and took a long draft from his newly filled cup. Senjit gestured to the pouring girl to keep it filled. "A few weeks after the Ta Hiera's departure, the temple received word that his body was found at the base of a mountain near the east coast. It appeared as if the priest died from falling a long distance. My brother said he was nearly unrecognizable! The speculation by most was that he was climbing the mountain in search of the mythical Shrine of Metis."

"Is there truly a shrine there to find?" Senjit asked with exaggerated astonishment.

"Who can say? If the Fire-Bringer to Kronos couldn't survive the search, what chance would there be for the rest of us?"

Senjit raised his cup. "To the Fire-Bringer!"

"The Fire-Bringer!" the man responded, took another long draft and continued. "The oddest thing about the remains of the Ta Hiera was that he was not alone. The bodies of a Chimera and a winged Pegasos were said to lay dead nearby. Creatures from legend, if you can believe! It's a great mystery. Sometimes I think my brother drinks too much!" He laughed.

This was precisely the type of information Senjit was looking for. There was no mention of demons, but just the rumor of the unusual creatures found dead next to the body of the Fire-Bringer was worth looking into further. Senjit lingered at the tavern a little while longer before he decided the dark, early morning hours would be the best time to leave Foronikon-Asty with the least attention. He set off into the cold.

A little while later, Senjit walked through the northern gates with a warning from the guards on duty to be vigilant and take care during his nocturnal travels. Outside the wall there were dozens of small wood-and-thatch built residences lined in rows near the main road. Some showed lights through curtained windows, while most remained dark for the night. Senjit continued on, soon passing organized campsites at the edge of the city where travelers who couldn't afford an inn stayed temporarily under the watchful eyes of frequent patrols. Looking ahead, the road leading north was dark and Senjit suspected that there would be no travelers until the morning.

As luck would have it, a bend in the road put the last camps near the city out of sight. Senjit strode toward the cover of the forest, but just as he was about to cross the tree line, he spied a group human forms quietly creeping toward him from the depths of the wood. With an exaggerated sigh, Senjit stopped and waited for them to approach. He knew what they wanted and what they were going to do. This was not Senjit's first dance with this kind.

The men hesitated when Senjit stopped and stared in their direction. They naturally expected to ambush him unawares. A few whispered words passed from one to another before they cautiously walked forward in a loose arc that they must have thought was very intimidating and stopped only a few paces away. To a man, they were dressed in leather armor and carried a combination of bows, swords, and spears. There were twelve of them in all and they must have been reasonably successful at their deadly craft considering that their apparel seemed to be new and their weapons of good quality.

Too bad, thought Senjit.

Their leader, a big man with a shaved head and a missing front tooth, spoke first. "Hello, friend. It's a bit late to be wandering alone in the dark with bandits and beasts about," he smiled. "Perhaps we can offer protection for a small . . ."

The man never completed his thoughtful offer as Senjit's slender blade interrupted the words in his throat. Before the dead man's body hit the ground, quick strikes sent three more on their way with him. Taken entirely by surprise by what the bandits must have thought an easy mark, the eight remaining men jumped backward and drew their weapons. Senjit never stopped moving, his brown cloak spinning behind him in one direction and then another as he wound his way through his adversaries. His speed was blinding and even before the first of their swords cleared oiled scabbards, two more men lay dead. Four others lost their will to move, victims of Senjit's psionics dominating their feeble minds, while the last two turned to run. Senjit evoked bolts of lightning from the fingertips of one hand that sent them sprawling onto the ground after a single step, their bodies twitching with spasms in leather armor smoking with the stink of their own cooked flesh. The battle was over in seven seconds, without much of a ruckus to attract attention.

Senjit immediately altered his form into that of a great golden dragon and stretched his massive wings preparing to take flight, nearly forgetting about the four men standing like human vegetables. *They are dead anyway.* He rationalized. *No point in prolonging their suffering.* With a single thought, he snapped their will to live and they fell to the ground, powerless to encourage their own hearts to beat. The last image the stricken bandits glimpsed, unable to comprehend the fast approach of their own death, was the glint of golden scales launching into the night sky.

Chapter 14

Aquilon

The central market was huge. To simply walk the lanes of merchant stalls would have taken days if one had the time and inclination to do so. Qel marveled at the expanse of it. *Not even the City of Atlantis had a marketplace such as this one*, he thought. There was jewelry fashioned from silver mined in Tartessos; colorful dyes from Gades; exotic spices, incense, and oils from faraway TaShemau and TaMehu; as well as fruits, vegetables and olives from local Atlantean estates. Farther down they passed clays, copper, lead and salt from the Mouillians; steel tools and weaponry from the dwarfs of Tirnan Yog; potions, healing tonics and cures from Eriu; metal and chain armor from Lyonesse; and thousands of varied items from places so far away that Qel could hardly guess at their origin.

Everything was a new and exciting experience. Each stall was decorated in a unique fashion that reflected the culture and tradition of the merchant within. It was a visceral experience for Qel. He favored the colorful banners, signs with unusual script and best of all, the strange clothing the people wore in the fashion of their native lands. Qel happily followed Havacian up and down the lanes of merchants through the remainder of the morning and into the afternoon exploring the endless treasures of the market before returning to the Wizards Tower for a light meal.

"I wish to go back to the market this evening," Qel said between bites of hartebeest stew. "There were several taverns nearby and we never had a chance to celebrate after graduation."

"That," agreed Havacian, "is the best idea you've had since we received those two day passes at the same time from our masters a few years ago."

Qel knew his friend was speaking sarcastically. "Aw, c'mon Havacian, we had a great time."

"Until we got drunk and you had me freezing the water in the fountains all over the city."

Qel laughed so hard at the memory that he almost snorted the broth out through his nose. "Artistic expression! We were so misunderstood."

"We caught hell for that," Havacian shook his head. "The masters never let us out at the same time again."

"Well, there are no masters around tonight," Qel smiled.

"Very well, but remember what Master Curatei said before we left. We represent our order now and our actions must always reflect well on the order."

Qel rolled his eyes. "We are not children anymore, Havacian. Let's go find out what grown-ups do on a night out in the city."

An hour later they were back at the central market. Qel was surprised that most of the vendors were still open and the throngs of browsers had only lessened by a little. The taverns were easy to find. Some had rowdy music and raucous patrons, others featured outdoor seating and small orchestras while still others were quiet with a minstrel playing a flute or lyre and reciting poetry. No matter the persuasion of the tavern, they were all very busy. On Qel's suggestion, they entered the liveliest of the taverns and sat together at one of the crowded long tables.

The tavern was a jovial mix of mostly humans, a few dwarfs and a small number of young Atlanteans all singing and laughing to the quick music played by a group of musicians on a small stage. Havacian ordered wine for them both and laughed when the server brought them mugs of fine Mekali from Qel's own family vineyard. The taste of the familiar burgundy was silky smooth on his tongue, exciting his taste buds with hints of fruit, chocolate and cedar inciting a heady response that cast blooms of blush on his cheeks and forehead. It felt nice. Qel was finally relaxing. After a while, the musicians took a break and the din of conversation in the busy room rose to such a level that Qel had a hard time hearing Havacian speak, but it hardly mattered, they were both enjoying the moment.

And suddenly there was a collective shout from nearly everyone in the tavern, "Wanderer!"

Qel tossed his head around and observed a middle-aged human man with dark hair that touched his shoulders and a short chestnut beard mount the steps to the stage. He carried a staff in one hand and waved to the crowd with the other, then took a seat on a stool that had been placed for him in the center of the platform. The room hushed with anticipation while the man adjusted his oversized, dull blue robes cinched at the waist by a thick gold chain. He was loosely covered by a grayish brown cloak that had one side flung over his right shoulder in the fashion of a noble or bard, yet none would have claimed him to be either.

"I have heard of this man before," Qel commented. "He is purported to be a great poet. My brother once said he draws his inspiration from traveling the world and a life-time of wonderous experiences."

"By the looks of those robes, he must have a great store of life experience!" Havacian jokingly replied.

Qel laughed. "I have heard that sometimes he will recite a poem or song in a language unheard of and without translation, making it even more mysterious."

Finally settled, the man looked around the room, as if searching for something or someone, then with a dramatic flourish of his hands bejeweled with rings on his thick fingers, addressed the gathered crowd. "Good evening, fine folk of the world. My name is Wodanaz, a wanderer of many lands among many peoples. I hope to entertain you this evening with a few of my favorite sonnets and poems. And when I am done, I pray my work has inspired some of you to seek out your own wisdom and knowledge with a clear and open sensibility beyond the place that you currently call home!"

Soon Wodanaz was spinning his prose with such grace and timbre that not a patron spoke nor a mug clanged. Qel could sense subtle magic woven into the beautiful words the Wanderer spoke and when he finished each oration, the crowd in the tavern applauded enthusiastically, calling for more with much vigor. The word must have quickly spread that the famous entertainer was performing in the tavern, for soon crowds began to gather, even overflowing into the street outside. Qel was glad of their fortuitous arrival at the tavern given that within minutes it was standing room only.

Wodanaz responded to the throng as if he completely expected it. Perhaps he did. Why wouldn't he? Qel thought. His name rose above even that of Boeger Pennhallow and Vyvyan who had theatres and libraries named in their honor. Not Wodanaz, he wouldn't have it, so Qel heard. He was a man of the people, walked among them with humility and served them with his talents without regard to profit. Qel wondered if the tavern keeper had even expected Wodanaz this night as it was rumored he never booked a performance, but instead, would simply show up.

Every eye and ear hung on every word and theatrical gesture. When the poetry was sad, the crowd cried with him; when it was fraught with humor, the crowd roared with laughter; when it was triumphant, they cheered; and when about love, the people were quiet and reflective. A little over an hour later, the performance ended, to the great disappointment of the entire room and Wodanaz yielded the stage back to the musicians flush with admiration who knew they could never measure up to the great man and loved him anyway. With a flourishing bow and flamboyant toss of his long cloak, he exited through a door at the back of the stage to thunderous stomps and applause.

"I wish we could have met him!" Qel lamented.

Havacian, grinning broadly and clapping with the crowd, spread his hands wide, pointed to his ears and rolled his eyes. The clamor was so loud that the roar of thunder would have been muted had lightning struck. And just as the noise died back down to the constant buzz of conversation with the musicians playing once again, Wodanaz emerged from backstage to renewed ovation cheers, before taking a place quickly vacated at the bar. There, he was plied with ale by adoring fans while he told short, funny stories that kept the drinks flowing and the patrons laughing.

Qel waved excitedly to Havacian and they abandoned their table to angle closer to where Wodanaz sat surrounded by his admirers and listened in on his stories of far-off lands. They heard tales of the Vikja in the north, the pirates of Tartessos east across the Primal Sea and rumors of a fantastic Golden Dragon said to fly the skies over the Isles of Gades in the south. These were among Qel's favorites. The tales inspired him to want to visit all of these lands and more.

Although there were many performances of music and prose on the stage that night, the real show was Wodanaz and he might as well have been sitting on stage for all the attention he was getting. Qel was fascinated by the man and found himself drinking into the early hours of the morning with no encouragement from Havacian to take their leave. His friend was clearly as enamored with the famous entertainer as he was. It wasn't until early the next morning that Wodanaz finally relinquished his chair and retired to a room offered by the tavernkeeper that the crowd began to disperse. Qel held onto Havacian giving as much as receiving support as they stumbled back to the Tower for a few hours of sleep.

Qel awoke the next morning to the worst hangover of his life. He would require the services of a priest if he could find one before his head exploded and he was sure Havacian must be feeling the same. Cleaning up as quickly as his limbs would allow, he got dressed in casual trousers, tunic and cloak before he went to retrieve his friend.

Qel knocked for a while until Havacian finally opened the door to his room. He was dressed, but his hair was mussed and the look on his face reflected his own pure misery.

"I was going to find a healer. Would you care to come with?" Qel asked.

"Without question." Havacian nodded and the two strode down to the common room together.

There was a different attendant at the administrator's desk that morning. He was from the Brown Hall, the Earth Wizards, introducing himself as the assistant to the House Administrator. This man was nearly their age and had probably graduated only five or six years before them.

"The healers are at the temple just a few blocks away. Shall I send a runner to fetch one here for you?" he asked politely.

"Thank you, no," Qel replied. "We will go there ourselves. The walk and the fresh air will no doubt do us some good."

Striding outside and into the perfectly sunny day, Qel regretted their decision almost immediately. The street was crowded and it was very bright. They pressed on despite their discomfort and found the Temple of Pontus in short order. The temple itself was on an island surrounded by a broad moat filled with water. It was symbolic of the temple in Atlantis, Qel supposed. From what he could tell through the glare of the morning sun reflecting off the water, there was a single wide bridge that led over to the main entryway. Had he felt better, Qel would have admired the white marble crossing that was adorned with a series of large sculpted fish that sprayed streams of water arcing high overhead, one way and then the other, when they passed.

At the end of the bridge was a wide-open courtyard with a massive fountain embellished with more fish, seahorses and a giant squid with tentacles reaching out of the water toward something imagined. Beyond that was the Temple of Pontus. Like the one in Atlantis, the main feature was Pontus himself holding his trident high and forward in the direction of the Primal Sea. This one, however, was much smaller and enclosed on the sides and back by great slabs forming marble walls and a propylon in the front supported by numerous tall marble columns. Surrounding the Sea God's likeness were smaller statues of notable Atlanteans from history and not only those dedicated to the priesthood.

A young, pretty priestess wearing a white robe approached them when they reached the end of the bridge. "How may I guide you, good sirs?"

Qel could barely keep his eyes open from the glare reflecting off of everything. "We need a priest."

"For healing or death?" she asked politely.

"For healing, of course," Qel replied irritably. "I'm standing here in front of you, aren't I? I'm not dead yet."

She smiled knowingly. "My apologies, I did not want to presume in case you were mourning."

"Oh, right," he said, a little embarrassed at his behavior. "We need a healer, please."

"Follow me," she gestured forward leading them across the courtyard and through a side entrance of the temple. Inside, the darkened room was lit only by a dim light globe floating near the ceiling revealing several chairs and a few cots. Otherwise, the chamber was empty.

"Please sit or lie down, as you please and I will inform our day healer that you are here."

The priestess disappeared through a door in the back and a servant came in a few moments later with a tray holding mugs of cold water. Qel was relieved to be out of the sun and thankful for the water. He couldn't get the thirst from his tongue no matter how much he drank, feeling as dehydrated and nauseous as he was.

They hadn't been there long when the priestess returned with an older man adorned in sea-blue robes and a gold medallion engraved with a blue wave and gold trident that identified him as a High Priest of Pontus. Qel immediately stood and greeted him respectfully; high priests were equivalent to the masters of his order.

"Sit here, child"—he beckoned to Qel— "and let me have a look at you."

Qel sat on the chair indicated and the high priest stepped up to place his hands over Qel's temples. There was a feeling of warmth that began to saturate Qel's body and he sensed the use of the power flowing over him. It was not magic as he would generally describe it if he were to observe it from another wizard, but there were some similarities. He learned early on that the priesthood did not rely on the orichalcum crystals for their abilities. Somehow, they drew their power from nature itself or the energy that surrounded and bound it together. Even the masters did not understand fully how they did it. The priests would only say that their power was a matter of faith and spoke nothing more about it. Qel could always tell that it was a source of frustration for Master Ampher and probably the entire order. To think of the priests as a kind of enigma that they had no hope of understanding was simply beyond the comprehension of the Imperial Order of Wizards.

The most striking thing to Qel was when he found out that the exception also applied to foreign priests, shamans, holy men, clerics and druids regardless of their race or religion. It was also true for magical creatures derived from nature like Dryads, Pixies, Fairies and Nymphs. His master once told him that the one caveat of the different conduits from which they gained magical power was that when the priests and the wizards collaborated in their research, it often revealed hidden knowledge to their mutual benefit.

"So, you have a hangover." The high priest's brown eyes capped by bushy gray eyebrows bore down on him with disapproval. "You are an Imperial Wizard and, more importantly, an Atlantean. I suggest you conduct yourself with more reserve in the future."

The priestess standing behind the high priest was a little younger than Qel and gave him a reassuring wink and a smile. She could appreciate the exuberant nature of youth that seemed to be lost to his people the moment they hit forty.

"You are correct, Revered One," Qel answered humbly. "My friend and I have only recently graduated and we took our celebration a bit too far."

"So it's the same for the other one, then?"

"It is, Revered One."

Suddenly the warmth he felt turned cold and his head and teeth felt like they would shatter before it was over. Then he felt wonderful, possibly even better than he usually did. The headache and nausea were gone, the sluggishness replaced by energy and vigor. The high priest walked over to where Havacian was slouched holding his head in his hands and sat down beside him. Within a few moments, he too was on his feet expressing his gratitude for the high priest proverbially bringing him back to life. Qel wanted to roll his eyes.

On his way out, the high priest called a warning over his shoulder, "I expect that you gentlemen will not be back here again under the same circumstances."

It was not really a question. Almost as one, Qel and Havacian were quick to assure him they would not, trying desperately not to laugh at the priestess who followed in the high priest's wake making funny faces at them.

Qel looked at Havacian, "I am so full of energy I think I could run to Avalon from here. Shall we tour the city before we go back to the market?"

"Great idea," Havacian agreed. "And let's find some food along the way. I'm starving."

When they departed the temple, Qel marveled at the great pools of pristine water complete with beautiful fountains and waterfalls designed seamlessly into the architecture of the temple itself. The waters were tended by aqueous elementals he knew as Oceanides, the children of Pontus, just like the ones that guarded the channels in Atlantis. In his previous state, he had ignored the beauty of the temple and was glad not to miss it again on the way out.

After finding a nearby tavern where they stuffed themselves with fresh fish and boiled Mahiz, they spent the remainder of the morning on a fast-paced exploration of the natural beauty and splendors of Aquilon. Along the way, they stumbled upon the perfectly plain and square granite building complex that served as the dwarf's trade consulate. It was so wholly austere and unremarkable that it could have been mistaken for a massive stone block if such a thing wouldn't have been considered absurd sitting in the middle of the city.

In the afternoon Havacian dragged Qel back to the central market. The dense crowds pushed them along like a river except when they stepped to the side to be assailed by the noise of incomprehensible haggling between buyers and sellers at nearly every stall. Qel's energy had waned somewhat since that morning, but he was still game to spend a few hours following Havacian along the endless lanes in search of the unknown. His friend's quest for knowledge was insatiable and even the little things, like a bamboo tool used by the priests of TaShemau to liquefy and remove a corpse's brains during mummification, was exceedingly interesting to him. Qel was just glad Havacian didn't buy the dreadful contraption.

When the sun finally fell below the horizon, even Havacian conceded that he was exhausted and the two walked back to the Tower, ate a light meal in the common room and went straight t. They planned to cross into forests of the Sylvan Kingdom the next morning. It would mark the beginning of a five-day journey that would take them to the fabled Avalon, capital of the elves, if nothing delayed them. Even though he would have liked to spend a few more days exploring the beautiful city of Aquilon, other than the central market, Qel was eager to be well rested and on their way the next day. He didn't want to miss a thing.

———

Rising just after dawn, Qel got dressed and checked on Havacian before packing his clothing and personals away for travel. Not surprised at all, he found Havacian ready to go before he was. They went down to the common room for a quick breakfast, then retrieved their horses and set off on the north road toward the border only a league away. Qel was excited and nervous at the same time, having heard many tales of the elves and their enchanted forest. He was sure that most of them were just fanciful stories written to entertain, but some might hold elements of truth too strange to imagine.

Remarkably few people were on the road with them that morning; even the merchants were scant. In fact, except for a few Atlanteans and a group of dwarfs transporting heavy ore in wagons, the road was empty. Most notably, not a single human was in sight.

"Havacian, why do you think there aren't any humans going north this morning?" Qel asked.

"Don't you know?" Havacian looked surprised. "The elves won't allow them in. They never have."

"They allow Atlanteans and dwarfs entry, but not humans? Why is that?"

"Master Curatei says they don't trust the nature of humans. He said they probably have other reasons as well."

"I suppose we are not much better," Qel conceded. "The emperor won't allow humans to own land in territory controlled by Atlantis, the high priests won't allow them to enter the priesthood and our own masters will collaborate but not allow them entry into the order."

Havacian sighed. "Master Curatei says that too many humans carry hidden agendas and that you never really know what their motivations are."

"My father told me much the same," Qel nodded. "It's truly sad, especially since there are *so many* of them."

The tree line appeared in the distance and when the road brought them closer, Qel could see two slender figures standing casually astride the entry into the forest. He didn't see them at first since they blended into the leafy background so well. It was only when one moved to speak to the other did he notice they were there at all. When they rode closer still, it was clear they were elves wearing uniforms in shades of green with breeches tucked into high, soft boots and both carried a curved sword at their side and a bow across their back. Qel thought that one appeared to be male and the other female, although each was just as exceptionally beautiful as the other. *How can they stand themselves?* Qel jested to himself. Their features were sharp, with almond-shaped, slightly turned-up eyes, slender noses and narrow jaws. And of course, their most notable feature: pointed ears. The male elf had natural brown hair not unusual to any humanoid species, but the female displayed a very strange silver tone that shimmered in the light when she moved. They both appeared young by Qel's standards—although, considering the long lifespan attributed to the elves, they could easily have been a hundred years old.

There was an aura of magic around the elves and from the forest itself, which was thick on both sides of the road where it crossed into the Sylvan Forest. Qel could sense it clearly. He wondered if it was anything like the orichalcum on the walls of Atlantis that served in some mysterious fashion to protect the city in times of need. Or maybe it was something else entirely. He couldn't be sure of the magics purpose, but he was sure of its presence.

"Good day, Atlantean wizards," the male elf greeted them formally when Qel and Havacian approached. "You are welcome in our home. Please remember to respect the laws of our land and people,"

"Thank you, good elf," Qel pulled up and dismounted so as not to appear to lord over the warrior. "Any advice for our journey to Avalon?"

The elf responded with a half-nod, "While on the road, you will always be safe and there are many way stations, so you do not have to camp in the wilderness. However, if you choose to wander the forest on your own, then your safety cannot be assured."

Although Elves were not exactly rare in Atlantis, Qel rarely had the chance to speak with one. He was so enthralled by their graceful movements and almost poetic way of speaking that he only just noticed that the road ahead was completely blocked by trees. *How strange that they would allow the wilderness to grow so wild and block the roadway,* he thought absently. And traveling off the road appeared improbable as well, with the underbrush choked with thorny bushes and entwined with vines and roots of other foliage along the entire tree line as far as he could see.

Qel motioned toward the overgrown road, "Good elf, how may we, or anyone, enter your beautiful and mysterious land when the trees have been allowed to block the road behind you?"

The elf smiled mischievously. "This is your first-time entering the Sylvan Kingdom, Atlantean? The Tree Guardians only keep out those who are not welcome."

With a wave, the trees blocking the roadway slowly retracted their entangling roots and *walked* to opposite sides of the road, leaving the space open for the wizards to pass. *Walked!* Qel watched in amazement. When he looked closer at the trees, Qel could make out vague outlines of legs and arms formed from the trunk and branches. He could even make out the forms of eyes, nose and a mouth high up on their massive trunks. These "trees" were intelligent magical creatures clearly placed here by the elves to intimidate and perhaps defend if called upon to.

Startling Qel from his fascination, the elf backed off the road and called out, "Farewell Atlanteans. Remember, stay on the road and you will be safe."

Qel mounted and kicked his Lambei forward. Havacian followed as they slowly moved past the elves under the watchful eyes of the Tree Guardians and into the ancient land of the elves.

Chapter 15

The Sylvan Forest

The dark forest was devoid of the usual wilderness chatter that Qel was accustomed to as he and Havacian followed the roadway north toward Avalon. On either side, the foliage was thick and impassable, forcing them to stay on the road, which had transitioned from the paved thoroughfares of the Atlantean Territory to a strangely hard-packed soil after they passed the elven checkpoint. Even much of the light was shut out by the canopy of branches that interlocked above them, giving him the impression of riding through a broad tunnel. The foreboding atmosphere was not at all what he anticipated the Sylvan Forest to be like. The stories always portrayed the wilderness in Sylvan Kingdom as a bright and happy place with fairies and gentle wildlife dancing playfully among fruited limbs. The reality couldn't be further from that idyllic picture of nature.

"I did not expect this," he told Havacian.

His friend turned to him with a hunted look in his eyes. "I feel like they are watching us."

"They?"

"The trees," he whispered. "Do you think they are all Tree Guardians?"

"If they are, then the elves take their isolation very seriously." Qel looked around nervously at the thought.

"They do," Havacian leaned in a little when he spoke. "Master Curatei says there are only two roads into the Sylvan Kingdom. The first connects the capital to their only port in Andlang in the northeast and the second is the one we are on now. Apparently, the elves are very strict about who enters their homeland and those discovered trespassing are met with expulsion and a stern warning. It's worse if they committed a criminal act, in which case the punishment could be as harsh as death or sold as slaves to the Vikja."

194

"It doesn't seem like the lands of the elves are a very friendly environment to outsiders." Qel suppressed an involuntary shudder. "I wonder why so many Atlanteans come here for respite."

Havacian shook his head and muttered in a voice vaguely hopeful, "It must get better."

They passed another league in silence and still nothing had changed. Then in the distance ahead, Qel observed a group of men wearing brown robes adorned with feathers, fur and knotted cords tied with colored beads that dangled and clacked together by their sides as they walked on the side of the road. When they drew closer, Qel could clearly see that they were humans, six of them. Some had red hair or brown and one was blond. Their hoods were down, leaving their features unhidden for any to see, displaying intricate blue tattoos that covered their faces. They chatted amiably with one another as if they were strolling the shopping boulevards in Atlantis. When Qel and Havacian passed, the men made no effort to hide that they were humans and instead waved and smiled. Each of them wore a peculiar smooth stone hanging loosely about the neck on a short thong threaded through the thumb-sized hole in its center. The colored patterns of the stones shifted and swirled in a manner that appeared much like storm clouds.

It was a strange sight, thought Qel, to see these humans who Havacian had told him earlier were unwelcome in the Sylvan Kingdom. He looked over at his friend who, for reasons Qel could not begin to guess, had an animated expression on his face, yet he remained silent until they rode past the men and out of earshot.

"Do you know who they were?" Havacian was bursting with repressed excitement.

"No, I thought the elves didn't allow humans . . ." Qel cut off sharply when his mount abruptly shied in close to Havacian's.

He looked over, expecting to see a snake or raccoon that had surprised the Lambei on the dirt road. Instead, he found himself staring into the eyes of the largest wolf he had ever seen trotting casually beside them. As big as his Lambei was, the wolf's head easily cleared the height of the horse's back. Qel immediately prepared a spell in anticipation of attack when Havacian grabbed his arm.

"Wait," he said quietly as five more wolves trotted up behind the first.

The lead wolf looked over at him with strangely intelligent eyes and seemed to smile with its tongue lolling partway out. Qel was jarred to see the same stone on a tight thong around its neck that he had seen on the men they so recently passed. Then the pack picked up speed and moved at a jog away from them and into a break in the forest.

"Was that . . ." Qel stammered.

"Yes!" Havacian practically shouted. "They were druids! The only humans allowed in the Sylvan Forest. Master Curatei spoke a time or two about their mysterious centers of worship deep in the forests so remote that very few Atlanteans have ever seen them."

Qel's felt the excitement then too. He had just seen real druids and they had changed into wolves. Only in stories did he know of the druids and was sorry to have missed the transformation. Druids were almost unheard of in Atlantis. They were welcome like everyone else, but from what he understood, they didn't care much for cities. *This must be what true adventure is like,* he thought. *Long bouts of boredom interrupted by spontaneous moments of excitement!*

Riding on, Qel was relieved to see that the forest started to open up and they were no longer riding through the gloomy shaft of branches and vines. The sun filtered through the leaves overhead and he could see small glades with ponds of sparkling water. Farther on, shallow creeks and clear streams meandered one direction then another with an abundance of wildlife that seemed unafraid when they passed by. And birds chirped and cooed cheerfully—wonderfully familiar sounds—from every direction. It was as if the appearance of the druids had transformed the forest.

"The wilderness has finally come alive." Qel was elated.

Havacian laughed. "I was just noticing that, so caught up with the druids!"

As beautiful and pristine as everything around them appeared to be, Qel still couldn't shake the unavoidable feeling that they were being watched. By something in the forest or even the forest itself, he had no idea, but he knew that the feeling was real. He decided not to mention anything to Havacian, who seemed to be enjoying the beauty of the scenery around them, as long as he didn't feel they were in imminent danger.

"Why don't we stop for lunch in that glade with the pond?" Havacian pointed to a clearing a few paces off the road.

"I wish I knew how to fish," Qel jested. "I could cook us up a proper meal."

"Be wary," Havacian replied with a chuckle. "The fish here might have teeth."

For an hour they enjoyed the relaxation of the soft green grass under their backs, the gentle lap of water from the nearby stream and the occasional splash of a jumping fish. They ate sweet honey bread and strips of dried hartebeest garnered from the kitchens in the Aquilon Tower and washed it all down with watery ale from one of the nearby taverns. Although the day had started very dreary, Qel was feeling comfortable again in his surroundings, even happy.

"No wonder the elves are such an amicable folk." He inhaled deeply of the cool crisp air. It felt good in his lungs.

Havacian looked over. "Why is that?"

"They live among such beauty all their lives. I mean, not that Atlantis or any other place on the Emerald Isle is unattractive by any means, but it is almost prosaic in comparison."

"Maybe the elves feel the same way," Havacian suggested. "After all, they live a long time. Besides, I've only known you a few years and you're becoming pretty prosaic yourself."

Qel hit his friend playfully on the arm and they laughed vigorously for the first time since they were drunk in a tavern a few nights before. After an hour, Qel reluctantly suggested that they continue on their journey. A sign they passed earlier indicated that the next way station was twelve leagues farther and at their current pace they would be lucky to make it before nightfall.

Back on the road hours passed and the day wore on, but not Qel's spirits, he was enjoying every moment of this fabled wood. Soon enough, the light seeping through the trees faded to a dim amber and another sign posted next to the road indicated that the distance to the way station was four leagues, or approximately three hours if they picked up their pace.

"Looks like we will be riding in the dark soon," Havacian commented nervously. "Should we press on or try to prepare a camp?"

Qel chuckled at his friend's assumption that they could manage to make a proper camp. "Don't worry, Havacian; the road is clear and well maintained. I doubt the horses will find a rut or unseen crevasse to step in."

Within an hour the sun set and unlike earlier in the gloom when they first entered, the forest was still beautiful in the darkness, illuminated only by the waxing gibbous moon that Qel could see through the limbs above them. Curiously, tiny lights began to appear throughout the forest. At first, Qel thought they were fireflies, but rather than zipping about and blinking, they were steady and held their positions. Some closer to the road appeared to come from nooks and hollows in the trees. And then a few began moving purposefully in one direction or another without the many random deviations expected from an insect.

Not wishing to stray from the road in the darkness, Qel slowed down to peek within the lit hollow of a nearby tree. The light shone from what appeared to be a small home, complete with a little door and windows. Peering through a window, he could see tiny furnishings and décor like one might find in a dollhouse or children's toy.

"Fascinating," Havacian remarked beside him.

Qel just stared, unsure how to process what he was seeing. As they continued their study of the unexpected scene before them, the door suddenly opened, presenting a very small creature resembling a female elf standing only about a hand's width in height. The figure wore a little brown tunic, matching breeches and tiny boots. Her dark hair was long, disappearing down her back, where sprouted a pair of softly florescent, sheer wings. From a distance, Qel could never have seen this detail, but standing so close to the tree where the diminutive creature resided and looking into her home, they were nearly face to face.

"She must be a Fairy," Havacian whispered. "I have only read about them in stories, but never believed. . ."

The Fairy, who stood tapping her foot impatiently, shouted something unintelligible in a squeaky, high-pitched voice and in the blink of an eye flew over and tweaked Qel's nose before retreating back into her home, slamming the door.

Havacian laughed almost hysterically while they retreated to their horses. Qel sneezed uncontrollably for several moments, then started laughing as well.

"I guess she didn't appreciate us disturbing her privacy," Qel laughed. "She cast a minor spell on me that nearly made my head explode from sneezing. We better take care not to upset them."

Havacian nodded in agreement, still in the throes of laughter, unable to speak.

When they regained their composure, Qel gazed at the lights in the dark forest with new eyes. He could see hundreds of the little homes all around them with fairies moving here and there carrying miniature light globes mounted on the ends of tiny poles. They stood quietly for a while, enjoying the fantastic sight, until Qel thought he heard something coming from within the depths of the forest.

"Can you hear that?"

Havacian was also staring into the dark forest. "I wasn't sure at first, but yes, it sounds like singing."

The melody was simple and pure—a song that reflected the serenity of the night and solitude of the forest. Qel felt calmed by the singing and wondered if the voices were those of the fairies or something else as yet unseen. Fearing their continued presence might cause further disturbance, Qel mounted his Lambei, followed reluctantly by Havacian, and they continued along the road toward the way station, leaving the fairies behind. They rode in silence for a while, the quiet of the forest occasionally broken by the hoot of an owl or the yip of a coyote beyond the plod of their tired horse's hooves on the hard dirt. No one else was on the road at this hour. Not even a merchant or farmer.

An hour later, they arrived at the way station. It was a large two-story house built of stone with the entire roof covered by the roots of two gargantuan trees that stretched high into the dark canopy above. The soft glow of lanterns spilled from the windows and Qel could hear the echo of conversations from the outside when they rode near. Dismounting in front of the house, they were greeted by a young elf who politely took their horses around to the back to be rubbed down and stabled for the night while Qel and Havacian walked up a short stairway to the open front door.

The common room was filled with travelers. They were mostly Atlanteans that appeared to be merchants, a group of elves who might have been couriers and a table full of rowdy dwarfs who couldn't have been anything but tradesmen. High drama was taking its course around them, with the dwarfs drinking heavily and singing loudly, drawing the ire of the elves and the amusement of the Atlanteans. Weaving in between the groups of patrons were several beautiful elven attendants with trays crowded with mugs and platters of cheeses, fruits and seasoned meat pies. Qel's stomach grumbled at the delicious scents of the delicacies that teased his senses. He beckoned to one of the attendants and asked for the innkeeper before she disappeared into the kitchen again. While they waited, they sat at the end of a long table and ordered mugs of wine. Qel was mildly disappointed that they did not have Mekali, but he wasn't really surprised. Outside of Atlantis, it was considered very expensive and only the very affluent could afford it.

A mildly pudgy elf wearing a long smock over brown breaches and a silky green tunic soon appeared at their side. He had straight brown hair that hung loosly to his shoulders, a kindly face and a quick smile that made him immediately likable. "Good evening, gentlemen. Are you looking for a room this evening?"

"We are, sir, if one is available." Qel returned politely.

"I do have one left if you don't mind sharing."

Qel eagerly accepted. It was better than sleeping in the stable or camping on the side of the road. He knew nothing about camping. Then he and Havacian went upstairs to stow their packs before returning to the common room to have a meal.

"Odd how they follow their emotions to such absurd extremes." Qel commented. He and Havacian sat once again at a long table, out of earshot of the turbulent dwarfs and watched them with delight. "Drinking, carousing, singing and laughing loudly without a care for how they affect others around them."

"They are a far baser and more boisterous people than ours or the elves," Havacian agreed. "At least more so than our more mature brethren." He nodded toward the other Atlanteans in the room, all older than they were and quietly talking among themselves and a few of the elves. "One thing about the dwarfs, though, if the rumors are true, is that their word is as solid as the rock they live under in Tirnan Yog. It is said that befriending a dwarf is a friend for life and that their allies can always count on them to do as they say." Havacian echoed much the same sentiment as Qel's father.

Qel laughed suddenly. "Imagine what Atlantis would be like if our people were half as rambunctious."

"It's unimaginable," Havacian chuckled. "Our people are way too cerebral and obsessed with obligations and duty to ever allow themselves to have that much fun."

"And what about these elves?" asked Qel. "What does Master Curatei say about their ways and personalities?"

Havacian turned almost serious for a moment. "They are a very fun-loving, happy people that cherish their families and enjoy a symphonic relationship with nature that is inseparable from their spirit. Maybe nature is their spirit. It's all very mysterious." Havacian leaned in closer so not to be overheard. "But Master Curatei says the elves have a dark side as well. They exercise absolute control over their land, over who they allow to enter and where they are allowed to go without regard to rank or stature. Even Atlanteans have restrictions and especially the dwarfs, although the one exception seems to be the druids, probably because of their dedication to nature as well."

Qel found it all exciting and was once again glad Havacian was with him. It wasn't only because they were friends, but also because he appreciated the depth of knowledge Havacian possessed on so many subjects. He supposed that was an additional benefit of being the apprentice to the Keeper of Records for twenty years.

A group of Atlanteans and elves came through the front door and sat down next to them at the long table. Before long they were all chatting together over spiced wine. To Qel's chagrin, Havacian couldn't resist entertaining their new friends with the telling of their encounter with the fairy earlier. They all laughed appreciably, even the elves, patting Qel on the back. Havacian was turning out to be quite the story teller. Qel briefly mused that if his friend didn't find his calling as the next Keeper of Records at the Enclave he could always fall back on a career as a traveling minstrel.

The evening went long with good food, drink and fine companions until well after midnight when Qel and the others decided it was time to retire to their beds. The dwarfs were still as raucous as when they had first arrived and Qel wondered if they would continue all night or if they ever stopped at all. He wanted to learn more about them, but their lifestyle might prove exhausting if he and Havacian ever managed to find their way to the dwarfs Undermountain known as Tirnan Yog. Qel yawned as he followed Havacian to their room. That was a thought for another day.

——

The spring morning in the Sylvan Forest was cool and misty. Qel awoke late with the sun already well above the horizon, filtering light through the haze of earlier morning rain. Feeling rested and energized, he looked forward to the day ahead as they would be continuing their travels through the beautiful Sylvan Forest on their way to Avalon. Qel's moving about disturbed the still sleeping Havacian and before long the two were washed and dressed and on their way downstairs for breakfast. To Qel's delight, they were served bowls of mixed fruit and berries with a dollop of a porridge-like cream on top. It was absolutely delicious.

"Looks like we are the last ones to leave this morning," Qel guessed by the empty common room. "Even the drunken dwarfs have packed up and gone after the late night they must have had."

"Well, the dwarfs are a legend with their peculiar constitution for that sort of thing," laughed Havacian.

Soon after, the pair were back on the road again. They passed several groups of Atlantean and elven merchants going in the opposite direction toward Aquilon. Some drove carts while others used large floating disks to transport their goods. Although the elves imported far more than they exported, they still had a fair amount of trade and Qel knew that the Atlantean merchants were their primary agents. Fruits, nuts, berries and sweet syrups from tree sap were the elves' primary exports along with the famous elven silk, which was one of the most sought-after and expensive textiles in the Western Kingdoms. The elves wore it commonly and sold it very expensively. It was a mystery as to whether the silk was produced by a spider, worm, or some other creature and if the elves knew, they wouldn't say. Even Master Curatei, according to Havacian, was unclear about the origin of the textile. Elven silk was valued for its light weight, ease of taking dye and surprising durability, not to mention that it was the most comfortable fabric of any silk anywhere. Qel's mother owned a few pieces and raved about them whenever they were part of her ensemble. If it weren't for her, he might possibly have lived his entire life without knowing so much about elven silk.

Qel enjoyed observing the vibrant wildlife of feather, fin and fur that had been a rare sight over the past twenty years he resided in the Wizards Enclave. Of course, he'd seen the usual rat or songbird perched nearby in the courtyards and he often observed guard patrols mounted on the massive birds called Roc flying in formations over the city. In fact, he even witnessed a wild Roc fly over a year or so earlier. Apparently, it was a very unusual occurrence for a wild Roc to fly so close to a populated area and it caused quite a stir. At the time, he wasn't even sure he was looking at a Roc until Havacian pointed out the much smaller size of other birds in the sky nearby. Sadly, that was pretty much the extent of his examination of nature since he had become an apprentice.

Around midday, they came to a split in the road, with the main artery continuing over a bridge north toward Avalon and another curving off to the east along the river. There was no indication where the road, a trail really, led, so they agreed to follow it a short distance until they found a beautiful spot to break for a bite to eat and rest their horses. They chose an area where the trail ran very close to the river, out of sight of the main road. It was a perfect circle of dry, green grass where they could enjoy the quiet except for the gentle lapping of the river on its stone-ridden banks and the music of the birds singing in the afternoon sun.

Qel was removing the bread and cheese from their packs when he heard something splash upriver from where they sat. It sounded heavy and far more substantial than a fish jumping to snatch an insect, if there were even fish of that sort in this river. Then it was followed by the sound of something large moving quickly and without regard to the noise it made through the forest. At first it came straight toward them and then suddenly angled away, snapping branches as it went. No wild animal would be so careless, even Qel knew that.

"Did you hear that?" he asked Havacian nervously.

Havacian's eyes were larger than goose eggs. "I did."

Looking back to the river, not far from where he heard the splash, Qel saw what appeared to be a large leather sack bobbing in the water, carried toward them on the swift current. He stared at it curiously, wondering what it could be and then something moved inside the bag. Qel's heart froze in his chest as he watched the movements become more frenzied in the quickly saturating fabric as he realized with horror that if they didn't do something quickly, whatever was inside would drown once the bag slipped below the surface.

"There is something alive inside the bag!" Havacian exclaimed, mirroring Qel's thoughts. "And it's sinking fast!"

Focusing intently, Qel began to cast a spell. Seconds later, he was levitating above the ground. Keeping part of his mind focused on maintaining the invocation, he slowly stepped off the bank and moved across the top of the water.

"Qel," Havacian shouted.

Qel was busy trying to keep his concentration from wavering and couldn't afford to be distracted. "Be still, Havacian."

He would have to time his effort perfectly to grab the bag. If he missed, he wouldn't be able to outrun the current by chasing it. The bag bobbed closer and closer until he could hear the sound of desperate crying coming from inside. It sounded like a child.

"Qel," Havacian repeated.

"I'm going to try to catch it," Qel replied. Was that an exaggerated sigh he heard from his friend? What was wrong with him?

The bag was close and moving more quickly than he expected. He tried to focus and time its movement, searching for the best place to grab it. Then it was suddenly below him and he lunged for it, his hands slipping off the slick edge of the wet material. *Damn! Now, what do I do?* Thinking quickly, he turned and ran back over the water toward where his horse stood nibbling calmly at the grass as if nothing unusual had occurred. Qel had only seconds to mount his horse and sprint down ahead of the sack for another try. In his head, he calculated that the bag would be long submerged before he could get ahead of it again, but in his heart, Qel knew that a child's life was at stake and he had to do anything he could to save it.

After only a few steps, Qel realized that running while levitated was not the same as when his feet were touching the ground. In his current state, it was more like swimming and he found his arms and legs flailing wildly in an effort to move forward quickly. His progress was agonizingly slow and he was growing desperate by the second. Even if he quit the levitation and dropped into the water, he would never be able to catch up to the sack by swimming and it would take him at least as long to swim against the current to the shore near his horse. His mind racing, Qel struggled with what to do.

"Got it!" Havacian's voice rang out. Qel looked over to where his friend was standing a little farther downriver and saw to his eternal relief that the bag was on the bank of the river in front of him. The flow of the river still held the unnatural current that had taken the bag to the shoreline.

Qel felt like an idiot. Havacian was a Water Wizard. So stunned by his own stupidity, he lost his concentration and fell into the river just a few paces from the edge. Fortunately, he fell into the same current that had taken the bag and seconds later he ended up nearly on top of it.

Havacian pulled the bag onto dry land and then helped Qel out of the water. "Are you OK?" he asked.

The only injury Qel had received was to his ego, but he put that aside for the moment and crawled over to where the bag was flopping around violently. "Stop!" Qel shouted at the bag. "Stop moving so we can cut you out!" Incredibly, the thing in the bag began to struggle even more desperately.

"Havacian, I'll hold it down and you carefully, *carefully*, cut it out!" he yelled to his friend and then flattened himself on the bag, doing his best to restrict its rapid movements. Qel was happy it was smaller than him, but it was strong and he felt blows to his legs and sides that could have come from a grown adult. From inside he could hear sounds of the child screaming and crying in a language that sounded vaguely familiar, but his attention was entirely on holding the child still and he couldn't spare the time to listen.

Finally, Havacian took hold of the crimped opening that was bound by a tightly knotted rope and cut the binding. Immediately, out popped a screaming little elf girl about the age of a human toddler. She was hysterical and attempted to run away, but Qel gripped one of her arms and whispered shushing sounds to calm her. Having no experience with children, since he was the youngest of four siblings, he had no idea what to do to quiet the child. Havacian apparently had no ideas either, as he stood wide-eyed and staring as if she were some crazed animal. Qel was almost at wit's end when he decided to do what he thought his mother would have done in this situation. He pulled the child close . . . and hugged her.

The little girl went limp in Qel's arms, exhausted and sobbing. He stroked her long blonde hair and quietly sang a tune his own mother often sang to him as a child. So many memories came flooding into him, beautiful memories of his childhood he had not thought about in years. It felt natural and right to hold this small child in his arms and he instinctively kissed her on the crown of her head. "You're safe now."

Chapter 16

Chasing Ogres

Havacian rushed over and knelt down beside Qel, who was still holding the young elf child. Qel looked up and smiled and then his attention was drawn to movement in the forest behind his friend. His smile disappeared. Three mounted elves burst out of the woods, leaped off their horses in a single smooth move and sprang toward them. Havacian only had seconds to react and to his credit, managed to conjure a wind barrier that surrounded the two of them and the child just before the charging elves reached them. Their attackers must have somehow sensed the barrier and just stopped short of running into it. Qel, still a little slower than Havacian, had a firebolt ready to burst forth from his hands in case the elves managed to overcome the barrier. Yet, they made no move against them and simply stood glaring from angry eyes under furled brows.

Qel thought the elves look young, two men and a woman armed with bows and narrow curved swords. Only then did he recognize that their swords were sheathed and their bows were strapped to their backs. The woman stepped forward, gesturing wildly and she was joined by the two males shouting loudly at them through the barrier. Qel could not understand what they were saying with all of them speaking at once, but the expressions on their faces weren't angry, they seemed more pleading and desperate—especially the woman.

Finally, the eldest male elf quieted the others and calmly turned to them. "This is the child's mother." He pointed to the young elf woman.

Immediately Qel understood. "Havacian, drop the barrier."

"Are you mad? They will tear us apart!"

"Trust me, Havacian. Their only concern is the welfare of this little girl." Qel was unconsciously stroking the child's hair and he could feel her breathing calmly with her face buried in his chest.

Havacian sighed. "I hope you are right about this." He released the barrier.

To Qel's relief, the elven men did not move. The female elf fell to her knees in front of Qel. He still held tightly to the little girl and only then realized the child was unconscious. The woman made no attempt to pull the child away. Instead, she put her arms out and patiently waited for Qel to hand the little girl to her. He tenderly lifted the child and put her in her mother's arms. The two male elves standing over them watched with looks of grave concern on their sharp features. With the child in her arms, the woman began to gently shake and speak to the little girl in their own language. At first, she did not move and Qel feared that the trauma had been too much for her to bear. Then after a moment, to his great relief, she stirred and opened her large blue eyes. Her mother clutched her close again and began to cry. The two male elves dropped to their knees beside her surrounding the woman and child with their arms in a group hug. Qel motioned to Havacian to slowly move away a few paces with him as they silently watched what appeared to be a happy family reunion.

A moment later, the older male elf stood up, calmly walked over and bowed. "Thank you for protecting this child. We were fearful that we would not be able to retrieve her from the monster that abducted her. My name is AelrindelRokalyn, you may call me Aelrindel if it is easier. The child's mother is my sister, VnaeStrindricina and that is her husband, TridiStrindricinia—Vnae and Tridi, if you please. Did you see which way the Ogre ran?"

"We never saw an Ogre," Qel replied, "but there was something big in the forest that must have been running with all the noise it made. I believe it was heading east."

A dark look came over the elf's face. "Three Ogres entered our village during the night and abducted two of our children. We killed one of the beasts and recovered one child safe and unharmed not far outside the village. Another ran east with a goat, pursued by warriors from the village and the third came in this direction with my sister's child."

Havacian spoke up, "Why would the Ogre go to all the trouble of abducting the child only to throw her in the river?"

"I believe the Ogre knew we were almost upon him." Aelrindel glanced at the little girl, now calm and nodding reassurances to her parents. "Most likely he threw the child into the river to create a distraction and get away."

"I'm glad we were here to help," said Qel. "Will the child be OK?"

"She will be fine," Aelrindel assured them. "If you had not been here to retrieve her from the water, I doubt we would have found her alive, if at all. The Sylvan Forest has a way of quickly reclaiming its own."

The female elf, Vnae, walked over to them, holding her now sleeping little girl. "Thank you for saving my child from drowning in the river. It is a service that will not be forgotten."

Before Qel could respond, Vnae turned to her brother. "You're wasting time," she told him harshly. "Take Tridi and go after them. I expect it to be dead before it can escape the forest."

Aelrindel looked at her skeptically. "We have the child back. What is the use of running down the Ogre?"

Vnae's pale complexion deepened visibly to her neckline, but when she spoke, her tone was calm and matter-of-fact despite her visible anger. "If you don't make examples of them, then others of their kind will do this again in our village or another. Next time those they abduct may not be so lucky. How would you like that on your conscience AelrindelRokalyn?"

The tall elf took the sharp rebuke stoically, responding with a simple nod. Qel wondered which of the siblings was the elder. He imagined one of his sisters speaking to him that way and guessed that Vnae was probably older, although it was difficult to tell with elves.

Vnae, apparently satisfied that her instructions would be followed, turned away and walked back toward her husband standing near the water's edge inspecting the bag that had held his child. Aelrindel quietly watched her back for a moment, then turned to face Qel and Havacian. "She is right. The Ogres know that they are not supposed to leave the mountains and they have to know that we will not tolerate invasions into our homes."

Aelrindel looked back to where Vnae stood in conversation with her husband and spoke loudly enough for them to hear. "Take the child back home, Vnae. Your husband and I will find the Ogre. Come quickly, Tridi. Time is running short."

Tridi brought his wife's horse and helped her mount with the sleepy child held securely in her arms. Vnae circled her horse back in the direction from which they had come, made a deferential nod to her husband and disappeared into the forest. No one spoke a word when she departed and then Aelrindel turned his attention back to Qel and Havacian. "You are wizards from Atlantis fresh out of the Tower." It was more a statement than a question.

"How do you know we are not masters of our craft on important business *for* the Tower?" Havacian stood next to Qel bearing a rigid, indignant posture. Qel almost laughed.

The elf returned his glare flatly. "You are far too young and you fumble your spells like children. Besides, where do you think all the apprentices go when they are released on 'Discovery'? Here, Avalon."

Havacian's retort was almost juvenile. "We stopped you with our wind barrier, didn't we?" Qel wanted to jab his friend in the ribs with his elbow.

Aelrindel laughed. "Boy, in the time it took for you to see us, decide what spell to cast, piss yourself and finally cast it, you would have been dead if we were trying to kill you."

Qel felt the prickling heat of embarrassment on his neck, but he was also irritated by this arrogant elf. They may have been "fumbling their spells like children," yet they had saved the life of the elves' little girl. It seemed to him that some gratitude might be in order. Rather than allow Havacian to continue the downward spiral the conversation was taking, Qel decided to stop the metaphorical bleeding of their ego.

"It is true that we are recent graduates of the Imperial Order of Wizards and we are, as you say, on 'Discovery'. It is also very true that we still have much to learn. What is your point?"

"Only this," Aelrindel's tone softened. "You want adventure? Ride with us. We might need a spellcaster even if there is barely a wizard between you." The elf shrugged and turned to walk toward his waiting mount.

Qel looked over at his friend uncertainly. "What do you think, Havacian? Are we ready for this?"

"It is only one Ogre," Havacian reasoned hesitantly, "and the elves seem competent enough without us. Why not? Avalon will still be there when we are done."

"I agree," Qel said. "And what better guides could we ask for to explore the Sylvan Forest?"

Both Tridi and Aelrindel were sitting on their horses a few paces away, casually waiting for them when Qel shouted over, "We'll go."

"I thought you would." Aelrindel's tone held no humor. "Now why don't the two of you mount up so we can get underway? I'm sure the Ogre won't have the decency to wait for us to work things out."

Once in the forest, it didn't take long for the elves to pick up the Ogre's trail. It was even apparent to Qel which way it fled with all the broken branches and trampled vegetation left in the lumbering beast's wake. Aelrindel rode a few steps ahead before turning in his saddle to face them. "Ogres are not graceful and will leave a trail that we can easily follow, at least as long as we are in the forest and grasslands. The problem is that they can run as fast as a horse can trot and keep it up for far longer. I doubt we will catch him in the forest. He is headed east toward the Azure Mountains, where their kind live. He will feel safe among the rocks and will need to rest. We will likely find him in a cave or a crack in the earth if we find him at all. The danger is that there may be others nearby willing to come to his aid once he is cornered."

Qel suddenly wondered if perhaps they were in over their heads. This Ogre hunt sounded far more dangerous than he initially anticipated, especially if they were going into the creature's territory to track it down. *We wanted adventure,* he mused. *Now we have it.*

"How long will it take us to travel to the mountains?" Qel was surprised he had not thought to ask earlier.

"When it gets dark, we will make camp, since it will be too hazardous for our horses to continue. We should arrive at the edge of the Ogres' territory by midafternoon a night and a day after that," Aelrindel called over his shoulder.

The small party followed in the wake of the Ogre for several more leagues before the light began to fade and the roots and potholes scattered along the way became challenging to navigate safely. Aelrindel led them a short distance farther and then announced his intent to set up camp in a small clearing. Qel was embarrassed when he realized that they had not come prepared to camp, but the elves proved to be helpful and gave them a crash course on gathering materials for shelter, starting a small fire and scavenging for edible roots and berries in the forest.

They worked quickly in the failing light and by the time darkness blanketed the forest, Tridi had several grouse and woodcocks roasting over the fire next to a stew of wild vegetables and greens. Qel half expect the forest to light up with a community of fairies, but to his disappointment, it remained dark and the chirps of wood frogs and crickets were their only company.

"What is the name of your village, Aelrindel?" Havacian placed a folded blanket on the ground next to the campfire where they were all gathered and sat down.

"It is not my home village. I am here to visit my sister and her family. In any case, the village you speak of is called Braetling."

"Are you from another nearby village, then?"

Tridi, who had spoken so little since they met, barked a laugh. "My brother is a pretentious elf from Avalon. He has graced our home with his visit. Perhaps some of his highborn culture will rub off on us country elves!"

Aelrindel pushed Tridi's shoulder playfully and they both laughed. Perhaps the elves had some humor in them after all. Qel turned to Tridi. "How often must you defend your village from incursions by Ogres and the like?"

Tridi sighed and traced the end of a stick through the dirt. "The Ogres know they are supposed to stay in the Azure Mountains. That is their territory and no elf will violate it without just cause. Once in a while, though, a young Ogre will enter puberty and its hormones will get the best of him. Sometimes they will come out of the mountains to pick a fight or steal livestock. It's mostly harmless and we can usually run them back into the mountains without any bloodshed, except for a few arrows in their bum." Tridi smiled briefly before turning serious again. "But this invasion into our village, and especially the abductions, are a new extreme, even for Ogres. If we had not recovered both children unharmed, half of Avalon would be in the Azures killing Ogres."

Qel had to ask, although he knew he might not like the answer, "Why would they want the children in the first place?"

Tridi looked at Aelrindel, then cast his gaze back to the ground. Aelrindel answered for him. "They are easy to carry and their meat is still soft with fat."

Qel felt sick. "You mean they would eat them?"

Tridi nodded. "Sadly, yes. That is why we have to track down this Ogre and make an example of him. Hopefully, their elders will see reason."

Aelrindel shifted to lie on his side, supported by his elbow. "We will make them see reason if we must."

Qel didn't like the sound of that. "What about these elders you speak of?"

"Ogres roam independently or for a while with a mate. They are not traditionally tribal and do not live in groups; however, the oldest and wisest among them are called the elders and they set the rules by which all Ogres must live." Tridi cast his stick into the fire. "There have even been cases of very intelligent Ogres with the ability to cast spells like a wizard or priest. How they could ever learn such a thing, we do not know, but like every secluded culture, the Ogres are probably far more complex than even the wisest among us realize."

Qel glanced over at Havacian. His friend's full attention was on the conversation and he almost laughed at how Havacian was naturally fascinated with the whole idea of a society of Ogres. They learned very little about Ogres during their studies at the Enclave and it was generally assumed, as Tridi stated, that Ogres were solitary and dim-witted creatures. Qel dozed shortly after Havacian took over the conversation asking questions about the Ogres until Tridi finally suggested they get some rest since they were planning to leave at dawn. Qel looked forward to getting a few hours of sleep and not even worry over Ogres could keep him awake, so tired was he from the events of the day. Pulling his blanket up close, he drifted off to the soothing sounds of the night deep within the Sylvan Forest.

———

Aelrindel woke everyone before dawn.

Qel washed his face in a nearby stream and joined Havacian for a hasty breakfast of nut butter and hard flatbread Qel's mother packed for them. Then they mounted up as soon as it was light enough to safely ride through the forest without risking injury to the horses. Aelrindel advised them that they were still about a day and a half from the mountains, twenty leagues or so, and needed to take advantage of every minute of daylight if they hoped not to lose too much ground on the Ogre.

"I feel surprisingly rested today," Qel commented to Havacian, who was riding next to him once again. It was a welcome change when the trees and underbrush occasionally thinned enough to afford them the opportunity to ride side by side and speak to one another.

Havacian nodded his agreement. "We are used to the sounds of the ever-busy Enclave in the center of one of the busiest cities on the planet. I suppose the tranquility of the forest allowed us to rest peacefully for the first time in two decades."

Qel chuckled at that. Havacian was probably more right than he knew.

"Have you thought about how we might deal with this Ogre if it comes down to it?" Havacian's tone had shifted. He sounded more serious – and fearful.

"I expect the elves to take the lead." Qel, too, was nervous about the idea of confronting an Ogre. Or Ogres. And he hoped that Aelrindel was not expecting to rely on their magic abilities to carry them through. "In the meantime, I'm going to continue to practice my lessons, just as I promised the Battle Wizard. I have a feeling our adventure will present far more peril than either of us expected before it's over."

The going was smooth the entire day, with good weather and a cool breeze that filtered through the leaves and branches with a hypnotic rustling that made Qel drowsy. Bright sunlight illuminated the dense deciduous forest with intense rays of sunlight that cascaded down through the canopy above them, showing the clear path the Ogre carelessly plodded. Aelrindel inevitably informed them that he was all but certain that the Ogre would make it into the Azure Mountains before they could catch up with it—even if only by a few hours.

By nightfall, they had successfully covered nearly fifteen leagues before stopping to make camp in a clearing near a slow-moving creek. Given the prior evening's instructions, Qel and Havacian were more capable of erecting their shelters and gathering the roots and greens for stew with little direction from the elves. Tridi found six forest grouse to add to the stew and again they ate well. Qel was impressed with how swiftly Tridi returned with the game he hunted each night. It was almost as if he just walked into the forest, picked them up and brought them back. He assumed the elf must be a very competent woodsman. From a young age Qel had read much about the elves' close relationship with nature. He nearly laughed out loud at the thought of the animals merely sacrificing themselves for the elf's dinner.

No different than the previous night, Havacian was full of questions about Ogres and the elves. Fortunately, both Tridi and Aelrindel were very accommodating and even appeared to enjoy the conversation. Qel was so tired from the long ride and mentally exhausted from continually working through his lessons that he decided to lie by the campfire watching the flames and allow the low murmur of voices lull him to sleep.

Qel slept that night undisturbed and woke before Aelrindel had the chance to wake him. Like the day before, they departed just after dawn and rode the last few leagues to the rocky foothills of the Azure Mountains. The trees thinned considerably as the ground became harder, scattered with rocks and boulders bigger than houses jutting through the softer earth, and by the time they stopped at the edge of the low mountain range, the forest had receded into scattered copses and thickets where the roots of the undergrowth could find bare purchase. It was summertime and although it was always freezing this far north, the snow and ice retreated to higher elevations. Qel was used to seeing the impressive Atlas Mountains, whose soaring spires were visible from the City of Atlantis and covered in white powder throughout the entire year. Still, the Azure Mountains were no less impressive, if not for their size, for their grace. Snow covered the long, smooth, dome-shaped ridges here as well, with vast swaths of green alpine trees and grassy plains that ran through the valleys and saddles between them. The flora was interrupted by bare rock shelves and rocky escarpments that were quilted with colorful lichen and dotted with shrub vegetation above the tree line. Qel wondered how they would ever find the Ogre they trailed with all the caves, cracks and crevasses that were visibly abundant at every elevation. Surely it would be like finding a moonstone dropped in the ocean.

"Are there many Ogres up there?" Havacian gestured to the rolling peaks spread out before them.

"It's hard to say since they are never observed in groups. We don't know if they have a religion, form family bonds, or even mate for life. They are certainly intelligent, some more than others, but they lead a brutish existence that is more akin to animals' than anything approaching what we would consider civilized behavior. Considering that they are a creature of the Tuatha De and therefore unnatural, we are not attuned to their behavior." Tridi scrunched his elegant nose in obvious distaste of the creatures.

"They are a creation of the Tuatha De?" Qel was surprised. That was never part of what he had read about them.

"Yes." Tridi smiled. "You must have been dozing when Havacian and I were discussing it last night.

That bit of information was a bit distressing to him. The histories were clear about the folly of the Tuatha De and their experiments over three millennia ago. They used powerful magic to alter and create hundreds of species—from Giants and Orks to Dragons and other monstrosities—for the purpose of utilizing their unique abilities laboring in the mines, constructing building in their cities and transportation. Centuries later, the Tuatha De's own accounts speak of how the results of their dubious judgment finally spiraled out of control when the more intelligent creatures became malcontent and violent, fighting among one another in competition for food and dominance. Soon after, the violence spilled over to the general population and the beasts went on a rampage, killing thousands of Tuatha De who were not of the Blood because they were vulnerable and an easy food source for the powerful creatures. That was the catalyst that split the masters of the Tuatha De, the so-called 'Blood', into factions that led to civil war before the creatures they had created were banished to the lands of Fomoire and any further creations forbidden forever.

Qel roused from his ruminations, focused on the view ahead. The expanse of the mountain range before them was overwhelming. "So now what? Do we wander around the mountains until we find one, or can you track it over the hard rock?"

Tridi appeared amused. "No, wizard, Aelrindel and I have decided on a new strategy: they will come to us." Saying that, the elf dismounted and pulled out what appeared to be a ram's horn from his saddlebag. This one must have been exceptional, as it was covered with gold leafing and bore several markings in the elves' ancient language that seemed to glow with a blue illumination of their own. Tridi walked a few feet ahead of the group and blew through the horn. Incredibly, the sound that erupted from it echoed across the entirety of the mountain range. He blew the horn one more time and then walked back to the others. "Now we wait," he said.

Aelrindel dismounted and hobbled his horse near the tree line. "We might as well build a fire."

Qel and Havacian dismounted as well and went about collecting scraps of wood.

Tridi blew the horn again around noon. For the next two hours the men sat at the edge of the forest around the small campfire, occasionally scanning the mountain range for any movement. So far they had seen nothing resembling an Ogre. Qel reasoned that the magically enhanced horn could probably be heard for leagues into the mountains and whoever Tridi was expecting to respond to the call might still be far away.

Another hour passed and then, to the apparent astonishment of even the elves, a boulder rolled over not fifty paces away where a head popped up from a hole beneath it.

"There," Tridi announced and gestured in the direction of the rocky slope. "They have arrived."

The head glanced around, squinting in the sunlight, its saucer-sized eyes adjusting from the darkness it must have come from below. After a moment, a massive body slowly emerged from the secreted hole.

"So that's an Ogre," Qel stated to no one in particular.

Tridi, very serious, nodded, "Yes, one of the smaller ones."

The elf's words sent a streak of ice up Qel's spine. This was a smaller one? He studied the Ogre carefully as it lumbered toward them. The beast was ugly. There was no other way to describe it. Every part of the Ogre's face was an exaggeration—large eyes, bulbous nose, wide mouth bearing a few grotesquely protruding teeth, elongated ears ending at a point on top similar to that of an elf and massively hairy. All of this atop a thick neck and an even thicker body ending with limbs as big around as many of the trees they had passed in the forest on their way to this place. With no other perspective to compare it to, one might think the ogre was very short. Just the opposite, this "small" Ogre easily towered over Atlantean and elf by at least its head and shoulders. They were, without a doubt, powerful humanoids capable of moving huge boulders and probably felling trees if they were of a mind to do so. The Ogre's clothes were a patchwork of leather, furs, skins and cloth with a pair of open-toed sandals laced up his muscular shins. From the top of his head, a tuft of unkempt brown hair swayed with each step he took on the hard rock.

The Ogre came to a stop a pace away and passed his gaze over them. Qel glanced at Tridi, standing like a stone statue facing the Ogre, Aelrindel a pace behind him, leaning casually on a tree and Havacian standing open-mouthed, as if unsure whether or not to believe what he was seeing. *Aelrindel was leaning casually against a tree?* What was wrong with that elf? The Ogre could be on top of them in half a heartbeat and he leaned there as casually as if Tridi were facing down a chipmunk.

A deep rumble drew his attention back to the Ogre as he began to speak. At least he realized the creature was speaking once the words started to form so that he could understand them. Qel was initially startled by the strange, harsh speech that the Ogre was practically spitting out before it dawned on him that his own language must be entirely different from the one they spoke among themselves.

"Tridi elf, why have you called me here?" The Ogre sounded annoyed at being summoned.

Tridi responded in the firm, confident voice of a man who expected to be listened to, but with respect as if addressing a peer,

"Elder, you know I would not call without urgent circumstance. For as long as the Elves and Ogres have lived in this land, we have depended upon each other for safety and survival. Your people guard the Azure Mountains against outsiders and ours guard the Sylvan Forest. Your people stay in the mountains in peace and ours stay in the forest in peace."

The Ogre shrugged. "So it is. But you are not here for peace."

Tridi shrugged back. "So it is. We are here because three of your own have come to our village and taken our little ones. One of yours died in the village and we found one child; another threw our child into the river and then ran away. We found that child. The third one of yours ran away with a goat, which we did not recover."

A thick, singular brow darkened the eyes of the Ogre. "Two of ours have returned to the mountains, two of yours have been found and one of ours is no more. The debt has been paid with the life of our own, unless you are here for the goat."

Tridi took a step forward, his voice heavy with anger. "I would not chase one of yours here for a goat! The debt has *not* been paid. You know that your own cannot come to the forest and ours may not enter the mountains. The two that violated the agreement between yours and mine must be punished."

The Ogre was silent as he considered the obligation of his people. Then he turned around and bellowed deeply to the mountains behind him. Qel thought the move strange and wondered if the creature was simply wildly vocalizing its frustration or if it was something else. Tridi and Aelrindel never moved or reacted and it wasn't long before Qel understood that the bellow was a call.

A call that was answered.

From behind boulders and out of the ground stepped three massive Ogres. Two were a head taller than and half again as wide as the Elder Ogre before them. They wore what appeared to be discarded parts and pieces of leather and metal armor, most of which looked to have once been worn by human-sized men. The style of it appeared like that worn by the Vikja. The third Ogre was about the same size and age of the elder and wore tattered robes in layers that hung down to his sandals and he leaned on a staff the size of a small tree. As they moved slowly down the slope to where the elder stood, Qel detected a rustling from behind. He swung his gaze back in a panic, fearful they were being surrounded, only to see five colossal trees moving from the forest to stand behind their group. Their trunks were split at the base to form massive legs and they had two thickly knotted arms that swayed as they walked. Looking closely, he could make out a rough outline of facial features high on their trunks just before branches split away, heavy with leaves. The most unnerving aspect of their features were their eyes, which glowed with a solid, silvery blue light from deep within. The last thing Qel noticed before turning back to the Ogres was that Aelrindel was no longer leaning on a damn tree. He appeared alert and ready. *Ready. For what?* Tridi still had not moved a muscle, standing his ground while he watched the Ogre Elders talk.

"That one must be a wizard or priest. I can sense something about him," Havacian whispered to Qel.

Qel nodded. "I think you're right. I can sense it too. If things go badly and this turns violent, let's focus on that one."

Finally, after some time in discussion with his fellow Ogres, the Elder turned back to Tridi. "It has been decided. The two who violated our pact will be beaten and sent to live by the sea until they learn wisdom. This should settle the debt." If the expression it held was anything other than a scowl, Qel couldn't imagine what it was, but the tone it took had softened.

Tridi did not immediately respond. Instead, he took a moment to consider each Ogre standing before him. "I agree to your terms. We leave the mountains and your own in peace."

The Ogre responded in kind. "We leave the forest and your own in peace."

Without another word, the Ogres disappeared into the rocky crevasses and holes they had so mysteriously appeared from while Tridi walked the men and horses back into the forest. The animated

Tree Guardians departed as well, in separate directions, disappearing into the shaded depths of the forest and leaving only a vague scent of oak in their wake.

Tridi expelled a deep breath and turned to face Qel and the others. "Well, that went better than expected. We are lucky to have had a reasonable Elder respond to the call rather than a belligerent one."

Qel gestured back toward the forest. "I'm sure your tree friends were a motivating factor as well."

Havacian sounded a little miffed. "You could have told us about the Tree Guardians in advance. I was so startled I almost loosed a lightning bolt."

Aelrindel laughed from behind them. "What fun would we have together if there were no surprises?"

Chapter 17

Belthagore

The dark shadow could sense it drawing closer, the powerful magic that it was seeking . . . that it craved. The shade glided through the air unaffected by the chill, the wind, or any other physical influence of this world, for it was not of this world. Its home was once the Infernal Planes, a hellish dimension created by the old gods as a prison for its kind and others like it far more powerful. But no longer; it was free again. It didn't know how or by what method it and the others won release, but when the cracks in their prison appeared, they burst through and never looked back to question why.

The dark mass was aware of the thickly forested mountainous region below, in the heart of what the inhabitants of this world called The Wilds. The lure of power was close, very close. It could almost feel the intensity, the delicious enticement of control within its grasp. Once he sensed it, the shade was drawn to it with relentless abandon like a moth to a flame. Except that this moth could control the flame.

In the distance, it "saw" a wide crack in the face of a high, sheer cliffside. That was its destination. That's where it would find the creature that wielded the power it so desperately desired. That would be the place of its rebirth into this world as a thing of supremacy, dominance and overwhelming command over this land's creatures great and small.

Entering the break in the rock, the phantom flew swiftly down the winding, rough-hewn passage that led into the darkest depths of the mountain until it widened into a massive cavern with several smaller natural corridors twisting away into the gloomy voids around the perimeter. Pausing at the brink of the vast expanse, the thing observed a darker shape than even the impenetrable darkness that surrounded it. The shade was not afraid, nor did it harbor any doubts, even if the outcome of this encounter was far from certain. It was driven by a singular motivation for power and if it prevailed in the struggle that was to come, then it would wield more power and influence than it had at any time during its entire existence.

Sensing that the dark shape below was dreaming, the incorporeal shadow plunged into those dreams with little effort. This one had few defenses in it's current state and although it was a creature of great physical strength, magical abilities and a strong will, it was deprived of the psionic talents essential to its survival in this contest.

Stirred from a deep slumber by an ancient instinct for danger, the great beast reacted with sudden violence. Fire erupted through the cavern illuminating the creature's huge form, the flash of light glistening briefly off scales black as a starless night. Broad wings beat ferociously against the stale air, while a long, flexible tail tipped with long piercing barbs whipped to and fro, seeking satisfaction. Claws, sharp as daggers, rent the air below a thick serpentine neck supporting a huge spiked head that flailed and snapped angrily at imagined dangers between wild bursts of flame from its sharp-fanged maw.

Inside the creature's consciousness, the shade began to take control. The first thing it discovered was that the beast was an ancient Black Dragon and that his name was Belthagore. It was furious that his long hibernation had been interrupted by something unknown. The invader permeated the unprotected consciousness of the Black Dragon's mind revealing the creature's thoughts, feelings and memories. It had successfully ambushed the ancient beast and could sense the distress and confusion of being awakened like this. Even still, the dragon possessed a strong will and as surprised as the dragon might be, the shade knew that it would not be easy to dominate this one's mind completely. Yet, that was what had to be done if the shade hoped to gain complete control of the creature and all of its powers. It could sense Belthagore's struggle to gain clarity in his own mind and banish his unwelcome invader. The shade responded with psionic strength fueled by unadulterated evil, anger and aggression innate to its kind, spinning barrier after barrier within the venerable dragon's cognizance, little by little depriving the beast of its own awareness, thoughts and intellect.

For many days the silent conflict raged back and forth on an invisible, mental battlefield. The shade could sense that Belthagore was not prepared for a struggle of this magnitude and the dragon soon began to give up control a little at a time. This great worm was used to dominating by brute force and magical abilities to gain the advantage in a world where his greatest challenges were chasing down forest animals or terrorizing the pathetic humans that populated the lands nearby. The poor beast had not had a serious challenge since the Breaking of the Tuatha De and if the shade could have felt compassion, it would have understood that its true advantage was not because of its own power, but the despair of a creature with barely a will to live.

In the last moments, before the Ancient Black Dragon known as Belthagore lost his identity forever, the shade sensed a final parting thought, *What does it matter?* And then the venerable worm slipped into oblivion. The shade, no longer just a shade, now possessed the form and abilities of a formidable, three-thousand-year-old Black Dragon, a commanding host that could challenge the gods themselves! With the dragon within his control, the shade known as Tephras, Greater Demon of Anger, would be ready for any challenge.

The demon searched Belthagore's memories to find out more about this creature under his control, its history and its potent capabilities. He learned that dragons were once fairly common before the age of humanoids, so many millennia ago. They were not magical creatures then, were physically smaller and lived together in clans. Most hunted in pairs or groups and in those days stalked prey like any predator with claw, tooth and instinct, living typical life spans of about forty years.

Their lives changed forever when the first primitive humans appeared.

At first, humans were a welcome source of food, but their populations grew very quickly and they began to expand farther and farther into the dragons' ancient territories. In only a few hundred years, humans developed the use of advanced weapons like powerful longbows and protective armor, machines that threw great bolts or boulders and they were no longer so easily hunted. Before long, the humans turned the tables and hunted the dragons for their colorful scales, blood said to cure disease and for sport. Thousands of the creatures died. No longer safe to live in clans or hunt in groups, the dragons fled to remote areas away from human habitation and they became solitary creatures that jealously defended their territories against each other.

Then the Tuatha De appeared in the north.

They were a magical race of humanoids, not at all like the humans except in appearance and they took a particular interest in dragon-kind. Over many centuries, hundreds of dragons were captured and compelled to breed new generations altered by the dark magic of the Tuatha De. These new dragons benefited from higher intellect, magic-like powers and the ability to speak. The goal of the Tuatha De was to utilize them for transportation, labor and eventually war. More centuries passed and the dragons' evolution progressed. They were split into several species identifiable by the color of their scales and they developed high-functioning capabilities that rivaled even their masters. In the end, the experiment was interrupted by civil war between factions of the Tuatha De. It became known as the Breaking. The dragons fought for the Tuatha De and against each other until they realized that they didn't need to be the tools of war for these humanoids any longer. They turned against their masters and those few that lived, escaped into The Wilds. Belthagore was among those that fled. He was a young dragon back then. The weaker dragons who stayed behind were captured and ultimately banished to Fomoire with thousands of other Tuatha De "experiments" when the Breaking finally ended.

Over the span of the next three millennia, the dragons magical abilities evolved with their environment and growing intellect. However, their instinctual need for survival forced them to remain solitary creatures and the dragons lonely existence was counterproductive to their populations. Very few were born over the subsequent years despite the benefit of their natural lifespans extended over a hundredfold by the genetic meddling of the Tuatha De. And it didn't help that the most powerful among them fought for dominance or that the humans, especially the ones who clothed themselves in metal, found it great sport to hunt them. Yet, those few dragons who kept themselves apart from those dangers slowly perfected their magical craft and grew more powerful. Some even learned how to change their form and live among men.

Belthagore had never learned that trick, Tephras noted with some disappointment. There were many other abilities of his new host that Tephras was eager to explore. The Black Dragon's most recent memories betrayed a mundane, listless existence that induced frequent, decades-long hibernation with almost no contact with the outlying settlements of the closest human kingdom known as Tarre. That was about to change.

But Tephras was no fool. Before he could begin terrorizing the lands into submission, lead vast armies in conquest and spread his dominion over these pitiful humans unlike the world had ever seen, he would have to master his new prize. Tephras's mental grin reflected itself on the lips of the dragon. Empires would fall to his tyranny.

Belthagore, wholly subjugated by Tephras, roared with brief satisfaction. Seething with anger and hunger, he flew from his lair into the night sky in search of prey to fill his belly or merely kill indiscriminately just for the pure pleasure of it.

———

Tephras had a very successful night. Apparently, the inhabitants of the region around Belthagore's lair either forgot or did not realize that they lived in the shadow of a mighty ancient dragon residing in the peaks above their homes. The demon found nothing more agreeable than feeding his anger with the killing of man, animal and beast. Over the past several hours he found satisfaction in all three—first, a griffon flying nearby, then several deer standing sedately in an open glen and finally a merchant camped in the forest with a retinue of at least twenty guards and servants. All died horribly and some of their gruesome remains satiated his host's need for food.

That first night, Tephras stuffed the dragon's gut with far more than he needed for the next several days, but the demon would fly out again the next evening to kill for the amusement of it. He never felt such power from a host before. This ancient dragon was strong, with unexpected magical talents that the demon discovered with every passing day. The havoc he could wreak among the nearby kingdoms would substantially spread his particular brand of terror and it gave Tephras confidence to think that for once, he could project his power far beyond the immediate area of Belthagore's lair.

So far, the only frustration he had with the great beast was that it required frequent rest to recuperate its strength. The downtime allowed Tephras the opportunity to understand its abilities better, delving deeper into Belthagore's shattered mind to discover hidden secrets, if he could be patient. Unfortunately, patience was not a quality the demon possessed in abundance and he often compelled the dragon far beyond its limitations, physically and mentally exhausting the poor creature. Tephras expected that word would go out about a rampaging dragon in The Wilds north of Tarre compelling so-called heroes to organize expeditions against him. They would be entertaining if only a small challenge to his voracious lust for killing and death. Except that he did not plan to wait around for them.

Tephras enjoyed terrorizing the lands around his lair for several more weeks before he decided it was time to test his host with more challenging prey. The wild boar, deer and occasional hapless human had become tiresome quarries. The dragon's energy, magic ability and life force were fueled and enhanced by the unrestricted fury the demon channeled into his host. To keep his anger hot, Tephras needed to amplify the scale of death and destruction by increasing intensities of violence if he was ever to regain the potency he lost while imprisoned in that insufferable pithos. Once he was back to his full strength, with the power of an Ancient Black Dragon as his host, he would be unstoppable.

Tephras searched the memories of the dragon to learn more about the geography farther away from the lair and soon determined his course would take him south. There was a Tarre city known as Pherti only fifty leagues away if he flew over the mountains. It was settled by hundreds of humans who would be ripe for feeding his need for killing and burning. Tephras needed no time for preparation. He launched the dragon from his lair, guiding him south, eager to reach his destination before dawn.

Flight over the high, bitterly cold mountain peaks covered by snow was devoid of turbulence as he rode the smooth flows of air at his back. They pressed him forward with little energy of his own. Tephras was pleased. At this rate, he would arrive above Pherti earlier than he expected and with lots of vigor to carry out the violence he planned.

Through the dragon's night vision, he could observe the details of the mountain range below. It was teeming with wildlife and the occasional hunting camp occupied by humans crowded around a fire. Tephras was tempted to dive down and kill them all. It was an enticement that he nearly found impossible to resist, except to give into it would leave the dragon too exhausted when he arrived over Pherti. That was where Tephras was certain to reap his greatest reward – destruction and death on a massive scale – and true pleasure.

The hours dragged by until Tephras could finally make out patches of land cleared of trees for agriculture and livestock. The dragon's stomach rumbled at the sight of sheep and goats lying in the soft grass tended by a few scrawny humans. Far in the distance, he could make out the dark silhouette of Pherti. Forgetting about the sheep, Tephras approached the city at high altitude to avoid the chance of causing alarm. He wanted surprise when he rained down his fury upon them. It was still a couple hours before dawn and there were very few lights visible except for the occasional torch carried by a soldier patrolling along the street or atop the wall. The dragon enjoyed excellent night vision, which Tephras enhanced further with his magic. He wanted to see every detail, to locate any ballistae or catapults that might threaten him later. He quietly circled the city, noting how much of it was built with wood and earth rather than stone.

This city will burn, he thought with glee.

Turning away from Pherti, Tephras angled the dragon in a wide arc that would take him close to the ground and put the mountains behind him, concealing his approach against the dark background. His host flew with surprising efficiency for its bulk. The demon would never have expected that to look at one. These creatures boasted a strange symbiotic relationship between their life-force, arcane energy and physical prowess that Tephras had yet to decipher. Not even Belthagore's memories held a clue about how it worked. There would be time for that later.

Tephras guided the dragon fast over the tops of the trees with only a bare flap of its leathery wings. This was what the demon was waiting for. The past several weeks stuck in that cave getting to know his host had left him desperate for this moment. The forest gave way to terrain cleared of trees within a quarter-league of the city. There were fields and stilted farm houses, penned enclosures holding domestic animals that huddled together in fear when he passed, but all was dark. Flying lower and faster he rushed toward the wooden palisade set atop a massive earth embankment. There the dragon's sharp eyes spied a cluster of several soldiers neglecting their watch. They would be the first of many to die this night.

"Odqvasb Prge!" he roared.

A spray of fire engulfed the men and the portion of the wall where they gathered. The only terror they knew was that they died almost instantly, never knowing why or by what cause. Tephras would remedy that. He wanted panic and fear. He wanted every soul in Pherti to suffer and endure the horror that he brought before they died. Rising higher, the dragon split the air with flame, randomly setting fire to as many of the wooden structures as he could on his first pass. And then he turned sharply to go back. Among the burning buildings elevated on wooden stilts, dozens of people were assembled outside to escape the flames of their homes only to find themselves consumed by the same death they thought to flee.

Those that survived knew the terror that they faced and they ran screaming. The lucky ones died immediately, the unlucky ran burning.

Tephras reveled in it all and continued to bathe Pherti in fire pass after pass. Hundreds died and hundreds more scattered in random directions, frantic to avoid the dragon's inferno. Pure chaos had taken control of the populace and not even the militia could organize a resistance. The soldiers ran as surely as the others and burned brightly in their polished bronze armor. The humans made his work too easy with their streets arranged in a quadrangular pattern that allowed him to fly straight and fast.

Idiots.

Despite his success, Tephras stayed aloft, raining fire down on the inhabitants below. As much as he wanted to land and tear a few of them to bits with his claws, he knew that was when a dragon was most vulnerable and the demon had not survived five millennia by acting foolishly. More, he could feel that the dragon was beginning to tire. After a few more passes, Tephras directed the dragon to fly to a higher elevation so he could inspect his work. Most of the city was ablaze. The city walls, the temples, the merchant's stalls, the residences and government structures—all were constructed with wood. The wooden stilts that supported the dwellings burned and collapsed into other structures next to them, spreading the fire. There were smoldering bodies everywhere and the cries of grief and pain played like beautiful music to the demon's sensitive ears, inspiring him to inflict further devastation. It delighted him to know, that without any more effort on his part, the entire city would burn to the ground before dawn.

The only area left untouched was the palace complex located on the southeast edge of Pherti. It too was surrounded by a wooden palisade and elevated higher than the rest of the city. He would have to be careful not to linger over it too long. No doubt the rulers had witnessed the carnage in the lower city and were better prepared to mount a defense. And the advantage of surprise was lost. Tephras cast a few protective spells on the dragon, climbed higher and circled for a closer look.

Nearly invisible against the night sky, he detected no overt danger and sent the dragon diving hard and fast toward the palace grounds. He was going to set fire to the entire complex before he went after the other structures around it. Perhaps he could chase the royals out and set them ablaze in front of their subjects, he thought with excitement. Drawing closer, his enhanced night vision revealed that there were men on the wall, many of them and they were armed with bows and spears. It was of little concern as long as he stayed out of their range.

A flash of bright light and the crackle of lightning from somewhere below forced Tephras into an evasive maneuver to avoid the deadly energy. It was followed by several more that sent the dragon spinning away from the palace walls into the protection of the night.

So, they want to put up a fight after all, the demon thought with no shortage of amusement.

Abandoning his plan to fly over and spray fire down upon their heads, Tephras cut to the right and dropped low to the ground behind the elevated earth-works. The humans had foolishly left the other parts of the wall unguarded. When he appeared again, darting fast from the west over the palisade, he found the humans gathered together in confusion, unsure of the direction he went in the darkness.

Perfect. He laughed. *I have them now.*

Cries of shock and horror at his sudden appearance rose from below and he was greeted with sporadic flights of arrows that harmlessly flew by or bounced off his shiny black scales. Hurried casts of lightning from what he could now see must be priests in brown robes crackled and sparked at the edges of the shield he had prepared earlier. Their concentrated fire might have harmed him severely before, but now it was too late. Tephras felt the dragon inhale deeply. Cold air rushed into his lungs to feed the fire fueled by oil jetting from glands that he pressed together with the muscles in his neck to spew out liquid heat that burst into flame as it streamed from his toothy maw.

The people tried to run and he watched them burn. Burning and running. Some did escape, but they had no thought to turn and fight. The only ones to hold their ground were the priests, a small group of them off to one side that his flames did not touch. They were moving their arms together, preparing a cast. Tephras flew over them toward the east as fast as he could compel the dragon to go. The lightning ripped into him from behind, so much that it tore through his shields, singeing his tail and wings. The pain was excruciating, but his course did not waver. His anger satiated for the moment, Tephras realized that the dragon was exhausted and had to rest soon. As much fun as he was having, the demon didn't want to kill or cripple his host by pushing harder than it was capable. The damn priests would not get another shot at him tonight.

Reluctantly, he turned the dragon away from Pherti, flying back across the river and toward the shelter of the mountains. He remembered the sheep he saw earlier and thought they would be a fitting feast. They were not hard to find and several of their number, including the humans in charge of the flock, died quickly for his meal. Then he flew the tired dragon a few more leagues west where he found a secluded wood to safely rest and tend his wounds.

Attacking cities is dangerous business, the demon supposed. *But very satisfying.*

Tephras allowed the Black Dragon that was once known as Belthagore to rest in the forest for several days. Even at this distance, he could smell the smoke of death and ruin floating on the gentle breeze from the direction of Pherti. He considered what he would do next. Certainly, Tephras could return to Pherti and finish off the palace and kill those priests, but they might be more prepared next time and he didn't want to risk further injury to the dragon. The word had probably spread to cities further south as well. His compulsive desire was to kill and destroy, but Tephras knew his best chance of enjoying the greatest success was when his prey was not expecting him.

The demon was not driven by a desire to conquer or rule anything, nor did he care to hoard loot. The thing that drove him was an absolute need to satiate his wrath with death and violence. For now, that meant seeking his prey randomly and in places with concentrated populations—cities, villages and trade caravans on the roads. It was his revenge on this world for what they had done to him and the others. Only after that rage was satisfied would he consider the greater things.

Feeling rested again, Tephras flew south toward the sea under the cover of darkness. Along the way, he set ablaze several isolated villages and killed anything that moved between them. Tephras steered the dragon wide around Pherti and avoided Fondo, its closest neighbor to the south – no doubt their priests had learned something from their counterparts and had prepared formidable defenses. He traveled only at night, and allowed the dragon to rest during the day. By the time he reached as far as Coni, settled on the shores of the Bodin River, Tephras was sure that his rampage in the north could be nothing more than a questionable rumor this far south. A rumor he intended would become terrifyingly real to the inhabitants in the south soon enough.

The dragon's night vision revealed Coni to be a much larger city than Pherti, with a high defensive wall constructed of stone and kiln-fired mud bricks. The buildings inside were similarly made with the addition of timber framing. From his high altitude, the demon could make out regular patrols on the walls and throughout the city along with a variety of tradesmen, merchants and citizenry strolling casually near the busy taverns and food shops. Considering the substantial defenses, Tephras decided that this city was not worth the risk and elected to destroy more villages farther along as he continued his southern route toward the coast. There he would find ports with very flammable ships and fishing vessels with lots of timber to burn . . .

A few days south of Coni, Tephras found himself flying along the coast where the mountains met the Great Sea. Continuing south and west, the dragon's memories revealed that he was entering the realm of Rasna and that the high mountains on his left were known as the Spine of Cel, named after their earth goddess. If he continued along the coast, he would soon have the port city of Funa in sight. With the dragon well rested and full of energy, Tephras was feeling a distracting hunger to burn and kill. He wasn't craving food—there had been enough goats and wildlife to satisfy the dragon's physical hunger. It was time to surrender to his basest desires. He maintained his course south.

Just after midnight, the dragon's keen eyes spotted the city lights of Funa in the distance. Tephras was delighted. Although Funa was constructed much like Coni, the city included a modest port where several ships swayed at their moorings. That was where he would strike.

Tephras didn't delay. Within an hour a dozen ships were burning while sailors, merchants and servants ran in terror in every direction. Just like Pherti, the people were taken completely by surprise and what followed was chaos and death. Tephras was growing stronger, he could feel it and he reveled in the full frenzy of bloodlust.

A few sailors with powerful longbows sent arrows against him, but the dragon barely felt their sting. None had the strength to pierce his scales. Only when spellcasters joined the defense did Tephras realize he had stayed long enough and with great reluctance, he flew south into the darkness. The dragon was tired again, although not exhausted like he had been after Pherti. The demon's host was growing stronger with him. Soon, even the best-defended cities would be vulnerable to his rage.

A little while later, Tephras found a natural cave along the coast that would serve as a good place to rest and heal his wounds. One of the spellcasters had managed to strike him with a bolt of energy that left his right front claw in significant pain. Tephras was not an accomplished healer, although he thought he could do well enough to take care of his own minor injuries.

Landing at the entrance of the cavern, he could smell the stink of the creatures that occupied it as their lair. He cautiously moved into the darkness and was beset from either side by a pair of griffons striking at his scales with razor-sharp talons and beaks that could chop a man in half. Initially, Tephras is not sure if they are trying to drive him off or get out, but it didn't matter either way. With a few quick strikes with his uninjured claw, a final death bite to one and a crushing tail swipe to the other, he removed the former inhabitants, tossing their lifeless bodies into the sea. He could have eaten them, but the feathers were such a burden to deal with that he would rather go hungry until he found something more palatable.

Over the next few days, Tephras allowed the dragon to rest and heal, leaving the cavern only long enough to find a few deer and a fat boar to squelch his hunger and constant desire to kill. Overall, the demon was pleased with his host, although he was surprised how vulnerable it was to focused attacks by humans, especially those who could fling spells. In small groups or one-on-one with anything that crawled or flew, he was more than a match, but these humans with their arrows and magic could be troublesome. Tephras would have to be more careful attacking their cities. Otherwise, Belthagore's head might be decorating some idiot king's throne room and Tephras would be looking for a new host.

Chapter 18

Braetling

"We are going back to Braetling now. Would you care to join us?" Tridi's left eyebrow was raised high on his forehead.

Qel shifted his gaze to Havacian, who nodded vigorously. Qel nodded and chuckled at his friend's enthusiasm, "We would be pleased to."

"Then let's get underway. It's going to be dark in a few hours." Tridi fluidly hopped up on his mount and led the small company north over the barren hard ground that bordered the forest and the mountains.

Qel rode up next to Tridi, leaving Havacian to chat with Aelrindel. "Why are we going north rather than back the way we came?"

Tridi gestured to the ground in front of them. "We can ride much faster without tiring the horses and avoid the hazards of the roots and pits hidden by the underbrush. Horses have never been a good choice for traveling through the Sylvan Forest."

"Is there a better choice?"

"Obviously not," Tridi smiled. "Otherwise we wouldn't be riding them, now would we?"

Qel felt like he had just been the victim of a joke he didn't understand. He was learning that elves had a strange sense of humor. "What about the disks? I assume elves have them just as we do. Wouldn't they be a good choice for moving through the forest?"

"We rarely ride the disks, except maybe in Avalon. You'll have to ask Aelrindel about that. And you can't carry packs on a disc like we can on our horses." Tridi shook his head as if the answer were obvious. "And a larger disc would be impractical in the dense forest."

Qel decided to change the subject before he came off any more daft than the elf probably already thought he was. "What happens when we get to the Rayfin River?"

"We ride along the bank, following it west until we come to my village."

Havacian must have heard the last part of their conversation as he rode up next to them. "Why do you call it the Rayfin River?"

"I'll show you when we get there," Tridi replied.

Show us? Qel thought. *What could that mean?* Hopefully not another monster of their realm like the Ogres . . .

Two hours later, Tridi led them back into the forest along a game trail leaving the mountains behind obscured by the leafy boughs. How Tridi knew which way to go, Qel had no idea. He knew enough about the stars and the passage of the sun that he could determine any direction with a clear view of the sky, but in the Sylvan Forest, the canopy was so thick that only a small amount of light filtered through, let alone a view of the sky.

"Tridi, how can you ascertain our direction in the forest when you can't see the sky?"

Tridi pointed to a tree ahead of them. "See that tree with the moss on it? In the Sylvan Forest, moss generally grows on the north-facing side of the trees."

"Fascinating." Qel bent over his horses' neck and studied the trees they passed. "I never would have thought of that."

"I'm sure that your 'Journey of Discovery' has been quite an education so far."

"It has been," Qel had to admit, "and in so many unexpected ways."

Tridi burst out laughing. Had Qel said something funny? "Just wait, young Atlantean. There is so much more to come."

Less than an hour later, they emerged from the forest and onto the banks of what Qel was sure must be the Rayfin River. Looking to the north, Qel could see the outline of the mountains, farther away than he would have expected and he guessed that the mountain range had curved east while they had ridden north and west through the forest. The river flowed from the higher elevations on a much faster current here than where they had first met the elves. It was also far wider, with less depth, than farther on and the flowing water was frequently interrupted by clusters of jagged rocks rising well above the surface.

Tridi pointed to the distorted images of large fish swimming against the fast-moving water, their silver fins cut across the surface of the river in sporadic jerky movements as they skillfully avoided the rocks. "Those are Rayfin. They are abundant in this river and a source of food for our village. We prefer to smoke the meat to store it longer and maintain the flavor."

"So, the river is named after the fish," Havacian observed.

"Very astute of you," Tridi replied wryly.

Havacian's face darkened a little with embarrassment, but he did not say anything further. *Poor Havacian, I hope you find I am good company in our troupe of imbeciles!* Qel thought with little humor. He desperately wished that their days of Discovery were not just a long list of other people pointing out how little they knew outside of the City of Atlantis.

They followed the river southwest for the rest of the day, only stopping once to let the horses drink from the river and nibble a few blades of grass. Tridi announced that if they kept up their current pace, they would arrive at the village before evening the next day. Qel was glad for it since he was still not used to riding a horse for long periods of time. He was sure that when they eventually arrived in Avalon, he would be walking bow-legged with thickly chaffed thighs.

By late afternoon, Tridi brought them to a stop to set camp in a clearing with dry ground. A little while later, with the sun not long for the horizon, Qel and Havacian got their first lesson in fishing for Rayfin under Aelrindel's tutelage. Somehow, they managed to pull four of the large fish out of the river, clean and set them to smoke over the campfire that Tridi had built before it was completely dark. A little while later, while sitting on a log soaking in the heat from the fire, Qel shivered. They were much closer to the mountains than when he and Havacian were on the Sylvan Road and without the shelter of the thick forest all around them, it was colder at night and the biting breeze that traveled down the river from higher elevations found every slip and crack between the folds of his heavy cloak. They all sat close around the fire in their heavy cloaks with their hands soaking in the heat from the flames. Despite the discomfort, he finally felt the tension of the day slipping away as they laughed about their encounter with the Ogres.

"You really handled yourself well," Qel remarked to Tridi. "I swear Havacian and I were trembling in our boots the entire time."

Tridi laughed, "I was going through the same thing, only it was all on the inside."

Qel gestured over to Aelrindel. "This one was acting as if he were witness to a discussion among milkmaids!"

Aelrindel feigned a look of innocence. "Did I miss something? I thought the whole thing was civil from the start!"

The men laughed.

Havacian turned to Tridi, "You seem to have some authority with the Ogres. In an unorthodox way, I thought they actually respected you."

"I am an Elder within our community, so I have dealt with the Ogres a few times in the past." Tridi pulled one of the Rayfin out of the heat and began separating the meat.

"An Elder! I have always thought of elders as old men with nothing better to do than spew their opinion to anyone who would listen." Qel was in a jovial mood now that he was warming up and about to eat hot food.

"For the Sylvan, elders are simply people who have knowledge and talent in certain specializations. It is true that many of those who are considered Elders are much older than I, but in our village, I am one of a group of Elders, even though I am only a little over a hundred and fifty years old. It was my family that was attacked, so the village allowed me to handle the infraction as I saw fit," Tridi explained.

"A hundred and fifty!" Havacian exclaimed. "Any Atlantean would be blessed to live so long. We learn few details about the elves, except in children's stories. I don't know why our people speak so little of your people."

"The Atlanteans are the center of the world. Because of your people, there is balance and the elves are safe to live their lives in seclusion." Aelrindel took a long leaf piled heavy with fish meat and handed it to Qel. "The Atlanteans speak so little of the elves out of respect for our culture."

"That is true," agreed Tridi. "Among the leaders of the elves and the Atlanteans, there is an important understanding. We bear the responsibility of protecting nature and the Atlanteans keep the Emerald Isle secure for us to lead our way of life."

"I'm glad we came to the Sylvan Kingdom, even though the first few days have left me trembling in puddles of fear." Qel paused to stuff a bit of the fish in his mouth. It was delicious. "We have learned so much about your culture and we have made new friends. I hope we can call each other friends with all we have been through."

"As well we should." Aelrindel agreed.

Tridi allowed them to take their time breaking camp the next morning. Qel enjoyed not being in any particular hurry, a nice luxury after the last few days. The low roar of the fast-moving water over the rocks and boulders in the river formed the baseline of soothing sound that allowed Qel to sleep soundly through the night. When he awoke, he felt refreshed and energized, stealing a few moments to watch several large brown bears on the opposite bank swiping at the jumping Rayfin or chasing one another in the shallows. While Qel was sitting at the edge of the river, Tridi brought out a net and invited Qel to join him.

"You have a net?" Qel was incredulous. "Why didn't we use that to catch the Rayfin last night rather than the poles we fashioned out of branches?"

"Did you know how to fish before yesterday?" Tridi countered.

"Well, no . . ."

"And now you do." The elf had a very smug look on his face. "And you know how to forage for food, build a shelter and set a proper camp. All these things may be important for your survival one day."

"You're right," Qel had to agree. "Thank you."

"See those bears?" Tridi pointed across the river. "They are called long-tooth brown bears. They are very dangerous. If they were hungry, they might consider us a source of food. Fortunately, the Rayfin are abundant this time of year and easy to catch, so they won't concern themselves with us as long as we keep our distance."

"Avoiding most animals in the Sylvan Forest is probably a good general rule," Qel volunteered.

Tridi smiled showing the whites of his sharply pointed teeth, "That is the most sensible thing I have heard you say since we met."

Qel wasn't sure if he should laugh at that or not.

After netting two large Rayfin, they walked back to camp and Tridi went about preparing breakfast. An hour later, they cleared the camp and resumed a brisk pace westward along the banks of the Rayfin. Tridi still expected to arrive in Braetling before nightfall even with their late start. It was still cold in the morning, colder than in the forest and the breeze stronger still as it blew down from the high altitudes of the mountains and west along the length of the river. It was the height of spring and the warmth of the sun slowly climbing above them eventually complemented the chilly breeze and made for perfect traveling weather.

Farther on, the river became less rocky and rapid. The Rayfins still jumped as they swam upstream to spawn, but the fish had more energy than they would when they reached the faster-moving water. Qel enjoyed the beauty of the sunlight sparkling like diamonds on the river and the wildlife that so often congregated along its shore. Because he spent so much time in the city or on his family estates in the country, the wilderness invoked a strange allure and mystery that he had never experienced before. Not to this extent anyway.

In the afternoon they stopped to rest the horses. Tridi pulled out his net again and gave Qel and Havacian a chance to fish up their own Rayfin while Aelrindel foraged for nuts and berries in the forest. The clean, fresh water was slow enough that they could strip down and wash in the river without fear of being swept away. The river was frigidly cold, but once his body acclimated, Qel enjoyed the swim. Havacian showed off his talents by dunking him with conjured waves, creating whirlpools and columns of water spinning here and there. Even the elves were impressed, if also mildly annoyed when he directed one at them.

They arrived at the village of Braetling just before sundown. At first, Qel was confused by what he was seeing. Elves were moving with purpose in one direction or another within the forest, disappearing into strange knots of foliage and cooking on open hearths in seemingly random glades. Children ran and hid from one another, their innocent laughter echoing through the forest while others playing games together in small clusters here and there. None of it made much sense until they came to a stop in a clearing and the details of the village became much clearer.

Qel was astonished.

The houses and public buildings were not constructed as much as they appeared to be *grown*. Each building was part of a tree or multiple trees depending on its size, yet there had been no cutting or shaping by tools of any kind. Tree trunks, branches and thick vines molded themselves to shape walls, ceilings and floors of each construction. There was no clear boundary between village and forest. As far as Qel could determine, the structures camouflaged seamlessly at different elevations within the trees themselves and merged into the surrounding forest. In fact, not knowing the village was there, Qel might have passed it altogether if no one made a sound. Perhaps that was the point. The elves had a symbiotic relationship with nature. They protected the forest, cherished and nourished it and the forest protected them in return.

Riding farther through the interior of the village, Qel observed how each home was personalized in a different way. Most had small gardens, some had small fountains or ponds and others attached to small play areas for tiny children. In many ways, they were no different from the homes back in Atlantis.

"How do you manage to force the trees into the forms they take and how long does it take to grow these amazing dwellings?" Havacian asked Tridi. Qel's inquisitive friend had also noted how the trees formed the homes they passed.

"The trees are not forced. Every year there are a few female elves, chosen by Niamh, born with the talent to whisper their desire to the trees. Over the course of time, the trees grow into the desired forms. These talented women are known as Traetling, or Tree Whisperers. Vnae is privileged to be among small number of elves with this gift."

"I have never heard of anyone with that ability," Qel commented, "not even in the Enclave."

Tridi brushed the long dark hair away from his face. "Only a female elf can be born with this gift. Never a male and no other species, anywhere."

"Who is this Niamh that chooses them?" Qel asked, "An Elder or ruler of the elves?"

Tridi looked at him with a mix of confusion and disbelief. "They really teach you nothing about us, do they? Niamh is the deity of nature and magic, goddess of the elves. It is by her will that we exist."

Qel felt his face heat from blushing. "I'm so sorry, Tridi. I didn't mean to offend . . ."

"You didn't offend," Aelrindel interrupted. "Tridi forgets that elves and even Niamh herself are endowed with a sense of humor. You cannot be faulted for something you don't know."

The farther they rode into the village, the more apparent it became to Qel that it was much larger than he expected. Had it been a village in the Atlantean Territory, it would have been considered significant, if only a fraction the size of Aquilon. Each clearing they passed was surrounded by at least a dozen homes at various elevations in the trees and each of those was connected to others by bridges molded from branches to points either on the ground or in other trees forming the greater expanse of the village. It was the time of day that families were preparing the evening meal on what were inherently communal outdoor kitchens located in the center of each clearing, but it was difficult to tell how or if each family was organized the way they all mingled together so familiarly.

"Why don't the villagers cook inside their homes?" Havacian asked Tridi.

"Each one of these clearings that we pass represents a micro-community within the village," Tridi explained. "The preparation of meals is a community effort, not one that's left to each family or individual. In addition, no elf would ever allow a flame within their home because of the nature of the structure. It is a living thing, not stones piled on top of each other like they do in your cities."

"Then how do you keep warm in the winter?" Qel asked.

"The trees provide excellent insulation. Along with that we have a thick layer of furs on the floor and we can always freely request warmth globes from any of the magic-crafters in the village when it becomes particularly cold in the winter."

"Magic-crafters?" Havacian asked.

"They are similar to what you define as a wizard in Atlantis." Aelrindel turned in his saddle to face Havacian. "Like your Imperial Order of Wizards, the magic-crafters are sorcerers that develop their abilities from a young age and typically attend the Demesne of Magic in Avalon."

When they reached the center of the village, there were many small tree-grown buildings dedicated to various trades and mercantile as well as several larger structures whose use was not apparent, except for one—a tavern. Qel was looking forward to finding out what sort of drinks the elves living deep inside the Sylvan Forest had to offer. Through the center of the village ran a narrow stream of clear water from the Rayfin on the northern outskirts of the village where stood several stands of fruit trees. Adjacent to the stream stood a wide-open space that was the only area not touched by trees and wild shrubbery. A tall sculpture, if Qel could call it that, created entirely of tightly woven living branches, leaves and vines displayed the incredible likeness of a woman that Aelrindel identified as the goddess Niamh. Her stern likeness and beauty were evident in precise detail, which was astonishing considering the medium. Wildlife was particularly abundant near the figure of the goddess. Small birds chirped and warbled from perches nearby while fuzzy chipmunks ran here and there in pursuit of one another as they danced from limb to limb. None of the villagers seemed to mind.

"There is a guest house in the community where my home is, not far on the other side of the plaza. The two of you may stay there while you are in Braetling. It will be more comfortable than staying at the tavern where the merchants from Atlantis and Tirnan Yog stop over. Not to mention that it is always noisy and crowded." Tridi pointed to the busy tavern on the other side of the clearing.

The elves frequenting the plaza were friendly and often waved and smiled when they passed. Tridi was evidently well-known and respected, receiving brief nods and even a few quick bows. It didn't take long to reach the other side and soon after that they arrived at Tridi's home, where they dismounted. Immediately, Vnae ran out to meet them, hugging her husband tightly. Right on her heels came their daughter, the little blonde one they had rescued from the river, prompting the Atlanteans to enlist in the chase after the Ogre. She enthusiastically joined her mother in hugging her father, happily giggling the whole time. Vnae then kissed her brother Aelrindel on the cheek and greeted both Qel and Havacian with a warm hug.

Qel was amazed at the change in her demeanor. The last time they met, she was seething with anger and focused on one thing—her husband and brother tracking down the Ogre that nearly drowned her beautiful child. He supposed it was understandable and wondered if he would have acted any differently if it were his own child. Now that they returned to the village, she could only conclude that they accomplished her task.

"Vnae, I have asked the Atlanteans to join us for the evening meal, if you don't object," Tridi raised his eyebrows in question.

"Of course, I don't." She smiled happily. "I look forward to hearing your tale. Have you offered the guest house for their stay, husband?"

"I have, wife"—he kissed her on the cheek— "and I will take them now so they may rest and wash before we retrieve them later."

"I will stay here with Vnae and Tolia and get a head start on washing up." Aelrindel dismounted and led his horse over to the side of the house. "I'll see you boys in a while."

Qel and Havacian waved to the family and followed Tridi to the guest house. They led their horses past two homes in the same clearing and stopped in front of a winding set of stairs formed by heavy roots and branches. Tridi whistled and a young elven boy appeared from the stables nearby to take their horses.

"The boy's name is PynterTacryniael; call him Pynter. If you need anything or have any questions, he will be more than happy to assist you." Tridi pointed to the stairway. "Your rooms are up there. I hope you find them comfortable. I will be back for you before dark."

After brief farewells, Qel and Havacian climbed the stairs to a door consisting of thick hanging vines and leaves that parted effortlessly as they pushed through them. The thought occurred to Qel how easy it would have been for the Ogres to enter the elves' homes if all their doors were the same. Even in the City of Atlantis, where crime was a rare and extraordinary thing, the doors were stout and fitted with locks or bars.

Inside, the guest house was surprisingly spacious. There were two separate bedrooms with comfortable mats atop a frame that was formed from the tree itself. Qel marveled at the detail. There was also a sitting room and another small room attached with a large water basin composed from tightly woven branches and big enough to sit in and bathe. It took Qel a little time and experimentation, but soon he determined that if he manipulated the position of two individual branches that were sticking out at odd angles, they would release cold and warm water. It was one of the most peculiar things he had ever seen.

A little later, as the twilight before nightfall descended over the forest, Qel and Havacian joined Tridi's family for the evening meal set up in the clearing surrounded by the residences. There were long stone tables and boulders that served as chairs that Qel had not noticed before. The furnishings were completely overgrown with ivy, which obscured their purpose and provided a comfortable cushion. Initially he assumed they were oddly placed hedges until Aelrindel motioned for him to sit on one as he sat upon another. The community prepared a beautiful presentation of boar, cheeses, a selection of fruits, fresh greens from their gardens and a local Sylvan fruit wine. They sat together at the end of one of the long tables with their elven friends and little Tolia while the rest of the community found their places all around them in loose groups of families and friends.

"Is it always like this?" Qel asked Vnae.

Children were playing and sometimes eating and there were lively conversations filled with jokes and stories and lots of laughter. Once in a while one elf or another would stand and sing a short tune or recite a limerick, and good or bad, there would always be wild applause. The little community visibly cared about one another and lived happily together.

"Oh yes," Vnae smiled. "You should see us when we get together with some of the nearby communities. Or worse yet, during the summer solstice when the whole village comes together to give thanks to Niamh."

Tridi had already told Vnae the short version of their meeting with the Ogres and she seemed satisfied enough with the results. While they sat together over the meal, Qel and Havacian took turns relating the details from their perspective, including how frightened they were confronting the monsters, Qel's agitation at Aelrindel's unexpected lack of concern when more Ogres showed up and how the Tree Guardians nearly made them jump out of their skins. Everyone enjoyed a good laugh.

"I'm curious to know how the Tree Guardians came about. The first time we saw them was at the border near Aquilon, but they were less obvious. Are there many of them in the Sylvan Forest?" Havacian asked Aelrindel.

The elf appeared surprised at the question. "Have you never heard of our forest protectors? They are creations of our Elder Magic-Crafters with some involvement of the druids. Great care is taken to grow them from small saplings with many sessions of various enchantments before they are the right age to begin their work as protectors of the Sylvan Forest." The elf paused to take a sip of the fruit wine. "It takes nearly a hundred years to grow one fully and I couldn't begin to tell you how many there are. The only thing I am sure of is that they never leave the Sylvan Forest and will always come to the aid of an elf in need. We call them Tree Guardians because that is their purpose."

After the meal, they spent a few hours talking before Qel and Havacian returned to the guest house for a much-needed night of rest. Walking the short distance to the guest house, the village was quiet except for the usual night sounds from the forest. Many lights were present from several of the tree homes they passed and Qel was pleased to note what appeared to be a Fairy habitation in the forest at the northern edge of the cul-de-sac. On this clear, crisp evening, he could see the bright sparkle of stars through the break in the trees and he almost felt like he was home.

Over the next few days, Qel became more familiar with the elves and their village. To his delight, Tridi and Aelrindel spent more time teaching them the ways of the forests and survival techniques in the wilderness. And every day, without fail, Qel kept up with the crucial lessons provided by Traegarlin, the Battle Wizard. He was noticing small increments of progress every day: a little faster cast, stronger potency and better insights when performing the complex combinations. Most importantly, he felt himself growing and becoming more confident.

"Are all the villages in the Sylvan Kingdom like this one?"

"More or less, with the exception of Andlang, which is much more like Aquilon considering it is our only international port." Qel was walking with Aelrindel through the forest, collecting walnuts for a red berry pie that Vnae was making that afternoon. "Even Avalon itself is very much like the villages except on a much grander scale. You would be impressed by the scale and beauty of the palace complex where the royal family resides. It is the oldest living structure in all of Avalon, self-renewing and always growing."

"When will you be returning to the city?" Qel asked.

"In a week or two. You and Havacian are welcome to travel with me if you like."

"That might be a good idea. And not just because you would keep us from getting lost," Qel quickly added. "We also enjoy your company."

"As I do yours," Aelrindel responded with a smile.

A smile that Qel was sure was genuine. He had a feeling that he and these elves he had only known a couple of weeks were fated to be friends for the rest of their lives. And he felt good about that.

———

The morning of their departure was a little emotional for Qel. He enjoyed his stay in Braetling and had become familiar with the elves of the community who lived there. Most importantly, he had developed a bond with little Tolia. Qel would think fondly about the games they played, her squeals of delight when she won and most of all, her tender hugs before she scurried off to bed every night. He had never thought about having children before now and he fervently hoped that one day he would meet the right woman and have many of them.

"It's time to go, Qel," Havacian said quietly from the doorway of his room. Qel was lost in his thoughts and appreciated his friend's subtle vocal nudge so as not to startle him. With a nod, he picked up the packs that were sitting at his feet, loaded with his clothing and supplies and followed Havacian out of the guest house.

"There you are," Aelrindel spoke jovially from the clearing where he stood smiling beside Tridi, Vnae and Tolia. "I thought maybe you boys decided to sleep in today."

The sun was only a few minutes past dawn and already the village was alive with activity. And it wasn't just the elves going about their business, but also the forest that was teeming with wildlife so present around them. Qel would miss waking to the pleasant chatter of birds, the patter of chipmunks running along the branches that formed the roofs and the daily occurrence of deer drinking, without a hint of fear, from the stream that ran through the village.

"It's not easy leaving this wilderness paradise," said Havacian, "but we are looking forward to seeing Avalon."

They all stood together in the clearing in which for so many evenings they shared communal meals and laughter and said their goodbyes. Genuine friendships and bonds had been developed that Qel hoped would last a lifetime, although he couldn't hazard a guess as to when he and Havacian might return. It could be years or even decades. And it was that thought that already had him feeling nostalgic. After he said a few words to Tridi and Vnae, he knelt down to where Tolia stood next to her mother.

"I will miss you most of all, young lady." He pulled a small object from his pocket and put it into her tiny hand. It was a small obsidian unicorn with a silver chain wrapped around it that he had been working on over the past two weeks. It was only the night before that he added the final enchantments.

"It is a charm that will protect you and keep you safe from monsters," he told her quietly, as if it were some vital secret between them.

"I love it!" She smiled broadly and fumbled to unravel the chain.

"I'll help you." Qel untangled the chain rolling the charm out to hang freely at the end of it. Then he placed it around Tolia's neck under her long blonde hair.

She held up the charm to her mother, "Look, Mommy, a unicorn!"

Vnae smiled down at her daughter. "Yes, it is and it's beautiful."

Tolia gave Qel a big hug. "Thank you, Qel! I will wear it forever!"

"I hope you do, little one." He was doing his best to hold back the tears that wanted to pour from his moisture-swollen eyes. "I truly do."

Chapter 19

Avalon City

I have a natural affinity for the natural naturalness of the completely natural biological structures of Avalon. Bah, enough of that! I would say such a city was beautiful if it weren't so unusual in its perpetual design and the centuries required to construct it. The astonishing abilities of the Traetling are evident in every aspect and form that no other magic or power could hope to duplicate. Avalon is unique in so many ways that the only thing that could possibly make it better is if there weren't so damn many trees! Naturally!

Wodanaz the Wanderer

———

There was a particular feeling that Qel had begun to experience while traveling for long hours over days in a place where he had never in his life tread previously. It was a sort of quiet wonder at the unfamiliarity and newness of everything around him that gave him a sense of freedom and excitement. Maybe it was the prospect of adventure and danger that could seize his circumstance at any moment or the natural perfection of the beautiful environment that whispered seductively, soothingly and calmed him to the foundation of his soul. Avalon was everything that he had hoped for and nothing that he expected. And it was thrilling.

Traveling the broad road north, Aelrindel, the consummate teacher, pointed out various points of interest in the forest. There were wild apple trees that became more and more abundant as they advanced closer to Avalon, the tracks of diverse forest animals imprinted on the soft soil along the side of the hard-packed road they followed and the singing of fairies that occasionally echoed through the forest, though none were ever seen. Each night they elected to camp in an open glade with a pond or small stream rather than the frequent way stations that dotted their way along the Sylvan Road. It was a chance to practice their camping skills and woodland survival techniques they had learned from the elves. Every moment was exhilarating and after a few days, Qel had even grown surprisingly comfortable with their self-supplied accommodations.

"Aelrindel, is Vnae your only sibling, or do you have others?" Qel was sitting at the campfire next to Havacian on their first evening out of Braetling.

"She is, in fact. Elves are fortunate to have a single child in their lifetime, let alone two." The expression on his face was almost serene as he spoke. "I guess by elven standards we have a large family. I wouldn't be the man I am today without Vnae."

"Why is that?" Havacian asked and then quickly added, "If it is not too personal to ask."

"You two are friends now and that means you may ask me anything without fear of reprimand. Regarding Vnae . . ." He put his hand on his chest in a motion that Qel thought must be symbolic of something. Love, perhaps? An endearment? "It is her strength that taught me courage when I was a child and she cared for me while my mother was away."

"Vnae cared for you as a child?" Qel was taken aback. "Surely she is only a few years older than you."

"You are right," Aelrindel agreed. "She is my elder by only twenty-three years."

Qel was astonished until he remembered how long the elves lived. To them, twenty-three years must be hardly a blink of an eye. "When did she know that she was Traetling?"

"She has known her entire life. Everyone knew." His features reflected a smug smile. "Our mother is also Traetling. You see, when Niamh chose her Traetling, she chose them only once, at the beginning of our people's birth, nearly five thousand five hundred years ago. From that time on, the Gift of Traetling has passed down through the generations, but only on the mother's side to daughters." Aelrindel sighed deeply. "Because of the Sylvans' low birth rate, there are far fewer Traetling today than there were in the beginning. We believe that when the last Traetling is born, that event will signal the last generation of elves upon this earth."

Qel was moved by the significance of what the Aelrindel was telling them. The elves prophesized the end of days that could come with the birth of a descendant in his own family line. Then it hit him. "That means that little Tolia is also a Traetling."

"Yes, she is."

"Do the Elders among the Sylvan have any idea when the last Traetling will be born?" Havacian was staring into the fire, the skin on his face a darker shade of blue from the heat.

"They say at least a few thousand years, but there are so many variables. It all depends on the rate of girls born within the Traetling line, disease, wars, or natural disasters." Aelrindel lay down on his blanket and looked up at the stars. "Maybe longer if there is a boom in the birth rate. Who knows? We don't worry about it. We live our lives happy and content if we can."

It saddened Qel to know that the Sylvan believed in such a tragic end for their people. As far as he knew, Atlanteans had no end-time prophesy and Pontus would rule over them for eternity. If that were the case, he wondered what would happen to the elves. Qel's sister was a high priestess to Pontus in the City of Atlantis; he would have to ask her more about that the next time he saw her, whenever that might be. He would sleep comfortably knowing that, whatever happened, it would be long after he had left this world. And long after Tolia.

The following day they found the road to Avalon busy with merchants, tradesmen and travelers going to or from the ancient city. Most were elves or Atlanteans, either mounted on horses or in floating carriages and those that were transporting goods slowly trekked along the road in a caravan of wagons. There were also frequent mounted elf patrols that moved deliberately one way or the other, although Aelrindel commented that the warriors rarely had anything more severe than a drunken dwarf or lost foreigner to deal with.

Qel was impressed with the elf warriors. They wore enchanted leather armor that barely made a sound when they rode by on their tall steeds, which Aelrindel had told him were bred to move quickly through the forest without losing their footing. Just like the elves that guarded the border in Aquilon, they all carried curved swords at their sides and bows on their backs. Aelrindel further explained that elf warriors were required to be experts with both weapons even when mounted. Although physically less powerful than Atlanteans, humans and especially the dwarfs, elves were astonishingly agile and swift in their combat abilities. Qel had seen Aelrindel and Tridi exercising their blades against each other in Braetling and did not refute the elf's assertion.

Once in a while, the patrols included a rather bored-looking sorcerer dressed in flowing robes of elven silk, multiple necklaces, rings and bracelets. Qel knew from his time in the Enclave that elf sorcerers were powerful, especially in magic related to nature and the foundational elements. Like the druids, they did not rely on Orichalcum Crystals for their power; instead, they drew it from the strength of nature. Qel was sure there was much more to it, but that was the extent of what he had learned. He didn't doubt that Havacian would know more and thought to ask him about it later when they were alone. Atlanteans and elves who practiced the magical arts had a healthy respect for one another and were often found collaborating for the benefit of both peoples. Qel knew of many elves who were training with the masters in the Imperial Wizards Enclave of Atlantis and others who came to the libraries in the Atlantean Towers located in foreign cities to do research. He was told that it was often the same for Atlanteans visiting the elven equivalent known as the Demesne of Magic in Avalon.

Once they were within half a day of the city, Qel began to see more patrols along the road and the obvious presence of Tree Guardians slowly moving one way or another in the forest near the Sylvan Road. Even in the air, through breaks in the forest canopy, Qel could see delta formations of elves patrolling the skies around the city mounted on great eagles the Atlanteans called Roc. The forest creatures hardly noticed their passing and apparently did not see them as a threat, although it was quite unlikely that even a wild Roc would attempt a dive into the forest after prey, considering their size.

That morning they found themselves trailing a small group of Tree Guardians carrying massive quarried stones along the road they were on.

"What are they going to do with those stones?" Havacian asked.

"The druids must be building another ceremonial site. The Tree Guardians transport the megaliths from the quarries near the mountains and place them where the druids desire," Aelrindel explained. "I've never seen the mysterious monuments of the druids, but others have told me that the Tree Guardians help build their triliths and stone circles. Apparently, there were once Tree Guardians in Eriu and parts of Lyonesse before they became the kingdoms they are today. What happened to them, none can say."

After an hour the Tree Guardians left the side of the road, striding deeper into the wilds of the forest, along no trail that he could see. He glanced over at Havacian, their eyes met and Qel knew they were both thinking the same thing. The druids megalithic stone circles just found their way near the top of their 'must see' list.

By late afternoon Qel noticed scatterings of tree-formed homes very much like those in Braetling except that they were far more numerous and closer together. Some were even formed quite high in the forest canopy and connected by a series of beautiful bridges and walkways that spanned impossible distances from one side of the clearing to another with very little support. Idly, Qel traced the network of bridges and found that one could walk the entire distance that they rode high among the branches of the trees.

"The Traetling must be akin to artists," Qel commented. "The elevated structures and walkways look as if they are not simply grown for efficiency but for natural beauty as well. Just look at the bridges, Havacian, they almost appear as if they have been carved with beautiful lacework so delicate that it should be impossible to support the weight of a mouse, let alone a grown elf."

"The bridges and walkways are deceivingly stable and capable of supporting an amazing amount of weight," Aelrindel spoke proudly. "Remember, every structure is *alive* and when there is undue stress on any part of it the forest compensates to distribute the weight more evenly."

Havacian was hanging on every word Aelrindel spoke and had recently begun to take copious notes in a magical journal he had brought from Atlantis. Qel had one as well and he wrote a note to himself once in a while, mainly cataloging the exercises he had learned from the Battle Wizard, Traegarlin. He would chart his progress on the pages of vellum that would never run out in a journal that would always maintain its original weight and volume, no matter how much he wrote. The journals were gifts from their masters on graduation day and although he didn't think much of the tome at the time, he certainly appreciated its value now. Undoubtedly, Havacian more than he.

After riding a little farther, Aelrindel announced, "We have officially entered Avalon."

Qel was puzzled as he gazed around and heard Havacian ask what he was thinking, "Where are the walls and towers? The city gates?"

Aelrindel laughed, "There are no fortified cities in the Sylvan Kingdom. The forest is our protection. How could any force on earth ever manage to move a siege engine through the tangle of woods that surround us? We had a tough enough time guiding our horses through it chasing Ogres!"

Qel found it frustratingly impossible to judge the size of the city considering that it was formed as part of the forest with the trees obscuring the distance it extended in every direction. The most notable difference was that the road over which they traversed took on an unusual texture. Previously, the Sylvan Road was incredibly hard-packed soil, easy on the horses and humid enough not to toss up dust. Now it had a slight silvery sheen as if the road was coated and sealed with a dusting of silver sand. The clearings they passed, surrounded by residences, were much more extensive than in Braetling, featuring open plazas with fountains, streams and ponds alongside grassy parks where children played.

Qel thought of Tolia again and had to smile. He learned from Vnae that it was a rare privilege to be chosen by Niamh to give birth to a child. She told him that nature, through Niamh, kept a proper balance on the elven population so that it always stayed relatively constant. In a year that there were many deaths, there would be many births. Nature somehow always knew and controlled the growth very carefully, considering their longevity. He thought back to the conversation with Aelrindel a few nights earlier and wondered why Niamh, or nature, didn't also keep the Traetling in balance. Perhaps the Sylvan didn't know either. Qel didn't know what the birth rate was among the Atlanteans and dwarfs, but it must have been far less than the humans that seemed to be popping children out on a regular basis. *The humans.* They would be a force to contend with one day. There was no joy in that thought.

The streets and walkways were busy with the citizens of Avalon going here or there on their daily errands. Just like in Braetling, they often smiled or greeted them with a "good afternoon" when they passed and always appeared to be in the best of moods. In this alone, Avalon was very different from anywhere else he had ever been.

The forest suddenly opened up when they arrived at the city center. There, spread out before them so unexpectedly, was a massive grand plaza which was currently being used as a marketplace.

"Five days of our seven-day week, this is a bustling market, but on the last two, the merchants must pack up their stalls and clear the plaza." Aelrindel waved his arm across the air in front of him as if willing the merchants in the plaza to disperse. "On those two days, our people gather to sing, feast and perform ceremonial dances. This is our way of honoring nature, the spirits of our ancestors and the nature goddess, Niamh. No business may be conducted on these days and the palace provides a grand feast. Foreigners, even the Atlanteans, are dissuaded from joining in what we consider our sacred holy days. Except for the druids, they are always welcome. The ones in Avalon pay homage to Niamh as much as they do to Eriu or Sunna. In fact, there are few outside of the Sylvan Kingdom who are aware of it, but we believe all three goddesses are related as sisters."

"I read that there is some controversy in the Western Kingdoms about Eriu and Sunna being sisters," Havacian said. "Imagine the pandemonium of throwing another sister into the mix."

Aelrindel nodded his agreement. "That's probably the primary reason we keep it to ourselves. In case you didn't notice, we generally care little for what outsiders think anyway."

"As much as you talk of isolation, your people intermingle well with the foreigners who are here." Qel was looking over the crowds strolling the market or sitting at tables outside the taverns along the perimeter of the plaza. Overwhelmingly, the elves were in the majority, but where there was an Atlantean, a dwarf, or even the rare human druid, there were several elves with them conversing, haggling or laughing as friends might do.

"We are a welcoming people to those we welcome," Aelrindel smiled with a shrug. "There is a section of the city where all the foreigners stay in select taverns and inns. The embassies for the Atlanteans and the dwarfs are located in this district. The few foreigners allowed in the city may go anywhere they wish as long as they respect the laws and customs of the Sylvan Kingdom and it is up to their elven hosts or host country to educate them on what that means."

Qel was momentarily taken aback. They had received no such instruction and he wondered if he should have asked when they were at the Wizards Tower in Aquilon. So far he didn't think they had offended any of the Sylvan, with the exception of that one fairy, but it wouldn't hurt learn what they could from Aelrindel before he left them on their own.

All thoughts of propriety vanished from Qel's mind as the royal palace came into view on the other side of the plaza. In their travels Aelrindel had mentioned what an astounding monument it was to the Sylvan people, the royal family and the long history of the kingdom. If anything, the elf downplayed the beauty and expanse of the natural architecture. Somehow, the thousands of trees, vines and foliage that had come together to create it must have taken a thousand years or more to accomplish. The structure of the palace, with towering spires, broad balconies and elevated walkways, seemed impossible to achieve without construction. Yet there it was, in front of them. Artistic details with vine, leaf and branch gave every surface a heightened level of magnificence he could never have imagined in any architecture. Adding to the mystery, Qel could sense that the entire palace was alive with magic and it appeared that the oldest sections of the palace had petrified rather than deteriorated or rotted when the host tree eventually died. The elves were the second oldest civilization on the planet behind the Tuatha De and Qel could only wonder at what this forest had seen over the millennia.

Aelrindel led them around the plaza to a comfortable inn within the foreigners' district, not far from the marketplace. "Will you both join me for the evening meal at my home tonight? It would be my honor to present you to my family."

"Of course, we will." Qel was eager to meet Aelrindel's family. "And the honor would be ours."

"Wonderful, I will return to retrieve you at sundown." With a wave, the elf disappeared back into the crowds of Avalon.

There were several Atlanteans in the common room of the inn, as well as a few dwarfs and the strange human-like people Qel recognized as Tuatha De. *The Tuatha De,* Qel mused to himself, *the most mysterious of all people, perhaps more so than either the elves or the reptilians.* They were known as an ancient people from a land north of Lyonesse. To all appearances, they were just a larger version of humans, except that they most definitely were not.

Generally, their features were dominated by blonde or red hair with blue or light-colored eyes, thin lips, long noses and deep-set eyes. Most exceptional was their high propensity for magic and aptitude for creations of magic. Often they traveled on discs that levitated off the ground using a cloud of dark air similar to the Atlanteans' floating disks. Qel realized that he really didn't know much about the Tuatha

De and made a mental note to ask Havacian what he knew from Master Curatei's teachings when they next had a chance to talk.

The inn where they stayed had a two-room suite available which they gratefully accepted from the Sylvan innkeeper. A young elf boy took charge of their horses while Qel and Havacian carried their travel packs to their room to clean up and relax before Aelrindel returned for them in a few hours. The room was strikingly similar to the guest house they stayed at in Braetling and Qel supposed that there must be a basic floor plan for rooms and residences that allowed for them to be created with more consistency.

"Shall we go back to the common room and enjoy a drink or two before Aelrindel returns?" Havacian looked as energized as Qel felt and he eagerly agreed.

A short time later, Qel was relaxing in a comfortable chair drinking the apple wine Avalon was so well-known for. He had to admit that it was surprisingly good. "Havacian, what have you learned about the Tuatha De?" There were several of them sitting at a table nearby acting half-inebriated, and having a good time just like many other races in the taproom. Not like the dwarfs, of course—no one could hold a candle to their level of intemperance, not even the humans.

Havacian furrowed his eyebrows and spoke as if he was conjuring the words. "The histories speak of them as different than they are today. You know about the 'Blood', right?"

"They are like the masters or the revered in our society, as I understand it," Qel offered, but he was not really sure.

"More than that," Havacian leaned toward him and spoke in almost a whisper, as if one among the crowd across the room might overhear him. "The Blood have godlike powers, or had, anyway. Not many of them are still alive today. So says Master Curatei."

Qel was intrigued now. "What happened to them? And how are they different from those over there?"

"During the time that the Tuatha De were creating monstrous species to serve them, there were many more Blood and only a few like the ones over there." Havacian gestured to the group of Tuatha De laughing in the common room. "Then there was an insurrection of sorts that occurred. The story everyone knows is that the creatures the Blood created rose up against them, but they were defeated and banished to Fomoire. However, that is not the complete truth of it." Havacian drained his cup of apple wine and poured himself another from the carafe on the table. "There was a book written in the Third Age of the Golden Aspen by the Watcher CrellianRafkarSil of Avalon and he records what really happened. Master Curatei happens to own a rare copy."

"The Third Age?" Qel was astonished. "Atlantis didn't develop as a civilization until the Fourth Sylvan Age. You are speaking of several thousands of years ago."

"Indeed," Havacian replied. "Three thousand three hundred seventy-eight years ago, to be exact. I was curious about that myself. Anyway, what CrellianRafkarSil reported was that the creatures did not rise on their own. They were led."

"A civil war among the Tuatha De?"

"Exactly."

"What happened?" Qel begged.

"Some of the Tuatha De Blood refused to give up their creations and violent conflict erupted between them." Havacian physically shuddered. "The Tuatha De were almost all of the 'Blood' then. Pure-born of their race, powerful and godlike. They tore one another to pieces. Many thousands died on both sides, including most of the Blood, before it ended. When it was over, the few who survived banished their creations to Fomoire. The ones that they could find, anyway. Some records reveal that many of the more intelligent creatures managed to escape into the Wilds. Now they can be found all over the world, the Trolls and Ogres among them. It has even been speculated that the dwarfs were an original creation of the Tuatha De," Havacian chuckled, "although any dwarf will vehemently deny that to the point of violence. In the end, what remained of the Tuatha De Blood divided the ruins of their four cities among the survivors."

It was Qel's turn to drain his cup and pour another. "So, what of these other Tuatha De? The ones that are not of the 'Blood'?"

"The few living Tuatha De of the Blood organized into families and elected a principal to head each one. They would become the royalty of the cities Falias, Gorias, Finias and Murias. The problem they faced then was that there were nearly no people to populate and rebuild their cities." Havacian ran his fingers through his brown hair, which was tinged with the mist of sweat from the drink and the telling. "The elves were secluded; the dwarfs were grotesque and the humans were just starting to build rudimentary civilizations. Yet, despite their lack of advanced development, the Tuatha De thought the humans were beautiful and decided to mate with them and populate their cities with their offspring."

"So, the first human cities were in the lands of the Tuatha De?" Qel was incredulous.

"Essentially half-human, but the Tuatha De born to human mothers were much different than that of the average human. They were a highly magical people that took their power from somewhere other than nature or Orichalcum Crystals. The masters are still unsure of the origin of their power."

"What of the Tuatha De Blood?" Qel asked.

"There are so few of them now, perhaps only a dozen or so from what Master Curatei says and apparently that will be the last of them. Either something happened during the conflict that ended their ability to procreate among themselves, or they never could. There are no records of children among the Tuatha De Blood. Even CrellianRafkarSil never recorded anything about it one way or another. There will be no more Tuatha De Blood when the ones alive today eventually die and all that will be left will be their progeny filtered down through their human mates."

"The Blood must live a long time," Qel observed, "if they are still alive after three thousand years."

"Apparently so," Havacian agreed, "but for how much longer? Who knows?"

When Aelrindel returned to the inn, the sun was already below the horizon and the tavern was swelling with patrons. Qel waved him over to where they were sitting and gestured to a chair. The room was so loud with conversation that not even the elf's sharp ears would have heard his call.

Aelrindel sat and leaned over the table. "Sadly, my parents are out of the city this evening," the elf practically had to shout to be heard. "So, if you like, I will take you on a tour of Avalon and we will have the evening meal at a tavern mostly patronized by locals."

"That is a fine alternative, although we are saddened that we will be unable to meet your family tonight." Qel stood, eager to see Avalon at night and get away from the noise inside the tavern.

Pushing through the crowd to exit the tavern, Qel paused outside to stare in wonder at the surrounding forest dwellings. Almost all emitted a yellow glow from their interiors, competing with the light-globes that lit the streets outside atop tall poles grown out of the ground at intervals. With the transition from day to night, Avalon appeared very different than when they went into the tavern. Following the curve of branches high above them, Qel was surprised to see many other dwellings and walkways that he had not noticed before. The numerous lights from their windows shone like stars in the dark canopy, giving the illusion of an open sky above. Considering the elevation of so many dwellings and the size of the city, there must have been several thousand elves that resided along the vast network of branches.

Prompted by Aelrindel, the companions were soon back at the grand plaza where the merchants hawking and trading continued in full force. "They will go as late as mid-evening before they are compelled to close for the night. At least for a few hours, the city must be quiet."

Qel agreed that the market was quite noisy, but now that the sun had set, the plaza was filled with magical light-globes hanging on poles, suspended from merchant's stalls, or carried by shoppers. Many were in colors other than natural light, especially those illuminating the merchant stalls blinking and whirling to attract attention. Brilliant tones of blue, red, green and yellow lent an almost carnival-like atmosphere to the area. A festive display that drew the eye to every corner and along each aisle eager to see something new.

Then there was the palace that loomed over the plaza like a massive guardian. The entire structure was somehow bathed in a frost-blue light that contrasted starkly with the colorful glow from the market and coolly with the warm illumination cast from dozens of windows and balconies facing the plaza. For Qel to say that the palace, with its glowing towers and natural façade, was profoundly beautiful, would have been an egregious understatement. He wanted to stare for hours and take in every detail, but Aelrindel was walking further ahead, no doubt finding the sights and sounds ordinary having lived among them for so long.

That last thought saddened him for a moment as he considered the long lives the elves enjoyed. To them, life must sometimes become so dull, like fish in a pond or a bird captured in a cage. Except that they had the free will to go beyond their borders and explore new places and experience new ideas, yet they rarely did. The elves seemed perfectly content in their fishbowl and it left Qel wondering why.

Taverns set on the edge of the plaza had moved more chairs and tables outside with nightfall so their patrons could enjoy their meal or drink in the open air of the chilly spring evening. Music drifted on the breeze from a minstrel playing a flute to entertain patrons seated outside a nearby tavern while several other songsters and troupes of musicians played merrily around the perimeter of the plaza, which was so expansive that they could all entertain their respective audiences without creating a cacophony of sound. Then there were the fragrances of cooked food that made Qel's stomach grumble loudly, reminding him that he had not eaten anything since midday.

His attention was suddenly diverted to an almost humorous scene playing out between a dwarf merchant and a tiny fairy standing on a display table full of hundreds of everyday household utensils forged from Dvergr steel. The two were embroiled in a heated argument until finally the dwarf shrugged and handed the fairy a small steel pin. The fairy, in turn, threw the dwarf a tiny bag and flew away with her hard-won item. Qel couldn't help but laugh, drawing a dark look from the dwarf, and he quickly held up his hands in a gesture of apology. The dwarf turned his back on him with a loud *harrumph*, then directed his attention to another patron. Still smiling, Qel followed along behind Aelrindel and Havacian around the outside edge of the marketplace, his gaze flitting from one curious scene to the next. Having just seen the fairy, Qel abruptly realized that there must have been hundreds of them buzzing around the plaza like bumblebees and dragonflies. Most carried tiny little light-globes bright enough to be seen by their larger brethren as they flew high above the crowd's heads to avoid being trampled.

As fantastic as the City of Atlantis was, Qel was utterly taken in by the beauty and ambiance of Avalon. They passed a wide street that Aelrindel said led to the Foreign District. Qel could see the southern edge of an odd stone structure. It had no windows that Qel could see and the entrance was blocked by two massive oak doors. The building was dark except for the illumination from the light-globes along the street.

"That is the embassy of the dwarfs," Aelrindel pointed at the oppressive grey block.

Qel thought the stone building looked so out of place in this city of natural beauty that he wondered why the elves allowed the dwarfs to build it. The next complex Aelrindel pointed out looked like any other structure in Avalon. The vine doors were pulled open allowing bright light and cheerful sounds to spill out. He could see several Atlanteans and elves gathered together inside holding goblets of wine in apparent celebration of some special event. Probably something to do with trade, anniversary or an official's birthday, Qel thought. His parents had hosted many of them when he was a child and still did as far as he knew.

"That is the Atlantean embassy," Aelrindel informed them.

Qel was relieved his people had proved more adaptable than the Dvergr Dwarfs. He knew that the Atlantean Empire had a small presence in nearly every major civilized city in the known world, overtly or not, and that they went to great pains mimicking the architecture of the host society. Sometimes blending with their religious icons, temples and sacred places. In many cultures the Atlanteans were considered representatives of the gods themselves.

The smell of cooked food coming from a dwelling that looked too short to stand in and completely woven with strange bulging roots made Qel's stomach rumble with more urgency. He recognized the smell of grilled hartebeest and mahiz, a staple of the Atlantean diet that he had enjoyed many times in his life and it left his mouth watering for a taste.

"That's a cookhouse," Aelrindel explained. "They are located near the residences and in the rear courtyard of every tavern and inn all over the city."

Havacian looked over at the elf in surprise, "The elves allow indoor cooking in Avalon?"

Aelrindel nodded, "The full-sized kitchens are sunken into the ground and built completely of stone on the inside. The roots and vines growing over them are perpetually saturated with water in case there is an accident. They also serve to hide the gross ugliness of the stone. Just like in Braetling, no flame is allowed anywhere in the city, with the exception of the cookhouses."

Finally, to the great delight of Qel's complaining stomach, Aelrindel stopped at a small tavern off the main street and they went inside. There was enough room for only about twenty people to sit in the small establishment and it was nearly full. Aelrindel found them spaces together at a long table where a number of elves were already seated. Qel noted that although there were only elves in the tavern, they didn't seem bothered at all by the Atlanteans intrusion.

"How long will you two be staying in the city?" Aelrindel asked when they were settled and mugs of fruit wine had been ordered.

Qel looked at Havacian. "At least a few more days. We don't have any particular plans, so we will probably explore the city thoroughly before we move on."

Aelrindel smiled. "Great. I have work that requires my attention tomorrow; however, I will return the next day and take you to the wild apple groves outside the city if you like."

"That would be wonderful," Qel replied appreciatively. "Everyone has heard of the legendary apple groves of Avalon, although few have seen them."

The server soon returned and they were treated to their fill of rabbit stew, crusty bread and wild asparagus porridge seasoned with local herbs before strolling back to their inn sometime later. It had been a long day of travel on the back of a horse and with the sweet taste of fruit wine lingering on Qel's tongue and clouding his senses, fatigue left him wanting for good night's sleep. He looked forward to a full day exploring the city the next morning and knew that Havacian would have him up early. Thanking Aelrindel for his hospitality, they retired to their room for the evening.

———

Morning greeted Qel with the sounds of chirping birds and the muffled movements of Havacian getting washed and dressed in the connecting chamber. He was excited about exploring Avalon further, but allowed himself a few more moments in the comfortable bed molded by branches and springy vines that grew around him like a cocoon. Light filtered through slender spaces between crisscrossed twigs that formed a small window above him casting flickering shadows against the opposite wall. He guessed that it couldn't be more than an hour or two past dawn. Torn by a desire to lay in the tranquility of his room and eagerness to start the day, Qel sat up and washed his face in a basin of water set within a nearby nook. He was glad they were here and he was grateful for the friends they had made and was feeling more confident than ever that he and Havacian would be okay on their own.

The first half of the day was spent at the market sampling strange food and perusing unusual wares from all over the world. By late afternoon, Qel suggested they take a break from the market and the two agreed to stop by the Atlantean embassy near their inn. Once there, they learned that the Wizards Tower was located on the other side of the city. They briefly considered moving their accommodations to the Tower, but decided against it, preferring to experience the city from a local perspective even if it was within the Foreigners District.

"We should check in at the Tower before we leave Avalon in case there are any messages for us," Qel suggested.

"It's on the far side of the city and the day is running short if we are to return to the market," replied Havacian. "Shall we plan to go tomorrow?"

"Tomorrow would be best," Qel agreed.

When nightfall found them once more, Qel suggested that they spend the evening enjoying the sights and sounds of the marketplace at one of the taverns with outdoor seating. It didn't take long to find one with seats at a small table and an orchestra that played pleasant music. From where they sat, Qel could observe the persistently busy market, the impressive canopy of lights cast from the natural structures high above them and the legendary Sylvan Palace that had to be the most inspiring building, if he could call it that, he had ever seen. Looking at it closer, Qel could see that the palace was much like all the other grown constructs in Avalon, at a much larger scale, with massive tree trunks and exposed roots forming its foundation, thick branches shaping its frame and thin vines that overlapped continuously like mortar that filled in all the spaces. The entire palace was covered with leaves and moss that formed intricate patterns between huge effigies of animals that seemed impossible to have been created with living foliage. Qel did not doubt that given its sheer size, stretching to the highest elevations above them and with the complexity of structures that it encompassed, it was easily as vast as the palace in Atlantis.

During the evening meal, Qel was gazing at the Sylvan Palace when he noticed a soft red glow emanating from high upon the very top of the structure. Considering the entire palace was illuminated in blue light, the dull luminescence of the red-glowing crystal at the apex of one of the palace's tallest towers was barely noticeable.

Qel pointed out the glow to Havacian. "I was wondering where the Source Crystal was located."

After a moment of quiet study, Havacian agreed. "I can feel the Source very strong in Avalon, stronger than I could feel it in Braetling and nearly as strong as our home. I was certain that a large Source Crystal had to be nearby and I just assumed it was atop the Wizards Tower."

Qel fingered the Crystal amulet under his clothing; he could feel it hum in close proximity to the much larger stone. "Have the masters ever told you how much of the Source Crystal they house in structures around the world? I mean, do you think it is as much as a cartload in there or maybe just a single large shard?"

Havacian considered a moment. "We have both seen the cavern under the Wizards Enclave, with the hundreds of man-sized Source Crystals stored there. As I recall, they were all generally the same size and shape and none appeared broken. I would guess one or more of those are relocated to the towers and pyramids around the world, but I have no idea how many."

"So the pure crystal at the top of the palace amplifies and radiates the Source Crystal's power for a considerable distance from where it sits now?"

Havacian nodded while he chewed the pulpy kernels of salted mahiz from the bowl of vegetable stew he had ordered. "That's just a finely cut and polished quartz fashioned into whatever form is most appropriate for its location. Usually, it's fashioned into the shape of a pyramid since that is a most efficient purveyor of power over long distances. I don't know why. The Source Crystals are far below, in direct line with the quartz, in a protected area that few have access to.

Qel had also ordered the vegetable stew and aside from the mahiz, he did not recognize any of the other vegetables that crowded the thick broth. In any case, it was delicious and he considered ordering a second bowl. Elf portions were somewhat smaller than what he was used to in Atlantis.

"How far does the power of each Crystal extend?" Qel wondered. "I mean, should we be worried about dead zones where we will not have access to our magical talents?"

"From what Master Curatei explained to me, the masters and high priests have created an overlapping power grid of sorts all across the world by placing the Source Crystals at certain points along predictable lines of longitude and latitude called ley lines."

Havacian always became excited when he was explaining something new. Qel wanted to laugh, but he didn't want his friend to take it the wrong way. His friend was a natural when it came to soaking up knowledge and teaching it to others in a simple way that was easy to comprehend. If Qel had to bet on which one of them would be a master first, he would have to bet on his friend.

"At those points, they construct towers, pyramids, or temples of various designs unless they are granted access by the local rulers to one suitable to their needs." Havacian continued. "Most importantly, the buildings must blend in with the local culture using architectural fashion common to where they are built. With the exception of the quartz, they typically look like every other structure around them."

Qel was intrigued. He knew the basics of what Havacian explained but had not learned many of the details about the Orichalcum Source Crystals from his own master. "So why are some of the Source Crystal locations tended by priests of Pontus and others tended by wizards of the Imperial Order?"

"It all depends on where they are located," Havacian explained. "Some cultures are theocracies ruled by representatives or avatars of their gods. Many of those cultures believe the arrival of the Atlanteans was prophesized and they see our people as children of their gods or even the gods themselves. Those cultures are very sensitive to their people's unwavering belief system and our priests are more appropriate to work side by side with their own. Obviously, the natives rarely know the true purpose of why we are there. An example of this type of interaction is with the people of Kur-gal, far to the east beyond the Great Sea." Havacian took a sip of wine before he continued. "The more advanced or enlightened cultures that accept wizards as part of their social norm are more likely to want to keep their religious matters separate and, in that case, wizards of the Imperial Order are a better choice. Ys, Eriu and Lyonesse are perfect examples of that."

"I envy that your master was the Keeper of Records and took the time to teach you about these things," Qel said.

Chuckling, Havacian replied, "I envy that you can light a campfire with your finger. And I doubt that it was an accident that our masters allowed us to be friends from an early age. Somehow I suspect the masters go to great lengths pairing their apprentices with others who they can learn from."

Qel laughed as well. "How clever of them!"

Chapter 20

New Friends

Qel stood staring up at the 'Tower' in awe. Havacian was right—the Wizards Towers were not always actual towers. Depending on where one was located, the constructs usually conformed to the standard architectural style of that city so as not to stand out as an obviously foreign structure. Here in Avalon, the Wizards Tower was a massive tree supporting a significant complex of natural dwellings that were interconnected extending into the farthest reaches of its highest colossal branches. Had he guessed at the magnificence of the Tower, Qel would have elected to stay here rather than the inn and based on the look of admiration on his friend's face he doubted it would have taken much convincing to get Havacian to agree.

Qel stepped through the main entrance followed by Havacian only a step behind. They were immediately greeted by a young clerk, "May I have your names please?"

"I am Qellel of House Mekali and this is Havaciante of House Talika. We are recent graduates of the Imperial Order of Wizards in Atlantis."

The clerk quickly recorded their names on a ledger held steadily in his left hand. "Will you be staying? I can direct you to the house administrator if you are." His response was formal and very polite.

"No," Qel responded with a tinge of regret. "We would like to go to the lounge as we already have accommodations elsewhere."

"Of course." The clerk showed no surprise or any emotion otherwise. If nothing else, he was very professional. "The lower lounge is through the hall behind me and on the right. The upper lounge, which is known as the 'Treetop Recline' can be reached via the stairway at the end of the same hall or the lift discs next to it."

Qel was confused. "Lift discs?"

"Yes," the clerk answered coolly. This was obviously not the first time he had addressed this question. "The lift discs will take you quickly and directly to the upper lounge without the exertion of climbing a little over two thousand steps."

Qel looked at Havacian. "The lift discs, then."

"Very good, it's located at the end of the hall behind me," he reminded them and then greeted the next guest, who had just walked up behind them.

Qel was eager to see these lift discs. Certainly, they must exist in the City of Atlantis, probably in the palace and maybe even in parts of the Wizards Enclave where apprentices were prohibited from venturing into. Qel was mildly surprised he had not heard of them before now.

They followed the instructions of the initiate, walking through the naturally formed tunnel of vine and branch studded with light globes along the way. It opened into a huge lounge crowded with dozens of men in muted cloaks or vibrant robes and women wearing colorful gowns that often trail behind them when they walked. Most were Atlanteans with nearly as many elves, a few humans and a handful of dwarfs engaged in lively conversation. But the sight that stopped Qel in his tracks were a pair of creatures he had only read about in history books between his studies at the Enclave.

"Incredible," Havacian muttered breathlessly next to him.

The two creatures, Qel couldn't think of them as beasts although they shared much in common with one, stood as tall as an Atlantean with the pale features of a human and the pointed ears of an elf. They wore white lacey gowns that covered lean feminine physics and their heads were capped by broad-brimmed hats decorated with feathers under which long dark hair cascaded halfway down their backs. When one shifted, the long leather skirts they wore embroidered with silver tassels moved hypnotically from side to side, but it wasn't enough to distract from the long arching spine that ran over their thick flanks and heavy hindquarters or legs, all four of them, that tapered down to sharp hooves.

"Centaurs," Qel excitedly nudged his elbow into Havacian's side. "All the way from Gades!"

"Ooof!" Havacian grunted. "I see them, Qel. How graceful they stand. How beautiful."

Qel couldn't agree more. The centaurs were a thing of beauty that no image or description in a book could have hoped to capture so eloquently as they appeared in real life. Their fluid movements and frequent smiles lent to an impression of kindness and decency that gave away their Sylvan origins, although as far as Qel knew, there were no centaurs in the Sylvan Kingdom. They lived on a cluster of remote islands, across the Primal Sea east of Atlantis, called the Isles of Gades. It was a small kingdom with close ties to the elves ruled by a Nymph Queen and her consort, a golden dragon named Senjit. A few years earlier there had been a flurry of news from Gades when the royal wedding had taken place and now it was said the couple had welcomed the birth of their first child. A very unusual little girl, so the rumors went, but such stories carried few details.

Qel pulled at Havacian's arm. "Let's not stand here gawking like first-year initiates. Perhaps we will see more of them in the Treetop Recline."

On the opposite edge of the lounge, another branchy corridor wound further into the 'tower'. When they reached the end, there was the stairway situated on the left side of an open landing visible through a wide nook that led outside. Glancing out, Qel could see that it spiraled around the outside of the colossal trunk of the tree they were in rising so high that it became lost in the cluster of leaves and branches far above them. But it was the strange contraption on their right that held their attention. The base of it was apparently a disc. It glowed and hovered just like every flying disc he had ever seen in Atlantis. What was strange about it, aside from the fact that ten men could have easily stood upon it with room to spare, was that it was enclosed in a kind of cage. Like the cage his master would keep the occasional songbird on the desk in his office. Branches surrounded the disc from top to bottom with enough space in between to extend an arm or leg if one chose to. There was a kind of door, also made of branches, which swung freely, as if inviting them to enter. Qel hesitated. The disc floated there attached to two thick branches, one on each side of it. The branches were smooth and sprang straight up from the ground where they stood to somewhere deep into the canopy above. Beside it, there was a vacant space and two additional branches marking the spot where another lift disc must rest when not in use. It was a thing of wonder, a thing of magnificent magic and it scared Qel half to death.

"Do you want to take the stairs?" Havacian spoke nervously and uncertainly, as if he just assumed Qel would agree. Qel couldn't agree. They had to get on this wondrous monstrosity and experience the terrifying adventure of it.

"No," Qel replied, unable to conceal the warble in his voice. "We're going to take the lift disc."

"Okay," Havacian agreed. "That's what I thought we would do anyway."

Despite their apparent resolve, neither of them made a move toward it. They just stood and stared and considered their courage.

"Going up?" The gravelly voice that came from behind shocked Qel nearly to his core. He caught an audible *yip* from Havacian and knew his friend had not heard anyone approach either.

The man came around in front of them after neither of them responded. "Are you boys okay? If you're going up, get on, or you'll have to wait for the next."

He was a human of middle years, with long black hair to match his equally long beard and mustaches. His gray robes were layered and long, cinched at the waist by a thick chain of gold and he held a staff in one hand. "C'mon, let's go. The best wine is in the Treetop—Mekali, I believe—and I intend to have a few cups before the night is done. I'll treat you both to a cup or two if you'll join me."

Qel struggled to speak. The human's smile was comforting and his deep-blue eyes were inviting, but they also held a glimmer of undeniable power that he had only seen in the learned orbs of the masters at the Enclave.

Clearing his throat, Qel finally found his voice, "Yes, yes, we are going up. Havacian, are you ready? Havacian?"

Havacian stood rooted as sure as the great tree they were about to ascend. Qel reached out and took hold of his friend's sleeve and to his relief, Havacian moved forward until they were both standing on the lift disc with the friendly human. The man stepped forward and closed the door, prompting the disc to hum beneath them.

"Take us up!" The man was looking at Qel when he said it. Qel felt panic rising. He had no idea what to do and considered just getting off as he was so embarrassed.

"You've never been on a lift disc before, have you boy?" There was no mocking in the man's tone, just a statement of fact.

"No, sir," Qel managed to reply.

"You just have to will it to ascend under your own power. It will go as slow or fast as you like." The human's face stretched into a wide warm smile, "Give it a try."

Qel heard the words the man spoke, but he wasn't sure if he comprehended what it was he was supposed to do. Quickly recovering himself, he closed his eyes and visualized the lift ascending. There was a jolt, the rush of acceleration, his stomach dropped to his feet and then the sensation of weightlessness. Havacian screamed in terror. Qel's eyes shot open and suddenly everything stopped. He felt himself using his power but in a very controlled manner. To his shock, he realized that the human was in control of the flow of his magic and tempered its surge, regulated it so the lift ascended slowly and smoothly. *How is this possible? Even my master has never taken control of my mind and magic the way this man does.* It made him feel helpless, but at the same time, he was *learning*. The man was teaching him how to control the ebb and flow of the magic that surged through him.

"We've got it," the man said with assurance. He showed no effort at all from where he stood casually on the other side of the cage. Qel looked beyond the thick branches and could see the lights from the city far below. There was the market, the palace, their inn. He felt light-headed from the height and clenched his teeth to keep a scream to rival the one released by Havacian from being ripped from his throat.

"Ah, a fear of heights," the man commented. *How does he know?* "I'll fix that."

Seconds later, Qel felt normal again. The fear and anxiety were gone and the lift disc was still ascending under his power. Well, the man's control of his power through him. And so it went until they were into the canopy of the trees and the city was only a twinkle of lights below. Then the lift disc abruptly stopped.

Reaching forward, the man opened the door of the cage. "Here we are," he said cheerfully.

Qel stumbled forward, dragging Havacian behind him. It was late afternoon and all around them, elves, Atlanteans and dwarfs sat in comfortable chairs drinking or having a meal at one of the many long tables. Servers wove in and out of the crowd serving cups of wine, ale and mead throughout the room. Except that it wasn't a room at all. It was more like an immense balcony. Looking beyond the chest-high wall of entangled branches that surrounded the open space, Qel could see the clear sky to the horizon in every direction. They were at the very top of the tree and below the green canopy of the forest stretched out before them.

"It's beautiful, isn't it?" the man said quietly beside him. "As many times as you come up here in your lifetime and it will be many, I assure you, the view will never be less astounding."

Qel was nearly in tears at the sight before him. This must be the view Pontus enjoyed every day looking down upon them. Someone put a cup in his hand and he absentmindedly took a sip. It was Mekali wine, from his home far to the south. He looked over to see Havacian holding a cup and staring into the vast expanse with as much ardor as he was.

"Join me for a few more, boys," the man said jovially. "The more you drink, the more philosophical you will become in a place like this! But first, tell me your names."

Qel pulled himself back into reality. "My name is Qel and this is Havacian." He gestured to his friend, who was slowly turning from the impressive scenery to join the conversation. "May we have the pleasure of your acquaintance?"

"Why certainly," the man replied with a broad smile. "The name is Myrllin, at your service."

Qel was distracted by two men, wearing earth-brown robes decorated with feathers and beads, who strode quickly by him toward the low wall he had turned from to address the human, Myrllin. Their hoods were up, so he couldn't tell if they were elves or humans, but it hardly mattered, for not a pace from where Qel stood the pair jumped up on top of the wall and casually stepped off the other side.

This time, Qel could not suppress his scream and neither could Havacian. Instantly, they were both at the wall looking over to see the fate of the two men. There was no sight of them and no ledge below that they could have landed on. The only life he could see were two eagles that flew away from them side by side.

Then the realization of what had just happened hit him. "They were druids," Qel told Havacian. "They walked off the edge and transformed into those eagles over there." He pointed across the growing distance to where the eagles flew.

"Thank Pontus," Havacian exhaled.

The room behind them was oddly silent and when Qel turned to see what was the matter, every soul was staring at them. Their urgent screams had apparently captured the attention of the entire room. He was never so embarrassed in his life.

Myrllin walked to stand between him and Havacian and with an explosive laugh, patted them both on the back. The room erupted in laughter with him and the sounds of music and casual chatter resumed. Myrllin had saved them from an awkward situation again.

He smiled slyly before steering them toward a long table with a few open spaces. "Let's go liberate a few more glasses of that fine Mekali wine from their barrels, shall we?"

———

Qel awoke with a slight headache and a horrid sense of dread. What had they done? He recalled that they drank Mekali wine throughout the night with their new human friend. What was his name? Myrllin? Yes, that was it. The man was quite the social entertainer with his stories and witty humor. Qel and Havacian enjoyed his company enormously and the wine kept flowing. At first, it was just the three of them laughing and spinning tales at the long table in the center of the upper lounge. Before long, others gathered with them at the table, including several elves, to join in on the fun. It was surreal sitting among these wizards, many of whom were quite accomplished based on their fine clothing and medallions of office. Qel was even surprised to see a pair of Atlantean masters, whom he did not recognize, seated at a nearby table. Many of the patrons of the Treetop Recline knew this man called Myrllin, especially the older ones and everyone treated him with great respect. Qel respected him as well after feeling the control and power the man had exerted over him in the lift disc. It was a sensation he would never forget. He wished he had the chance to ask Havacian if he felt it as well.

The afternoon had lengthened into evening and food was brought out for everyone to share. It was a good thing since Qel was ravenous after all the drinking. If the night had ended there, Qel thought he would have departed the upper lounge as a respectable Atlantean wizard of the Imperial Order who had dined with what some of the patrons referred to as a legend of the magical arts. Unfortunately, things had taken a very different turn.

Just after they finished the fine meal of roasted vegetables and braised pork, a man walked into the lounge. To Qel's utter shock, it was the Wandering Minstrel—or the Wanderer, as most called him—

Wodanaz. A great shout of recognition greeted the minstrel from the crowded room of patrons prompting him to wave and smile in return. He looked around the room until his gaze landed on the table where they were sitting and without hesitation began weaving his way through the room, receiving pats on the back as he went. When he arrived, the man sitting next to Myrllin quickly vacated his seat and with a nod of thanks, Wodanaz replaced him.

"I was hoping to speak with you about a matter of some importance tonight," Myrllin told Wodanaz, "but I found these two and they needed a bit of mentoring."

"I got your message, brother," Wodanaz had replied. "If you're sure they need us, you know I'm here to help. Besides, it's nice to see you loosen up once in a while." He turned to them and put out his hand, "I'm Wodanaz. I believe I have seen the pair of you before. Well, no matter, you're about to have the wildest night of your lives . . ."

Everything was a blur after that. Qel remembered Wodanaz playing his golden flute and singing fanciful tunes. There was dancing on the tables and bawdy songs and raucous laughter from the patrons of the lounge. More were always arriving as the word got out that Wodanaz was entertaining. All the while, Myrllin encouraged both Qel and Havacian to perform small feats of magic, like creating dancing flames or fireworks in the air. Havacian invoked a light mist to appear throughout the lounge during one of Wodanaz's dramatic tales before sending hundreds of floating water-filled bubbles spinning about the room that others would pop, showering their friends with water to everyone's delight.

Qel never drank so much of his family's wine, or any wine, in his life and if things had stopped there, even then, they could have departed with their dignity. But there was more, much more. Myrllin never let up and continued to encourage them to greater and more challenging feats. Qel did things that he had no idea were possible, let alone something he was capable of. The power he wielded was absurd as he shot magnificent orbs of fire and jets of flames into the air high above them, lighting up the night as if it were daytime. He even produced a line of half-clad dancing women, formed by flames, swaying seductively on the wall of branches that kept the patrons from tumbling off the side of the platform. Havacian somehow conjured a thick pillar of water underneath each of them to keep Qel's flaming women from burning the branches causing sizzling steam to cover the lounge in a smoky haze. The crowd cheered them on and cried for more . . . and they gave more. The spice in the pie, as his mother would say.

By the end of the night, he and Havacian each managed to inexplicably commandeer the pair of lift discs, racing them up and down the length of the great tree under their own power and control. Qel remembered *jumping* from one to the other as they moved together at impossible speeds, clutching with one hand to the outside of the cage surrounding the discs, laughing about not spilling his wine when he landed. Until that moment, Qel had no idea that his family vintage could cause people to lose their minds.

He cringed under his blankets, recalling more and more details of the previous night. At least they survived it and managed to find their way back to the inn, although he remembered none of that part. *He* survived it anyhow; he would have to check on Havacian in his room. Qel wondered what his master would say when he got the report about their behavior in the Treetop Recline. There were masters there that would be sure to have noticed. He didn't want to think about it.

Finally emerging from his bed, Qel was still a little shaky on his feet. He stood a few moments to regain his balance and then took his time washing and getting dressed. His stomach rumbled, reminding him he had not eaten for several hours and with food as the goal in mind, he left his room to find Havacian. To his surprise, his friend was already up, staring up at the ceiling from a chair in the sitting room that connected their bedchambers in the suite.

"Do you remember what we did last night?" he said when Qel entered.

"Some of it," Qel replied. "Too much of it."

Havacian visibly shuddered. "There's going to be hell to pay, you know. I hope the masters don't recall us."

"The Tower knows where we are staying," Qel said, "if they decide to send us a message."

Havacian sighed. "There's nothing we can do about it now, I suppose. Are you hungry?"

Qel let himself laugh. "I could eat a whole hartebeest by myself!"

———

Qel and Havacian were just finishing up with their breakfast when Aelrindel walked into the inn. He had a grin on his face as wide as the Primal Sea when he spied them sitting at a nearby table. "I heard you two had an impressive evening at the Wizards Tower last night," he said while taking a seat at the table with them.

Qel was bewildered. "How could you know that?"

"Two Atlanteans stood toe to toe with Wodanaz and his brother Myrllin in a contest of magical feats and . . . drinking." Aelrindel laughed. "Word is all over the city after your little light show last night, not to mention your antics afterwards on the lift discs."

Havacian visibly sank lower in his chair. "We are definitely going to be recalled now, Qel."

Qel glanced at his friend and then back to Aelrindel. "No one knows who we are, I hope? Our names?"

"You don't remember, do you?" replied Aelrindel dubiously.

"Remember what?" Qel was feeling irritable now. Apparently, the entire city remembered more than he did about last night.

"Well," Aelrindel cleared his throat. "With all the commotion you boys were making up there, more than a few citizens became concerned. Some of those citizens were quite influential and before long the High-King ordered his Griffon Riders to investigate. From what I heard, you two were just getting off a wild ride on the lift discs and fairly close to passing out when they arrived. Myrllin assured them that everything was fine and requested that they return you to your inn to sleep off the effects of the evening."

Aelrindel leaned back in his chair, crossed his arms and displayed his infuriating smile again. "And that's how you got back to the inn last night."

"Are you saying that the High-King's elite Griffon Riders *flew* us back to this inn and put us in our beds?" Qel was incredulous.

Havacian just groaned.

"The innkeeper's staff put you in bed, but yes, the Griffon Riders flew you here," Aelrindel finished triumphantly. Qel had a feeling he had planned this entire conversation just to watch them squirm. This was the dark side of elven humor he had heard about.

Havacian groaned a second time.

"I guess we are done here," Qel blustered. "I'm surprised we haven't been run out of the city or had a visit from the Atlantean ambassador. Surely this will be viewed very badly at the Enclave. Our masters will probably fetch us back, strip us down to initiates and keep us locked up in the Enclave for another twenty years!"

"I doubt it," Aelrindel replied coolly.

"You doubt it? *You* doubt it? Who are *you* to doubt anything?" Qel exploded on the elf with a fury he had never felt before. He and Havacian were facing severe repercussions for what they had done and it wasn't entirely their fault. And this *elf* was telling him that he *doubted* anything would come of it. Didn't he just say that they were flown back to their inn on the orders of the High-King of the Sylvan Kingdom? They were in serious trouble and he knew it.

"Be calm," Aelrindel spoke softly, soothingly. "Don't you know what you have done?"

Qel was out of energy, exasperated and defeated. "What have we done besides act like fools for the world to see?" he replied calmly.

"You have spent an evening with Wodanaz and Myrllin, the two most prolific figures of our age and many ages besides," Aelrindel told them. "If anything, you will be hailed as friends of the famous duo."

Qel was doubtful. "That remains to be seen."

"So how about I take you to the apple groves as I promised?" Aelrindel's sprightly mood was not catching.

"Sure," Qel replied blandly. "That would be great." Somehow the appeal of the famed apple groves had lost its luster, but at least they would be away from Avalon for a while.

"Great. I'll tell you some good news on the way."

Aelrindel led them to the stables to obtain their mounts. To Qel's surprise, the horses had been readied for their departure and they rode from the inn with little delay. Avalon was crowded and busy this time of day, inhibiting their movement as they made their way around the market and through the northern districts of the city. Here, many of the natural structures were grown quite large and complex. Aelrindel explained that the dwellings were mostly government and administrative complexes, with the most important offices at the lower levels and the lesser ones set higher among the branches in the canopy above. After what seemed like a long time, the crowds thinned and the noise reached a tolerable level, allowing Aelrindel to speak without shouting.

"My father returned yesterday and suggested that I travel to Ys. Apparently, strange things are happening in the city and he asked me to investigate the rumors on behalf of the High-King. How would you two like to join me on another adventure?"

Qel, feeling sorry for himself up until then, found the idea of escaping the city and possibly the wrath of their masters before they could be summoned appealed to him greatly. "When can we leave?"

"Qel . . ." Havacian began.

"Do you really want to go back to Master Curatei and the rest of the Enclave a failed wizard barely into our 'Journey of Discovery'?" Qel chided. "I certainly don't. If we can leave the city and get on a ship to Ys before an initiate from the Tower can find us, then technically we haven't done anything wrong."

Havacian rolled his eyes. "Except evade their summons. You know it must be coming."

"Well, *they* don't know we are evading anything. We're simply moving along to a new destination."

"What happens when we run out of money?" countered Havacian. "As soon as we show our faces in the Wizards Tower in Ys, or anywhere for that matter, the summons will be waiting for us."

"Then we will make our way on our own," Qel retorted. "I'm sure two talented wizards of the Imperial Order can earn a few coins doing something useful to get by."

"Perhaps we can open for Wodanaz. You can create pretty fireworks and I can juggle balls of water. What a pair we would make!" Havacian was being sarcastic and irritable, Qel knew. In the end, Havacian would not want to return to the City of Atlantis after their night of overindulgence any more than Qel did.

"Boys, boys," Aelrindel interrupted. "Everything will be fine. I'm sure of it. I have already booked passage on a ship to Ys that departs in two days. I reserved for the three of us in case you wanted to join me. Let's enjoy the groves this afternoon and we will worry about getting you on the ship without the Tower discovering your deception once we return."

Chapter 21

Shrine of Metis

Senjit arrived in Sesklo in the afternoon and as usual, he set up in a busy tavern to canvas their patrons for information. Almost immediately he heard the same story related to him in Foronikon-Asty. As fortune would have it, he arrived in Sesklo a few days before the Ritual of the Summer Solstice which was traditionally performed by a Fire-Bringer. Unfortunately, the last one died in his bed of old age the year before and there was not another to replace him. The subject of Fire-Bringers was a popular one at the moment and there was no bigger tale to tell than that of their most famous one – a club-footed priest named Akakios. Although the details were sketchy, from what Senjit could gather, the story involved Anesidora, the beautiful daughter of the deities Kronos and Metis. Enter Akakios, apparently smitten by her image in dreams and a plea for help, ventured on a pilgrimage to the Shrine of Metis, which legend asserted lay high in the Othrys Mountains, to claim his love.

A love story.

Senjit was surprised. He still wasn't sure what, if anything, it might have to do with the Chaos Demons, but it was the only interesting pursuit he had at the moment. Without further consideration, he decided to find this Shrine of Metis and investigate further. According to the story, it was located in the peaks above a remote village far to the east on the coast of the Sea of Waves. Of course, no one had ever been there, except for maybe Akakios and he was long deceased. Senjit calculated that it would take him a little over an hour to reach the coast and with a bit of luck and the advantage of flight, he would find the shrine without too much effort. Before he departed, Senjit thought it might be prudent to speak with the Hierophant in the Naos of Kronos. If anyone had reliable details about Akakios's circumstances, it would likely be the Hierophant of the order the Fire-Bringers belonged to.

The next morning, Senjit was up with the first light of dawn. He wanted to get to the temple before the priests began their morning rituals and he fervently hoped the Hierophant was not a late riser. Whatever the case, Senjit was determined to see the Hierophant, even if from the man's bedside, and be quickly on his way to the coast.

There were only a few people in the street at such an early hour. Tradesmen and servants mostly, moving sluggishly in their short chitons and sandals through the haze toward their varied destinations, unhurried by the slowly rising sun that had yet to cast its rays upon the single-story buildings in the mountain city. It was cold here, much colder than Gades and it was summertime. In his human form, Senjit felt the chill far more acutely than when he was a dragon and he was glad that his journey had not brought him here during the winter months when thick layers of snow covered the mountainside.

Up ahead, he could see the flames from the iron braziers reflecting off the polished white marble columns that rose from a base of carved steps to an impressive facing embellished with images of Kronos highlighted by accents of red-gold plating. He climbed the steps and strode through the forest of columns to a doorless entry so large that he could have easily passed even as a dragon. A long dark hallway with sculpted images on the walls and many more columns stretched beyond to an altar set with a bronze bowl containing a flickering red flame at the far end. On each side a guard in broze armor holding a shield and an unusual-looking sword stood at attention facing the holy display.

Not hesitating a moment, Senjit strode with purpose down the hallway. He barely made it half-way down when a man stepped out from between the columns directly in his path only a few steps away. He was short, middle-aged, with a shock of greying hair that formed a partial ring around his balding head. In one hand he carried a chisel and in the other a hammer, both held low and unthreatening against wool raiment typical of a priest. He smiled warmly as Senjit approached closer.

"Eukomai se . . ." the priest began.

Senjit stopped and waved his hand in a swift gesture. The man's features immediately smoothed, his body relaxed and his eyes stared ahead blankly. Humans were easy to charm, especially the least intelligent of them.

"I need to see the Hierophant," Senjit stated flatly.

"Of course," the priest agreed as if he was about to suggest it himself. "Please follow me."

Senjit followed the priest past the guards and through a series of corridors with open doors that revealed large rooms filled with sculptures and reliefs in various stages of completion. Several priests and priestesses walked by or looked up from their work as they passed, most smiled and waved, but none attempted to delay their progress. A few moments later, they arrived at a door with two young acolytes sitting on the floor beside it.

"This is the Hierophant's office," the priest pointed at the door.

"Thank you," Senjit smiled at the man. "Now, please return to what you were doing and forget that we ever met."

The priest nodded and casually strode back the way they had come.

Turning his attention to the two boys, Senjit could see uncertainty in their eyes and a little fear. Clearly the short conversation with the priest had unsettled them more than a little.

Before either one could speak, Senjit crouched down to their eye-level and whispered, "Sleep."

Eye lids suddenly very heavy, both acolytes' chins fell to their chests and their bodies slumped together in a deep slumber. Senjit walked through the unlocked door.

"What's this?" A man in the next room demanded when Senjit abruptly entered unannounced.

The chamber was illuminated by a pair of light-globes floating near the ceiling and a shaft of light cast through a small window on the other side of the room. There was a round table with four chairs neatly tucked under it near the window, several rows of shelves carefully stacked with rolled parchment and precisely aligned books and a padded kline against one wall.

The man had risen quickly from his stuffed chair nearly toppling it over behind a desk littered with scrolls and stacks of parchment. He held a quill in one hand and there was a small splatter of dark ink on the white chlamys covering his slight frame that glistened damply on the fabric. The Hierophant was late in his years, but no so old to be considered elderly, his angry eyes were bright and intelligent and his head was shaven completely bald.

"I am the drakon Ladon," Senjit shifted his form slightly to expose his golden scales and slit yellow eyes.

The Hierophant's face lost its color, his eyes widened, the quill fell from his fingers and he took a step back almost stumbling against his chair. Senjit needed the Hierophant to take him seriously, but he didn't have time to wait for the man to come to grips with facing a creature from legend and mythology. Senjit decided to hasten the process by implanting a suggestion in the Heirophant's mind with his psionic powers.

"Be calm and relax," Senjit sat in one of the two comfortable chairs facing the desk and waited.

Slowly, the Heirophant reached behind to find his chair without ever taking his startled gaze off of Senjit. Then he sat, his eyes reduced to their normal size and the blood returned to his tanned features. "I didn't believe . . ." he began and then chose to say something else. "Why are you here?"

Senjit didn't want to say more than he had to, only what was relevant for him to find out more about Akakios and the Shrine of Metis. But the Heirophant might know something about the Chaos Demon Alseid had captured and the story about the Fire-Bringer might not have anything to do with it at all. He would just have to ask and let the answers lead where they may.

"My . . .I captured a demon," Senjit tried to sound casual about it. "Don't worry, it was not a very powerful one. Before I destroyed it, the thing told me it had come from Hellas. That's why I am here."

"A demon? From Hellas?" The Heirophant practically stammered.

Senjit wanted to just take control of the man's mind and be done with it. He might yet be forced to do so, but it had to be a last resort since he was far to clever for a simple charm. Dominating another person's mind, especially if they were unwilling, often resulted in intellectual and emotional damage that they would be forced to live with the rest of their lives. The Heirophant didn't deserve that.

"From Hellas," Senjit confirmed. "I am here to find out if there could be others. Has anything happened in Sesklo within last few years that stood out as unusual or remarkable?"

The Heirophant pulled himself up to the desk and appeared to regain a measure of his composure. "I have been the Heirophant of this temple for the better part of three decades and I can tell you that some years have been better than others. Just last year we lost our Fire-Bringer and there is not another ready to replace him. Our city has suffered disease, bad weather, food shortages and lost a few shepherds to wolves. We have also enjoyed bountiful harvests, a spike in our population because more infants and mothers survived childbirth and no wars." The Heirophant spread his hands apart on his desk. "But there has never been talk of demons or blaming demons for the natural occurrences in our lives.

Senjit leaned back in his chair. Maybe the Chaos Demon came from somewhere else in Hellas and he was wasting his time here. Or perhaps the demon came from Hellas many decades or centuries ago and the memory of anything it had done here was long lost to history.

"What do you know of the Fire-Bringer Akakios?"

The Heirophant's raised his eyebrows high upon his bald forehead. "Now that is a strange story, but a tale from long before my time. He died over a hundred years ago."

Senjit was intrigued, "Is there any record of what happened to him?"

"There is," the Heirophant rose from his chair and walked over to one of the book cases. "Miltiades was the Heirophant at that time. He was originally a blacksmith, if you can believe it, but he kept meticulous records." The man rummaged through one shelf and then another, knocking some of the rolled parchments onto the floor in his haste, as he pulled books off and then put them back in their place. "Every Heirophant reads Miltiades journal to glean some hint as to the mystery of Akakios. Apparently, they were close friends. I doubt anything more will ever come of it. So many years have already passed. Ah, here it is."

The Heirophant returned with a large, leather-bound tome and lay it heavily on top of his desk face down. With great care he lifted the back cover and gently turned the pages. Senjit looked on in silence.

"The pages are old and brittle," he muttered to himself as he slowly worked his way through the volume. Then he glanced up at Senjit, "The passages are near the end of the journal as Miltiades died less than a year after Akakios. His successor documented his death as the result of madness. It appears that he went insane and demanded that all the temples in Sesklo not devoted to Kronos be torn down, even going as far as trying to raise an army to force other cities to do the same! What a sad end to his remarkable life. Here we are, I will read what he wrote about Akakios."

Senjit leaned forward. What the Heirophant mentioned about Miltiades was very provocative, particularly in light of his relationship to Akakios and the way he died so soon after his friend. Another clue perhaps.

The Heirophant cleared his throat and began reading from Miltiades journal, *"The pitter-patter of rain on the hard marble of the temple walls fits my mood today. The Ta Hiera Akakios is dead. The Fire-Bringer is dead. My friend is dead.*

Just this morning, from a village overlooking the Sea of Waves, a messenger arrived with the sad news that the Ta Hiera's body had been discovered under very mysterious circumstances. He related that a shepherd was moving his goats to a more remote area of the Othrys to find fresh grass when he stumbled across the mangled remains of a man on a rocky slope near a shallow river where his goat drink water. What added to the already disturbing story were the equally disfigured bodies of two incredible creatures nearby.

The hieros from the village came to the site to confirm the unbelievable claims of the shepherd only to find they were true. Further, he was able to identify the Ta Hiera by his symbol of rank—a silver headband with the flaming sickle-scythe, the symbol of Kronos, twisted and bent around his neck. What remained of the body was broken and dismembered, as if he had fallen from a terrible height. It was only the presence of his club-foot that readily identified him as Akakios.

To the shock of everyone, the claims of the two creatures were accurate as well. They were mythical beasts created by the gods in ancient times. From the descriptions of the creatures, I know one to be a Chimera and the other a Pegasos. Their bodies were broken and torn like the Ta Hiera and appeared to have fallen from the sky. Most interesting was the hieros's observation that the Chimera's claws were buried deep in the Pegasos's flanks and that both creatures had injuries suggesting they were in a violent struggle before crashing to the earth.

The hieros ordered the creatures burned, their bodies sent to Elysium so as not to displease the gods and the remains of the Ta Hiera were prepared for his sad return to the Naos. I have no doubt that every citizen of Sesklo will turn-out when we build the pyre and send his body back to the gods.

I wonder if he ever found his beautiful Anesidora."

The Hierophant looked up from the tome, "Miltades never wrote another thing about it."

Senjit had heard enough.

With barely a word of thanks, he exited the Heirophant's office, removed the spell on the acolytes snoring on the floor and quickly made his way out of the Naos of Kronos. Once outside, he transformed into his dragon form and took flight paying little heed to the astonished few near the temple. They would have quite the story to tell about witnessing the fabled drakon, Ladon, the golden serpent, taking hasty leave of the temple.

An hour later, Senjit was flying high over the east road, using its direct line to the sea as a compass. He flew over three small villages before he found the one on the coast. There couldn't be more than two or three hundred people living in the small settlement below him. He supposed that if he wanted isolation while still receiving the occasional convenience of a merchant, then this was the place to live. It had no port, just a few small fishing vessels dragged up on the shore and he knew by the looks of the choppy breaks in the Sea of Waves that it must be a challenging trade.

Senjit gazed up at the outline of the Othrys overhead, but their peaks were obscured by swirling clouds that concealed the details of what lay beyond, even from his piercing vision. He supposed the mountains were always shrouded in a billowing haze at the higher altitudes and more so in the winter. Gathering his strength to navigate through the strong winds above, he expected it would be a rough ascent and hoped that it might be calmer above the clouds. Fortunately, the coastal winds were steady closer to the ground and he managed to ride the air currents in a zig-zag pattern without using too much energy until he was just below the clouds. Then, as expected, the wind blew chaotically from one direction then another. Senjit skillfully maneuvered to avoid tumbling over and spiraling out of control, fighting his way through the clouds and up the side of the mountain. When his vision cleared, the tumultuous gusts suddenly subsided and he was above it. Although the winds were still strong, at least they blew more consistently from the east and he could begin searching for the shrine without too much distraction from the weather.

Senjit possessed keen vision and it didn't take him long to catch sight of the landing in front of a massive propylon that had to be the shrine. The elevation where the structure was built was far too high for any human construction, leaving only the gods capable of such a feat. He knew who they really were, or suspected, anyway and felt a little shame because of it.

Drawing closer, his sharp eyes were able to make out the details of the columned propylon covered with magnificently sculpted reliefs depicting glorified images of the goddess Metis. Beyond the stone facade stood a pair of high double doors set into a shiny metallic frame on the side of the mountain. He knew they must be made of solid bronze with yellow flame from elevated braziers reflected from the doors' perfectly polished surfaces. One stood slightly ajar.

There didn't appear to be any living thing on the landing or flying nearby that might challenge his presence. Still, Senjit remained cautious and diligent. He didn't want to be caught by surprise. If the stories he heard about the Chimera and Pegasos were true, then there could be more. It was very windy and cold at this altitude; however, as soon as Senjit landed on the open terrace in front of the temple and transformed into human form, the wind slowed to a light breeze. And although the temperature was cold, it was not unbearable.

Comfortably altered in his human form, he allowed himself to be represented by a gold tunic, trousers and matching cloak with a rampaging Golden Dragon emblazoned on the back—the attire he was so well-known for. Anyone that he met here would know who he was, so there was no need to hide it. Senjit glided through the opening between the bronze doors and entered the temple. Before him stood a long corridor framed by smooth white marble with occasional light globes set high on the wall for illumination. He walked down the hallway, confident and without fear, into a massive circular room with a tremendous domed ceiling decorated with historical images from Hellas's ancient past. Spaced a roughly equal distance from one another in a circle around the perimeter of the room stood several white-marble statues of Metis in various costume and poses. There were other statues of creatures from legend seemingly placed randomly throughout the chamber. Most notably, were a life-size sculpture depicting a Pegasos and a Chimera locked in a fierce struggle. Although he took it all in with one glance, none of these details mattered at all to Senjit. His attention was on the strange scene in the center of the room.

A raised dais of seven steps terminated at a circular platform two paces wide that held a waist-high marble pedestal. What was on display there at one time was no more. All that was left were hundreds of broken shards of glazed pottery scattered on the pedestal, around the platform and on the steps. Senjit could only guess by the larger pieces that it was once a very large, decorated pithos. What it had held, he did not know. There was no evidence of wine or grain or anything else that would customarily be stored inside such a vessel. Deep in thought, Senjit realized that he could hear his own calm breathing in the eerie dead silence of the chamber, as if the room itself were patiently waiting and expecting . . . something.

And then she was just there.

Senjit was surprised by the instant appearance of a woman standing atop the dais. She was smiling wickedly and her dark eyes seemed to stare directly into his soul. To say she was one of the most beautiful creatures he had ever seen would have been an understatement. The ghostly white peplos she wore clung like a second skin over her perfect pale frame leaving nothing to the imagination, her long blonde hair cascaded over her shoulders and down her creamy back and she moved with the grace of a leaf on a gentle breeze.

"Greetings, Revered Dragon. I am Anesidora, daughter of Metis," her silky, feminine voice dripped with self-assurance.

Senjit returned her smile and replied with polite formality, "Greetings, Anesidora, daughter of Metis. It is my greatest pleasure to make your acquaintance."

"You are on a heroic and brave expedition that will surely be legendary. Your name will be sung in ballads and your great deeds will be recorded for future generations." She moved closer. Her revealing peplos without a strophion was exceptionally alluring to his eyes as she stepped down the stairs.

Senjit felt a tingling at the edge of his consciousness and realized that this beautiful woman, Anesidora, was trying to distract him with seduction while using powerful magic to probe his mind for weakness. He might have been a young dragon, but Senjit was especially adept when it came to psionic ability and well aware of her intent. He began to weave a counter-trap that would make her mind his if she pressed forward.

Anesidora continued to compliment his nature as she posed her sensuous body at perfect angles to reveal just enough to hold his unwavering attention. It was all a show. The real struggle was inside his head and Senjit could sense Anesidora's lack of experience in the way she tried to force her will upon him. A few more seconds and he would spring the trap that would allow him to dominate her completely.

It was done. All he needed was for Anesidora to open her mind again to probe him and he would have her. Senjit, smiling all the while, felt her mental touch . . . and then nothing. He was utterly cut off from his own psionic power. *How was this possible? Did she have him trapped somehow?* Anesidora stood silently with an expression of horror on her face. Someone else had them both . . . someone very powerful.

As if on cue, a second woman appeared next to Anesidora. She fit the perfect image of the statues and reliefs. The goddess Metis herself stood before him.

Metis was beautiful, even with the expression of anger that she wore now. She turned her angry gaze upon Anesidora and scolded, "You are taunting a being that could destroy you easily if he wished."

"Mother . . ." Anesidora began to protest, but Metis waved dismissively and her daughter disappeared.

Senjit felt mild disappointed at Anesidora's departure and then relief a second later when Metis removed the barrier in his mind. He didn't feel threatened by her, although he was sure that if she wanted him dead, he would be so already.

He knelt respectfully. "Revered Metis—" he began before she interrupted him.

"I know why you are here." Her tone was cold, matter-of-fact.

Motioning for him to stand, Metis continued, "My daughter has acted like an impetuous child luring a Ta Hiera of Kronos to open a pithos in *my* sanctuary simply to satisfy her curiosity."

Senjit could hear the anger in her voice.

The goddess continued on, "This childlike, innocent action has set into motion events that will change the world forever."

She bent and picked up a shard of the once beautiful pithos. The glossy blue pigment on the piece she held reflected coldly in the ambient light of the room. Senjit wished he could have seen the beautiful container when it was in one piece.

Shaking her head sadly, Metis effortlessly crushed the pottery to dust and let it fall slowly through her delicate fingers. "The Ta Hiera knew the truth in the end. He prayed." Metis threw back her head and laughed. "How he prayed! Not for himself, but for the world. And he made promises to right what he had done. But it was too late."

"What happened to him?" Senjit was agitated by the lack of sympathy displayed by Metis. A great man had died, the Fire-Bringer, and terrible evil had been set loose upon the earth. For what? A god-child's curiosity? The gods were overindulged and immodest in their appreciation of the adoration they received from the multitudes that scraped out their meager lives below them. As far as he was concerned, the world would be better without them.

If Metis knew what he was thinking, she didn't let on. "We trapped these demons in the pithos after it was discovered that they had escaped through a rift between this world and the Infernal Planes, or what most humans call the Underworld. How the rift came to be is a long story in itself. Needless to say, the gods repaired the rift and captured all of the demons that escaped through it. In doing so, this world was nearly ripped apart. Now, those same demons are free to sow chaos throughout the world once again. And the gods have no will to intervene this time."

Metis strode close to Senjit and twirled one of his long golden locks around her finger. "But know this: even the gods are vulnerable to prophecy and breaking the seal of the pithos not only released this dangerous scourge across the land, but also corruption that could alter the destinies of the gods themselves. Although the demons can be returned to the Infernal Planes, the corruption cannot. That is why the Ta Hiera of Kronos was allowed to die. He had been touched by the corruption and would have eventually been used as a tool against us. Prophecy has been altered and riddled for the gods and not even we can see the ramifications this will have on our future, let alone that of anyone else."

"What about your daughter?" Senjit asked bluntly. "Is she also affected by the corruption?"

An expression of profound sadness crossed the goddess's face. "She has been touched by the corruption and will spread it if allowed to stay among the gods or the peoples of this world. She is not a god, but a demi-god, meaning that she will have to face her mortality. However, her father Kronos and I will not allow our child to die so easily as we did the priest. Instead, she will be sent to Edin to live her life in happiness among the Enlightened Ones."

"Will she not corrupt Edin as she would anyplace else?" Senjit countered.

Metis patiently shook her head. "Edin is the only place within the planes of gods or man where the corruption cannot exist. Not even the gods know the reason why this is."

Senjit remained silent. Apparently, the 'gods' loved their children as much as mortals did and he could imagine how heartsick he would be if he had to send Alseid away. The thought tempered his anger with the goddess and he felt sorry for Metis. The corruption was beyond even her divine powers.

Metis peered at him closely, searching his features as if looking for something familiar in them. "It is no accident that you are here. Your father altered the path of the Chaos Demon so it would eventually send you to us. You are the only Golden Dragon to ever exist and you have a very important role to play in the future of both gods and mortals. For now, you must do your best to help humanity track down the freed demons and return them to their own realm."

Senjit felt the heat rising inside, an instinct from the part of him that was a dragon, through his ancient blood. "You said my father sent a demon to threaten my child in an effort to lure me here? I don't even know my father. He probably doesn't know about me either."

Metis replied, unmoved, "He did not send it. He manipulated its path. Originally, he expected it to attempt to control your wife. It might have succeeded. Fortunately, it was drawn to your daughter, who is much more capable of defending herself from this kind of attack."

Now, Senjit was angry. "Who is this man that can manipulate demons that you call my father? And what evil is in him that he would put my family at risk just to get my attention?"

"You don't know?" Metis appeared genuinely surprised. "Your father was produced from a union of love between the divine Nyx with Erebus before the Breaking. He is Aether, god of light. And he is not evil; he is a god. Your wife is a mere nymph, queen of them though she might be. The gods have no evil intent; our view of the universe is simply much larger than yours. Besides, your daughter was likely in no danger anyway. She has much larger prophecy to fulfill."

"My father is a 'god'? And what prophecy of the 'gods' will my daughter be mixed up in?" Senjit demanded. His calm demeanor was giving way rage. He wanted nothing more than to transform and roar his displeasure.

"That is not a discussion for today," replied Metis. "Your task is what is important now and you will not be alone. Many heroes around the world will rise to combat whatever evil the demons spread. It is our hope that the good of humanity will prevail, for hope is all that remains for the Second Breaking that will soon enough be upon us all."

The goddess paced back to the steps that led up to the dais where the pithos once stood and sat down. Incredibly, Senjit could almost see a weariness about her.

"How can they be destroyed?" he sighed. "Or, at the very least, driven back to the Infernal Planes?"

She raised her downcast gaze and fixed him with intense brown eyes. "The Chaos Demons are more nuisance than a threat. They can be killed by your breath or the fires of the Ourea. They can also be exorcised by certain holy people. It's the Greater Demons that will require expulsion through exorcism or banishment and only with the knowledge of their True Name. Even now, the Demon of Anger has managed to possess a powerful, Ancient Black Dragon and is rampaging through the lands of the Tarre people causing death and destruction."

Metis turned as if startled by something from behind and then disappeared as abruptly as she had first appeared. Senjit sensed nothing in the room, only that he was alone in her shrine once again.

Another Breaking? he thought. She sounded like a typical Tuatha De. He knew that what she spoke of was the truth, but also a lie. What were the 'gods' up to that they would allow such evil to be released upon the earth again?

Senjit left the shrine and flew south and west. He had a date with a Black Dragon and the sooner he found it, the fewer people would die. Along the way, he had much to think about. If it were true what Metis said about his father being the god Aether, then that would make Senjit a demi-god like Anesidora. And what effect might his own divinity have upon his child born by his nymph wife, Lysithea?

He thought about her then and his lovely Alseid. His mate was probably worried sick about him, knowing that he was going into harm's way. Now it seemed inevitable. With a little concentration, he used his psionic talent to send a message, or more like an impression, to Lysithea confirming his well-being. He sent messages to her in this manner often when he was away, so he knew she would recognize the thought when she received it and he hoped she would find some comfort.

The cruel goddess Metis had told him things that night with little or no explanation as if he were incapable of understanding their purpose. What greater prophecy could his daughter have to fulfill? Now or a hundred years or more from now? He was determined to protect her from anything that would threaten her, even the gods. It would be a struggle to decide whether or not he should say anything to Lysithea about what Metis said. She deserved to know, but did he have the heart to tell her?

Chapter 22

The Grove House

Qel sat astride his Lambei next to Havacian riding close behind Aelrindel who guided their route through the crowds north along the road and out of Avalon. The air was crisp, stained by little humidity, promising a beautiful day ahead. Any other time such weather would have lifted his spirits and garnered his enthusiasm, but not today. Not yet anyway.

"The apple groves are only a league north of the city," the elf announced cheerfully over his shoulder.

Qel still worried about being dragged off to the Enclave in Atlantis. He hoped Aelrindel's plan worked and they could escape to Ys before anyone from the Imperial Order of Wizards caught up with them. Qel knew that if they really wanted to find him and Havacian, they could quite easily, but he doubted that they would expend that much effort. Besides, he knew that they knew an initiate with a summons would compel them to return as surely as an armed contingent of Imperial Atlantean Marines and Battle Wizards.

Not far from the outskirts of Avalon, the forest began to open up becoming less dense and the bright rays of the sun cast frequent beams of light between the thick boughs overhead. Travelers coming and going were far fewer than the road from Atlantis and soon there was no one in sight at all. For the next hour, Qel enjoyed the comfortable light breeze that carried the light fragrance of honey on wispy currents of air until they broke from the forest into a clearing lined with rows of enormous apple trees.

Qel was in awe at the sight before him. "I never imagined that apple trees could grow so big." Easily three times the height of an Atlantean, the trees spread their broad limbs over an area equal to fifty paces high enough for the trio to ride under without disturbance.

"We are fortunate," said Aelrindel, "the harvest has not yet begun." Each one of the trees appeared heavy with apples the size of

Qel's hand, beautifully ripe and red, tempting him to reach out and sample a bite of their juicy flesh.

"Are we permitted to remove one for ourselves?" Havacian asked.

"Not without penalty," Aelrindel laughed. "And you two don't need any more attention than you already have. There is a stand near the Grove House where we can purchase as many as you like."

"That would be sensible," Qel agreed.

"If we stay on the road, it will take us around the grove," Aelrindel steered his mount onto one of the rows between the lines of trees. "Instead, I'll lead us through it to the other side and save ourselves an hour."

The straight pathways between the perfect rows of apple trees were wide enough for ten men to ride side by side underneath the tangled canopy of the heavy, fruit-laden branches. Riding down one of those pathways, Qel's stomach growled at the abundance of the juicy orbs, but Aelrindel was right: they didn't need any more trouble, especially if it involved filching fruit.

The hooves of their mounts clopped over the soft soil, stirring up the scent of freshly turned earth, which lingered in the still air. It was oddly quiet under the shade of the apple trees. The absence of chirping birds and critters skittering over branches was a little disconcerting. Qel realized how comfortable and aware he had become with the natural 'chatter' of the wilderness since he and Havacian had come to the Sylvan Forest.

"Where are all the workers?" Qel was surprised that they had yet to see anyone else in the grove.

"The week before harvest is known as Quiet Week." Aelrindel spoke softly as if to emphasize the point. "The trees are allowed to rest without disturbance before the Tenders of the Grove return to accept the Gift of Apples, or harvest, as you call it. Even the animals of the forest respect this time. The druids help with that, I'm sure."

"Why do you call it the Gift of Apples? Don't the Tenders pick them from the trees just like other fruit?" Qel didn't want to offend Aelrindel if it had something to do with a religious ceremony, but he was curious about how the elves interacted with the grove.

Aelrindel smiled. "The Tenders will bring their baskets on hover discs, elevate them below the branches of each tree and sing a song of appeal. If the tree is ready, it will release its apples into the basket and the Tenders will move to the next. If a tree refuses to release its apples, then the Tenders will come again the next day. An apple will never be forcibly separated from a tree unwilling to give it up."

"I will never think of an apple in the same way again," Havacian leaned over his mount's neck squinting to look closer at the plump apples they passed.

"There is no other grove like this one on the planet." Aelrindel was clearly proud of his people's grove. "Not even the nymphs' life-giving grove on the Isle of Gades can compare."

"All I know is that twice a year, the markets in the City of Atlantis are crowded with thousands of baskets to be traded and shipped to lands near and far." Qel recalled his mother preserving the apples when he was a child so they could enjoy them in the wintertime. He used to eat so many that his stomach hurt.

"And that's only about half the production! The balance we keep for ourselves or trade with the dwarfs and Vikja through the port of Andlang northeast of here." Aelrindel abruptly brought his horse to a stop. "Can you hear that?"

Qel strained to listen. And then he heard it. Someone was singing somewhere in the grove. It was a beautiful melody of such clarity and purity that he was moved by its perfection. There were words, words he could not understand from a single voice, unaccompanied by instruments that would have ruined its transcendence. He listened as it grew closer and then diminished into the distance. He couldn't help but feel disappointed when it was gone completely.

"What was that?" Havacian whispered, as if afraid to disturb the moment with the sound of his voice.

"It was a druid," replied Aelrindel. "They come here to sing to the trees. Most frequently during the Quiet Week. We don't know why, exactly, but it is said that their singing soothes the trees and eases their anxiety in preparation for the Gift of Apples."

"Your land is full of wonders, Aelrindel," Qel remarked with appreciation. And it truly was. When he and Havacian first decided to begin their Journey of Discovery, he was sure that they would be amazed by the Sylvan Kingdom. Yet even away from the city they had stumbled upon many more unexpected curiosities that surprised and delighted him.

It took less than an hour to reach the far side of the grove. In a clearing dominated by a copse of maple trees, Aelrindel pointed out the expansive natural structure that formed the Grove House. The entire design was just like all the other dwellings in Avalon except that it was restricted to the modest height of the giant maples that stretched forth their limbs to shape its walls. Without the comparison, it was a rather large two-story structure, but having recently been in Avalon, the Grove House had a very quaint appearance.

Qel thought it strange that there was no one about. Had they been approaching the great house of the vineyards that his family owned, there would have been dozens of people in sight by now, even if it was a farmer's holiday.

"Has the entire household retreated before the Gift of Apples next week?" Qel looked around. Not even the apple stand was staffed and not a soul strode the grounds.

Aelrindel furrowed his long dark brows in concern. "This is not usual at all. The last time I was here, there were scores of our people going about the business of the grove and household. Perhaps they are all inside for the evening meal, although it is early yet."

The elf dismounted and tied his mount to a tree near the front of the house. Qel and Havacian followed suit before they approached the tangle of thick branches that served as the wide double doors of the main entry. Hesitantly, Aelrindel pushed the door inward. It did not resist, revealing a dark tunnel into the interior. The corridor could hardly be considered narrow nor was it short in height. In fact, it was just the opposite and would have been thought grand had there been any light-globes in use to illuminate the mystery of the darkness. As it was, the light-globes hung suspended, inanimate and black as if somehow burned-out from within.

Qel, almost without conscious effort, brought forth from his hand light that shone forth in an expanding cone illuminating the way forward. He was surprised how it appeared with hardly a thought, requiring no concentration whatsoever. He was further surprised that Havacian, standing nearby, produced the same light with seemingly as little effort. They would have to discuss this development later, but for now, Qel was nervous about the current state of their situation at hand.

"The entry should have a doorman and proper illumination." Aelrindel voiced his own concern. "Something is wrong." As if to emphasize the point, he drew from its scabbard the long, curved blade that he always wore at his side.

Qel had only seen him draw that sword one time before and that was when they first met after pulling little Tolia out of the river. The fact that he drew his blade now concerned him a great deal and heightened his presumption that something was indeed terribly wrong.

"Stay behind me," Aelrindel ordered as he moved slowly ahead into the corridor. Qel exchanged a glance with Havacian, who shrugged with an ignorance as great as Qel's own, before they hurried after the disquieted elf.

Qel had an eerie feeling about their trespass and hoped they would soon find someone who would contradict their fears that anything was wrong. Perhaps the unstaffed and darkened entry was just an unfortunate neglect of protocol. Yet as they tread further along the silent corridor, he detected a stench in the still air that smelled decidedly of rot and death similar to that of a recently deceased animal.

"Do you smell that?" Havacian whispered to Qel.

"I do. This place is making me nervous. I can sense magic all around us, yet not from any specific source."

Havacian nodded in agreement. "I noticed that as well. There must be someone here somewhere. How can a house such as this be so empty?"

Any further thoughts of neglectful stewards were shattered when they turned the first corner. Ahead, just within the forward edge of their light spells, lay a body, bloodied and battered on the ground before them. Cautiously, Aelrindel led them forward for a closer look. When they were only a pace from the decaying remains, the head of the elven corpse slowly turned toward them at an impossible angle and spoke as if from a faraway place, "Those who oppose me choose not to heed my words; those that will listen, hear me now."

Qel froze. He took little comfort that Aelrindel and Havacian froze with him. What terrible thing had they encountered? This was supposed to be a distracting jaunt into the country to see the legendary apple groves of Avalon. Instead, they were faced with an animated corpse. *How was this even possible?*

"We heed your words, venerated spirit." Aelrindel spoke to the corpse as if it were an elder or master. "Speak freely to our benefit or peril, as you must."

Qel felt ice flow up his spine. *What strange ceremony are we witnessing?*

"Beware!" it spat from its bloody maw. "For the Old Haig dwells in this place."

"The Old Haig!" Aelrindel repeated with repugnance.

The lifeless corpse made no reply as the glow that briefly surrounded it faded away.

"What is that?" Qel felt frantic. *What monster are we faced with now?*

"If the Old Haig is here, then we must proceed with caution." Aelrindel cast his gaze down the hallway uncertainly. "She is a witch of unpredictable power from one of the lakes north of here. It should be impossible for her to have left the water to take over the household of the grove. There is more going on here than we can know."

"What do we do now?" Havacian looked as if he might bolt back through the door.

"We proceed." Already Aelrindel was walking down the corridor, leaving the now still and inanimate corpse where it lay. "I have a duty to dispatch this creature before it can escape."

Qel nodded. He was impressed with their elven friend if more than a little apprehensive. The look on Havacian's face was far from reassuring, but Qel knew they could not leave Aelrindel to face the thing alone. Quickly he caught up to the elf, with Havacian only a step behind.

They followed Aelrindel cautiously through the long corridor until they reached the next turn. He noticed that the earthen floor had become damp as if a bucket of water had been spilled over, but the thin layer of mud glistening in the conjured glow of the light-globes, presented only the challenge of the slick surface. It wasn't until the depth of the water rose high enough to reach his ankles did Qel become uneasy. Worse yet, it smelled of fetid rotting vegetation and the constant sloshing caused by their forward progress only heightened the stink and made it impossible to walk quietly. Qel worried that anything up ahead would know of their approach. He deftly transferred the light from his hand to a light-globe pulled from a pocket within his robes. He might need both his hands if things took a sudden turn for the worst. Havacian knowingly followed suit.

"What should we expect from this Old Haig? Is there something we can do to prepare in case it is still here?" Qel was glad he was wearing his riding boots to keep out the wet, but the cold water relentlessly numbed his toes as he walked.

Aelrindel stopped and turned to face them. "You are right, young wizard. We need to discuss what we are walking into." Qel was not sure, but he thought he caught a slight reddening on the elf's cheeks from embarrassment. Perhaps he realized the folly of their hasty charge.

"An Old Haig is the spirit of a corrupted female elf. She haunts the shores of rivers and lakes in the Sylvan Forest searching for vulnerable souls, living and pure . . . to consume." In the dim light of the corridor, Aelrindel's features appeared gaunt and haunted, like the creature he was describing. "The souls she takes do nothing to improve her corruption, yet she takes them still, believing in her insanity that if she takes enough of them, she will eventually become innocent and pure herself—as she was once before."

"How was she corrupted in the first place?" Despite his fear, Havacian had the look of intense curiosity that Qel knew so well.

"It is not known, exactly." Aelrindel shook his head in sadness. "We know only that they were once powerful sorceresses that grew too ambitious and sought to use their power to pervert nature to their advantage and to feed their adulterated appetites. Our goddess, Niamh, looked upon what they had become and what they created and considered it blasphemy. In her own name, she invoked a curse upon them and any elf that would use the power from her to desecrate nature. We call it Niamh's Curse."

"Are there no elven men who have been so ambitious? Has it always been only the women?" Qel would have laughed if he wasn't so terrified. His friend must have momentarily forgotten where they were and what they were about to do, allowing his curiosity to overwhelm him.

"Of course, there are. They are known as Troglodytes. This isn't a story from the distant past. Every few years we hear of one of our people becoming struck with the curse." Aelrindel seemed lost in thought for a moment. "Especially recently."

Qel was cold and he knew he wasn't the only one, as evidenced by his companions' violent shivers. They needed to get moving and finish whatever they were going to do before they froze to death standing in the cold water. "What is her power and how can we defeat her?"

As if waking from a dream, Aelrindel stared at him blankly for a moment. "She will still be powerful with her magic, although it will not work for her in ways she, or we, might expect." The haunted look the elf had before was replaced with determination and anger. "She may also have the ability to call upon profane creatures if she is strong enough. Apart from that, I'm not sure what to expect. I hope you boys are up to it."

Qel's teeth were beginning to chatter and the constant shivering was becoming more than a minor distraction. "Havacian, can you do something about the temperature of this water?"

Havacian threw up his hands. "I can. Why didn't I think of that?" He spoke a few words, crouched low and placed his palms on the surface of the sludge. Almost immediately the water warmed until Qel no longer shivered. "The water around me will stay tolerable as long as you are within a span or two."

"Thank you, Havacian. This Old Haig apparently likes water, so prepare yourself as best you can." Qel gripped his friend's shoulder tightly. "We may need your best tricks."

Aelrindel drew his narrow, curved sword once more and turned back toward the corridor ahead. "Let's be done with this, then."

They traversed a long hallway with a series of doors obstructed with dangling vines and then around another bend.

"Where is this deluge coming from?" Qel wondered aloud. The water was no longer cold, thanks to Havacian, but soon it was higher than his boots and his feet were soggy. To make matters worse, the stink of rotten vegetation had become nearly intolerable.

"The corrupted ones are bound by Niamh to haunt the darkest bogs of lakes and rivers, making it impossible for them to travel over clean water or land." Aelrindel glanced back at Qel with a shrug.

"Somehow she has managed to bring it with her." He pointed to the foliage that was part of the construction of the house. "See where the water touches the healthy branches and vines? Her dark magic will accelerate its decomposition until the whole place is in shambles."

The corridor wound and curved through the first level of the Grove House often passing natural stairways leading away or branch-formed doorways. Aelrindel passed them all with little hesitation. He was clearly following the path of knee-high water that slowly flowed from wherever their destination was ahead. Then, from around another bend in the corridor, Qel could just make out the glow of green light from something beyond. Aelrindel saw it too and motioned for them to darken the light-globes they carried.

Stowing his light-globe securely in a pocket, Qel, followed by Havacian, crept up with Aelrindel toward the corner that separated them from the origin of the green luminescence. They all moved slowly, trying not to disturb the water more than necessary and when they arrived at the bend Aelrindel cautiously peeked beyond. The elf stiffened, giving Qel a second of warning before he peered over his friend's shoulder.

Qel's gaze locked onto the improbable scene before him, the hair on his arms rose and his heart thumped so hard it made his head pound. What he saw there was more terrifying than anything he had ever experienced, even counting the Troll and the Ogres they had somehow survived. The long, high-ceiling of the room was bathed in a green glow that radiated from hundreds, no thousands, of sickly branches covered with rotting vines and slimy leaves that coated the interior walls of the room. Even below the surface of the water, Qel could glimpse the glow through the stinking and nauseating murky broth they would be forced to wade through if they entered. If this were all that the room contained, it would still be a fearsome place to tread, but that was not all. Not even close. Movement caught his eye among the wasting branches draping the ceiling. They were slow and deliberate and once his vision adjusted fully; he could see many more that did not move at all. They were black and spindly, with hair covering their bodies and multiple red-glowing eyes that peered from the depths of dark sockets. They were spiders of a sort he did not know. Qel had never seen spiders of that size; easily the thickness and width of a man's chest with long legs that made them appear much larger. His frozen brain managed to count nine of the creatures, unless there were more somewhere unseen, but even one would have sent him running in panic under normal circumstances. These were not normal circumstances. He would be expected to help expel them from the Grove House if Aelrindel decided that's what they would do.

Then he remembered that they had not come here for spiders. Qel's eyes desperately searched the room. The Old Haig had to be here, didn't she? There were no other exits that he could see other than the rippling of water in the center of the room that indicated the source of the putrid brine, as if it came from some corrupt spring. Something was tugging at the back of his cloak, breaking his concentration. He slowly turned his head away from the frightening scene to find Havacian's hand holding a piece of the fabric in a tightly clenched fist, but rather than tugging to get his attention, as Qel thought, his hand was violently *shaking*. Standing very close, his friend's eyes were glued to the room just as Qel's own were a moment before.

He drew Havacian back around the corner a few paces. "Are you OK?" Qel's whisper was almost inaudible.

Havacian's eyes were wide like oval saucers before he forcibly closed them and took his hand from Qel's cloak. It took a moment, but when he opened his eyes again, he had calmed measurably. "I am now. Are we really going in there?"

"Yes." Both he and Havacian practically jumped clear of the water at the hiss from behind them. Aelrindel had silently joined them. "I will handle the spiders while the two of you dispatch the Old Haig."

"Is she there? I could not see her anywhere." Qel had excellent eyesight and could not believe he had somehow overlooked her.

"She is there." Aelrindel removed the bow from across his back and carefully dried the reverse-twisted bowstring with a linen cloth. "Straight ahead, near the opposite wall. Her eyes are closed. Perhaps she is asleep."

Qel moved back to the corner, careful not to make any noise and peered around its edge once again. The back wall of the room looked like the rest of it—just a mass of rotting branches and foliage. *Where is she?* He looked closer. There was something odd about the shadows there. Or was it his imagination? His eyes followed a vertical line that seemed out of place, then a curve. He almost gasped aloud at how perfectly camouflaged she was. Her "dress" was actually formed of the same branches and leaves that extended around the room and her arms, flush next to her body, were colored green with brown textures. Then there was her haggard face blended perfectly with the pattern of wilting leaves. Aelrindel was right. Her eyes were closed and she appeared to be asleep. If they were lucky, maybe they could slip in quietly and . . . the Old Haig's eyes popped open. Her bloodred orbs stared out from the tangle that shaped her grotesquely misshapen features. A chill ran down Qel's spine. She was looking directly at him.

"*Ol uran gi,*" it cackled.

Qel slowly rotated his body, breaking the gaze he held with the monster and stood with his back against the wall. He realized with a start that he was breathing rapidly. "She knows we are here."

Aelrindel didn't seem surprised. "Then we must go, now."

Qel heard Havacian let out a sigh of relief and, in truth, he felt relieved as well until Aelrindel waded around the corner, bow drawn and ready. Reality crashed down on Qel as he realized the elf had meant *go forward* and almost without willing to, he followed.

Everything felt like slow motion. Qel saw Aelrindel wade into the bog, loosing arrow after arrow in quick succession. He was sure it must have been at an incredible speed if time was passing at a normal rate for him. Looking ahead, the Old Haig's eyes were glowing bright crimson and her arms were moving in strange patterns. Then the water around his boots suddenly lost its depth and a thick wall of fluid liquid formed in front of him, blocking his view of the witch. At first, he thought he might be drowned in it. Instead, it moved away from him and slowly crashed over the Old Haig. She screamed. A long, visceral scream, which went on and on. It was deafening along with the frequent *thwang* of Aelrindel's vibrating bowstring. To Qel's right, there was movement. He looked over just in time to see one of the giant black spiders launching itself toward him. Instinctively, he thought to catch it. Then the rational side of his brain kicked in and he knew that if he did, it would kill him. He raised his arm to knock it away, fend it off, something, anything. Arm straight out, palm toward it, the thing was almost on top of him. So slow. Then there was heat, incredible heat that rushed through his arm from somewhere inside of him and it did not cause him pain. It sprang fluidly from his open palm and exploded on the falling spider, the force of it sending the flaming creature away from him to land sizzling in a tight ball in the stinking water.

Time returned in a rush.

Black spiders were everywhere. Some floated in the water around him, full of arrows and others were falling nearby from above. The *thwang* of Aelrindel's bowstring was no longer distinct, just a constant hum of vibration, he loosed his arrows with such speed. From behind, Havacian was sending liquid jets of water into the spiders nearly as quickly, piercing their bodies like daggers and at the same time sending walls of water at the Old Haig to disrupt her spell casting. Qel knew they couldn't keep this up forever and decided that he had to do something about the Old Haig if they were going to survive.

Qel worked to dispatch the nearest spiders with flames from his hands until they were no longer any near him. Aelrindel was out of arrows and was fending off the spiders with his spinning sword while Havacian focused his full attention on keeping the waves of water exploding on the Old Haig.

"Torzu toltorg!" The witch spoke words of magic Qel could not understand, but he knew that something had changed.

Bubbling up from shallow depths, two massive shapes emerged from the mire disrupting the walls of water buffeting the Old Haig. She moved her arms from low to high and with each dramatic gesture seemed to pull the creatures up as they grew in front of her.

Qel sent flames into them, but nothing happened. They looked strange, he thought, generally humanoid with thick arms and legs and a featureless, faceless head covered in rotting vines and leaves. When they reached their final height, taller than even he, they began to move toward them. Qel sent more flames into them. Still nothing and it appeared Havacian's water walls were no more effective. One came close to Aelrindel and he swiped at its arm. His blade sunk deep and stopped, held tight in the mud-like composition of its form. The elf pulled his sword free barely in time to dive away before the thing could strike him in the shoulder with its other heavy hammer-like fist. In the meantime, the Old Haig was waving her arms again.

"Havacian!" Qel cried as he maneuvered his way away from a mud monster. "Can you extract the moisture from them?"

"I can try!"

Qel looked around wildly. The spiders were all dead and Aelrindel was hacking ineffectively around the slow-moving mud creature on the far side of the room. He looked back at the Old Haig just in time to see a cloud of projectiles hurled his way. There was nowhere to go, so he dropped to the water in front of the mud creature nearest to him. The heavy collision of numerous dart-like objects impacting the heavy form from behind was satisfying until he felt the shock of pain in his side. It burned deep in his right hip, but he had no time to agonize over it as a heavy blow to his chest sent him tumbling through the air toward Havacian. Qel couldn't breathe. With the breath knocked out of him he lay gasping. Above him, Havacian had his arms in the air with what looked like a fast-moving mist flowing all around him.

Seconds later, Aelrindel was next to Qel, pulling him away from Havacian. He tried to stumble to his feet while the elf swatted at the mud creatures, keeping their attention away from the Atlanteans. The Old Haig was preparing another cast when Aelrindel tossed a dagger that lodged in her midsection, interrupting her invocation. She screamed something that sounded like a curse and pulled at the blade to dislodge it. Qel was amazed at the pure skill of the elf to almost single-handedly keep them alive and he resolved to pull himself together and get back into the fight.

Qel was confident that Aelrindel could kite the mud creatures around the room and away from him and Havacian as long as Qel could keep the Old Haig's attention. She had just managed to remove Aelrindel's dagger from her abdomen and where it pierced her, he saw a greenish-brown liquid oozing from the wound. The smell of it reached him almost as quickly and he gaged involuntarily. It was far more putrid than the water in the room, if that were possible.

The water.

Just then he realized there was no more water on the ground and even his feet felt dry inside his heavy boots. Risking a quick glance, he looked over at Havacian. His friend was exactly as he was before. Then Qel's attention was back on the Old Haig.

Ignoring her wound, she had her hands on the mass of branches that grew out of her back and stretched around the rest of the room from the wall behind her. She was chanting. Qel cast a sheet of flames, engulfing the Old Haig and the wall of branches around her. She screamed in pain, but the damage appeared minimal. Qel surmised that the branches that covered her must still be saturated with water giving her some protection from his flames. The room flashed with blue light and the next second he was on the ground writhing in pain. Qel could hear the screams from Aelrindel and Havacian echo his own. When it finally ended, he stood unsteadily and attacked the Old Haig with more flames. She shrieked with rage, but there was no more visible damage than the last time. He looked around. Aelrindel somehow just managed to stay a step ahead of the mud creatures despite the lightning attack and Havacian was attempting to resume whatever he was doing to dry out the room. Odd, Qel thought absently, the chamber seemed smaller than it was before.

Qel scanned the branches around the room. The ones furthest away from the Old Haig appeared brittle and dry and there was a distinct creaking sound that came from all around him that he had not noticed before, as if the branches were contracting. Aelrindel was much closer now, moving in a zigzag pattern at the edge of the room, which was smaller than a moment before. The mud creatures, no longer wading through water, looked dry and cracked, leaving thin patches of crumbled earth on the ground behind them. The creaking continued and Qel realized what was happening. He ran over to Havacian, who was slowly being forced toward the center of the room by the branches behind him.

"Havacian! The Old Haig is contracting the branches to bring us all within reach of the mud creatures. I need you to focus on removing the water from them, not the entire room." Qel was feeling desperate. The room was a quarter the size that it was when they first entered and the Old Haig was unreachable behind the branches on the wall she occupied. "Hurry, Havacian, or they will crush us!"

Qel could no longer feel his right leg. He collapsed on the ground in front of Havacian. With all the adrenaline flowing through him, he had forgotten about the wound in his hip. He reached down and found the head of the missile lodged there and pulled it out. He gasped at the pain. Blood began flowing freely from the wound like a crimson river draining his life. Qel glanced at the projectile that he removed from his flesh and threw it aside. It was a colossal thorn with a point as sharp and deadly as any dagger. Evoking a small ball of flame in his hand, he shoved it into the open wound to cauterize it. His scream nearly outdid that of the Old Haig before he passed out.

"Qel!" Someone was kicking him. "Qel, wake up!"

Qel opened his eyes to see Havacian standing over him with outstretched arms. Magical flows of power passed through him and into the mud creatures that were approaching closer and closer. "Put some fire into them!" Havacian implored urgently.

Qel was groggy and exhausted, his head swam with an explosion of pain from the wound in his hip when he tried to stand, causing him to lose his balance and fall back to the ground. Somehow, he managed to rotate his body to face the direction of the mud creatures and sent a column of fire plunging into them. Large chunks of dried mud burst from their bodies in a hail of bits and dust, yet they shambled on hardly missing a stride toward Aelrindel, who was nearly out of room to maneuver. So close were the enclosing branches compressing the space around them that the dry ones ignited into flames.

Aelrindel was a blur of movement not only barely avoiding the pummeling of the mud creatures, but also dodging the flaming branches falling from above. "Damn the flames! Finish these monsters!" By the look of the haggard elf, he was nearly exhausted and would fall soon if Qel didn't act quickly.

Flames poured from his hands in thick jets conjured not just for the power of their flames but for the force of their impact. The first blast sent a mud creature's arm exploding into a million pieces; the next one shattered a leg and another evaporated one's head. Still, they lumbered on while the branches surrounding them became nothing less than a flaming cage. Looking on in horror, Qel feared that even if they destroyed the mud creatures, they would all die by the flames of his own making.

The Old Haig shrieked, purified pain reflected in her agony, the pain of flame that they too soon would be experiencing. Shoving those thoughts aside, Qel was quick about his business, blasting parts and pieces of the mud creatures until they could no longer threaten. When it was over, Aelrindel and Havacian huddled with him, sweating from the heat, near collapse from the smoke, under the flaming canopy that would soon be collapsing upon them, entertained only by the serenade of death sung by the shrieking Old Haig.

It might have been a dream, a vision, or a delusion, Qel couldn't be sure and he didn't care. In his last moments of consciousness, he was sure he felt the fresh, cold, wet and beautiful patter of rain cascading down upon his face. And if anyone ever found his remains, with his friends pulled close around him, they would find the death mask of an Atlantean with a mysterious smile.

Chapter 23

Recovery

Qel awoke in a room that he did not recognize. It was a chamber grown in the style of the elves, to be sure, but it was not the inn where they stayed in Avalon. He shifted his weight to have a better look around. The abrupt movement caused an excruciating pain to shot down his right leg and up through his abdomen. Wincing, he carefully adjusted his body into a position that caused the least amount of discomfort. *The thorn,* he thought. *At least that proves I'm not dead yet.* He still didn't know where he was. Cautiously, Qel rotated his gaze around the room. To his surprise and happiness, Havacian was seated in a comfortable chair not far away, asleep. The dim light-globe that illuminated the room was the only source of light and there was no window for him to guess at the time of day or night.

Qel decided to stay quiet and not disturb his friend. As much as he wanted answers, he was satisfied that they were both alive and safe. The answers would come soon enough. Besides, he was still so tired. Nearly asleep again, a thought jolted his mind back to awareness—where was Aelrindel? The thought brought him starkly awake as he tried to remember the last details about their encounter with the Old Haig. In the end, he couldn't recall much right before he lost consciousness . . . except rain. There was something about rain.

"Qel? Are you awake?" The sound brought him back to the present. It was Havacian speaking to him. How long had he been daydreaming?

"I am. Are you okay?"

"Yes, besides feeling exhausted and the pain in my throat from the smoke, but I'm none the worse." Havacian's voice was hoarse, wavering when he spoke; he needed as much rest as Qel did.

"Where is Aelrindel? Is he?" The last part was left unspoken, but there was no doubt in his meaning. Qel realized his own throat was sore from the smoke as well, but he had to know what had become of the elf.

"That one?" Havacian smiled and shook his head. "I don't think two Old Haigs could have stopped him. After you passed out, I brought rain to stop the fire and cleanse the air. Aelrindel cut through the dead branches to get to the body of the Old Haig and removed her head for good measure while I checked you for injury and found the wound in your hip. He left immediately for Avalon to retrieve a healer."

"Where are we now?" Qel tried not to shift too much to see his friend more clearly.

"We are in the Grove House still, in one of the bedrooms on the second level." His friend seemed entirely unperturbed about remaining in the house where the spiders and mud creatures and the Old Haig had almost finished them.

"Nobody minds that we are here?" Qel felt uncomfortable about sleeping in someone else's bed uninvited, no matter his injuries.

"We checked most of the house." Havacian lowered his voice. "There is no one left alive that we found. There were only a few."

"Maybe the others are hiding." Qel was hopeful.

"Maybe," Havacian sounded doubtful, "Aelrindel thinks the spiders took the rest to feed on. Their remains will probably be found in some isolated place in the house."

"That's dreadful. I hope it's not true." Qel could imagine the horror since he had almost been among them and he wished fervently that they might be found unharmed. "So then, we wait?"

"We rest here until Aelrindel returns." Havacian yawned and tried to hide it. "He should return before morning if he can manage not to kill his horse at the speed he left out of here a couple hours ago."

"Very well, let us rest until he returns." Qel's words were more for the benefit of his friend than himself. After hearing the likely fate of the residents of this fine house, he wouldn't be able to sleep a wink.

——

The crack of lightning brought Qel fully awake, jolting him into a sitting position in his bed amongst a tangle of sweat-dampened sheets and he found himself looking directly into the eyes of Aelrindel. Havacian was in the background, wide-eyed with panic, jumping up from the lounge chair where he had been sleeping.

"Good morning." Aelrindel calm demeanor almost immediately settled Qel's anxiety. "Are you able to stand?"

To Qel's utter surprise, he thought he could. The pain in his hip was no more than that from a deep bruise rather than a severe injury from a hand-length thorn. "I think so." As if to prove it to himself as much as anyone, he threw his legs over the side of the bed and stood steadily as if he had never been injured at all.

"Good." Aelrindel poured himself a cup of water from a pitcher on the side table. "We can leave now."

"Is it morning?" Havacian yawned and stretched his limbs.

"It is almost noon." Aelrindel looked like he needed a bath. There was dirt on his face and greenish-brown stains covered his fine cloak and tunic. Qel detected the scent of rotten foliage and smoke, but that could have been from his own clothing as much as the elf's.

"Are we returning to Avalon?" All Qel wanted to do was go back to the inn and wash.

"We are if the healer I brought back with me did his job well and you can stand a few hours of riding." Aelrindel was in a serious mood. Considering what they had been through, Qel supposed that should be expected.

"I feel fine, just dirty and tired." Qel's stomach rumbled as he spoke. "And hungry. Otherwise, I look forward to returning to the inn to wash up and order a warm meal."

Havacian was rummaging through his pack and produced a link of preserved hartebeest meat. He handed it to Qel. "Hopefully this will take the edge off."

"Alright, let's go." Qel chewed on the meat as they exited the room. "By the way, is there a storm? I thought I heard the crack of lightning."

Aelrindel gestured vaguely with his hand over his head. "Those are the sorcerers clearing the remaining spiders from the house."

"Sorcerers?" Aelrindel didn't have to respond, the house was crawling with elves of every sort—sorcerers, warriors, priests and even a few human druids. None of them paid them much attention, other than a curt nod, when the trio departed the house.

Outside, the scene was even more astonishing. At least a hundred elves, some mounted on enormous Rocs, both on the ground and in the air, as well as a dozen Tree Guardians occupied the open space between the Grove House and the lines of apple trees. It appeared as if Aelrindel had returned with a small army.

We could have used them last night, Qel thought to himself bitterly.

Aelrindel must have read his mind. "My people are here to cleanse this place and the entire grove. It must be clean for nature to repair itself. Soon the High-King will appoint a new family to manage the groves and this experience will be but a sad memory."

"Do you have any ideas about why the Old Haig came here in the first place?" From what Aelrindel told them earlier, the witch should never have been able to come so far from the water – a very disturbing detail in Qel's mind.

"Maybe." The elf's features twisted in distress. "Let's move away from here and we will talk more about it where there are fewer ears.

They retrieved their horses and rode away from the Grove House in the same direction as they had arrived the previous day. Aelrindel led the trio without a word or a glance backward, leaving Qel wondering what could have disturbed the sturdy elf so grievously. Yes, the battle with the Old Haig was dangerous and nearly killed them all, but there was something more only Aelrindel knew and he was unwilling to speak about it until they were alone.

There were no singing druids on their return through the grove and the hour it took in the filtered sunlight to reach the other side was spent in silence. It wasn't until they entered the forest again that Aelrindel spoke again.

"Qel, I'm sorry I had to leave you back at the Grove House when I went to find help," Aelrindel spoke the words but would not look him in the eye as he did.

Qel had thought nothing of it. "What choice did you have, Aelrindel? I was injured and unconscious."

"It is true that you probably would have died if I had tried to bring you with me, but that is not the only reason I abandoned you with such urgency." *Abandoned?* The elf's voice was genuinely sorrowful and still he refused to look at him directly, as if ashamed to meet his gaze.

"Aelrindel, you didn't abandon anyone. You left me in a safe place with my friend to care for me. I needed help and you flew like the wind to find a healer to mend my wounds." Qel was incredulous at the conversation they were having. "You saved me."

Aelrindel swung his horse around to face him then, abruptly halting their progress in the middle of the road. "I ran!" the elf shouted; his voice thick with emotion. "And I am ashamed of it."

"Aelrindel, relax. You are among friends." Havacian tried to calm the elf. The look on Aelrindel's face was pure distress.

If Qel didn't know the elf, he might have thought he was about to lash out and strike him, but he knew that was not in his nature. Something was terribly wrong. "You had nothing to run from," Qel assured him. "Havacian told me you finished off the Old Haig and the few remaining spiders went into hiding. If anything, you are a hero!"

Aelrindel dropped his head to his chest and spoke more calmly, "You don't understand. There was something else. Something I have never experienced before and I fear my people may not be finished with it yet."

"Tell us," Qel implored. "Tell us so that we may know your fear and share your burden."

Aelrindel sat in silence for a long while before he finally looked up with an expression that Qel could only define as . . . defiance? His eyes were red from exhaustion and he smelled of earth from the dust his mount had kicked up in the previous hours. This proud elf had not had one minute of rest since they left Avalon the day before, while Qel had been laying in a comfortable bed for hours because of a damn *thorn* in his side! Qel suddenly felt the burden of shame that Aelrindel had admitted to and it was his own to bear, not that of the elf who nearly sacrificed his life to save him.

"Havacian was correct in what he told you. I did cut through the dead vines and strike the head from the Old Haig to ensure she could no longer threaten us." Aelrindel paused as a shudder rocked his shoulders. "There was . . . a black void. It rose from her lifeless body and fear like I have never felt before in my life engulfed me like a dark shroud. It was all I could do to find a safe room for you and Havacian before I fled." The look in his eyes had changed from determination to shame again as he spoke, reflecting the elf's misery.

"What was it?" Qel didn't know what to say. He had never heard of anything like it before. "Did it harm you?"

"No, it . . . left. It didn't dissipate or evaporate in the air. It simply went away and I am certain it will not be the last the Sylvan Kingdom will know of it."

"Then there is nothing you can do about it." Qel couldn't understand Aelrindel's fear—he didn't experience it himself—but he knew they were powerless to do anything about it unless they were confronted by it again.

Aelrindel nodded his agreement. "That is likely true, but I must inform my father so he can warn the High-King and the Demesne of this potential threat. I don't know why, but I believe that the thing will return in some other form and harm more of my people. That is my concern."

"Then let us return to Avalon swiftly so that you may unburden your fears to your father and then we shall sail to Ys." Qel snapped the reins of his horse and took the lead, not waiting for Aelrindel's response. To his relief, both the elf and Havacian quickly followed behind him.

———

Qel had been waiting with Havacian in the common room of their inn in Avalon for over an hour past the time Aelrindel said he would meet them.

"He should have been here by now." Qel was irritated at the elf's delinquency. Everything seemed to annoy him lately and Aelrindel was no exception. He was feeling the weight of responsibility like never before since their encounter with the Old Haig. He could sense the change in Havacian as well. Neither of them joked or even laughed in the two days after their return which was completely unlike either of them. Qel wondered if this was the change all wizards of the Imperial Order went through on their Journey of Discovery and if maybe they were suddenly maturing faster because of their recent experiences. He knew it would happen eventually. Over the years he watched many young exuberant wizards depart the Enclave only to return, years later, solemn and wizened – a shadow of their former innocent naivete.

"He told us he might be late, Qel." Havacian was the vision of coolness, sitting calmly on the opposite side of the table with a cup of Mekali wine in his hand. "Especially if his father took his concerns about the black void he encountered seriously."

"True enough," Qel conceded. "I am simply restless to move along to the port of Andlang."

"Do you still think the Order will summon us home? The innkeeper said no one had come looking for us while we were away."

Qel barked a soft laugh. "Pontus knows why, after our performance at the Tower."

"Ah." Havacian was gazing toward the entrance to the inn. "Guess who has arrived."

Qel turned to see Aelrindel walk up to their table. He still had a haunted look in his eyes that had not diminished since they departed the Grove House, but at least his smile had returned.

"I'm sorry to be late." The elf sat on the bench next to Havacian. "Are you boys ready to leave?"

Qel stood right away. "We are. The stable should have our horses ready."

"Good." Aelrindel stood and so did Havacian. "Then let's get underway before the day is lost to us."

They traveled out of the city along the Sylvan Road toward Andlang. Although the merchant and farm traffic going both ways was far busier than they experienced on the road south of Avalon, the going was still steady and unhindered. Aelrindel had previously told Qel that he expected the journey to take no more than two and a half days and he hoped that in that time the elf would return to his old self at some point along the way. Although it seemed to him that despite what he wished, their meeting with the Old Haig changed them all irrevocably.

The quiet hours on the road gave Qel time to consider some of the changes he was feeling. Indeed, they were not unexpected. Every Atlantean went through them around his age and much of the time they were welcomed. At least by the older folk who had already gone through them. The difference with him was that these changes felt as if they were happening much more rapidly than they should. He noticed the change in Havacian as well. His friend was also unmistakably going through a very rapid maturing and it concerned them both. So far, there was little discussion about it, although Qel knew that they would find some comfort in the fact that they were going through much the same thing together. Until then, he would try not to brood on it and enjoy the beautiful land they passed through. Who knew when the next time would be that they were here again? Or for that matter, when they would return to the Emerald Isle? He would have to remember to send his mother a message before they departed across the sea.

Just before dusk, Aelrindel silently led them off the road and a short distance into the forest. Qel didn't need to ask why; they had done this several times in their travels. Before long they found themselves dismounting in a narrow clearing to set up camp for the night.

"There is a stream nearby," the elf muttered while he sharpened the end of a stick he had picked up off the ground. "If you two will prepare a fire and clear the area, I will see about catching us something to eat."

"Would you like company?" Havacian cast his gaze around for another stick.

"Not this time. I'll be back shortly." Without pausing for a response, Aelrindel disappeared into the forest.

"I hope he talks to us soon." Havacian was clearing a space for the campfire while Qel collected fallen branches nearby. "He is hiding something more than what happened at the Grove House."

Qel dropped an armful of branches next to the clearing and began to break them into smaller pieces. "Something to do with his father, I would bet. He was determined to speak with him as soon as we returned to Avalon."

Qel started a comfortable fire and organized the stack of dry branches ample enough to last through the night when Aelrindel returned with a string of large silver fish over his shoulder. The evenings were a little chillier the farther north they traveled and the warmth of the fire felt good on his skin. This was the first night since before they arrived in Avalon that the three of them made camp together and the scent of burning wood under a clear starry night made him feel at ease.

Within an hour, they had cooked and devoured the sweet tender meat from the fish down to the bone, then sat in silence around the campfire. Not much was said after Aelrindel returned with the fish, other than what needed to be said to adequately prepare their meal. It was a striking change from the laughter and playfulness of previous camps, especially since Havacian was not asking a million silly questions. Qel missed those days. He was feeling a little nostalgic and a little sleepy from the belly full of fish he had eaten.

"I'm not supposed to discuss this." Aelrindel's voice startled Qel from his lethargy. "But I need to speak to someone about it and I know I can trust the two of you, my friends."

Qel nodded in agreement. "We *are* your friends, Aelrindel. After what we have all been through together, I think we share a deep bond that few others can claim."

"Thank you, Qel, well said." The elf poked his fishing spear into the fire, stirring the embers. "What I am about to tell you must be held in the strictest of confidence." Aelrindel looked a little embarrassed before he continued, "I know that I didn't have to say that."

Qel said nothing, waiting patiently for the elf to come around to what he needed to say. He appeared to be struggling with something in his mind as he methodically shoved his fishing stick into the ashes of the campfire like a poker. Havacian looked over and raised an eyebrow uncertainly, as if he wanted to say something, but Qel responded with a quick wave of assurance to maintain the silence.

The poker prodding suddenly ended with the stick shoved forcefully into the fire, where it ignited in a flare of angry flames. Aelrindel looked directly at Qel, then he shifted his gaze to Havacian and back again. The tension in the air was palpable.

"I told my father everything that happened at the Grove House and with the Old Haig . . . afterwards." Aelrindel bowed his head a moment and swallowed. For a few seconds Qel feared he would not speak again and then the elf looked back up, his eyes fierce with intensity. "You don't know my father. I expected him to dismiss what I saw as my imagination, tell me that I was seeing things, or blame it on the fog of battle. What I didn't expect was that he would take my words seriously. So seriously, in fact, that he immediately took me to speak privately with High-King TatharonCalithIlon, Ruler of the Sylvan Kingdom."

Qel was astounded. He secretly thought some of the same things that Aelrindel mentioned when he first heard the story. He was glad now that he kept those comments to himself.

"So what happened?" Havacian was leaning forward on the overturned log, thoroughly engrossed in the elf's tale. *He hasn't lost his curious nature.* Qel smiled. He hoped that would never change about his friend.

"Have you ever heard of the Nine?" Qel wanted to laugh, but the look on Aelrindel's face was grave. The Nine were a children's tale, nine powerful beings who met secretly to determine the course of world events.

Qel glanced over at Havacian. His friend had the same look of surprise on his face that Qel must have betrayed. "The Nine are a children's tale in Atlantis. What does that have to do with the Old Haig?"

"They are a children's tale in the Sylvan Kingdom as well, or so I thought until last night. The Nine are real. Your Emperor, my High-King, the Dvergr Mountain King, Wodanaz and his brother Myrllin are among them." Aelrindel sat back, quiet again.

Qel didn't know what to say. Had the elf lost his mind?

"The High-King told you this?" Qel did his best to keep the skepticism out of his voice.

"That and more."

"What more?" Havacian sounded incredulous.

"During long hibernations, Myrllin has visions about the future, which he shares with the others." Aelrindel was pacing now. "Not long ago he awoke with a vision about evil unleashed across all the lands of the world. He cautioned them to stay vigilant and keep watch in their kingdoms for strange occurrences. The fact that the Old Haig attacked the Grove House, that she was able to leave the water to do so and what I saw when she died qualified as one of those strange occurrences."

"What is the evil Myrllin spoke of?" Qel's heart was racing. He had learned in the span of a few seconds that the Nine were real, Myrllin had premonitions in the form of visions and they had come face to face with unspeakable evil and managed to survive.

"The High-King didn't say and I was in no position to press him." Aelrindel shook his head as he paced. "He *did* say that what I saw would not be the end of it and to stay vigilant."

"What are you to do now?" Qel stood up and so did Havacian, as if they would all mount and rush off in pursuit of evil somewhere. "Can we somehow track and follow this thing that was in the Old Haig?"

"I don't know. I was thanked and dismissed with no further instructions." Aelrindel shrugged. "The only reason I was allowed to know the little they told me was because my father is one of the High-King's closest confidants. My father advised me this morning to go ahead to Ys as planned. What we experienced here may have links to the strange events taking place there."

Qel settled back down and stared into the fire. "Then that's what we shall do. When you promised adventure the first day we met, you certainly delivered."

Finally, there was a laugh from the elf, a laugh like one expected from him just a few days earlier. "It has been just as much of a surprise for me as for the two of you. And unless I misinterpreted the High-King's dire warning, this is just the beginning."

Chapter 24

Confrontation

Senjit crossed the Great Sea in the direction of the Sican coast, fishing for shallow-swimming fish and other sea creatures to fill his belly. The Golden Dragon enjoyed a unusual proficiency—the ability to spot large fish beneath the water while cruising over the surface and pluck them from the sea with claw and maw for a quick meal. He mastered this talent over the centuries while living in his island lair, watching the majestic cormorants dive to depths twice his length in the Primal Sea. Senjit chuckled to himself. He was quite an ardent adolescent dragon back then, willing to test his skills against almost any challenge, mainly when he was hungry and without other dragons behavior to emulate. He had always followed his instincts and the conditions of his environment to develop unique skills that would benefit his circumstances.

Flying mostly at night and resting during the day to avoid causing a stir to any population he might fly near, Senjit searched for the rampaging Black Dragon. He had never fought another dragon before and could only guess at this one's capability. Without actual combat experience, he would need to rely more on his natural competence rather than brute force. The one thing Senjit knew about Black Dragons was that they grew quite large and as far as dragons went, he was on the small side of the scale. He hoped he could observe the dragon unseen for a while and find some advantage to exploit before it was time to confront him.

For two days, Senjit flew roughly southwest away from Hellas and over the Great Sea without encountering anything unusual. It wasn't until he was passing over the eastern coast of the lands occupied by the Sicans when he was suddenly aware that he was being watched by something . . . powerful. Senjit didn't know how he knew these things. It could have been an instinct common to all dragons as far as he knew or something to do with his innate psionic aptitude. Whatever the cause of the feeling, it was always accurate. At first, Senjit feared the Black Dragon was nearby and had spotted him before he was aware, but the source of whatever creature noticed his passing was on the ground. *Odd,* thought Senjit. He was not far from the massive active volcano the Sicans called Etna. He could see the perpetual dark plume of smoke that it coughed into the air. As long as Senjit could remember, the volcano was always in the same state of near violence, punctuated by small eruptions every hundred years or so, disgorging hot lava and ash high into the atmosphere. For miles around it, the land was barely tolerable for human settlement. Why any intelligent being would be crossing this wasteland on foot was beyond his imagination.

The next day he rested on the west coast of Rasna a few leagues south of the city called Cara. There were no settlements along the jagged coastline and he relaxed easily out of sight of the hilltops above and the water far below. Just after sunset, he took off again and started westward across the open water. Senjit was not sure where he was going, only that soon he would turn north if there was no sign of the dragon he hunted.

The night was cloudless and beautiful, revealing a sky full of stars shining brightly from the heavens as Senjit flew across the calm oscillations of the waves below. Far into the distance, his gaze stayed steady on the flickering lights of a city in the darkness. He was sure it must be Gallu, a midsized port on the eastern coast of Nurozieri. Senjit knew the Nurozieri well, an agreeable people welcoming of outsiders and trade and never aggressive toward one another or their foreign neighbors unless provoked. There were several city-states on the island, each controlling vast agricultural lands around it and ruled by a single dominant family. Their port cities employed modest merchant fleets for trade but no real navy to speak of and hardly presumed to control the waterways around their small island.

Unfortunately, their peaceful nature was viewed as a sign of weakness to those that would raid or invade their lands. However, their significant defensive structures were often overlooked and their adversaries often found their cities and villages far less vulnerable than they anticipated.

Senjit had spent a number of years among them a few decades previous, in the city of Ruju on the northwest coast of the island. He appreciated the Nurozieri style of construction, utilizing clusters of cylindrical towers of different elevations that were interconnected to form substantial walls for protection. To see one of their cities from the sea or air was awe-inspiring—the elegant towers were numerous, making up the bulk of the construction. The Nurozieri were clever builders, always erecting their cities on hills or gradations backing up to the natural slope of a mountain or cul-de-sac in a valley. With the additional height of their foundation, the towers looked even grander than they would have on a flat plain. At the central and highest point of the city, an inner complex of towers and walls rose high above all the rest. This was where the ruling family lived and played. The Nurozieri had reason to build the high solid walls to defend their people, for their enemies were not always human.

Senjit could recall the villages for their uniqueness as well, with structures of small stone huts and circular walls supporting a wooden frame with a ceiling of boughs, some erected on poles driven into the ground. The pavements were composed of limestone slabs of basalt cobbles or clay. The villages often featured megalithic towers with a truncated cone shape that were defensible home sites inclusive of their rounded barns and silos. He spent a year in one of these villages learning the language of the Nurozieri and the Giants with whom they shared the island.

Senjit found the Giants to be an unexpected surprise. The Nurozieri had a strangely symbiotic, yet servile relationship with the tribes of Giants that populated the island's mountainous interior. Each of the city-states was obligated to provide the Giants with regular peace offerings of livestock, grains and vegetables to keep them pacified.

Often, the priests preached that it was the will of their deity, the so-called Dark Mother. Senjit didn't believe it and suspected that they had some advantage espousing such views. Perhaps control over the people. Sadly, the offerings represented much of the agricultural surplus of the island and in lean years they were forced to import food stock to supplement their contributions. In return, the Giants kept the interior of the island secure from invaders and when called upon would quarry and transport huge stones from the mountains for the construction of dolmens where the Nurozieri interred their kings. Otherwise, the Giants kept to themselves, not bothering their human neighbors as long as the offerings continued uninterrupted. Senjit had gotten the feeling that the Giants were in some way considered holy or divine, but the priests were deliberately vague on that point.

Once, while hunting in his dragon form over the mountains near the city of Monte, Senjit came into close proximity with a few of the Giants he heard so much about. They were a furry, brutish-looking people who exhibited prominent brow lines, large eyes, broad noses and weathered faces framed by blonde or red hair. Except for the fact that they were easily five times the size of a human, they would have been considered short and barrel-chested, with a robust build looking very much like the secluded tribe of wild people that lived in The Wilds east of the Western Kingdoms. Their dress was just as unusual, covering themselves with furs and scraped skins, with leather sandals on their feet. Most of them carried a huge club, spear, or axe made of wood and stone for protection and hunting. By the look of the skulls hanging from a few of their belts, animals were not always their only prey.

When the Giants interrupted Senjit, he was consuming a red deer he had found for a meal. Apparently, they were just as threatened by a dragon as any human might have been and they threw large boulders at him until he flew away. Senjit certainly didn't want to fight them over a deer; the Giants weren't evil, just primitive and protecting their territory.

One aspect of the Nurozieri culture that Senjit never quite understood was their worship of a mysterious deity they referred to as the Dark Mother. Her consort was a bull "god" that the people believed was the representation fertility. The Dark Mother was worshipped in religious centers featuring a pyramid-like temple built more in the style of the ziggurats he had seen in Kur-gal than the pyramids of Ta-Mehu and Ta-Shemau. The temple at Monte was considered the high temple of the Dark Mother and housed Orichalcum Crystals, projecting their power through a rotating quartz crystal in the shape of a pyramid levitating above its apex. Senjit was sure it would still be there, along with a handful of Atlanteans to look after it. There were other smaller temples in the country, but it was only this one that held the Orichalcum and was tended by Atlantean priests, or the "Enlightened Ones" as they were commonly known throughout that part of the world.

While living in Ruju, Senjit had the opportunity to learn a little of the Nurozieri magical arts through their priests. They did not know him as a Golden Dragon, of course. To them, he was a priest of Gersemi, sent by the nymphs of Gades as a cultural ambassador. Senjit was more than a little surprised that the priests serving the Dark Mother practiced a form of necromancy and earth magic. Their magic was not evil, much like the necropolises that they painted in red ochre to represent the Dark Mother's menstruation, the raising of the dead and speaking to spirits was a form of rebirth to the Nurozieri. Senjit did not understand it all exactly, but he did understand the spiritual connection they had between themselves, the dead and their unusual goddess.

Snapping out of his reminiscing, Senjit realized that he was not far from Gallu. He looked forward to experiencing the city and its people once again and was already drooling over the variety of locally caught fish that their inns and taverns prepared grilled, baked and in stews that were always delicious. It was a delightful indulgence to consume cooked food once in a while, rather than what he plucked from the land or sea to devour raw. He began a slow descent toward the forest where he could safely alter his form and walk into town.

Unexpectedly, Senjit was jolted by a sudden, urgent feeling in the core of his being, a sign of recognition, an instinctual sensation different from the one he felt before—he was in the presence of another dragon somewhere nearby. Arresting his descent, he drifted quietly on the wind. It was only a moment before his keen vision picked up the familiar shape of the creature flying above the city. Without warning, a band of fire lit up the sky, engulfing one of the towers and igniting fires nearby. Then there was another and another. Senjit was filled with dread. He had found his adversary.

By the gods, the thing was enormous.

Senjit was more than a little intimidated by the massive size of the Black Dragon. It was easily four times his size and it obviously employed a dangerous, fiery breath weapon. A dragon of that size had to be at least a thousand years old or more. During the first few centuries of his life, Senjit explored nearly every part of the world and immersed himself in many cultures and civilizations, but he never met another of his kind. There were always rumors, legends and myths of dragons in every culture he encountered. Sometimes he filled the role in those traditions himself and Senjit naturally assumed that he was the only dragon in existence outside of Fomoire. He was still a young dragon with unique abilities, including psionic powers and a talent for magic—a very dangerous combination, to be sure—but a physically large dragon he was not. Senjit watched the huge Black Dragon with trepidation. It was a giant compared to him.

He had to think this through. If it came down to brute strength, this thing was going to rip him apart. Senjit decided his best chance would be to go invisible, get close enough to ambush the monstrosity and possibly control his mind with psionic intrusion, avoiding a fight altogether. Even knowing the dragon was possessed by a Greater Demon, he hoped to end the confrontation quickly, although he had little real confidence it was going to be that easy.

He cast the spell.

Senjit, camouflaged by invisibility, cautiously approached the Black Dragon circling the burning city. He opened his mind and began to gently probe at the other's. Strangely, the Black Dragon's conscious mind was devoid of thought, almost as if it didn't exist at all. Then Senjit's heart sank to the pit of his stomach when his adversary abruptly swiveled its head in his direction and stared directly at him. Senjit might have thought it a coincidence, except that the Black Dragon immediately altered his course to intercept.

Dammit to all the hells! Senjit swore. This was going to go down the hard way.

Even with Senjit invisible, the great creature seemed to know exactly where he was and flew directly toward him. Dropping his invisibility spell, Senjit hoped his unique appearance would make the other take pause while he conjured protections against fire, lightning and mind intrusion. He had no idea what the other dragon's capabilities were and as the Black Dragon quickly closed the distance, Senjit felt uncertainty creeping in. This was not how he planned this confrontation in his mind; he wanted to study this ancient creature for a while before they met in battle.

When the two were still well apart, Senjit opened with a volley of lightning that made the Black Dragon recoil against the sudden attack. It paused only briefly, then pressed forward, mostly unaffected— except that it was angrier. The Black Dragon countered with a stream of fire from its maw that burst upon Senjit like a violent wave against the bow of a ship, but his protective shield repelled the majority of its damaging effects, leaving him unharmed. After that failure, the great beast surged forth faster than seemed possible for a creature of its size and Senjit, unable to avoid the rush, took the full impact of the massive beast.

The physical force of such a great body was almost overwhelming as it propelled Senjit violently backward, nearly causing the two to tumble end over end through the air. Then there was a sharp pain in his sides . . . as the Black Dragon sunk its sharp claws deep into his flanks. With a gasp, Senjit could not think for a moment from the pain, let alone concentrate enough to cast a spell and the two of them, wings flapping chaotically, began to plummet toward the sea.

Senjit knew he was not prepared for a physical struggle with such an overwhelming adversary; he couldn't have been more than a quarter of the other dragon's size. And the pain from its deeply piercing claws, impossible to ignore, was excruciating. Senjit involuntary threw his head back and emitted a roar of pain. The sound was cut off mid-release when the Black Dragon snapped his jaws tight over Senjit's exposed throat in a final death hold. Somewhere in Senjit's reeling mind, he admired the skills of his rival and acknowledged that if he didn't do something quickly, his struggle would be at an end.

With supreme effort, Senjit calmed his mind and reached out to the Black Dragon. Immediately he sensed the anger and rage coming from a dominant source inside—the Greater Demon of Anger that Metis warned him about. Probing further, he detected an impression of the former dragon's consciousness. Belthagore was his name and he was too far gone to be of any help. The demon had done his work well. Senjit's only hope was to attack the demon's mental hold on the dragon directly, with the danger that if he failed, the demon might be strong enough to control and subjugate his mind as well.

What choice do I have? He thought bitterly.

Aggressively, Senjit brought his formidable psionic abilities to bear and attacked the other's mind with everything he had. With a sudden gasp, the Black Dragon released him and the two arrested their fall. Apparently, the demon was not expecting his adversary to attack his psyche and as the two bodies separated, they mutually flooded each other with fire.

Then time seemed to sit still.

"*Esiasch . . .*" the Black Dragon spoke inside Senjit's mind.

Senjit was confused, 'Esiasch?' How could the demon know his father's language? "*Zir ip g esiasch,*" he spat back.

To anyone else, the two great beasts must have looked as if they were frozen high in the air, facing each other, with the only hint of what was happening beneath the surface of their scales betrayed by the intensity in their eyes. Senjit threw devastating psionic attacks at his foe and the demon, a worthy opponent with similar psionic abilities, rebuffed his attacks at every turn. Outwardly, neither of them twitched a muscle except to magically hover in flight.

It was an impossible struggle. Senjit assumed that he could easily dominate the disembodied consciousness of the demon. He was wrong. *How could I have been so arrogant?* This demon was not just as capable of using psionic power; he was the most adept with it that Senjit had ever encountered. Even more so than the Wizards of the

Yellow Hall that he had met in on occasion at the Enclave of the Imperial Order of Wizards in the City of Atlantis.

In an effort to disrupt the Black Dragon's focus enough to give him some little advantage, Senjit combined his mental attacks with a physical assault. Sharp rakes with his claws and vicious bites drew deep gashes in the scales of the demon dragon, sending blood misting into the air between the two. Conversely, blood loss from the grave injuries on Senjit's neck and torso were starting to take their toll and he was slowly becoming cold and fatigued.

His time was running short. Senjit allowed a small part of his mind to close his wounds. He would have to heal them properly later—if he managed to escape from this beast.

"Foolish little Dragon," the demon laughed inside Senjit's head. "Do you think your paltry few centuries of life on this pitiful rock have made you a master of the mental arts? I have existed for millennia! I will block your feeble attacks until you are exhausted and then take your mind. Yes, little one. I can control you and this one with little more effort." The demon's laugh trailed to a quiet echo.

Senjit knew he would have to find a way to evict the demon from the Black Dragon if he had any hope of surviving this battle. Physically he was outmatched by the much larger dragon and the demon had brought their psionic struggle to a stalemate. Still, he was not hopeless or despondent, merely pragmatic about his current situation. With part of his mind continuing a relentless attack against his opponent, Senjit had to consider self-determination. Under no circumstance could he allow the demon to take control over his own power and do harm to others.

His situation deteriorating by the minute, Senjit accepted that he was not going to win this battle. There would be only one of two outcomes: he would either escape or die. Then it occurred to him that the Black Dragon had not demonstrated a potent ability to use magic. That could be the only advantage Senjit had over him and he quickly developed a plan that might just get him out of this alive.

Partitioning off a section of his mind, Senjit conjured a series of spells that would activate in a precise sequence that he hoped would give him enough time to break off and flee. He knew of a place in the mountain range called the Spine of Cel between Rasna and the Sicans. This place was known to the humans as Vers Patna—or Bowl of Fire in the language of the Rasna—and it was quite literally hell on earth. If he could reach it before the demon dragon overtook him, Senjit hoped he could use the treacherous terrain to his advantage.

With an enormous intake of air, Senjit built his fire deep in his chest. He could expand it until it reached capacity and exploded within his body, perhaps even taking them both out together. If it came to that. His mind fought the psionic battle and his physical claws brought him tighter against the Black Dragon's body. It was an enormous effort of concentration to do both, but if he failed, he would not survive.

Forgive me, Lysithea, he thought sadly. *Forgive me, Alseid.*

They were nearly locked together. Soon the time would be right, but he needed a small distraction before he triggered the first spell. "You seem challenged by a mere mortal so much smaller than the physical form you have taken, demon!" he taunted.

The demon replied with a voice full of fury, "You are nothing to me, little dragon! I will wipe you from the sky and sink your body to the lowest depths of the sea!"

Senjit could feel the demon's anger rising. Perfect.

"Then why have you not done so already? Instead, we dance together as if we were lovers at a ball. Shall I curtsy or bow?"

Mental waves of energy coursed around the edges of Senjit's consciousness. He anticipated the rage-driven attack when he insulted the demon and he put all his power into building an impregnable defense.

"This is no dance, you worm! I am a Greater Demon of the Infernal Planes! I have no match! I have no equal in this world! I shall eat you instead and defecate your body into the sea!"

If the demon dragon wasn't in a hot rage before, he was now, digging claws deep into his sides again. The pain was maddening.

"Do you have no equal in the Infernal Plane as well?" Senjit forced a convincing laugh through the excruciating pain. "Then what a docile place it must be! Look how you struggle against one so much smaller and weaker than you. Maybe you choose large creatures to possess to compensate for your shortcomings!"

The demon's rage was now at such a height of frenzy that he could barely control the body of the Black Dragon. His head slithered back and forth, spewing great sheets of flames without direction into the air.

"I will . . . rip . . . each . . . scale from your body!" he roared.

"Will you, now?" Senjit was weakening fast and if his plan didn't work, he would be done. "Is that what they call you in your world? The great and powerful scale-ripper?" Senjit's mocking laugh boomed loudly through the air and projected into the mind of the raging demon.

A monstrous roar ripped through the Black Dragon, who was by now apoplectic with fury. "I am the Great and Mighty Lord of Rage! And I will crush your skull with my might!" The Black Dragon lunged forward, maw open, neck extended toward Senjit's head.

It was time.

The fire in Senjit's chest was hotter and more volatile than ever before. He released the flanks of the Black Dragon and grasped its massive head, thrusting toward him. With every bit of strength he possessed, Senjit held the dragon's maw open wide with his foreclaws and breathed a stream of liquid heat into its unprotected and vulnerable bowels. The demon reacted with complete surprise and horror when Senjit blasted the massive fire and energy directly into the Black

Dragon's body, forcing him to release Senjit in an attempt to disengage, but it was too late.

The unexpected physical attack from the smaller dragon interrupted the demon's relentless psionic assault long enough for Senjit to trigger the first spell he was holding back. Immediately, a thick cloud of blinding smoke enveloped the Black Dragon, obscuring Senjit's movements. The next spell automatically released and seconds later Senjit was teleported almost half a league away, putting some distance between him and the furious dragon just breaking through the black smoke in pursuit. The third spell activated, flooding Senjit with energy and he fled east, toward the mountains.

Senjit glanced behind to gauge the distance between him and the other dragon. Somehow, the gravely injured, demon-possessed dragon was keeping up with him. Maybe even gaining a little. Fortunately, the demon was still too far away to assail him with his psionic power, but Senjit wasn't confident that would be the case for long and he kept up his mental defenses just to be safe. It was exhausting but necessary if he was going to survive.

Still, he was almost fifty leagues from Vers Patna, about three hours with the active haste spell he was under. With some luck, Senjit could keep the haste spell up that long, but it played hell on his body the longer it was in use and it could ultimately kill him from exhaustion. He didn't have much of a choice. If the Black Dragon caught up to him, he would be dead anyway.

By the time the moon began to wane past midnight, Senjit was high over the Spine of Cel mountain range and the Black Dragon showed no signs of slowing behind him. In fact, the beast appeared to have closed about half the distance on him. The strenuous effort of keeping his mental defenses up and the effects of the haste spell were beginning to take their toll. Even if he made it to Vers Patna, he might fall dead of exhaustion on its nightmarish slopes. Maybe the Black Dragon was just as exhausted as he was. Senjit fervently hoped so. He didn't know much about demons, but this one, the Lord of Anger, must be mighty indeed to keep such a huge host flying so long and so fast. Senjit was smaller and leaner, built for speed and agility, whereas the Black Dragon was bulky, massive and physically powerful—not the type of dragon that should be able to keep up with him for so long.

Senjit felt the first evil caress on the periphery of his mind and he was struck by the shocking level of rage and promised violence in those initial probes. *That Demon is a determined one,* thought Senjit. He loathed to engage him again, although soon there would be no choice in the matter.

He was not far from Vers Patna. In the distance, Senjit could see the orange glow of the massive caldera tucked neatly within a ring of high ridges over a league across. Occasional flashes of bright light illuminated the sky like distant heat lightning dancing through the dark haze suspended above it. The whole display looked surreal and it gave Senjit hope.

Energized by adrenaline, Senjit dove toward the caldera. The frigid mountain air pressed wisps of long chin hair against his face where moisture from his eyes was trapped and crystalized almost instantly. *Follow me if you dare.* He sent the thought back to the demon already diving hard to follow him down. Quickly, the temperature swung wildly from freezing to hot the closer he approached the caldera and soon his scales glistened with sweat. *Now we will see how agile this demon is with his dragon.* Senjit kept that thought to himself and closed his mind off to any possible intrusion. It also meant he would be unable to attack the demon with psionic power or use many of his spells, but he doubted it would matter and chose the safer route of protecting himself first. Besides, he had another plan in mind that might just swing the advantage back to him.

The full fury of the caldera came into view as he leveled off just below the ridgeline. Bubbling pools of liquid magma quilted the craterlike patchwork, broken only by the constant ejections of steam from cracks in the earth and fountains of lava that stretched higher than any tower. These were the dangers that were easy to avoid. His sensitive ears caught the shrill sound of a whistle among the cacophony of noise and altered his course sharply. In the line that he was traveling only a moment before, a magma jet shot high into the air, briefly igniting the ash above him. Molten rock heated to incomprehensible temperatures would have killed him easily enough if he had the misfortune to suffer a direct hit by any of it. That was the real danger of this place—the random bursts of lava traveling faster than an arrow from a longbow.

Senjit was not unfamiliar with this place and he knew the signs that forecast the micro eruptions. When he was a young dragon living among the Nurozieri, this place was one of his playgrounds. Years later, he hoped he remembered the caldera's turbulent nature well enough to save his life.

Angling lower, he slowed just enough to goad the demon dragon into following his erratic line of flight as closely as possible. The heat was intolerable at low altitude even for him and if it wasn't for the spells protecting him against heat and fire, he knew he wouldn't last long. He glanced back at the Black Dragon; the environment was taking a tremendous physical toll on his body. Black scales steamed and flesh blistered and tore. Nevertheless, the demon kept it coming, heedless of the physical damage it suffered. Senjit almost felt sorry for the treatment Belthagore would have suffered if he had still been present in his own body. That was no longer the case and there was no doubt that the demon retained a singular objective – to kill Senjit.

Briefly, Senjit considered just staying in the caldera until the Black Dragon died of exposure, except that the longer he remained, the higher the risk that the Black Dragon would catch him or Senjit might make a mistake. And as exhausted as he was, he wasn't sure he could keep up the chase much longer. Another high-pitched whistle caught his ear and Senjit broke to the right. The Black Dragon wasn't close enough to get caught by the brief molten spurt and avoided it as well.

Senjit slowed down and let the demon dragon get close. It was a dangerous ploy, allowing the monster within a few spans of him. One surge forward and it would have him. If that happened, Senjit wouldn't have the strength to fight him off again. He was sure of it. Pressing on, he desperately zigzagged through the caldera, listening for the distinctive whistle. Geysers of lava erupted here and there, but none were close enough to help him. He was glad of one thing – the Black

Dragon no longer had the use of his breath weapon. That would have been the end of Senjit. Not for the flame or heat of it, but for the force of it. At this range, it would have easily sent him tumbling. He considered the use of his own fire against the demon and then discarded the idea almost immediately. By the time he turned, it would be too late. As close as the demon-dragon was, Senjit had only one viable plan and that plan was based on pure chance.

A quick burst of speed and the Black Dragon was snapping at his tail. Senjit couldn't look back; that would only slow him down. He had to put everything he had into keeping his motion unpredictable until fatigue overtook him. Another whistle warned him of an eruption close by and he lunged toward it, just barely avoiding a direct hit on himself. He felt the hot spatter of smaller drops burning through his leathery wings—he couldn't make that kind of miscalculation again.

The extreme edge of the caldera appeared through the acrid haze just ahead and Senjit knew that in moments he would run out of room to maneuver. He would have to either turn or ascend. Neither choice was a good one for him, since it would cause him to slow and that would be the demon's best chance to finish him.

While he was still unsure of what he would do, a chorus of sharp whistles rent the air around him. There were too many to know which way to go. He tried to focus on avoiding the nearest ones ahead of him and hoped he guessed correctly. Banking sharply right, he just missed a lava spout venting its deadly bile high above. The angle of it rained down portions of the liquid fire behind him. He heard the Black Dragon roar in pain. Senjit could still sense him close. Whistles to his right: he banked left nimbly. Several streams shot into the air and missed them both. A little farther away more geysers appeared and he had no choice but to fly straight toward the ridge that formed the western wall.

The choice was made for him—he would have to ascend. The earth was whistling in every direction and Senjit tried to gain a little altitude early. To his horror, the demon dragon anticipated his move and he felt the sharp daggerlike fangs latch on to his tail almost immediately, preventing his forward motion. Senjit flapped his wings in a desperate attempt to wiggle free, but he knew it was no use. It would be over as soon as the Black Dragon's massive claws got ahold of him.

All his hope and energy entirely spent, Senjit hit the ground hard. He tried to dig in his claws into the igneous rock to pull himself forward, but the rock was too hard and his last reserves of strength were spent. He couldn't even find the energy to keep up the psionic barrier. His will was seeping away as the demon entered his mind with a wave of triumph. Senjit felt as helpless as a hartebeest in the clutches of a lion.

Then he heard the whistles, a rush of thick magma pushing through the earth and he waited for the final pain of death. Instead, there was screaming, loud and desperate, both in his head and the air around him, or so it seemed. And then the Black Dragon crashed into him so violently that Senjit nearly flipped over himself when his tail was suddenly released.

Senjit lay heaving, trying to regain his feet. The best he could do was to push himself up to the base of the ridge to stay clear of the magma. Looking back to where he had been, he saw the body of the Black Dragon smoldering in a shallow pool of cooling lava. Yet, to his dismay, the presence of the demon was still in his head. There was something different about it now—it no longer held the force and power that it had before. It was somehow . . . fading.

With every twitch of the dragon's body, the demon grew weaker. He was no longer on the offensive or desperately fending off psionic attacks from his adversary. Senjit dared to have hope and within minutes, the heart of the Black Dragon stopped forever, taking away all of the demon's power to resist. With a final scream of rage and fury, the Lord of Anger released the body of the dead Black Dragon and departed.

Senjit watched as the black void, blacker than the blackest hole in the night sky, rose from the remains of the Black Dragon. He felt a shiver of fear, almost terror, run through his body just to look at it. It was a terrible thing that Senjit feared he might have to battle again one day.

Hovering for only a moment, the black void departed into the distance at an impossible speed, accompanied by a high-pitched screech of anger that left Senjit's ears ringing.

Senjit lay exhausted and triumphant. The departure of the demon gave him the strength to believe he might still make it out of there alive. He had to go soon before his protection spells failed. Otherwise, he would die right here next to Belthagore. He was tired and injured and just wanted to get home. He wasn't even sure if he had the strength to fly.

Somehow Senjit managed the strength to climb to a shallow ledge on the nearly sheer ridge and glide out and away from Vers Patna. He found a secluded glen within the forest a couple of leagues west of the caldera to rest and recuperate. He counted himself fortunate to have survived the encounter with the demon that possessed a Black Dragon and worried about how the world would handle the other six Named Demons. He would have to educate as many leaders as possible about the demons and the challenges they would face against them. Otherwise, they would continue recycling until they found themselves in a body, like the Black Dragon, that could do serious, possibly irrevocable harm to civilizations around the world.

Wanting nothing more than to fly home immediately, Senjit accepted that he needed to rest and heal. This was the first time in his life that he was so close to death and he vowed to be better prepared when next he faced it. He had not employed his impressive array of psionic and magical abilities to his best advantage. He needed training if he was going to protect his family and competently face another demon and the terrible creature one might possess. For now, he would patiently rest until he was strong enough to return home to the Isles of Gades, where his wife and young Child of Gold awaited him.

Chapter 25

The Departure

"There it is, Atlanteans. Only a league or so down this road and we will be in the port city of Andlang." Aelrindel sat atop his tall stallion, looking down the escarpment in the direction of Andlang and the deep blue waters of the Primal Sea beyond it. Qel was relieved that the elf was nearly himself again since unburdening his disquiet regarding his conversation with the High-King. It was only a day and a half since they spoke about it and they'd breathed not a word afterward. There was nothing more to say and Qel didn't want idle speculation to send his friend back into the dark malaise he had so recently escaped. Fortunately, Havacian must have been of the same mind and kept his thoughts on the matter to himself as well. Only a week before, Havacian would have been relentlessly questioning Aelrindel every waking moment to satisfy his curiosity. But that was a different Havacian. That was before Myrllin, Wodanaz, the Old Haig and the revelations about the Nine.

Qel admired Andlang from his perch upon his own horse. He could see tall white towers, multistory buildings, wide boulevards and merchant kiosks adorned with vibrant fabric. The city was open and unrestrained by curtain walls or fortifications. In many ways, it was a twin of Aquilon, except that Andlang had an extensive port.

"It doesn't appear to be a city formed from trees and vines like the others we've seen in your kingdom," Qel remarked curiously.

"It would be unpractical with all the foreigners." Aelrindel pointed with his thumb back to where the Sylvan Forest abruptly ended behind them. Just like in Aquilon, several elven warriors and a pair of Tree Guardians stood watch over the gateway into the enchanted wood, keeping out the humans and anyone else they didn't approve of. "That's where the Sylvan Kingdom really begins."

The forest was dark, thick and impassable except for the Sylvan Road that passed through the guarded entrance. Qel surmised that all of the Sylvan Kingdom must be surrounded by the natural barrier to protect it from unwanted intrusion.

"Who governs Andlang?"

"The Potentate, WhritarianSendalvil and the Sylvan Authority." Aelrindel's gaze was fixed on their destination. "Andlang is still a city in the Sylvan Kingdom, so it is governed and protected by our people. The Dvergr Dwarfs built Andlang and gifted it as a gesture of eternal friendship to the Sylvan almost fifteen hundred years ago, just like they gifted Aquilon to the Atlanteans." The elf spurred his horse forward. "Let's get moving so we can find a ship to take us to Ys this week before all the captains start getting drunk."

The wind rushing up the windward-facing slope had a chill bite to it that the forest had insulated them from over the past two and a half days. Qel drew the edges of his heavy cloak in tighter before urging his Lambei to catch up with Aelrindel and Havacian. The road leading to Andlang curved in a long zigzag pattern to compensate for the steep descent. The terrain around them was open grassland broken by occasional copses of pine and patches of loose rocks around partially buried boulders.

Even here, life was abundant. There were long-haired goats with curled horns that blended into their surroundings so effortlessly that Qel only knew they weren't part of the landscape when they moved. Wild pheasants took to the air spontaneously when they rode too close and field mice ran from the protection of nests in the rocks to the tall grass in search of food while avoiding the sharp eyes of a pair of eagles that circled high above.

It was a fascinating environment that Qel was unfamiliar with and the small dramas performed by the animals on the steep escarpment kept him entertained along the slow course they traveled. Andlang was visible the whole way down and Qel observed the busy port with a mix of excitement and trepidation, watching the ships arrive and depart in every direction knowing that soon he too would be westward bound on one of them. It would be the first time in his life leaving the Emerald

Isle and the irrational fear that crept through him almost made him want to turn and run for home.

Less than an hour later, they rode into Andlang and there was no doubt they had just entered a port city. A blind man would know by the unmistakable scent of salt air combined with the strong stench of freshly cleaned fish. Aelrindel said that the fishermen processed their catch right on the dock to be packed in salt for transport inland. It wasn't so different in the City of Atlantis, except that the fishermen's landing and market were on the far side of the outermost segments and too distant for anyone on the inner rings to notice.

Aelrindel skirted the perimeter around the south of Andlang to enter nearer the docks to save time. It was getting late in the day—the sun had not yet set but was no longer visible behind the trees—and already groups of loud, rough-talking sailors were making their way toward their favorite taverns.

"We will stop at the dockmaster's shack and inquire about the next ship departing for Ys." Aelrindel seemed to know where he was going. Qel was more than happy to let him lead the way.

The dockmaster's office was not far away. The small wooden building sat just off the boardwalk opposite several moorings designed for the largest ships. Without hesitation, Aelrindel tied his horse to a post and walked inside not bothering to knock. Qel glanced uncertainly at Havacian, shrugged and quickly followed. Inside, the main room was bigger than he expected, with nautical paraphernalia of every sort hanging on the walls or crammed on sagging shelves. Most of it appeared to have been salvaged from old wrecks. Qel knew from the stories he read that there were hundreds of shipwrecks littering the waters around the Emerald Isle. Most were due to bad weather, but no few were caused by pirates, especially the Vikja, that hid among the hundreds of small islands and preyed upon vulnerable merchant ships laden with cargo.

In the center of the room sat a skinny human man with pale features and a shock of dark hair behind an equally small desk. Oddly, the clerk's clothing appeared completely out of place with his surroundings. He wore a fine, fox fur–lined cloak over a white silk tunic with upturned collar and thick wool trousers despite the warmth of the fireplace only steps away. It was as if he were sitting out in the unsheltered cold. He stood and bowed to Aelrindel and then separately to both Qel and Havacian when they entered. *Strange,* thought Qel. He would have expected an elf to be handling the affairs of the dock rather than a human.

"I am Forley, assistant to the Dockmaster. How can I be of service?" he asked politely.

"We came to inquire about the next ship leaving to Ys," Aelrindel spoke nearly as politely as the human, leaving Qel to wonder at the strange dynamics in Andlang. Not that he expected the elf to be rude, but he knew that most elves looked upon humans with indifference, more often cold indifference. "One that might include comfortable amenities, if possible." Aelrindel turned and winked.

"One moment while I check the register," Forley sat down again and ran his finger down what appeared to be an inventory of ships. Qel's sharp eyes could make out some of the lines noting where the ships came from, where they were going and what sort of cargo they carried. "Ah, yes. There is a Mouillian merchant vessel called the *Wave Breaker* that should meet your expectations. It will be leaving at first light tomorrow morning. I suggest that you check with the captain right away. They may have spots for passengers available yet."

Aelrindel nodded without a word of thanks and turned to leave. Quickly, the human stood from his chair respectfully. The poor man was apparently confused about what he should do when Qel smiled and waved goodbye. The humans might be a mostly ignorant, under evolved species, but they responded well to kindness and if there was a difference between the Atlanteans and the Sylvans, it was compassion.

Fortunately, the Mouillian trade vessel was one of the larger ships in port and was docked nearby. Qel knew about the Mouillians as a seafaring people from the lands across the Primal Sea and along the southern coasts of the Great Sea, far to the east of the Emerald Isle. Like the Atlanteans, the Mouillians plied the seas in some of the most advanced sailing vessels in the known world. During his lectures at the Enclave, Master Ampher enjoyed discussing any subject having to do with sailing ships and frequently referenced the Mouillians as a people born of natural ingenuity.

Qel marveled at all the ships lined up so close together at the expansive docks. There were at least a hundred vessels of every size and origin docked at the busy port with all manner of goods still being loaded and off-loaded even this late in the day. Of course, Qel was not unfamiliar with many of the ships from faraway ports. He and Havacian saw them often in the City of Atlantis and recognized their flags. The two of them used to sit together on a wall overlooking one of the many docks and watch the ships sail in and out of port when they had a few hours of freedom from their studies. That was when their dreams of traveling the world began, more than a decade ago and now here they were about to embark on an adventure of their own.

"Stay here while I find the captain." Aelrindel dismounted and walked amidships, where planks were laid down to allow for boarding the ship, leaving Qel and Havacian to stare up at the towering stern.

"That is a big ship." Qel felt small next to it, even mounted on his Lambei.

Havacian smiled at him. "They do look a bit smaller from a distance. Look there! A ship flying the colors of Ys!"

Thanks to his master, Qel knew all about the ships that came to the Emerald Isle and the treasures they carried. He had seen vessels from Lyonesse laden with copper and tin, from Eriu bearing bronze and sandstone and from Ys bringing beets, beef and cereals to market. From the Great Sea came the pirate traders from Tartessos, dealing in precious metals from slave mines and the Mouillians with their exotic dyes and clays. From even farther west came the Nurozieri trading agricultural products and leather and then there were the Sican merchants loaded with obsidian, lemons, sardines and olive oil.

But the most ominous ships, the ones that made Qel's heart race, were the black-sailed long ships of the Vikja. Their ships flew a gold banner emblazoned with a red hammer above their sails, indicating that they were heavy with goods from the Dvergr Dwarfs in Tirnan Yog. They usually transported a variety of ores, precious gems and steel bars. The dwarfs were not a seafaring people and although they had a few ships of their own, preferred to contract most of their sea trade to their local neighbors, the Vikja. The Vikja were reputed to be savage raiders that would not hesitate to prey upon merchant ships and vulnerable villages along the coasts and deep within the inland waterways. However, when they flew the merchant flag of the dwarfs, they were under contract and forbidden any acts of aggression. Everyone knew that an attack on a Vikja ship while they flew the Dvergr flag was considered an attack on the dwarfs themselves and would be met with harsh retribution.

Even so, Qel heard the rumors about some of the more enterprising Vikja who had tried to use the Dvergr trade colors to their advantage by raiding under its protection without fear of attack themselves when they returned to the sea. And according to Master Ampher, once the dwarfs caught word of what the Vikja were doing, they sent warriors to round them up and bring them back to Tirnan Yog, where they were subjected to a brief trial, convicted and sentenced to death. Their execution was a brutal hanging by the neck from the cliffs of the island kingdom facing the sea, with their bodies left to rot and be devoured by the carrion birds. From that moment on, the Vikja self-policed their own people and hung any violators themselves. Despite that history, they still struck fear into anyone they encountered on the seas and raided as much as they always did, just never under the banner of the Dvergr Dwarfs.

"The captain had one room left that he said would fit three mats." Qel had not heard Aelrindel's approach and was startled when he spoke. "I took the room rather than wait for the next ship headed to Ys."

Recovering quickly, Qel handed the elf back the reins of his horse. "That is aggregable to me. I'm looking forward to seeing Ys."

"It's fine with me as well," Havacian chimed in.

"Good, then let's find an inn away from the stink of the port, but not too far away." The elf began to chuckle. "The captain made it clear they would be shoving off one hour after dawn with or without us and I already paid him!"

Leaving the docks, they rode through the crowded streets toward the center of Andlang to find a decent inn. They passed several along the way without stopping and Qel decided that Aelrindel must have had a specific one in mind. Already he had learned to look for inns the elves or Atlanteans patronized. They were the best assurance of sanitary accommodations and good food. Although Andlang was technically a Sylvan city within the boundaries of the Sylvan Kingdom, there were far more humans visible in the street than any elves. Even the patrols of the city guard were formed by humans. Qel made a mental note to ask Aelrindel more about the governance of Andlang when they were settled.

Before long, they arrived at an inn near Andlang's center. The shingle over the door identified it as the *Fickle Sprite* with a faded illustration of what appeared to be a winged Fairy. Qel smiled to himself, thinking about his first encounter with one in the Sylvan Forest. It felt like ages ago, but it had only been a few weeks. The interior of the main hall was bright with lanterns and light-globes and crowded with Atlanteans, elves and a few affluent humans sitting together at round tables or booths. It was loud with the conversations of so many voices and music played by a minstrel with a stringed instrument in the corner. Qel wished it was Wodanaz sitting there, knowing what he knew now, although he would not have known what to say.

Qel found a table and sat with Havacian while Aelrindel rented rooms for the evening. They were all tired from the long day on horseback and after an excellent meal of mahiz porridge with a thick side of fresh grilled tuna, and warm crusty bread, Qel was ready to retire for the evening.

Later that evening, as he lay in a comfortable bed with ample blankets and a warm hearth, he rested awake thinking about all the possibilities that might occur in their future. He never would have guessed at the unexpected adventure he and Havacian would find among the Sylvan and knowing this, could hardly hazard a guess as to what might lay ahead in Ys. Whatever it was and where ever it took them, Qel was excited about the prospects. Yet, in the back of his mind, he worried that their journey home again might not come so soon or so easy.

———

Qel woke before dawn. He could feel the wet chill of the night fading and knew that soon he would be sailing across the Primal Sea for the first time in his life. Up until this moment, he had felt the thrill of excitement at the chance to adventure beyond the Emerald Isle. But now he faced the stark reality that he was leaving his home, his family and the places familiar to him and wondered if he was ready. Yes, he and Havacian had been through a lot in the past weeks and grown because of it. Still, the prospect of leaving everything familiar to him behind suddenly left him questioning his resolve to go forward. In the minutes before dawn, alone and in the dark, staring up at a foreign ceiling, Qel was sure he was making the wrong decision and steeled himself with the words he would say to Havacian. Would his friend go on without him or cower in a blanket of comfortable familiarity beside him? Havacian was not the same as he was when they left the Enclave in Atlantis and maybe his friend thought the same of him. Would it change their friendship? He prayed to Pontus that it would not. What would he say to Havacian?

Washed and ready to go, Qel sat on the edge of the bed and waited for the knock at the door he knew would come. He rehearsed his speech over and over in his head, planning rebuttals against the protests he expected and the logical arguments he had prepared to plead his case. No matter what, he would not be crossing the sea with them today. He was not ready.

The expected knock finally came and Qel slowly rose with his pack over his shoulder. He opened the door to find a wide-eyed Havacian standing next to a determined-looking Aelrindel. In an instant, Qel knew that Havacian was of the same mind as he and his heart rejoiced.

Then Aelrindel looked him square in the eye, "Are you ready to go?"

Qel's will utterly collapsed.

"Yes," was all he could reply as he exited his room and followed the elf down to the stables.

Dawn in Andlang was much colder this time of year than in Atlantis. Qel shivered in the damp air that quickly seemed to pervade the open folds of even the heavy cloak he wore. He hoped Ys would not be so frigid. Otherwise, they would be forced to find a Wizards Tower to withdraw enough money to purchase warmer clothing. That thought made Qel shiver as much as the cold. Their adventure could abruptly end if word had been sent out to order he and Havacian back home.

They arrived at the *Wave Breaker* early in order to safely board their horses before settling themselves into their small cabin. Qel was impressed by the professional conduct of the sailors on board despite their rugged appearance. To a man, they wore colorful, loose-fitting silk blouses with full sleeves, calf-length trousers and a thick leather belt to hold a cutlass and dagger. Master Ampher described them as the wealthiest men on the sea given the unusually substantial cut of profits the crew traditionally received. The Mouillians, once a pirate nation, were now known to be talented seafaring people who traded across the expansive waterways of the world. Master Ampher spoke at length about the exotic goods and animals they brought for trade in Atlantis. He cautioned that although they were merchants, as sailors, they were as fierce as any. The crew always went about their duties fully armed and were trained to perform any onboard task without removing their blades. Even the Vikja and Tartessos pirates tended to avoid the Mouillians' trade vessels when encountered at sea.

Precisely one hour after dawn, the *Wave Breaker* departed the port and tacked out against the chill wind that blew across the icy glaciers far to the north. Qel stood with Aelrindel and Havacian at the aft of the vessel and watched Andlang slowly shrink in the distance. The fear and uncertainty he felt earlier that morning was gone and he was glad to be on a ship headed into the unknown with the promise of adventure that lay beyond.

Cast of Characters

AelrindelRokalyn (Aelrindel). Elf warrior and master archer. His father is a trusted advisor to the High-King of the Sylvan Kingdom.

Aether. Hellas God of Light. Known as Dhroghan to the Tuatha De.

Akakios. The TaHiera known as the Fire-Bringer responsible for dedicating forge and flame in the name of Kronos.

Anesidora. Daughter of Kronos and Metis. She is a demi-goddess with a wicked curiosity.

Anlawd Dormont. First King of the humans in what would later become the Western Kingdoms.

Chaos Demons. Minor demons from the Infernal Planes. They are highly intelligent but driven by a hunger for sowing evil and chaos in whatever manner they are able.

CrellianRafkarSil. The Watcher. He was an elven chronicler during the Third Age of the Golden Aspen.

Dagda-Dana Laghfrin. Tuatha De Wizard Queen of Falias in the North. Founding member of the Five.

Dhroghan. Legendary hero of the Tuatha De (deceased) and founding member of the Five. Known by the name Aether in Hellas.

Emperor Zamfer. One of the earliest Emperors of Atlantis who reigned over one thousand years ago. He was a founding member of *The Assembly of Nine* who assisted the Tuatha De in closing the rift to the Infernal Planes that was a result of The Breaking. Zamfer later led the combined forces of multi-racial allies to imprison the remaining demons in the pithos that Phalaeh (Metis) produced.

Emperor Liltanian of House Atlas. Current ruler of the Atlantean Empire. Formerly of House Straeter, he is known by most as simply Emperor Liltanian.

Empress Chartria of House Atlas. Wife to Emperor Liltanian. Her older sister, Secria, is the wife of Terrikan of House Elbian, Ambassador to Eridu in Kur-gal.

Grand Wizard Tochthon. Highest authority of the Imperial Order of Wizards in Atlantis.

Havaciante of House Talika. Wizard of the Blue Hall from Atlantis. His closest friend is Qel.

Hierophant Miltiades. Head Priest of the Temple of Kronos in the Hellas city-state of Sesklo.

High-King RalnapianCalithIlon. Ruler of the Sylvan Kingdom (deceased) and founding member of the Five. He is the grandfather of the current ruler, High-King TatharonCalithIlon.

High-King TatharonCalithIlon. "Willow Tree in the Moonlight", current ruler of the Sylvan Kingdom.

Kronos. Patron god of Sesklo, deity of blacksmiths, artisans, fire and harvests.

Master Ampher. Master of the Red Hall in the Enclave of the Imperial Order of Wizards.

Master Curatei of House Sevreckly. The Keeper of Records for the Imperial Order of Wizards, Master of the Blue Hall and mentor to Havacian.

Metis. Goddess of wisdom in Hellas. She is known by the name Phalaeh to the Tuatha De.

Mountain King Brak Iron-teeth. Lord of the Dvergr Dwarfs (deceased) and founding member of the Five. Great-grandfather of the current Mountain King, Sulyen the Breaker.

Mountain King Sulyen the Breaker. Lord of the Dvergr Dwarves in Tirnan Yog.

Myrllin. The Mad Bard, the Prophet, the Sage, the Wizard of Hy-Brasil. Rumored to possess the ability to foresee the future with varying degrees of clarity, he is a powerful wizard with an obscure past. He makes his home in a fortified palace on the mystical island of Hy-Brasil where he will sometimes hibernate without aging for hundreds of years at a time. He is the son of Dhroghan, a legendary hero of the Tuatha De and the older brother to his twin Wodanaz by less than a minute.

Niamh. Nature goddess of the elves.

Nomios and Agreus. Paein brothers who helped Akakios find his way to the Shrine of Metis.

Qellel of House Mekali (Qel). Wizard of the Red Hall in Atlantis, he is the youngest of three sisters and a brother. Their family is known for their prized production of Mekali wine grown in groves north of the City of Atlantis.

Queen Lysithea. Ruler of the Isles of Gades. She is a nymph, wife to Senjit and mother to Alseid the Child of Gold.

Senjit. A Golden Dragon, he is married to the Nymph Queen Lysithea. They have a daughter, a Child of Gold, named Alseid. His mother was a dragon named Findyl and his father was the god of light, Aether. Senjit is known by many names throughout the world including—Huanglong by the Huaxia, Culebre by the Astriense, Ladon in Hella, The World Serpent by the Vikja, Usum in Kur-gal and the Earth Monster by the Olmec, among others.

Tephras, Demon of Anger. Possessed the ancient Black Dragon Belthagore.

Traegarlin. A Battle Wizard or 'Exalted One'. The Battle Wizards are a specialized group of the Imperial Order of Wizards in the City of Atlantis trained specifically for combat. They patrol the territory of Atlantean Empire on the Emerald Isle and act as part of the emperor's personal guard.

TridiStrindricinia and VnaeStrindricina. Elves living in the village of Braetling. They have a daughter, ToliaStrindricina (Tolia). Vnae is the sister of AelrindelRokalyn. She is a Tree Whisperer, or Traetling, as was her mother. Tridi is an elder of his village

Wodanaz. Wanderer, minstrel, poet, entertainer, seeker of wisdom and Chronicler of the Fourth Age. He is the younger twin brother of Myrllin by one minute and son of Dhroghan, a legendary hero of the Tuatha De.

Glossary

Abbas. A low-level priest in Hellas.

Amphora. Container to transport wine, water, etc. in Hellas.

Artos. Loaf of wheat bread typical in Hellas.

Aurinium. An extremely hard translucent blue, glass-like 'metal' that only the Atlantean Forge Wizards have the knowledge to create. It is highly valuable and strictly controlled. The material is used in the forging of armor, weapons, tools and magical jewelry.

Bargina. Sweet bread from Eriu.

Chiton. Worn by the men of Hellas, it is a tunic fastened at the shoulders with a belt at the waist. The length of the tunic is typically short when the weather is warm and longer when cold.

Chlamys. A woolen robe generally worn by men in Hellas.

Dagda or Dagda-Dana. Wizard King or Wizard Queen of a Tuatha De city.

Demesne of Magic. Located in Avalon, it is the center of power for the Sylvan Magic-Crafters, Wizards and Sorcerers of the Sylvan Kingdom similar to the Imperial Order of Wizards in Atlantis.

Dvergr Dwarfs. Those dwarfs who live on the island of Tirnan Yog, northwest of Eriu.

Dvergr steel. The hardest and most finely crafted metal available to anyone who can afford it. Only the Dvergr Dwarfs have the knowledge to forge it. It is commonly used to produce armor, weapons and tools.

Elysium. The afterlife, 'Place of Perfection', according to the priests in Hellas.

Exegetes. City Official who was an expert in religious matters, although not necessarily a priest.

Harpyia. Creature of legend with a head and torso of a human and lower body of a great eagle or Roc.

Harpe. A sword with a protrusion in the shape of a sickle near the tip of the blade.

Hellenes. People of Hellas.

Hierophant. Head Priest of the primary temple to a specific deity in the city-states of Hellas.

Hieros. A priest.

Himation. A heavier outer garment worn like a wrap going over the left shoulder and under the right. It is typically worn over a chiton or peplos.

Hy-Brasil. The legendary home of Myrllin and Wodanaz gifted to them by the Tuatha De. The island is almost always obscured by fog and rarely visible to passing ships. A red dragon is said to inhabit and guard the island against intruders, discouraging adventurers and curiosity seekers from attempting to explore its secrets.

Hydruntin Ass. A breed of donkey common throughout the Western Kingdoms, Hellas and the Capsians.

Hypokrites. An actor from Hellas

Kithara and lyre. Musical instruments with strings.

Kolpos. An upper garment similar to a blousy tunic typically worn with a chiton in Hellas.

Lunula. A crescent-shaped jewelry traditionally worn as a necklace in Eriu.

Megeiras. A cook or butcher.

Miniver fur. Soft white fur from the underbelly of the red squirrel's winter coat.

Naos. Temple, dwelling place of a god, in Hellas.

Neokoroi. Caretakers who maintain a temenos. They are not necessarily priests.

Oinochoe. Pitcher of wine typically served in taverns throughout Hellas.

Oinos. A flavorful wine common in Hellas

Orichalcum. A precious crystal that is known to originate only in Atlantis and perhaps not from this world if the legends are true. It is said to have unique attributes of storing and conducting vast amounts of magical energies. It is extremely rare and valuable.

Ourea. Massive volcano in the Atlas Mountains on the Emerald Isle.

Peplos. A long garment pined at the shoulders. Worn by the women of Hellas.

Pithos. A traditional vessel for transporting wine, olive oil and other liquids in Hellas

Salik. Herb originating from the bark of a willow that has the healing properties of an anti-inflammatory, usually mixed into warm tea.

Strophion. A breast-band worn over the outside of clothing for support.

Sylvan. All creatures natural and magical related to the elves including fairies, sprites, centaur, dryad and nymphs. Most, but not all, reside within the borders of the Sylvan Kingdom.

Ta Hiera. High Priest of a temple in Hellas, second to the Hierophant.

Temenos. A sacred area dedicated to a specific god, usually fronted by a Propylon, a symbolic gate or entry.

Thaumaturgists. Sylvan masters of magical crafts that form the highest council of leadership at the Demesne of Magic in Avalon.

The Assembly of Nine. A group of nine of the most powerful beings on the planet who come together every few decades to determine the course of world civilizations to maintain peace and resolve significant disputes.

The Breaking. A civil war that occurred between factions of the Tuatha De who believed in genetically altering life on the planet for use as slaves and controlling humanoid civilizations versus those who believed just the opposite. In the end, a truce was declared only after most of the Tuatha De Blood had been killed and thousands of commoners died. A bargain was struck to banish all of the creatures they had created to Fomoire, but they would still maintain influence over humanoid civilizations in a very unexpected way.

The Order of the Five. A legendary group of explorers who initially came together to defend humanity against the evils and tyranny caused by demons that plagued the world.

Triskele. A symbol with three spirals radiating from a common center.

Tuatha De. A mysterious, magical people that are the oldest humanoids on earth, according to their lore. There are two distinct groups – the 'Blood' and the ordinary citizens. The Blood are the rulers of the people and are purely born to the original Tuatha De. The commoners are the descendants of Tuatha De Blood that have bred with humans. Commoners have different levels of magical inheritance based on their interbreeding. Most of the Tuatha De Blood died during The Breaking and none have been born after.

Enochian Translations

The language of devils and angels

"Parm, apachama! Zir Teloc!" – Run, Slimy things made of dust! I am death!

"Micma a ialpon a unph!" – Behold the burn of anger!

"Saanir oi sor ol zonrensg a loagaeth piadph coraxo bahal de allar a babalon pir pambt oi zizop bagle tol cocasb." – By this action I deliver with speech from god within the depths of my jaws the thunders of judgment and wrath cried with a loud voice to bind the wicked ones unto this vessel for all of time.

"Zir g teloch!" – I am your death

"Irgil a unal chis caosg?" – How many of these are upon the earth?

"Ol uran gi," – I see you.

"Torzu, toltorg!" – Arise, creatures of the earth!

"Odqvasb Prge!" – Destroy with the fire!

"Esiasch" – Brother

"Zir ip g esiasch," – I am not your brother.

About the Author

Born in Homestead, Florida, Ravek Hunter grew up in the United States and Belgium. He earned a bachelor's degree in marketing from Florida International University and went on to become a sporting goods executive. He currently serves as a consultant in the same industry and occasionally assists his wife of fifteen years at her floral design company. The proud father of two boys, Ravek counts reading, exercising, and family travel among his leisure hobbies.

Over the past thirty-five years, Ravek's passion has been researching ancient civilizations with a focus on the origin stories behind their mythology. His writing style attempts to immerse the reader into the story by bringing to life historically accurate and rich details of the culture and time period that frame the narrative.

Inspired by classic fantasy authors like Robert Jordan, Terry Goodkind, and R. A. Salvatore, Ravek writes to entertain and provoke his readers, who, he hopes, share his fondness for mythology.

Connect with Ravek Hunter

Thank you for choosing this work of blood, sweat and tears by *Ravek Hunter*! If you enjoyed reading this novel please consider posting a review, telling me what you think on one of the social media platforms listed below or reach out via my direct email:

Friend me on Facebook:

https://www.facebook.com/Ravek-Hunter-Literary-LLC-238417183579740/

Follow me on Twitter:

https://twitter.com/RavekHunter

Subscribe to my blog:

https://www.goodreads.com/author/show/17885196.Ravek_Hunter

Visit my website:

https://www.WorldsofAtlantis.com

Email: Ravekhunter@gmail.com

www.ingramcontent.com/pod-product-compliance
Lightning Source LLC
Chambersburg PA
CBHW022144010726

47493CB00002B/329